Book Three

The

Reawakened

Forest

Sally Stout

Sally Stout

Story Weaver Press - Frankfort, Michigan

For information contact:
Story Weaver Press
155 Beech St.
Frankfort, Michigan 49635
Or see our website at www.sallystoutbooks.com

ISBN 13: 978-0-9795580-4-7
ISBN 10:   0-9795580-4-2

First Edition: October 2020

10 9 8 7 6 5 4 3 2 1

For

Clyde Alexander and Betty Ann

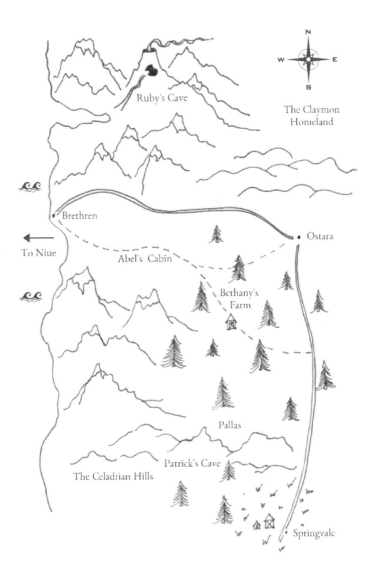

Ruby's Cave

The Claymon
Homeland

Brethren

To Niue

Abel's Cabin

Ostara

Bethany's
Farm

Pallas

Patrick's Cave

The Celadrian Hills

Springvale

1

SINK OR SWIM

HER RESCUERS HAD COME too late. With the next big wave Kathe lost her grip on the dolphin's smooth body. She tried to tread water one more time, but it was too rough, and she was heavy with cold. Although her spirit fought to live, her limbs, which had always been so dependable, would no longer obey. She took a last breath and slipped underwater.

Eventually her body would wash onto the shore, and someone might find it there and drag it out of reach of the tide. They might even say a few words over her corpse and bury it in the sand.

Even though it seemed long ago, it had been little more than an hour since Kathe jumped off the *Goshawk* and started swimming towards the stretch of beach south of Brethren. She was young, and a strong swimmer. It had seemed her best chance to elude the Claymon, who had already rowed halfway to the ship by the time she climbed through the captain's quarter's window and dropped into the sea. When she began swimming, she felt strong and hopeful, but now her strength was sapped by the cold, and that hope was less than a dream.

As her body slowly sank and the light receded, Kathe started to accept her fate. It was as if the healer in her was a clear-eyed realist, fighting as long as possible but finally acknowledging what could not be changed. And what did it matter, really? All mortal lives must end – often much too soon. Why should hers be different? Though she was afraid, it helped to know the friendly dolphins would be nearby at the end. She sensed them swimming around her in a tight circle. She tried to remember how it felt to be standing on the deck of the *Goshawk*, surrounded by friends, on the day the dolphins appeared and played around the ship for the first time.

In the moment before she released her last breath of air and filled her lungs with sea water, one of the dolphins darted between her legs. As it tilted her sideways, she groped blindly for its dorsal fin, and it carried her back to the surface in a burst of speed and bubbles. Back under the sky, with the waves once again churning around her, Kathe choked and gasped. Before she could sink again, two more of the creatures appeared. Others bobbed nearby, making their strange squeaks and clicks. Kathe couldn't understand their talk, as Meg could, but they seemed to be urging her to try.

Kathe didn't understand how they hoped to help, and she was sure she couldn't hold on for long, but she threw her leaden arms over the dolphins on each side of her. As best she could, she clasped their fins. She knew the creatures were not made for this, and she thought she might be hurting them. They swam slowly, stopping each time she lost her grip. In this way, she allowed herself to be carried like a rag doll until she was close to shore. She slipped off the center dolphin, and her toes touched the sandy bottom. Even then, when she would have been knocked over by the surf, the dolphins stayed close. Finally, she fell to her knees and crawled to safety.

Kathe didn't know how long she sprawled half in and half out of the water before she became aware of the sounds of the sea and of the warmth of sun on her shoulders. When she did, she dragged herself forward until she felt dry, warm sand; pulled herself to her knees; and squinted up and down the beach. Like a butterfly that has just emerged from its chrysalis, she was completely vulnerable. She had to find a place to hide, and it had better be some place touched by the afternoon sun. The shadows were already lengthening. Night would fall too soon, and if she could not dry and warm herself, she still might die.

Her skin was pale, almost blue, and her teeth chattered. She wrapped her arms around her body while her fogged mind struggled to decide what to do. This section of the beach looked deserted, and the town and harbor were out of sight around the curve of the shore. At least that part of the plan seemed to have worked.

Gazing out over the sea, she saw no sign of her saviors. She closed her eyes and thought, *Thank you. Thank you. Thank you*, in case the dolphins were not too far away and might be able to hear and understand.

Kathe slowly stood up, testing joints stiffened by cold and the swim. Bending double, she vomited. She wiped her mouth with her arm and stood again, swaying until her vision cleared. The headland looked very far away. It was as if she were seeing it through the wrong end of Captain Fischer's telescope.

Kathe thought about a time when she fell ill as a small girl, barely old enough to talk. Her mother, who never left her side during Kathe's delirium, fell into her own bed soon after the fever broke, when she believed her daughter was safely asleep. When Kathe woke that morning and found herself alone, she was thirsty. She felt better, so she went to find water. Her mother found her lying on the cold stone floor in the corridor, swept her up, put her back into bed, and tucked the warm blankets to her chin. Then she gave Kathe the cold water she craved. Tears welled in Kathe's eyes as she remembered her mother's hand brushing the hair from her forehead. She was just as thirsty now.

A low dune lay between the sea and the high, forested headland. Since it was the only cover in sight, she crossed the beach towards it, walking backwards. When she reached the base of the small hill and looked back, she saw the sand had captured her bare footprints. As she hoped, it looked as if someone had walked towards the sea. She knew her trick might fool a townsperson, but a skilled tracker would know exactly what she had done.

Kathe crawled up the dune on her hands and knees through thickly growing clumps of dune grass, making an obvious trail in the sand and, she hoped, making it look as if someone had slid down. Once she was over the top and out of sight of the shore, she stopped to rest again. She hitched up the cabin boy's pants and tightened the rope she was using as a belt. She now was completely coated with sand, like a cake covered in sugar crystals. Even the tears drying on her cheeks were streaked with sand. The thought made her laugh out loud, and that worried her. There was nothing funny about her situation. Bethany had taught her how to identify the symptoms of shock, and Kathe recognized a few of them in herself.

To warm herself, she kept moving down the back of the dune, out of the shade and towards the intense sunlight shining on the bluff beneath the forested headland. She thought about the things she carried that could help her to survive. There weren't many. She had the rope she was using as a belt. Her knife was still in its sheath under her clothing.

She stopped again, took the knife out, and wiped it dry as best she could, fingering the jewel on its hilt. The ruby sparked in the sunlight. The blade was short, but very sharp. In addition to its usefulness as a tool and a weapon, it was Kathe's talisman. She had thought it lost until Patrick brought it back to her. She returned the knife to its sheath and plodded on. She fingered a buttoned pocket where she could feel the hard shape of a firestone. Once she reached a dry place, maybe she would start a fire. Gale had given her the tool and taught her how to use it.

At the thought of her companions, she abruptly sat down again. Since the beginning of her life, whenever trouble found her, she found friends or her family nearby to help or just to suffer by her side. Now Bethany and Gerard were marooned on the Island of Niue. Gale and Meg were off on their own journey in the service of the dragon. She might never see any of them again.

Maybe her mother would find Patrick waiting in the town of Brethren. If she did, she would tell him how Kathe planned to escape. She was sure he would search for her, but for now she had to depend on herself. She felt the brush of loneliness and shuddered. Sitting in the shade and brooding had chilled her even more. She pushed her fears to the back of her mind, instead studying the slope of the high bluff and convincing herself she had enough strength to climb it.

It would be easier to hide here or in the brush at the base of the cliff until darkness, but by now the Claymon must know she was neither among the refugees nor aboard the *Goshawk*. If they had not done so already, they would begin to look farther away from Brethren along the shore. Peter Greystone, whose forces were pushing ever farther south, seemed to think he needed to put her on display in Ostara to cement his hold on the city. After running for so long, she must not allow herself to be captured now. Still, Kathe couldn't bring herself to move. Dully, she watched as her footprints began to fill with sand. There was a strong breeze. That was another piece of luck. The wind, waves, and tide would soon erase her trail.

When she reached the base of the bluff, she found it was even steeper than it looked from a distance, and unstable. There were some roots she could use as handholds, but her feet slipped in the crumbly sand at every step. As she set herself to the work of reaching the top, her heart pounded, as much from knowing herself to be exposed like a fly on a wall as from exertion. She risked a glance over her shoulder. She could see over the top of the low dune now. The beach still looked deserted.

She was about two-thirds of the way to the top when she heard a shout, followed moments later by a shrill whistle. She had heard sounds like those when her father was hunting. They were the sounds of discovery. The whistle was to summon the rest of the hunters. Her heart leapt in her chest, and she no longer was Kathe. She had become the fox.

She clawed her way towards the top of the slope. It was almost within reach when she put too much weight on a root, and it snapped. She slid part-way down, losing precious time before she caught and bruised herself on a large rock protruding from the hillside. She swallowed a cry and tested an oath she had learned from the sailors on the *Goshawk*.

"Try again."

She didn't hear the voice with her ears. It formed inside her skull and she knew without seeing that the friend she needed was waiting at the top of the bluff. She began climbing again, more carefully and with such focus that she was surprised when her fingers brushed the grasses growing along the top.

The last few feet of the climb were almost straight up, and she struggled to find toeholds. She tried to keep her mind on the next tiny movement that would bring her closer to her goal, but then she heard the breathing of someone climbing the slope below her.

When a hand touched her ankle, she gasped. She kicked hard, lost her grip, and fell backwards, knocking into the Claymon soldier who was below her. Together they tumbled back down all the way to the bottom of the bluff.

Neither moved for several moments. Then Kathe tested her arms and legs. One arm was twisted behind her. It hurt, but she didn't seem to have broken any bones. She supposed it was too much to hope the Claymon had snapped his neck. She scrambled back and away from her enemy on her elbows, then groped for the hilt of her knife. Her braids had come undone, and she used a precious motion to brush the hair and sand from her face.

The Claymon soldier was rising slowly, facing away from her, and even in her panic, she thought that was strange. He should not be leaving her this opportunity to attack. He was on his knees, and he seemed to be testing his limbs as she had done. This was when she should leap on his back and slit his throat. It would be her only opportunity, but she had never killed anyone, and she wanted to keep it that way if she could.

Also, something about him seemed familiar.

"It's you." She hissed.

"You didn't have to kick me," Stormer said in halting Ostaran as he turned around.

"What do you mean, I didn't have to kick you? You were trying to capture me, and I warn you, I will not be taken." Kathe's knife flashed in her hand. She glanced at the young soldier's sword, which he had not yet drawn. She would not be able to best him.

"I will kill myself first."

Just then, a black shadow poured down the bluff and stood between the two angry humans. The panther growled deep in its throat.

Kathe had to give the young Claymon credit. He blanched, but he showed no other reaction.

"I owe you my life," he said, keeping his eyes on the panther. "A life for a life. I want to help you, but we have lost too much time. I whistled for my comrades, so that they would not guess I plan to betray them, and I tried to confuse the trail, but they will be here soon. I was right behind you, and maybe I touched your foot, but I was not trying to catch you."

Katherine closed her eyes. She knew there wouldn't be time to climb the bluff again. As soon as she was above the top of the low dune, the soldiers would have her.

"Maraba. What should I do?" Kathe asked.

"It is nice to see you too. Follow me." The big cat padded away, following the base of the bluff.

"You are looking well," Katherine said, forcing a normal tone, as if Stormer was just an acquaintance she hadn't seen for a while. How had the only Claymon she knew managed to be here to find her? She tried to count how many days it had been since she found the young soldier lying on a deer trail in the forest. Then he was injured and struggling to breathe. Now it looked as if he had gained weight, and his face had the ruddy glow of health.

"No matter what happens, I will not regret the day I healed you," she said. "You can still choose. If you stay here…"

"I am coming with you."

She held out her hand, and he pulled her to her feet. She wasn't sure it was a good idea to take him with her, but there was no time to argue now. Together, they followed the panther into a cleft in the hillside.

2

The Spy

Stormer trailed a distance behind Kathe, who closely followed Maraba through the thick brush along the base of the bluff and up the course of a stream flowing down from the forest above. The stream's flow lost itself in the sand before it reached the beach. Even if Kathe had searched on her own for an easier way to reach the headland forest, she wouldn't have noticed this route, disguised as it was by plants crowding around the trickle of flowing water.

Later, when Stormer told the story, he would say he lagged behind Kathe and the panther so that he would be the first to confront and mislead the Claymon trackers, but the truth was he did not want to follow the big cat any more closely. His heart still pounded from meeting her, and he knew he would be hearing that growl in his nightmares.

Just about now, he thought, his comrades should be studying the traces on the beach. If the Claymon had learned one thing over the last year it was that it was no easy thing to capture Katherine Elder. She should have been friendless on this day, and after swimming to shore from the ship and tumbling down the dune, she certainly looked helpless, like some almost dead thing the tide had carried onto shore. However, that changed the instant Maraba stepped between the two of them.

The stream grew more active the farther they climbed. The closer they came to the top, the more steeply the dune rose on each side. The trees of the headland were almost within reach again. Stormer saw Kathe glance over her shoulder at him, confusion and mistrust still written on her face. She was right not to trust him. He wasn't sure, himself, what he would do if the others in his patrol caught up with him and he had to make a choice. There was a chance he could still betray her.

Since the day when Kathe healed him, not only of the injuries inflicted by the sow bear but of the illness that had weakened and slowed him since childhood, Stormer had been trying to figure out who he was before he met her and who he had become. He didn't say anything to his fellow soldiers or his commander about what happened in the forest. He didn't even show them the marks from the bear's claws, which had nearly healed in the days since the attack, much more quickly than they should have. He simply took his punishment for getting lost, as they thought.

They must have noticed he had changed, but no one said anything to him about it. He went from being the weakest member of his team to one of the strongest, and he owed it to this girl. He had decided to help her if he could, but he was still a Claymon soldier, and he knew his duty. There was a chance he might change his mind and return her to Peter Greystone instead.

Stormer pictured himself approaching Greystone in Ostara, kneeling, and receiving his praise. There would be a reward, and maybe some leave time. He hadn't seen his family in more than two years. He stopped and imagined the scene while the water flowed around his ankles. His boots were soaked, and his feet sloshed inside the leather.

It's too bad she didn't fix this daydreaming when she fixed the breathing, he thought in frustration. Kathe was out of sight. He listened for sounds of her passing and pushed more quickly through the brush. In the beginning, she had been shocked to see him, and then she seemed resigned to his company, but he had no doubt she would lose him as soon as she could.

After the bear attack, and after Kathe healed him, Stormer had known who she was as soon as he opened his eyes. Every

Claymon soldier had heard about the Lady Katherine Elder and how much Peter Greystone wanted to find her. Her name and description were in every speech he had heard from his leaders for more than a year. What Stormer didn't fully understand was that, in order to heal him, Kathe had to intertwine the edges of her mind with his. And although she did not know it, and he could not express it, Stormer also understood her very well.

This meant Katherine knew he was struggling to make choices that would determine the course of the rest of his life. If he continued to travel with her, he would become another quarry of the Claymon, and the hunt would not end until he had been captured and put to a slow death in the public square of Ostara. He would never see his home again.

At the same time, Stormer knew beyond any doubt that Kathe would keep her promise to use that small, lethal-looking knife on herself if he or his comrades tried to capture her. It was one of the things he knew about her. She did not bluff. It seemed less likely that she would have to make good on that threat, though, now that she was under the protection of the panther.

Stormer guessed the big cat must be one of the talking animals. He had started to hear stories about such creatures as soon as the Claymon army began to push south, and he scoffed along with the other men when they repeated the tales around their fires at night. Still, ever since his healing he wondered. If Katherine could do that, other things might be possible too.

He stopped again and retraced his steps a few paces downstream. Three men were following closely, just out of sight. Although Stormer had been expecting them, he hadn't heard them coming until now. The Claymon had learned a few tricks from the Woods Runners. He cursed silently and prepared to greet them, wiping all expression from his face.

"I had her." He spoke first, forcing himself to meet the eyes of his commander. "You heard my signal, and you saw the place where I pulled her down the side of the hill."

Stone faced, the man waited for the rest of Stormer's report.

"The vixen kicked me hard in the side of the head, and we both fell. It knocked me out for a few minutes." He touched his temple, hoping it looked as bruised as it felt. "As soon as I came to, I started tracking her again."

The stream had immediately erased all sign of Katherine's footsteps as soon as she began to walk in its sandy bed, but it was the only direction she could have gone – up into the forest. There were broken stems and bruised leaves to find for anyone who knew how to look for them. The young soldier, who had been scouting the beach with Stormer and who he had gone to whistle for the others, splashed ahead, pushing through the bushes and peering into the place where the stream emerged from among the trees of the headland. When he returned, he shook his head.

Stormer waited for the officer to respond. He was afraid if he said anything more the man would sense his deception.

Finally, the commander swore and spat into the stream. "She's a tricky one, but she can't get far. It would serve her right to spend a night alone in the forest. Where are her friends now? If we don't catch her before dark, the Runners will find her for us tomorrow."

She is not afraid to sleep in a forest, Stormer thought. *And she isn't alone.*

The leader pointed at Stormer and at the man on his right, an older soldier who outranked Stormer. "You two. Go back to Brethren. Find a Runner as quick as you can and send him here. I'll keep following the stream and see where it takes me. She can't be far." He gestured at the younger soldier to follow him. Under his breath he added, "We aren't going to lose her again."

Behind his neutral expression, Stormer's mind raced. He didn't see any choice. He had been ordered back to Brethren, and that is where he must go. He knew he would never find Lady Katherine again on his own even if he managed to slip away later. That meant there was no way to warn her that the Claymon were closing in on her. She would think he had chosen to betray her after all.

If he was honest, and Stormer was honest more often than most, changing his mind about helping Katherine was never really a possibility. As soon as the other soldiers caught up with him, he knew he would never expose the healer. He had tried to be a good soldier, like his father before him, but even when he rose strong and healthy after being healed on the forest trail and even after he rejoined the other Claymon troops, he remained a misfit among his unquestioning comrades.

Stormer watched the officer's broad back until it was hidden by the brush upstream. He wished he could see the man's face if he did catch up with Katherine. He'd like to see that stony expression slip when the panther snarled and leapt.

Blood oozed from deep scratches on Kathe's arms before she walked among the tall trees of the headland. She was grateful for the patched canvas of the cabin boy's trousers that mostly protected her legs from the briars that arched over the stream. As Maraba led her into the deep shade of the forest, only fear of pursuit kept her moving. Though the climb had finally warmed her, she would have to rest soon.

Kathe hadn't seen Stormer since the day she healed him, but she would have known if he had changed his mind about helping her. He must have been intercepted by other Claymon. If that was what had happened, there wasn't anything she could do about it. Even though she sensed he wanted to help, she would have to go on without him.

Kathe stumbled forward, keeping her eyes on the tip of Maraba's long, black tail as she had so many other times in the past year since she left Ostara. She was so intent on keeping up with the big cat she nearly fell forward onto her knees when something swept over her shoulder, close to her ear. She felt the slight breeze of wings as a great-horned owl swooped down, circled the tree just ahead, and landed.

She ran to catch up and stood panting beneath the branch where the owl was sitting. This was not just any owl, but Oro, her oldest friend among the talking animals. She must be in very great trouble if two such helpers had come to her.

"Where are you taking her?" Oro asked.

Maraba turned so that both animals faced Kathe. *"I am taking her far away from the men who are following her."*

"That is what you are leaving – not where you are going," Oro said, like a teacher patiently correcting a pupil. *"Where are you going?"*

There was a silence. *"I don't know. Where do you want to go?"* Maraba asked Kathe in a rather sulky voice.

Kathe was so tired that she almost snapped, '*When have you ever taken me where I want to go?*' but she knew the owl and panther were trying to help.

It was a good question. Where did she want to go now that she was back in the stream of time? Not Ostara. That was where Peter Greystone was, and though it was tempting to go home, she was not stupid enough to think she would be able to hide there. She couldn't go to her father's camp in the hills, either. She had changed so much he wouldn't know what to do with her, and anyway, it would be impossible to keep her presence among the rebels a secret. Their struggle would become even more dangerous.

Pallas? That was Patrick's home. She pictured the mellow stone of that city slowly disappearing into the forest. Could she wait for Patrick there? She had not thought it possible, but she suddenly felt even more tired. She had no way of knowing what had happened when the refugees reached the beach in Brethren or whether they would immediately make their way home to Pallas. Anyway, Patrick's father would be the one leading them there. Not Patrick.

The animals continued to wait for her answer. She knew it was urgent that she decide. Finally, she said, *"Take me to Bethany's farm."*

Stormer had been one of two men sent to scout along the southern shore that day to look for traces of Katherine Elder. The other soldier was barely a teenager, a raw recruit newly assigned to the regiment. Neither of them had been present for the fight that began on the beach after the refugees arrived. They didn't see the black cloud that was Honorus's enchantment, or Patrick running across the sand with his sword held in front of him. They didn't see the dragon swoop low over the beach, changing the balance of power in an instant, just as Maraba did when she bounded down the dune.

That morning, the two soldiers had left Brethren and walked side by side on the wet sand close to the waves, where Stormer knew they were unlikely to find any footprints. His young companion was still cowed by his punishing initiation into the Claymon army, and he would have had trouble following his own tracks back to Brethren, so it wasn't difficult for Stormer to take the lead. He soon found the place where Kathe left the water. When he saw how she had walked backwards across the beach, he quickly misdirected the younger soldier's attention. It wasn't until they had walked a long way farther along the shore and were heading back toward the town that he stopped and pretended to examine the trail more closely. By then it had been mostly obscured by the wind. That was when he sent his companion to signal the others while he went on alone.

Now the commander and the young recruit had moved off toward the headland, and by this time the two of them must be combing the forest for Katherine Elder. The man returning to Brethren with Stormer was as old as his father, and he was a sergeant. He was also in Brethren for the fight on the beach and everything else that happened, though Stormer didn't know anything about that yet.

Stormer's companion remained stone faced as the two of them marched back towards the town. That wasn't unusual, but he stopped so abruptly as they approached the broad swath of sand in front of the harbor that Stormer almost bumped into him.

Stormer shaded his eyes with his hand and squinted. He saw a group of about thirty people sitting on the sand half-way between the sea and the town and an ornate chair tipped on its side by the edge of the water. That looked like the counselor's chair they had lugged over the mountains, but it shouldn't be lying there, within reach of the rising tide. No fishermen were in sight, but the empty boats swayed in the shallow water close to shore. It was easy to see there were things wrong with the scene, but that didn't explain why his fellow soldier seemed so uncomfortable.

He couldn't have known that the gawkers from the town had fled directly to the inn as soon as the dragon disappeared over the horizon. That's where the fishermen went too. It was the sturdiest building in Brethren, and they all badly needed drinks. The people of this port would be talking about the strange, ghostly refugees; the fight between the Claymon and the strangers; the shapeshifting magician; and especially the dragon, for generations.

Stormer's comrade stood frozen in place. He stared at the sky as if he expected to see something fearful there. When he spoke, it was just to himself. "I'd think I made it up except everyone saw it. The black cloud. The old man young again. The lizard flying. I didn't join Greystone's army to fight any of that."

The man was so pale Stormer put his hand on his arm. This was the first time he had ever touched a fellow soldier, except during hand-to-hand fighting while training. It was obvious stepping back onto the beach was the last thing this soldier wanted to do.

"Listen," Stormer said. "Why don't you go straight to the inn and start asking around for a Woods Runner? It shouldn't be hard for you to find the rest of our men. I'll join you there soon. I want to see what those people have to say." He pointed at the group he'd noticed on the beach.

The other man nodded, and Stormer stood there a few moments longer, watching his companion quickly skirt the landward edge of the beach heading for the town. He doubted either of them would find a Runner. The Claymon had not brought any of the trackers with them across the mountains to Brethren, and from what he knew of them, the Runners wouldn't come to a place like this on their own. There weren't enough trees.

Asking the people who were sitting on the beach would be a place to start. As he approached them, Stormer saw right away they weren't from Brethren. The design of their clothing was simple and unfamiliar. Everything they wore was a shade of dun blending almost perfectly with the sand, and he had to adjust his count to include people who were lying curled on the ground. When he reached the group, he could see at once that some of them had been crying.

Stormer realized these must be the refugees the counselor wanted so badly, but if so, Stormer didn't understand why they were important enough to pull the old cripple and a force of Claymon soldiers across the mountains to Brethren. But then, none of the Claymon claimed to understand the counselor. He gave Stormer the shivers.

Holding his hands forward so they could see he carried no weapon, Stormer walked closer to the group, but before he reached them, he realized he wouldn't understand their language even if he could get them to talk to him. He was turning away and already thinking about where to try next when a woman rose to her feet and called to him in the common tongue, "What do you want?"

She wasn't dressed like the others. She wore a deep hood against the intense afternoon sun, and he couldn't see her face.

"I want a Woods Runner." Stormer said.

"For what purpose?"

He wasn't certain how to answer this question, so he gave the obvious response. "We want a tracker."

"For what purpose?" she repeated.

"To track someone."

Stormer noticed the refugees were gazing up at the woman, but they avoided looking directly at him. They might not understand everything she was saying, but it seemed they had already learned to mistrust anyone in a Claymon uniform. For the first time, he noticed a man lying on his back at the center of the group. No one was near him. His eyes were closed, and he was completely still.

The woman hesitated and came to a decision. She pushed her hood back.

He blinked. This woman was with Kathe when she healed him after the bear attack along with another, even older, one. He remembered she was cross that day. She snapped at him to get to his feet and on his way. She must have come to Brethren on the ship with the refugees. She knew why he needed a Runner, and she was afraid.

"I remember you," he said, looking around to make certain there was nobody else around who could understand him.

"I am Katherine's mother," she said sharply, "and I was once a prisoner of Greystone." She waited for his reaction. This was the moment when a Claymon soldier should have taken her by the arm and marched her into the town. Greystone wanted the daughter, but the mother would be almost as valuable a prize. Instead, Stormer just stood with his mouth hanging open, as if he wanted to say something but couldn't form the words.

"Did Katherine reach shore?"

Stormer hesitated. This woman reminded him of his own mother when she was interrogating him. She made him feel uncomfortable in the same way. Lying didn't feel like an option. He nodded.

"Have you spoken with her?"

"Yes."

"Then I ask you again. Why do you need a Runner?" Ellen was beginning to understand that the healing of this young Claymon might have unexpected consequences.

Stormer had already betrayed several of the vows he made on the day he joined the Claymon army, and each time it was a little easier. "I was trying to help her, but other soldiers caught up with us. She was ahead of me, and they didn't see her, but they are looking for her." When she didn't answer, he continued. "I don't think they'll find her. She has a big cat with her."

The Lady smiled for the first time, and Stormer immediately felt something ease at the center of his chest.

"My name is Ellen, and you still haven't answered my question."

"My commander sent me to find a Runner to find Katherine Elder and bring her back here, but I want a Runner to help me find her so that I can help her. I promised I would even though she doesn't want me."

"Ah, now I see," said Ellen. Then she fell silent for so long that Stormer's eyes began to wander over the group of refugees before settling again on the prone figure at their center. Stormer was a soldier, and he had seen corpses. He could tell the old man was dead.

Finally, Ellen turned to one of the female refugees and showed her through gestures and the few words she knew of the forest language that she had to leave, but she would be back very soon. Then, walking so swiftly he had to trot to keep up with her, she led Stormer across the beach and through the alleys of Brethren until they reached a steep path up the hillside behind the town. Along the way, Ellen was careful to avoid being seen, but as far as Stormer could tell, the streets were deserted. The windows of the houses they passed were all shuttered.

Ellen and Stormer kept climbing until they reached a house with a blue door, where she stopped and rapped sharply four times, peering over her shoulder once more to make certain they had not been followed.

"You do not know Patrick yet," she whispered. "He is inside this house, making a plan for the people you saw on the beach. He has to find a safe place to shelter them and some food to keep them alive until they are ready to begin their journey," she said.

The door opened a crack, so small that Stormer barely glimpsed an old woman's prominent nose and whiskery chin. He could not be sure whether it was the same old woman who was with Katherine and her mother when he first he saw them in the forest.

"Don't speak unless someone asks you a question," Ellen ordered as she pushed the door open. She took him by the wrist and pulled him inside. "Leave this to me."

In the time it took Stormer's eyes to adjust to the darkness, five men had circled him. None of them looked happy to see him. He decided to heed Ellen's warning to be silent. He wasn't sure what might happen if he said the wrong thing.

"Take off your shirt," Ellen said.

Stormer didn't want to do it, but he could hardly have felt more vulnerable than he already did. He stripped it off, letting it drop onto the floor. He had set something in motion when he promised Katherine he would help her. Now he had decided to follow her mother to this house, and he knew this was another of the moments that would determine how it was going to play out. He slowly turned around to get a better look at the men and to let them have a good look at him.

"Here," said Ellen with a trace of pride, pointing to the faint white scars on Stormer's chest, "is where a bear hurt this man. Katherine healed him. He says he wants to help, and I believe he speaks true."

After a moment, she added, "I was uneasy after that healing. She and I have a gift, and we are bound to help without asking too many questions, but this man is an enemy."

Stormer had been struggling to understand what she was saying about him, and he forgot her warning. "I am no enemy. I am a Claymon soldier, but I want to help."

One of the men, an old Woods Runner, muttered, "If that is so, then you are the first Northerner I've met who can think for himself."

Stormer had seen what happened to rebels when they were captured by the Claymon, and he had been warned about what would happen to him if he were to be captured by the Claymon's enemies. He glanced around the room. Would they torture him? Would he be flayed first, or would they kill him quickly?

Though he had wrapped his arms around himself to hide his shaking, Stormer slowly turned around again to read the faces of those who were judging him. He was surprised to see two Runners along with three others, a man in a bloodstained shirt who leaned heavily on the younger Runner; a youth who looked like a sailor; and a stocky man, perhaps thirty years old, who stood a bit apart from the others. His hand rested on the head of a rangy, wolfish dog. Like Katherine's mother, that dog looked familiar.

This was the man Ellen addressed. "Patrick. What must we do? The Claymon Commander sent Stormer back to Brethren to find a Runner to track Kathe. Yes," she said answering his unspoken question, "she made it to shore, and Maraba is helping her."

When the man called Patrick spoke, his grasp of the common tongue was nearly as simple as Stormer's, and his accent was strange. "I have a duty to my people, few and damaged though they are. Otherwise, you know I would go to her. And Abel is too hurt to go."

Stormer decided it was a good sign Ellen had used his name.

Patrick turned to the runners. "Will you go, Patch? I will need your son's help in the days ahead, but you are the best tracker I have ever known. Follow her, find her, and do what you can to keep her safe."

These must be the Woods Runners his commander had in mind when he sent Stormer back to the town, but if so, the officer had mistaken where the trackers' loyalty lay.

After talking quietly with the younger Runner for a few moments, the old Runner came over to Patrick and clasped him by the shoulder.

"I'll do it," he said. Without another word he picked up a small pack from the corner and, after sorting through its contents and adding a loaf of bread the old woman handed to him, he slipped it onto his shoulders and would have left at once except that Ellen stopped him.

"Tell him everything you told me," she told Stormer.

The Runner wore a stern expression. Stormer could tell that, like the others, he was not happy about their new ally.

Stormer said, "If you follow the base of the dune below the headland, you'll see a place where Lady Katherine tried to climb, and a little farther along is a brushy place that hides a stream. That's where the big cat led us up the hillside." He took a deep breath and blurted. "And I am coming with you."

Patch didn't bother to answer. He simply turned away, and in the next moment he had slipped out the door. When Stormer took an involuntary step to follow, Patrick seized his arm and pulled him back. "We thank you for the help you have given the Lady Katherine, but you will not go with the Runner."

It sounded like a dismissal

"But I promised...," Stormer said.

With a glance at Patrick, Ellen picked up Stormer's shirt from floor and handed it to him. "Maybe you can help in another way. Are you good at making up stories?"

No fool, Stormer assumed she was asking whether he was good at lying.

"I haven't had much practice," he said.

"Can you find the other Claymon and convince them you found a Woods Runner to track Katherine? Tell them you sent him on his way with a promise to reward him when he brings her back to Brethren. They must believe Patch has changed sides again. Some of them fought him not long ago, and they will be nursing hurts they received from him."

Stormer thought the commander must have been very confused when he found himself fighting the Woods Runners. Maybe he thought they were trying to protect the refugees, since like them, the refugees were from the forest and once shared their ancient home. Stormer had never met a Runner who wasn't in the service of the Claymon, however, and he knew they were well-paid. The commander must have decided he would try to use the trackers to find Katherine, hoping they'd be willing to sell their skills to seek the most valuable quarry of all. After all, she was from Ostara, not the forest, and the Claymon could not have known about her unlikely collection of allies. No, it wouldn't be so difficult to convince his fellow Claymon that is what had happened.

He smarted with disappointment that he would have to rejoin the other Claymon wherever they were hiding and licking their wounds. Now that he had made the decision to sever himself from that life, it was hard to accept going back. On the other hand, he was already an outsider before he met the three women in the forest. He tested a new word. Spy.

"I will do it," he said.

Patrick spoke to the rest of the group as if Stormer wasn't there. "What do you think? Should we trust him?"

Abel was in too much pain to voice an opinion. He had insisted on standing when Ellen and Stormer arrived, but now Patch had settled him into one of the chairs by the fire. The younger Runner knelt by his side, sponging Abel's injured shoulder with a cloth he rinsed in water from a shallow bowl. The wound must have been deep. It was still bleeding. The old woman brought a fresh basin.

The young sailor also had nothing to say. Stormer could not know it, but this teenager had just returned from the strangest voyage of his short life. He had been to an impossible island, where time had no meaning. He had gone from being a deck hand to a warrior in an afternoon, and he knew he would probably be dead right now if not for the arrival of a dragon just at the moment when the fight seemed to have been lost. This boy hadn't seen any sign of Captain Fischer yet, but when he did, they would both have stories to tell. Neither of them would have to buy their own drinks for a long, long time.

Patchson also remained silent. If he had spoken, he would have said Stormer was either trustworthy or not. There was no way to tell just by looking at him.

Ellen repeated, "I believe we have to trust him. He has already taken a great risk to help Katherine, and you know what the punishment will be if he is discovered. He seems to feel he owes a debt to her, even though she had no choice but to heal him."

"He owes nothing to the rest of us," Patrick snapped. He seemed to have aged years since fighting his brother. Honorus ran away from that encounter stronger than ever, and Patrick had watched his father die on the sand. Now he had to take Meier Steele's place and somehow lead the refugees over the mountains to Pallas.

The young Claymon she called Stormer was tall, and he looked strong. It is just like Kathe to heal an enemy soldier and turn him into another pet, Patrick thought irritably.

As if reading his mind, Ellen repeated, "She had no choice, but you do. Stormer may be able to tell us what the Claymon and Honorus will do next. Why not let him prove his worth?"

She turned to Stormer one more time, "Why are you so set on helping us? You could already have captured my daughter, and you would be a hero to your people."

Stormer wasn't sure how to answer this question, and he hesitated. This was another time to be truthful, but it was hard to put it into words. "I'm not so sure I could have captured the

Lady Katherine. She had a knife, and she threatened to use it if I tried."

"On herself," Patrick said flatly.

"Yes, not that I wanted to capture her. It seems she healed more than the hurt I got from the bear when she found me in the forest that day. When I joined the Claymon, I became a soldier like my father, but the people of the North have changed under Peter Greystone. We never felt the need to range from our own lands until he came along. We used to trade with those we now have conquered. And even though I followed orders, as I was taught, it became harder to do it after my healing. I started thinking."

He glanced at Ellen. "For one thing, I thought about what my mother would have to say if one of my sisters was forced into marriage."

His face twisted in an outward trace of his inner struggle. "I have got to do something."

"You had best make plans while I tend to Abel," Ellen told Patrick, as if the matter had been settled. "Tell Stormer what to look for and where to report. And then I have to return to the beach. I don't want to leave the People alone any longer. I hope it will be a while before Honorus will dare to leave the inn, but we can't be sure, and when we do meet him, he will be changed."

There was silence as the others in the room remembered the brittle old man on the beach. He had stolen enough life from the People to make himself young and strong again before the dragon swooped down and chased him off. Everyone could see how frightened Honorus was. Shame and anger would make the magician even more dangerous from now on.

"You had better warn Stormer about that, too," Ellen said. "Honorus can climb right inside your skull and steal your thoughts. I have felt it. Stormer will only be safe until your brother notices him."

"When you go to the People, I will go with you," Patrick said. "I have not forgotten Honorus. Maybe he will give up his insistence on ruling in Pallas now that he has seen how few and weak they are." His tone told Ellen he knew this was wishful thinking. "I will lead the People a short way into the hills and return to Brethren for supplies. There can be no refuge for them here. The sooner we are away from this place, the better." He glanced at Abel, lowering his voice, "And we may suffer more loss before we see the walls of Pallas again."

Turning away, he knelt and stroked the silky ears of the dog sitting by his side. "I know I said you would see your girl again soon, but it seems you will have to wait a little bit longer."

3

HALF-LIGHT

OF COURSE, MARABA AND Oro knew the Claymon were coming long before Kathe did. In their short time together, as they followed Maraba toward the headland, Stormer told her he did not signal the other Claymon the first time he spotted her trail. He wanted her to have time to get away. But he admitted he eventually sent another soldier to whistle an alarm for the Northerners. She still didn't understand why he did that. Was he protecting himself in case he changed his mind about helping her? Or maybe he was so used to following orders it didn't occur to him to ignore this one.

When shadows started to lengthen under the trees, Kathe sat down and would have curled onto her side next to the trail, but Maraba and Oro wouldn't allow it. They urged her back onto her feet even though she protested that she only needed a few moments to rest. The second time it happened, Oro nipped Kathe's ear, startling her into a yelp, which the two animal guides promptly shushed. After that she walked, rubbing her earlobe until it stopped smarting, but she did not stop again.

Instead of leading as she had been, Maraba paced by Kathe's side, pressing against her knee, murmuring nonsense words to keep her awake. Often, the panther stopped and listened with erect ears and twitching tail.

Kathe soon gave up trying to decipher the panther's speech as Maraba soothed her along. It was something like the music of poetry by the fire at home, and she imagined herself sitting with her head against her father's knee while a travelling bard told a rhyming story in a language she could not understand. Though not truly sleep walking, she was nearly asleep on her feet. She yearned to cross the line into oblivion.

The next time Maraba stopped to listen, Kathe shook herself alert and noticed that the pools of darkness under the trees had grown deeper. Soon it would be fully night. Surely Maraba and Oro didn't expect her to walk much farther without rest or food. It was far too early in the year to find any berries in these woods, but she kept her eyes to the ground around her feet. She picked a mushroom and held it in front of her face for a better look. Then she carried it in her hand like a treasure, trying to work up enough courage to eat it.

A few minutes later, she broke off a piece of fungi growing near the base of a tree. Most likely it was last year's growth. She struggled to remember what her mother had told her. Which ones were good to eat, and which were poisonous? She tossed away the mushroom that might have been a toadstool and chewed on the shelf fungi. It was tough, tasted earthy, and it didn't do anything to quell her hunger. She picked a couple of fiddleheads and chewed them even though they were bitter.

Kathe was still looking for things to eat when Maraba left her side, doubled back, and growled. Before this, whenever Maraba stopped to listen or when Oro flew out of sight behind them, Kathe thought the animal guides were just being careful. They had not said anything about pursuers, and her trust was so complete that she hardly spared a thought for the Claymon. Anyway, the Northerners were too large and clumsy to be good trackers, weren't they? That's why they used the Woods Runners.

Maraba had been leading them along a faint deer trail that led more or less towards the base of the mountains. They would have to cross those peaks again to reach Bethany's farm, but when Kathe felt the brush of a wing against her cheek, she knew she had to follow Oro off the trail instead. It was the same signal he used to get her attention when she first met him, more than a year before.

She left the path and pushed her way through the undergrowth in the direction she thought he had flown, searching for an owlish shape in the dusky light. Before they had gone far, Oro landed on top of a massive, fallen tree. Kathe started to climb over it, but the owl waddled along the trunk until he reached the base, where the tree had tipped from the ground, leaving a deep hole and a mound of soil.

"In. In. In," he said, hopping up and down to emphasize the urgency of his command and to deter argument.

Katherine peeked over the mass of roots fringing the base of the trunk and saw the tree was hollow as far as she could see. And it was dark. Anything could live in there.

"In. As far as you can."

She crouched in the opening, and Oro hopped down to sit on the mound of soil that partially obscured the hole. He brushed at the dirt with a wing and scratched at it with his talons. She realized he was trying to cover her tracks, and she reached out to stroke the feathers on his head.

"Thank you." She said. *"I haven't had a chance to ask you about your owlets."*

"There are three," he said grumpily, *"and they are always hungry, like you. Soon I will catch a mouse for you."* His voice took on the wheedling tone he probably used with his own young. *"You'll like that won't you?"*

Then he flew away, back to where Maraba awaited him on the path. Kathe gingerly scooted a little farther into the tree trunk and deeper into darkness, disturbing tiny, skittering things. She brushed a cobweb from her cheek, shaking her hand violently enough to dislodge a spider she could not see but imagined was there. She strained to hear what was happening back on the deer trail.

Danger must be close for Maraba and Oro to make her hide like this. What did the animal guides plan to do when the

Northerners came? She hoped they too would hide until the Claymon gave up and went away. The trackers wouldn't see the panther or the owl unless they showed themselves, and even if they did, they wouldn't connect them with Kathe unless Stormer had told them about the animal guides. Kathe didn't think he would do that. On the other hand, where was he? Maybe she had misread him. Stormer might be leading them here.

A poorwill began to call. The night bird's song was so loud and persistent that Kathe felt more than heard the rumble of distant thunder. When the breeze freshened, it didn't reach her hiding place. Between the enthusiastic bird and the rustle of leaves, it was hard to hear anything else. Now that she was no longer walking, she could have curled up and fallen asleep in this dark, dry place. Then she might forget her hunger for a while. Asleep, she wouldn't notice if insects crawled on her. The decaying wood was soft. She rested her head on her arms.

After a few moments of lying with her eyes closed, she realized she was completely, unreasonably awake. Also, she was alone again with only the sounds of the forest to keep her company. It helped to know Maraba and Oro were nearby even if she couldn't call them.

Kathe had been lost and lonely many times since running away from her home in Ostara. For one long, hot summer she worked in the Springvale kitchen and roamed the fringes of the manor's holdings after dark. That was before she and Meg became friends. Not long ago, when she and Patrick were swept down a mountainside by an avalanche, she was separated from all her companions by more than an arm's length of suffocating snow. And this morning on the beach she had thought herself alone. She could not have known she would find friends so quickly – first Stormer and then the panther and owl. Kathe reminded herself that she couldn't depend on finding help. She had to be ready to take care of herself and, for the third time that day, she fingered the knife.

Kathe knew the guides would be in danger if the Claymon discovered her in her hiding place. If that happened, they would fight to defend her, and they might be hurt or even killed. She couldn't let that happen. Talons and claws, however fearsome, are no match for a steel blade. Even though Oro had chosen this hiding place for her, the hollow log felt more like a trap with every passing moment. A rough oval holding the last trace of twilight marked her escape route to the outside, but it was too dark inside the hollow tree to see her hand in front of her face, let alone a centipede on that hand. If a face appeared in the opening, she would have no way to escape.

Suddenly claustrophobic, Kathe scrambled out of the hollow trunk, fell behind the tree and squirmed into a low place underneath it. It wasn't necessarily a better hiding place, but at least she could hear what was happening, and she would be able to run if she had to. Unless she made a noise, she was sure no one would find her.

Kathe did not know how to speak the Claymon language, but she recognized it when she heard it. Even though her parents kept her away from the soldiers when they began to congregate in the streets of Ostara, they couldn't keep those guttural voices from echoing up the stairs from the hall below. And even though, thanks to the healing, she knew Stormer as well as she knew her brother Bard, understanding that particular Claymon soldier did not come with any knowledge of his language, not even "Hello" or "Who are you" or "You are making a big mistake."

Because of her guides' behavior, Kathe knew the Northerners were getting close, but it was still a shock to hear the voice of one nearby. It came from right above her. She could have reached out and grabbed his ankle. He wasn't trying to be quiet, and he sounded angry. It wasn't Stormer's voice. It sounded deeper and older. Was Stormer there too? Was he the one listening to the words that were growing louder and faster?

Kathe curled herself into a tighter ball. She hugged both arms around her belly, which was beginning to make noises she could not control. Maybe she chose the wrong mushroom to eat. She hoped the Claymon was talking too loudly to hear the sounds.

A second male voice answered. This one sounded younger, squeaked like a teenager, and was much less certain. This also was not Stormer. She heard both men move off towards the base of the tree, and she imagined rather than saw them looking into the hole where she had been hiding a few minutes before. They took some time there. It sounded as if they were poking into the darkness with a stick. After a few more words, which sounded like curses, one of them kicked the trunk hard. Kathe jerked. She bumped her head, then buried her face in the leaves under the trunk. She vomited as quietly as she could.

The silence that followed was worse than the voices. She wiped her mouth with the back of her hand. What were they doing? She tensed, ready to run.

"Looks like you've come to a dead end here."

This third voice made the gruff Claymon gasp. He shouted words that sounded like cursing again. Kathe realized she could understand what the third man was saying. He spoke the common tongue, a simple version of Ostaran used by traders and other visitors to the city.

"Don't you know better than to sneak up on us like that?" the Claymon growled, switching to the same language. "It's a good way to die."

"You don't want to kill me," the newcomer said, sounding unconcerned. "You sent for me to find the girl."

The new voice was familiar.

"The trail leads here, but it is too dark to track her any farther tonight," the Claymon said. He didn't sound happy to see the newcomer, whoever he was and even if he did send for him.

"And why should we trust you? You did your best to kill us back at the town."

"I am glad you recognize me," the third man said. "Runners serve the Claymon, but we have older loyalties. That man on the beach, the one with the sword?" The speaker paused. "We have watched over him since long before Greystone was a mewling baby. And the old man your leader is using? The one you call the counselor? That one brings trouble wherever he goes."

Kathe held her breath. The man with the sword had to be Patrick. The dragon must have carried him safely to the mainland, and for some reason he was in a fight with the Claymon on the beach. Knowing he was safe eased her heart. But why was he fighting? She could put a name to the newcomer now. It had to be either Patch or Patchson. She never could tell their voices apart.

The Runner continued, "You might not be able to track in this light, but I can. Follow me."

Kathe heard the crunch of leaves as the runner moved away, followed by one set of footsteps. But where was the other Claymon? She felt panic as she listened to someone moving slowly along the fallen tree.

When she felt the toe of a boot in the small of her back, she jerked and hit her head again on the underside of the tree trunk.

"Come back! Here she is!" It was the older Claymon, and his shriek was so shrill his voice cracked. Kathe squirmed out from under the opposite side of the tree trunk and away from the boot, which kept kicking at her. Staying low, she scuttled into the woods, farther away from the path she had been following with the animal guides. More curses followed as the Claymon scrambled onto the tree trunk and fell to his knees on the other side.

Kathe half ran, half crawled through the brush until the Claymon's voice faded, and she reached a gash in the earth. She barely saw it in time to stop herself. After a moment's hesitation, she sat down on the rim of the ravine and slowly lowered herself over the edge. Swallowing a cry, she let go and tumbled to the bottom, unable to protect herself from the brambles that covered the steep bank.

She knew the trackers would easily follow her trail, but it was even darker at the bottom of the gorge than in the hollow log. The thorns that had slowed her descent would be a barrier to them too. She was lying in a shallow stream. She made herself breathe slowly. When she put her hand to her chest, it felt as if her heart was trying to escape.

Kathe drank deeply and crawled out of the water. She paused before starting upstream. She hoped that way would take her toward the mountains and away from the sea. Even though it was springtime, there didn't seem to be much growing in the gully except blackberry brambles and some other, even pricklier, vine. She wrapped her hands in the bottom edge of her shirt and held them ahead of her, pushing her way through the dense vegetation. She squinted, trying to make out shapes in the gloom.

This must be what it is like to be blind. Because she had lived outside for most of a year, she knew nights are rarely completely dark. There is usually enough moonlight or starlight for walking. Until now, that is. A few minutes ago, up above, she was still able to make out the grainy shapes of bushes and rocks in her path, but now deep blackness loomed in every direction.

Kathe tripped and stumbled a few steps forward. Her hands, outstretched to break her fall, brushed something unexpected. Warmth. Hair. The back of her neck prickled as she recognized a scent. It was the same as the one that lingered in the clearing where they found Stormer lying, nearly lifeless. It was the musky scent of a bear.

Heedless now of the tearing thorns, Kathe threw herself sideways and crawled towards the side of the ravine. She let out a sobbing breath and scrambled, for the third time that day, to climb.

"Hey there! Where are you going, Flame Child?"

Shocked into stillness, Kathe pressed her cheek against the ground. She looked back into the darkness and remembered another night in another forest. Oro was the first of the animal guides to talk to her and the first to call her Flame Child. He came to her where she waited for Abel at the edge of Springvale, and he led her deep among the trees. There, he showed her a wide circle of animals, and he told her to look at them until she was sure she would recognize each of them if she saw them again.

Since then she had come to trust some members of that circle. Maraba the panther was there that first night. Was there also a bear? She struggled to remember. There must have been, because here he was talking to her. Animal guides were the only ones who could do that.

Doing her best to swallow her fear, but still shaking, Kathe slid back down the hill and made her way towards the spot where she had felt the coarse hair of the bear under her fingertips. *"I was afraid,"* she told him. *"But now I know you."*

"Good reason to be afraid. The night bird told me you are in a heap of trouble."

Though she still couldn't see him, Kathe glimpsed the rising moon reflected in his liquid eye.

"Climb on." He said. *"It is time to sort this out."*

He had to lie on his belly for her to do it, but soon she was clinging to the rolls of fat and fur along the beast's massive shoulders, rolling back and forth, riding high above the brambles as he climbed up the side of the ravine. Katherine slid to the ground, and the bear lumbered into the forest towards the men who were chasing her.

"They're in for a surprise." He sounded as if he were looking forward to it.

Patch paused when he reached the tree. Here was where Katherine Elder had lain curled like a fawn under the trunk. She had vomited, and even though he was too good a tracker to believe in such things, Patch thought he scented her fear. He couldn't have prevented the Claymon from poking around. It was bad luck that the Commander had flushed the Lady from her hiding place. Patch had to give her credit, though. She hadn't made a squeak as she fled.

Oro flew forward over Patch's shoulder, following the course Katherine had taken through the trees. The young soldier was staring after his leader, and he didn't notice the owl. He hesitated. Patch and the boy could hear the officer crashing through the forest on the other side of the big fallen tree. The noises were growing fainter, but he had not received an order to follow, and he was scared of doing the wrong thing.

"You stay here, in case she circles back," Patch said calmly, hoping his status as a Woods Runner would convince the frightened boy. Patch didn't blame him for being afraid of the darkness, of getting lost, or especially, of displeasing his leader. It was lucky the young soldier had already turned towards Patch when Maraba silently leapt over the log. He would probably have soiled himself.

"Is that what I should do?" the soldier asked.

"Yes. And stay right here by this tree. Don't wander off. We don't want to have to look for you too."

Without waiting for an answer, Patch walked to the end of the tree, clambered over the mound of dirt, and followed the sounds of crashing branches. His body ached from the battle on the beach. He was getting too old for this. He told himself that, as soon as the Lady Katherine was safe and the People were back where they belonged, he was going home to Maron, and they would tend their garden in the forest together.

4

THE EMPTY SKY

GALE STOOD ON THE grassy hillside above the crescent of Niue's harbor, shading his eyes against the glare of sun on water. He had been squinting into the distance since before sunrise.

"Where is she?" he muttered for the hundredth time.

He heard Bethany and Gerard talking quietly, down below on the beach. They were busy planning their life together on this pile of rock that thrust skyward from the middle of the blank ocean. This accursed island wasn't even on any real maps. He didn't count the Changeful Map, which showed just as much as it wanted to. To his mind, it would be no life at all to stay here, yet all day the two of them had been moving around the beach together first studying the trickling spring, then disappearing into the darkness of Padraik's cave. Now he watched them poking at the sand with pieces of driftwood. What were they doing?

Gerard gave a whoop and held something over his head. With a grunt, Gale turned back to watching the sky.

"I found a clam, and where there's one, there'll be more," Gerard crowed. "We'll eat well tonight!"

Gale slid down to the beach and snapped, "Are you going to make a fire with that wet piece of wood in your hand? And what about tomorrow, and the day after that? What will you eat then?"

He had so far refused to think about what would happen if Meg and the dragon Padraik didn't return to the island. In that case, he too would be collecting scraps of flotsam to dry so they could make a fire to cook whatever the sea granted them. And he'd be doing it forever, as far as he could tell. Or at least until he decided he'd had enough. He pushed the thought away.

It was too soon to worry about that. He walked to the edge of the sea and kept his fierce attention on the sky until it turned the color of ripe apricots and longer, until it deepened to cobalt and the first star appeared and glittered coldly.

He might have stayed there, sitting on the sand all night, but Bethany came and led him to the end of the beach where Gerard had somehow made a small, lively fire. She handed Gale a piece of hard biscuit from the supplies left behind from the *Goshawk* and a bowl of salty broth to dip it in. He ate the shreds of shell-fish at the bottom of the bowl with his fingers. He was too tired and worried to acknowledge how good they tasted.

When he finally closed his eyes and fell asleep, Bethany covered him with a blanket. Then, for a time, she and Gerard stood where Gale had spent the entire day, watching for the shadow of a dragon to pass across the stars.

The breeze died overnight. When Gale awoke in the grey before dawn, the first thing he noticed was how quiet it was. The sea was calm, with only the slightest lapping of waves against the shore. He got up and poked at the remains of the small fire. There were still a few coals under the ashes, but he couldn't see any way to keep them alive. There simply was not enough fuel. Today he would help Gerard break up the boxes that held the supplies left behind from the *Goshawk*, but those wouldn't last long. Pensively, he fed the coals a shred of dry sea-weed, and the glow briefly brightened into flame. Well, there was plenty more where that came from.

He hobbled to the high-water line on morning-stiff legs and gathered an armload of the stuff. It was well-dried from the sun. He knew more would wash in on each tide, but it would burn fast. He started twisting it into tight bunches so it would last longer.

His compulsion to look at the sky had faded. Instead, he turned inward as he worked, thinking about Meg. He could almost hear the sound of her laugh, and realized he knew what to do to earn it. Even the silliest joke or play on words would make her smile, at least. He wished he had known her sooner, back when she was his father's servant. They might have become friends. Maybe she would have trusted him enough to tell him about the book she found.

This was just a daydream, and he knew it. He could never have been on such terms with a kitchen girl. It wouldn't even have occurred to the old Gale to talk to her. And the old Meg would have been too shy to reply even if he did.

It took Katherine to break them both free of their old lives and to begin their journey to finally becoming equals. When Kathe hid from the Claymon in the Springvale kitchen, and later when she fled into the forest and took them with her, she bridged the divide between their positions. If Gale was honest, Meg was now more than his equal. She had learned to read better than he could, and though she had no healing gift such as Kathe's, she knew so much herbal lore that she could name almost every useful or edible plant along their way. She was the only one who could talk to the dolphins or to Padraik. He'd never tell her so, but she had more common sense than he did – and a calmer head.

He took a single, steadying breath and glanced up at the blank sky, which was now too bright with the rising sun to see anything at all. He wouldn't give up on her yet.

He carried his small pile of fuel back to the fire. Laying the first seaweed bundle across the embers, he watched it closely to see how it burned.

It was another clear morning, which meant it would be another hot day. Gale suspected this was the only kind of weather on the island called Niue, so when a shadow fell across his shoulders and darkened the section of beach where he was sitting, it carried as much weight as a shout.

He leapt to his feet and ran towards the opposite end of the harbor where Padraik had landed and was lying with his neck and head stretched out on the sand. The sick tension Gale had been fighting ever since Meg and Patrick climbed onto the dragon's back fell away. As he came closer he saw Meg struggling to untie the rope knotted around her waist. She slid down Padraik's side, and crawled crab-like to the beast's head. She was crooning something.

When she rose to her feet and turned towards him, her expression stopped him. She looked bleak, like a soldier returning from battle or a sailor after a storm. Her face was grey with fatigue, with dark circles under her eyes. The hand resting on the dragon's neck trembled. Without saying a word, she told Gale she had doubted whether Padraik could fly all the way to the mainland and back again. Gale shuddered, as if he could feel the ice that had nearly formed in her blood.

She smiled slightly, looking away from him, out over the sea. It was as if she had heard all the words he should have said. "Help with the ropes, will you?"

Gale took the few steps to close the distance between them and hugged her. Her cloak was wet, and she couldn't stop shaking.

"He will have to eat," she said. Meg turned away from Gale and knelt by Padraik again. He heard her take a deep breath. "Do you know what he said to me after midnight? He told me he was sorry. That he didn't think he could make it all the way back to the island. I told him he had nothing to be sorry about. Just then I doubted I could hang on much longer. My hands were nearly frozen."

Gale took her hands and warmed them inside his own. Meg whimpered a little as they thawed.

"I don't know how he found the strength. I thought I would never see you again."

"I knew you'd come back," he lied.

They worked in silence to remove Padraik's harness and walked back to the fire together. Meg held Gale's arm, but whether for strength or comfort Gale didn't know. Bethany had already added his seaweed twists to the coals and had nestled the pot in the center. She was cooking more of the shelled creatures she and Gerard had dug out of the sand. Bethany hugged Meg, then held her at arm's length before settling her in the sun.

"Is there anything I can give Padraik?" Meg whispered. "He will need to be warm before he can hunt for himself."

"I will catch a fish," Gale said. He was eager to do something. The last time he fished was back at Springvale, and it was with a metal hook. The small fish he brought home that day would hardly have fed a hungry man, let alone a dragon, but fishing was fishing, wasn't it, whether in a mill pond or the ocean?

Gerard lent his walking staff to use as a shaft, and Gale used a piece of rope to lash one of his arrows to its end. Then he waded hip deep into the warm water and waited for his prey. The sand was soft under his feet, and with the sun on his shoulders, it would have felt like play if his task were not so urgent. The water was calm and clear. Gale could easily see the fish. There seemed to be plenty of them, and they were much larger than the ones he used to catch at home. None were within striking range yet, but they would swim closer if he stayed still.

He glanced back at the beach. Padraik still had not raised his head, but by now the sun should be warming him, and if Gale could catch a fish, he would be fed. Then they would wait to see whether the dragon would ever be willing to fly again.

Because of the nature of this island, it felt as if they had been here forever, but it was only a few days ago when Meg sighted Niue from her perch in the *Goshawk's* crow's nest. A pod of playful dolphins led the *Goshawk* here; and even though the landing boat had to fight its way through the turbulent harbor entrance, they thought their quest was coming to an easy end.

The travelers had been prepared for a sea-journey of several weeks before reaching Niue, but it took them barely three days to spot the unmistakable shape of the island's mountain. They thought they only needed to find the refugees to fulfill their promise – to take the lost people of Pallas home to their forest. On such a small island, how difficult could that be?

The sudden appearance of the dragon on the beach was shocking, but it was even worse when they realized the treasure it demanded. Meg was able to understand the dragon at once, and she told the others Padraik wanted an object the refugees were hiding, a music box that played a plaintive melody from their past. But now that the dragon had discovered he could talk to this human girl, Meg became the most precious treasure in his hoard. After a lifetime of loneliness, it was clear Padraik would never give her up. She would stay here to be the dragon's companion. Even worse, since no one on Niue ever grows old or dies, unless by accident or by choice, her imprisonment would last forever.

On the first day on the island, Gale cursed his hands, which had not healed properly after the beating he endured in Peter Greystone's prison back in Ostara. So many bones had been broken that he would never be the archer he once was. While the others climbed Niue's mountain to look for the refugees, Gale lay on the headland and watched Meg as she made her bargain with the dragon. That day, Gale wanted to send an arrow into its eye or into the unarmored place under its throat. He thought if he crept close enough, he could have seen its heart beating in the most vulnerable place.

Today, standing perfectly still in warm water, willing the fish to come closer, Gale realized he no longer wanted to destroy the dragon. This wasn't just because Padraik had become his best hope of leaving the island. Yes, the dragon had killed some of the refugees, but those deaths were the result of the dragon's nature, not malice. Would he blame a lion for killing a human who had wandered into its territory?

Gale couldn't believe his thinking had changed so much. He now saw those refugee deaths as the result of a misunderstanding between the People and the dragon. In their yearning for home and in a superstitious attempt to soothe the dragon, they had sent a series of singers to the rocks above the harbor to chant an ancient ballad about a hero of their people, one Patrick Steele. The dragon loved the song. He took the hero's name as his own, but he freely admitted he killed some of the singers who displeased him. He didn't eat them, and he seemed to think that should make a difference.

Padraik's dragon ways were hard to understand, but in the time since they met him, he had proven himself willing to do nearly anything for Meg. He flew Patrick to the mainland, and now he had returned to Niue even though it had almost killed him. Gale wasn't sure how she did it, but Meg claimed she had even taught the dragon that people are not for killing, no matter how displeasing their voices. But to be fair, the new rule had not been tested yet.

The first fish to swim within range of the spear was as long as Gale's arm, with bright blue streaks along its side. He threw the spear too soon, burying the tip deep in the sand. The fish put a little more distance between itself and the disruption on the seabed, but it hardly seemed to notice its close call. This wasn't going to be as easy as he hoped. It took two more failed attempts before Gale learned to allow for the way the water bends light. When he speared his first fish, he held it overhead and splashed back to the beach.

Cooked in Bethany's soup, it would have been large enough to feed the four of them for the whole day, but Gale hurried to the dragon. Padraik raised his head a little as Gale approached. Without thinking, Gale laid one hand on top of Padraik's massive nose and tried to say, *"I caught this for you. Thank you for bringing her back."*

Padraik winced. He said, *"You caught the best kind,"* and swallowed the wriggling fish whole. Encouraged by his first conversation with a dragon, Gale set off to spear another.

Before dawn, long before she saw the shape of Niue's mountain rising from the sea, Meg was sure she and Padraik were going to drown. She told herself that if they did make it back, she would never fly again. Now, two days later, lying on her back on the warm sand next to Gale, she was surprised to notice that her fear of flying had already dulled.

When she first met Padraik, after he poured out a flood of images that nearly burned her alive, he had become a dragon of few words. She knew he was thinking about everything she had shown him of the world beyond his island because at long intervals there were questions that seemed to come from nowhere.

Yesterday, when the ropes were laid out on the sand so she and Gale could test every knot, and as they talked about how to make the harness more comfortable for the dragon and more secure for themselves, Padraik asked, *"Why was there only one big cave in the place you called Springvale?"*

"What do you mean?" Meg said, pausing in her work to look up at the dragon. His eyes were closed. She had thought he was asleep.

"There was one big cave inside a tall wall, and there were a few small caves along the edge of the forest. Who lives in the big cave?"

Why was he asking this? Did he think the manor house was the home of a dragon? *"His father and mother live there."* Meg said, nodding towards Gale.

Padraik must have decided to mull over this new information for a while, since he didn't ask anything else.

Since returning from delivering Patrick to the mainland, Padraik had not said anything about making another flight. Meg tried not to make too much of that. She didn't much feel like talking about it either.

Gale had fallen asleep in the sun. She adjusted the angle of his hat to shade his face and focused her attention on the dragon.

She tried to read what Padraik was thinking, but he was also asleep, or pretending he was.

Meg rose and stretched, making her way to what had become Padraik's end of the beach. She stood to one side and rested her hand on the side of his neck. The dragon had caught what seemed to be a slight cold on his first journey to the mainland, and she had learned it could be dangerous to be standing in front of him when he sneezed.

"Padraik. I want to talk to you," She said aloud. "Padraik, you faker. You're awake aren't you?"

There was still no response from the dragon, who started to snore.

Gerard's voice startled her, "When the two of you came back, Padraik was exhausted. He is still tired, but now he sleeps because his belly is full of fish. Gale is getting better at spearing them, and now that he is hunting on his own, your dragon is finally full."

Meg smiled at the old healer, who had taken to going barefoot. He had made broad sun hats for each of them from the reeds growing near the spring.

"It is the way of reptiles," he said. "We have to be patient."

"He isn't my dragon," Meg corrected patiently. "It's just – I'm not sure how he will feel about our bargain when he wakes up. Now that he can talk to any of us, maybe he will think we are company enough. Maybe he will be too afraid to fly again."

"He will do it for you," Gerard said.

"Perhaps," Meg said thoughtfully. "But I wouldn't want him to do it just for me. He must want to find another dragon. He has to believe she, or maybe he, is out there somewhere. I admit I am hoping for a she, though. Now that I have met this dragon, it is hard to imagine the world without at least one of them."

"It has taken me a while," Gerard said, "but I am coming around to that way of thinking too."

Meg swung in a circle to encompass the whole island, trying to make Gerard understand. "I wish you could know how it felt to see nothing but water in every direction and to know – absolutely know – he lacked the strength to make it here. The flight to Brethren with Patrick was short, though it didn't seem so then. It took much longer to come back. It was as if the island was testing us, playing tricks with time. Who knows how long the third flight might take if we are not meant to escape?"

She gazed down the beach to where Bethany was sitting in the shade, reading a book. "Leave, I mean. This isn't a prison, is it?"

Gerard followed the direction of Meg's gaze. "Beth believes she is destined to stay here. I am not as certain, but after so many separations, I am content."

"The world will miss you," Meg said.

"I think you are wrong about that but come with me. I want to show you something."

Meg followed Gerard further along the beach and they circled around a heap of tumbled rock that extended into the sea at the far end of the harbor.

"Bethany hasn't seen this yet, and when she does, I'm not sure what she'll say."

There, upside down on the sand, was a small boat she had last seen on the deck of the *Goshawk*. It was half the size of the longboats that had carried the people out to the ship. There were oars too. She could see the ends sticking out from underneath. Meg glanced at Gerard to see what he was thinking. He looked pleased with himself. Meg knew this craft would be too frail to cross the wide expanse of water she and Padraik had just traversed. At least, she wouldn't dare to try it.

Gerard's eyes twinkled. He obviously was proud of his secret.

"She might be angry, but she will forgive you," Meg said.

Gerard held one finger to his lips. "For now, let's keep this between ourselves."

Padraik half opened one golden eye when Meg and Gerard passed him on their return to the other end of the beach. Since Meg was standing next to him, she saw her reflection, as well as

Gerard's behind her, and the steep cliff leading up to the mountain. It seemed the dragon had been listening.

"You will guard my hoard?" he asked Gerard.

Gerard and Bethany had already explored Padraik's cave with an eye to living there themselves after the dragon flew away for the final time, and they found it surprisingly clean and dry, with his small collection of treasures neatly heaped along one wall.

"I guess that means we are going to fly again," Meg said, and she tasted something sour at the back of her throat. "I can't promise…"

"Don't be afraid," Padraik said. *"You don't want to stay here, do you?"*

Was he leaving it up to her? She imagined living here with Gale. It would be good for a while. They could rest and soak up so much sun that her memory of the icy flight would fade to nothingness. But as soon as she considered this possibility, the haunted faces of the refugees filled her mind's eye. Those faces were enlivened by hope only when they hurried to board the boats that would carry them away from the island and into the future.

As tempting as it was to stay on Niue, Meg knew she and Gale had to leave. If they stayed here, they would fish and explore the island, but that wouldn't take long. After they had seen everything there was to be seen, every day would be the same. They wouldn't grow or learn or ever see their families again. Meg didn't have to ask Gale. She knew it wouldn't be enough for either of them.

"No," she said. *"I am afraid, but I don't want to stay here."*

"Send Loudmouth over here," Padraik said. *"I have a couple of ideas for the ropes."*

5

THE HERO AND THE SPY

WHEN PATRICK AND THE refugees reached Abel's old cabin, there was time to rest and wait before the cold hours after midnight. That's when they would have to cross the snowy ridge that lay ahead. Even though the cabin had been recently inhabited, it already felt abandoned. When Patrick stepped inside, he heard the rustling of small creatures living in the roof, and he saw the bed in the corner had been raked into a pile in the center of the floor by wild claws. Abel's precious books had been chewed by wood mice. Soon every volume would be transformed into nests for their young ones.

Patrick recalled the other night he spent in this cabin. Then it seemed like a celebration of sorts, with stories, stew and a dancing fire. Now Abel wasn't here, and that was another worry. The cut Abel received in the battle on the beach was deep, and he had lost too much blood to make the journey. As much as Patrick regretted leaving him behind, there wasn't a choice. When Abel tried to protest, Patrick didn't have to respond. The effort of arguing wore Abel down so quickly that he allowed Fischer's mother to lead him back to his bed. Once there, Abel turned his head away and said nothing when Patrick stepped into the bedroom to say goodbye. Together, they gazed through the room's round window, over the town to the sea. Patrick hoped it would help that he had given Abel something to do while he waited to heal. The boy Stormer would need someone to report to – assuming he ever had anything to report.

Even though food was scanty and they couldn't all sleep under the cabin's roof, the sight of the little dwelling cheered the refugees in much the same way it had cheered the earlier travelers who passed this place on their way to the Port of Brethren not long before. All of Abel's wine was gone, but Patchson had made a fire in the hearth before he disappeared to hunt. At least it wasn't raining this time. In fact, since they last visited this place, the year seemed to have made a giant leap towards spring. Small white flowers glowed in the clearing, and the air would be soft for those sleeping outside under the deep eaves.

Later, standing next to the door of Abel's cabin, Patrick measured two fingers' width from a loaf of bread, tore it off, and handed it to the next refugee in line, who had been waiting patiently for his portion. Although much changed, with deep lines marking his sun-browned face, the man was familiar. Patrick knew him long ago after he left the house of his father to become Leonides's apprentice. In those days, when Patrick was just the younger son of Meier Steele, this man had a bake shop a short distance up the hill from his master's work room.

In those days, round, flat loaves of chewy bread appeared on tables throughout the city every day, but this baker was the only one who sold flaky pastries filled with ground nuts and honey. Whenever this confection was in the oven, the fragrance wafted through the open windows of the carpentry shop and mingled with the scent of wood shavings. Patrick had forgotten about it until this moment, but now the memory of the delicacy returned so strongly that he looked down at the plain loaf in his hands, and his mouth watered. He didn't have much pocket money back then, so he couldn't buy the treat every day, but whenever he went into the shop, he always spoke with the baker. Patrick remembered his name. It was Marios.

Marios hadn't yet shown any sign that he recognized his long-ago regular customer, the boy who always had sawdust clinging to his cuffs and knees. Somehow, Patrick had become a hero and their leader.

The refugees knew Patrick had recently seen the city of Pallas. He had described to them the ways it had changed. How the buildings of the forest city now were open to the sky and full of moldering leaves. He wanted to prepare them for the damage they would find, but instead they grasped at the familiar.

He heard one of them say, "Did you hear? The spring is still running. We can repair the aqueduct."

Another said, "Those good stone walls! Roofs can be replaced." There were murmurs of agreement.

Patrick remembered the people of Pallas as creative, impatient and even quarrelsome, but now their jokes and good-natured bickering had been replaced by uncomplaining endurance. He hadn't heard them talk among themselves about what happened on the beach in Brethren even though it was their arrival from the *Goshawk* that started the conflict, and they were in the center of it all.

That final night, before Patrick led the refugees away, Fischer's mother stayed up to bake because she knew they would be leaving Brethren before dawn. Patrick had planned to ask for food from Captain Fischer, but the well-supplied *Goshawk* remained at anchor far from shore, and there was no way to reach the ship. In the end, Patrick had to spend a portion of Gerard's gold, sending Fischer's grandson to buy whatever he could from the tavern and the one other shop in the town. It wasn't much. On the coast, spring is a lean season in the best of years, and the Claymon had already emptied the shelves in the town. The refugees would have some dried fish, the bread, and a little soft cheese made from the milk of the skinny cows that grazed the hillside. It would be enough if they were careful. It would have to be.

Patrick looked uneasily from the dwindling loaf of bread in his hand to the refugees who were still standing in a line behind Marios. Their trust unsettled him. Without discussion or ceremony, they had transferred their loyalty from Meier Steele to Patrick Steele. To them, he was the man who once marched out to save the town from Ostaran raiders, who they believed to have been killed in that battle, and who now had returned by magic or miracle to lead them home.

Although he might seem a hero to the people of Pallas, Patrick knew himself to be a fraud. He was badly hurt fighting against Ostaran raiders, and he should have died, but the battle that seemed so important at the time was no more than a scrimmage. When he marched out from Pallas to meet the enemy, he was only a boy - a carpenter, not a soldier.

He had no memory of being spirited away by the Forest Lady after the battle. In fact, he didn't remember anything else until Katherine woke him from his enchanted sleep. None of it had anything to do with courage.

Kathe. Where was she? Was she safe? Patch must have caught up with her by now.

Before Marios turned away, he laid a hand on Patrick's arm. "When we get home, I'll open my shop. The ovens will still be there. I will make something special again, you'll see. You used to come to buy my pastries. I haven't baked for a long time, but I still have the recipes," he said, tapping his forehead with a finger. He looked directly into Patrick's face, something none of the other refugees had done. "We will be a city again. You'll see."

"Thank you," Patrick whispered. For the first time he felt a connection with one of the refugees that went beyond duty. He hoped Marios was right, but he knew these were the same people who had once listened to Honorus and followed his command to run away from their homes in Pallas and hide themselves on the island. Before that, these same refugees had turned against Patrick's parents for a time. Some of them probably still blamed his sister Bethany and her husband Gerard for their troubles.

No matter how hard they might work, these few, worn out refugees would never be able to recreate the Pallas they remembered. One day they would understand that, and on that day, their allegiance might shift again.

The refugees moved with maddening slowness, weakened by the deprivation they had experienced during their exile and by their encounter with the magician. Now that Honorus had regained so much strength at their expense, he would have easily caught up with them on the road if Patrick had chosen to lead them that way. Honorus could have demanded the Claymon track the refugees cross-country through the mountains, but Patrick believed he would now wait until the People were home in Pallas before troubling them again. He understood his brother better than anyone. Honorus was too lazy to lead the People home himself, but his pride would bring him back to the forest eventually.

Tonight they would rise in darkness to set off on the next, most treacherous, part of their journey. Patrick had good reason to remember Maraba's advice. If he could, he wanted to be well down the other side of the mountain before the sun started to warm the snow. Even though he couldn't see it from here, he glanced in the direction of the ridge and pictured the route they would take.

He missed Maraba. Stormer said the panther was guiding Katherine, which was as it should be. Still, he and Patch would be on their own tomorrow, and they were both men of the forest, not the mountains. The last time they came here, he and his companions had crossed in one long day, but he feared the people of Pallas couldn't match that pace. Once they started walking again, there would be no place to rest until they reached the other side. There were three babies, five other small children, and too many old people.

Patrick retreated to the edge of the alpine forest and forced himself to eat his share of bread. It tasted of nothing. When he heard a twig snap behind him, his hand went to his sword.

"You're jumpy," Ellen said. After a pause, she added, "I don't blame you."

Together, they looked back at the cabin. Some of the refugees sat leaning against the outside wall wrapped in blankets. Slivers of firelight danced through the windows and around the clearing.

"I wish I had more to give them," Patrick said.

"You have given them hope. That will have to carry them."

Before he opened the inn's door, Stormer paused and listened to the voices from inside. He couldn't make out any words, but it was noisy in there, and some of his comrades sounded drunk. Well, who could blame them? Before he left the house on the hill, Lady Ellen had told him everything that had happened in Brethren since the refugees returned from Niue. She thought it was important for him to know in his new role as a spy. He might not have been on the beach for the battle, the dragon, and the business with the old magician, but he had a better-than-average imagination.

Stormer took a deep breath, scenting smoke and sour ale, then pushed the door open and stepped inside. It took a few moments for the soldiers to notice him, but when they did, the room silenced. No townspeople were there. The soldier who had accompanied him back to Brethren was sitting in a corner away from the hearth with his head on the table. There was no sign of the magician, Honorus. That was good. If the old man didn't see him come in, maybe he wouldn't pick him out from among the other soldiers.

"Where've you been all this time?" Soren said loudly. The blocky Northerner had been conscripted into the Claymon army at the same time as Stormer, and the two of them had been in the same training group. That didn't mean they were friends. Sweat ran down Soren's flushed face in the overheated room. It was a mild spring night, but the shutters were closed tightly and latched, and a fire roared in the hearth. Based on the number of empty glasses on the tables, Stormer would be surprised if any drink remained in the Port of Brethren by tomorrow morning.

"He got back a while ago," Soren jerked his head in the direction of Stormer's companion. "Long enough anyway…Long enough to drink 'n forget. Where've you been?" he demanded again.

"I had to find a Woods Runner. To track the girl. She's running again." Stormer didn't want to say any more than he had to, but he knew this explanation wouldn't be enough to satisfy Soren and the others who were waiting with their eyes trained on him. They were looking for an excuse to vent their anger at losing a fight they should have easily won.

"I was ordered down the beach, remember?"

Stormer had never been a spy before, but from his experience as a low-ranking soldier he knew it was dangerous to talk too much. The more he said, the more likely he was to be caught in a lie. From the way Soren and the others were staring at him, though, he knew he would have to give them another piece of the story. "I tracked the wench as far as I could, but then the commander caught up with me and sent the two of us back. It took me a while, but I finally found a Runner hiding at the edge of town. That way," he added, pointing toward the hills, but at an angle away from the house with the blue door. "It wasn't easy to talk him into going after her."

Stormer had always been a loner, and he didn't have any close friends among his fellow soldiers. This was the most any of them had ever heard him say at one time. Desperate to move the focus away from himself, he said, "I heard there was some trouble down on the beach this afternoon."

"Trouble?" Soren snorted. "That's one way to put it."

"The Runner didn't want to talk about it," Stormer said.

Soren suddenly pushed himself to his feet, lost his balance and knocked over the table, tipping his own drink and several others onto the floor. He staggered forward and would have stood nose to nose with Stormer if he hadn't been so short. Still, he was close enough that Stormer could smell his vinegary breath. If it came to a fight, Soren's drunkenness would be to Stormer's advantage, but only if the other soldiers stayed out of it, and that wasn't likely, especially after the day they'd had and with their drinks pooling on the floor.

"You think you're special? Always off by yourself. Too good to fight and die with the rest of us? That's right," he said, seeing the shocked look on Stormer's face. "The Runners turned on us. Them and some others we never seen before. One of us is dead, and another will follow him to the nether world before morning. And look." He took a step back and pushed away the hair hanging over his forehead. "They did this to me." A purple, egg-shaped bruise pulsed on his temple.

"I was following orders. I had to look for the girl," Stormer said, holding his hands out, trying to soothe his drunken comrade. "I'm sorry I missed the fight," he added, not because it was true but because it was what he was supposed to say.

"A pint for Stormer," Soren shouted, his anger draining away as quickly as it had risen. Then he said mockingly, "He must be dry after his walk on the beach. Is that sunburn I see on your face? Another round for us all. And he's paying."

Stormer told himself he was lucky to be buying a round instead of paying in blood or teeth for his absence from the battle.

As soon as everyone was drinking again, Stormer took his own pint and made his way back to the table where his erstwhile companion gently snored. He shook his shoulder. The sergeant outranked him, and that meant he was technically in charge while the commander was in the woods looking for Lady Katherine.

"Wha…Wha…Leave me 'lone," he said.

"I found a Runner, sergeant," Stormer reported. "He agreed to track the girl, and I promised him a reward."

"Can't trust him," the soldier said, though it wasn't clear who he was referring to. "You better go tell th'old man."

Stormer hadn't yet drunk any of his ale, but he took a big gulp now. It immediately soured in his gut. A meeting with Greystone's counselor was exactly what he most wanted to avoid.

"Shouldn't you be the one?" he said. "I mean, I found the Runner, but you have a lot more experience. I'm just a private. A nobody. The old man has Greystone's ear, and you must have dealt with him before." Stormer glanced at the sergeant and realized he was talking to himself. The man's head was back on the table.

Stormer sat for a time with his pint in his hands, not drinking, trying to work up his courage. He didn't trust himself to take another gulp. He placed the drink on the table, and as if it belonged to someone else, he noticed his hand was trembling. Stormer knew this was an opportunity to learn something of the old man's plans, but it was too soon. He wasn't ready, and he was pretty sure he never would be.

So far Stormer had managed to stay out of the counselor's way, but other men in his cadre had been on duty when the old man questioned prisoners for Greystone. They used words like squeezed and crushed to describe the process he used to extract information. It sometimes fell to Stormer to clean up afterwards, and it looked to him as if those words were an exact description of what had happened.

When Lady Ellen was telling him about the events on the beach, and she came to Honorus and how he had changed, she stopped talking. She stared out the window at the sky for a long time before she continued. That told him more than anything she might have said.

No one was paying any attention to Stormer anymore. They had resumed the business of turning an embarrassing defeat into a victory, or if that turned out to be impossible, of forgetting it altogether.

Putting this off would only make it worse.

Stormer slowly eased around the edge of the room and pulled open the heavy door at the bottom of the stairs that led to the sleeping chambers above. Just inside, a guard leaned against the wall, dozing. His empty cup lay on its side on the bottom step.

"I have to report to the counselor," Stormer said. To his own ears, his voice sounded higher than it should have.

The guard managed to rouse himself enough to wave Stormer by. Between here and the top of the stairs, he would have to fix that and somehow slow his heart. It was trying to leap from his chest and escape the inn on its own. He climbed slowly, breathing deeply, but he felt worse with every step. Maybe climbing these steps and facing the man at the top of them was a mistake, but Greystone was far away in Ostara, and for better or worse, the counselor was in charge. By now he would know about Stormer's mission along the coast, and he would also know about the signal that alerted the others about Katherine's escape. He would be expecting a report.

As it turned out, after hearing the tale from Ellen, he thought he might have done the right thing by signaling he'd found Katherine after all. If he hadn't, the Claymon might have continued fighting on the beach, and if that happened, all the men he met in the house on the hill would surely have been killed. On the other hand, he heard there was a dragon. Even though he had never seen one, its appearance alone would probably have been enough to stop the fight. He noticed that, besides his growing nausea, he had a bad headache, and once he did notice, it was hard to think of anything else. He had had his fill of sun and sand, soldiering and, even though he had barely begun, spying.

Two things were certain. Regret was pointless. For better or worse, the day's choices had brought him to this moment. Second, if he could get through the next half hour without soiling himself, the coming meeting would be a success.

A second guard stood in the short passage outside the old man's room. This one was awake and showed no signs of drunkenness.

"I have to make my report to the counselor," Stormer said. He thought his voice sounded almost normal, though it seemed to come from someone else who was standing behind him and speaking over his shoulder. "If he's busy I can come back later," he added.

"You went to look for that girl from Ostara," the guard said, studying Stormer's face in the light of a lantern that hung from a hook nearby.

Stormer nodded his confirmation.

"Then you haven't seen him since what happened to him on the beach." He jerked his head in the direction of the room behind him.

Stormer shook his head.

"Well, try not to show you notice a difference."

"What do you mean," Stormer asked.

"Try not to make him angry. That's all the advice you're getting from me," the guard said, and he turned and rapped on the door.

6

HUNTED

WHEN THE CLAYMON COMMANDER told Patch it was too dark to track Katherine any farther that night, he was right. It was just frustration that made him kick along the bottom of the fallen tree one more time before following the Woods Runner. When the toe of his boot made contact with the girl's body and she ran, instinct took over. As soon as he spotted her shadowy shape darting away through the trees, he threw himself over the log. Although he continued weaving his way in the direction she had been heading, he soon had no choice but to stop and listen. The undergrowth was getting denser, and in the near darkness he couldn't spot the signs that, in daylight, would have allowed him to follow her.

This Claymon was a man of the frozen northern plains, not a Woods Runner. To the commander, the forest felt claustrophobic, especially at night, and he strained to hear the voices of the recruit and the Woods Runner behind him or any sound of the girl's flight. Not even a cracking twig told him her direction, and after turning around a few times, he was no longer certain which way was behind and which was ahead. He thought about calling out, but he wasn't ready to admit he was lost.

She was right there! He should have grabbed her before she ran off. That is what Greystone would say when he made his report. When the commander returned to Ostara, he could tell Greystone how hard he tried to track Lady Katherine in the darkness. No one could contradict him, but the basic fact would be clear. He had failed. He would end up demoted. If lucky, he'd end up as a guard in Ostara. If unlucky, he'd end up in prison himself, or worse.

No. Going back without Katherine Elder wasn't an option.

"You won't get away from us this time," he roared. Then, realizing there was no 'us' and that his tone would hardly coax a frightened girl to surrender, he tried to gentle his voice, without much success, "It is dangerous to be in the woods, girlie. Might be wild animals out here. Come towards the sound of my voice, and I'll protect you."

In response, he heard only the usual sounds of the forest at night. Ever since his first step into trees he had hated those sounds because he didn't know what was making them. He jumped and choked on an oath when the old Woods Runner appeared at his side, startling him for the second time that night.

"Whose side are you on, anyway?" he growled.

The Runner didn't answer, but he cocked his head and took a few steps forward as if he could hear something the Claymon had missed.

"You're right about one thing," Patch finally replied without looking back. "There are animals nearby. I wouldn't get between them and the girl if I were you."

The commander could not have known that Patch was listening not to the sounds made by Katherine trying to get away, or to the sounds of wild beasts, but to the voice of Maraba, telling him the plan she and Oro had made to frighten the Claymon out of the woods and back to Brethren. Patch doubted the commander could be warned off so easily, but he agreed it was worth a try. As frightened as the Claymon might be of the beasts of the forest, Peter Greystone's all-too-real anger if Katherine escaped again would be the Claymon's most important consideration.

"I asked you a question." The commander sneered. "Are you going to track the girl, or not?"

"I have been tracking her, and the signs led me to you." Patch said, continuing to walk forward slowly and pretending to study the ground for Kathe's trail, as if he could follow it in the dark. The commander trailed behind him uncertainly, wondering what the Runner was seeing and whether he had really answered his question. A little distance grew between them, and not for the first time, the Claymon noticed that he could never hear a Woods Runner moving through the woods. Sneaky good-for-nothings! The Runners would have some explaining to do when Greystone heard about the business back on the beach.

The commander would be glad when Peter Greystone broke his ties with the Runners, and that would be as soon as he brought the girl to Ostara, trussed like a pig if he had to. Illogically, he felt more optimistic about catching her now that the old man had reappeared and was on her trail.

He looked forward to making the report. Disloyalty was one of many faults Greystone would not tolerate. Anyway, the Claymon had learned so much about tracking from watching the Runners they didn't need them anymore. He had found the girl's hiding place without any help, hadn't he? Even if he had to wait until morning to follow her, she couldn't go far in the darkness.

As he found himself alone again, even though he despised the Runner and told himself he was well rid of him, the commander felt the seed of unease begin to grow again. He told himself there was no shame in being afraid. Long experience had taught him fear could keep him safe. The shame would only come if he refused to face his fears. Or if he failed in his duty.

The breeze freshened, and the first drops became a steady rain that had been marching towards the headland forest since sunset. The Runner couldn't be far. Even he couldn't keep tracking the girl in this weather.

"Stop. Wait for me," he called.

He expected obedience, and when the Runner did not appear at once, the commander quickened his pace to catch up even though he knew it was a mistake to move any farther into the unknown. He was already cold, but not as cold as he would be before he found his way back to Brethren the next day – with Katherine Elder in tow. Where was that recruit? He should be here. At least then there would be two of them, though the boy was worse than useless.

He was still pushing through the undergrowth when a scream shattered the silence. It came from a distance, and his first thought was the girl, but then he realized it was something else. He dragged his sword from its scabbard and held it in front of him, whirling around. Rain streamed down his face, and he brushed it away with his arm. Maybe he had imagined the sound. It could have been two trees rubbing together in the wind. He had heard that often enough and mistaken it for an animal.

When he heard the scream again, it came from the branches directly over his head, and it was followed by a deep snarl right behind him. The commander spun towards the second sound. He couldn't see what it was, but an immense, dark shape loomed over him. A pungent smell overwhelmed the scent of the rain, and without having ever seen a bear, he knew that is what it was.

He slashed forward, but his sword didn't touch the animal. It snarled again, even louder. It must be his imagination because it shouldn't be possible in this light, but he thought he saw the bear's gaping jaws. Its teeth were as long as his fingers. It swiped at him with one enormous paw, tossing him onto his side and knocking the sword from his hand.

He dragged himself to his knees, wondering why he wasn't already dead. When he fell, the bear should have finished him off, but before he could follow that thought any further, the scream of the unknown creature above and the bear's roar echoed again in unison and sent him scrambling back, out of reach of deadly claws.

The commander leaped to his feet and ran, careening against trees as he put distance between himself and the beasts. He swore when he heard branches breaking behind him and changed course. The bear was pacing him.

A few more steps, and he thought he might finally have found some luck. The way ahead seemed to be clear. He increased his speed, and then his groping arms felt nothing. He was flying.

Kathe waited close to the rim of the ravine. That's where the bear had paused just long enough for her to slide down from its back. He didn't tell her anything else except to wait, so she sat down and stayed where she was, arms wrapped around her knees, unable to think of anything to do except stay out of sight. It had started to rain.

There had been some cold nights, rainy nights, lonely nights, frightening nights, and she had just decided this was the worst night of them all when Patch found her sitting there, making herself very small behind an oak tree. She didn't recognize him until he whispered her name, and then she jumped up and hugged him.

"Shhh, now," he said, awkwardly patting her back, even though she had not made a sound. That's when Kathe heard Maraba scream, and the hairs pricked on her neck. They had both heard that sound before, but it was still dreadful. And then came the bear's roar.

They were still clinging to one another when the commander shot past them flailing his arms and legs and flew over the rim of the ravine.

As Kathe had reason to know, the ravine, though not very wide, was deep, and it had very steep sides. When she came to it during her flight from the Claymon, she slid to the bottom and paid her way in scratches and bruises. The commander had no chance to slow himself. He didn't scream or make any other sound, but they heard a sickening thud when he hit the bottom.

Patch and Kathe knelt on the edge and stared down, but they couldn't see anything. By then, Maraba and the bear had joined them.

Oro flew into an overhanging tree and peered into the ravine with his owl eyes. *"He isn't moving,"* he said. *"Did you hear me?"*

At first Kathe didn't understand what he meant, but then she realized all three companions had made sounds to frighten the Claymon. Maraba snarled, the bear roared, and Oro must have hooted. Even in her exhaustion, she knew she could not laugh at him.

"I did," she lied solemnly. *"What do we do now?"*

In a moment Maraba was at the bottom of the ravine. She sniffed the commander and gingerly touched him with one paw.

"Dead," she said matter-of-factly. *"Looks like his neck is broken."*

Katherine swallowed hard. She had somehow kept herself from laughing at Oro's pride, but she couldn't keep herself from crying now, and it didn't make any sense. The man lying below was alive a few moments ago, and now he was dead. He shouted threats at her, and he was determined to take her back with him to Ostara. He would have done it too. She had no choice but to run away, and she knew she should be glad he was dead.

"Why can't they leave me alone?" she sobbed, her tears flowing and mingling with the rain dripping from her hair.

"He was a Claymon," Patch said. "He was following orders."

"Don't be stupid," Maraba told her, her fluid shape appearing over the ravine's rim. *"The man is dead because he was afraid of us and didn't watch where he was going. Jasper and I just wanted to scare him, or maybe make him fight us instead of following you. We wouldn't have killed him."*

"Unless we had to," the bear named Jasper said laconically.

The four looked down into the darkness. There was no choice but to leave the body where it was.

Patch thought of the recruit, who surely had heard the sounds Maraba and Jasper made. "Speaking of scared to death, I'll deal with the boy. He can take some version of the news back to his comrades. That is, if he hasn't already run away. You three had better wait here." He didn't say so, but Patch doubted the Claymon would come to this place to claim the commander's body. Even if they did, Katherine would be far away by then, and the trail would be cold.

The bear settled onto the ground, and Kathe leaned against his warm side. "Jasper," she murmured. "I am glad to have met you." The rain had become a drizzle.

"And I am glad to meet you again, Flame Child," he said, but she was already asleep.

The guard knocked sharply. Stormer didn't hear any response, but then the door swung open and he was standing just inside the room without a clear memory of how he got there. It was a typical inn bedchamber, maybe a little larger than most. A single bed with a deep sag in the middle occupied most of the space, and on a table under the window a single candle shed a circle of light over a book that was lying open. Its pages lifted slightly in the breeze from the open window.

The candle had dripped yellow wax onto the wooden surface of the table and even onto the edge of one of the pages, which was a shame. Stormer could barely write his name, but he knew books deserve respect, and this one looked like something special. It was bound in black leather, and it seemed to be written in a tiny, precise hand. From here, the words looked like ants marching across white sand.

Stormer was glad the candlelight did not penetrate the darkness as far as the door. He focused on the details of the room, but finally he could no longer avoid looking at the man sitting in the chair by the table. When he did, he was relieved to see the counselor was staring out the window towards the sea.

Stormer felt dizzy. He squeezed his eyes tightly shut and then blinked. Even though Ellen had warned him, it was still difficult to recognize the man sitting at the table as the old cripple the Claymon had hauled over the mountains like so much baggage. He was no longer old. But he wasn't young either – not exactly.

He seemed to be naked underneath an old blanket he had dragged from the bed, except for a sagging pair of socks that drooped around his ankles. Strong looking shins covered in goosebumps poked out from underneath the blanket. Based on the counselor's erect posture, his formerly crooked spine was now straight. However, he was still completely bald, and the network of veins on his scalp still reminded Stormer of a map.

It was no wonder Ellen skipped over the details of this transformation when she was telling the story. She couldn't explain how Honorus did it, but she told him the refugees from the island were almost killed in the process.

Please, please don't let him look at me.

As if he had heard Stormer's thought, the counselor turned towards him, and it was Stormer's turn to look away. He studied his boots as he had been trained to do when in the presence of his superiors. He reviewed the information he had been given by Ellen. This man had a name. Honorus.

"Well, what is it you have come to say?"

Stormer swallowed. "I was ordered to patrol along the shore to search for Katherine Elder because the commander thought there was a chance she escaped from the ship and made her way to land. I found her trail, and I sent my companion to signal the others while I followed it. We came to a steep bluff, and I almost had her, but then she kicked me, and we both fell. By the time I came to, she was running again. I had tracked her partway up to the headland when the commander and the sergeant caught up to us."

This was almost the truth. Stormer knew Honorus could sense a lie. That is why Greystone used him as an interrogator. He had to stay as close as he could to the facts.

The sorcerer lifted his head and gazed at the young Claymon with dead eyes. "Look at me."

Stormer forced himself to look in the direction of Honorus's face, focusing on his chin.

"What happened next?"

"The commander ordered the sergeant and me back to town. He and the other soldier went on to track the Lady. The commander ordered us to find a Woods Runner to help him. We were supposed to find one and send him right away."

"Did you find one?"

"It took a while," Stormer said, taking an extra breath, trying to calm himself before giving the rest of the report. He was going to have to leave out an awful lot now, and he was sure Honorus wouldn't need sorcery to hear his heart pounding. "It took some time, but I finally found a Runner. He was hiding behind some rocks partway up the hill at the edge of the town."

As soon as he said it, he knew it was a mistake. Nobody can find a Runner who is hiding unless he wants to be found. But there was no going back. "At first he didn't want to track her. I didn't know about the fight on the beach until I got back to the town, and I didn't know the Runners were a part of it until I got to the inn tonight. That's why I didn't understand why he didn't want to track the Lady. The commander had told me to offer a reward, so I did, and then the old man said he'd go."

Stormer slammed his mouth shut. His fear had made him say too much. He should have just stuck with the facts even if that meant leaving big holes in the story.

Honorus was looking out the window again. Stormer waited to be released.

"That is all. Sir."

Stormer noticed the floor of the room wasn't clean. The wide cracks between the floorboards were full of debris, and in places he could see flickers of light shining up through the dust from the room below. There was a dark stain near the toe of his left boot, as if someone had stumbled and spilled something nasty.

Stormer was no magician, but he had a talent, very useful in the army, for distracting himself and taking himself elsewhere when he was someplace he would rather not be. Sometimes he sang songs to himself, sometimes he counted his steps or his breaths, and sometimes, as now, he just absorbed the minutiae of his surroundings. He could not have known it, but this well-developed skill was a defense, maybe the only possible defense, against Honorus's probing.

Out of the corner of his eye, Stormer noticed that the pillow on the bed looked grimy. He wasn't sure he would have been willing to lay his head on it himself – and he was used to sleeping rough. Turning his attention to the desk, he told himself he would teach himself to read one of these days. It seemed like the people who could read books had most of the power in this world. He was aware he was growing very cold, but the magician had not released him yet, so he just stood there pretending he was alone as he slowly turned into a block of ice.

Just as he started to feel a new compulsion to meet the magician's eyes, Stormer heard Honorus give a snort of disgust. "You can go, but not far. What is your name, soldier?"

"Soren, Sir." He didn't know why he gave his comrade's name. He just knew he didn't want this man to know who he was.

7

NORTH

MEG WANTED GALE TO understand what it meant to fly. She told him that at first he might think he'd never get used to the feeling, but before long it would be natural for him to look down on clouds and to see the shape of a coastline or a mountain from above. The fear of slipping from the dragon's back would also fade. Once you have made the choice to ride on a dragon, there is no point in worrying about falling. Also, Gale would be cold on a long flight over the sea – as cold as he had ever been. No matter what season it might be in the lands below, the sky is a frozen place. The longer the flight, the harder it would be for him to hang on to the ropes, and even though it might seem strange, there was also the danger of falling asleep.

The dragon Padraik liked to bask on sand hot enough to burn human feet, but he was somehow able to fly steadily through the icy sky. She thought there must be a fire inside the dragon that kept those fragile looking, but powerful, wings moving. During the two long nights she spent on his back, she had come to trust Padraik, but she knew that by the end of the second flight his fire had almost gone out.

When Padraik told her he was ready to fly again, Meg asked him to take Gale up alone to circle the island. Meg didn't have the luxury of time to practice before she flew the first time, and she wanted Gale to have this chance. The practice flight was as much for the sake of the dragon as to give Gale a taste of what it would be like to fly. Padraik would have to judge Gale's weight, which was less than Patrick's, thank goodness, to prepare himself to carry them both north along the coast. That's where she planned to search for another dragon until the three of them were convinced such a creature did not exist.

She had no evidence to support this plan, but at least the search would represent a leap back into the stream of time and into some kind of a future. She squinted as she craned her neck and gazed straight up at the marvelous, shining beast she had trusted with her life and would soon trust again. Was he the last of his kind? It seemed impossible!

Bethany and Gerard stood with Meg, equally mesmerized by the sight of Padraik circling the mountain.

"Someday, I'd like to do that," Bethany said unexpectedly, shading her face with her hand.

"Why not today?" Meg said. "It is good for Padraik to fly. No matter what he says, his confidence took a beating on the way back to the island. And he needs to exercise his wings with some weight on his back."

Gerard didn't say anything, but he looked at his wife as if he were seeing her for the first time.

"Not today, but someday. I know what you'll say," Bethany added. "The next time you and Gale fly away, you won't return. When will I have another chance?" She took Gerard's hand and smiled as if at a private joke.

Padraik appeared from behind the mountain one more time, flew out to sea, made a wide circle, and approached the beach at a gentle angle. His usual landing technique was to swoop down the mountainside at a heart-stopping rate before turning at the last moment and plowing into the sand. This morning he was being unusually considerate. Meg hoped this was a sign of the developing friendship between the dragon and the man he called Loudmouth.

After Gale slid off the dragon, he stood with his hands on his knees for a few moments. Meg knew he needed that time to make his legs stop shaking. Even though his knees had gripped the dragon's sides for only a short flight, it was the first time. When Gale recovered, he walked to where Padraik could see him and bowed.

Meg couldn't tell if they said anything. After the first terrifying days, when Padraik could speak only to her in images that seared themselves into her mind, he quickly learned to soften his speech and to communicate with all four of them in the usual way of the animal guides.

This dragon now could have private conversations, something she had never encountered among the talking animals. Somehow, he had fine-tuned his speech so that his words only reached the person he intended to hear them. Meg was not sure this was a good development, but when she thought about it, it didn't surprise her that a dragon would be the first talking animal to learn how to keep a secret.

Gale came up to them, grinning widely, "You didn't tell me it's like riding a horse, only better!"

"Maybe that's because I never rode a horse," Meg said. She couldn't help laughing, and she unexpectedly remembered standing in the kitchen garden back at Springvale and watching Gale race across the meadow on a roan mare. She didn't even know she had that memory, yet there it was, and she thought about that girl and the way she watched the boy, admiring the way he controlled a horse she knew to be headstrong.

On that day, Gale was as remote as a figure in one of his mother's tapestries. But now…"

Gerard's voice broke her reverie. "You'll be leaving soon."

"How do you know?" Meg asked.

"Come with me."

He led her to the fire end of the beach where a book lay open on the wooden packing crate he and Bethany were using as a table. Meg had reason to know that book. Until last year, when Gerard reclaimed it, she even called it her own. It held beautiful, embellished script, and illustrations so vibrant that the plants and animals in them seemed alive and ready to walk or grow off the pages. The book also contained the Changeful Map, and Meg knew they could not have reached this place without it. This is what made the book so valuable. Other ships, depending upon the same map, might have broken on rocks and been lost forever. Now the book was open to a page Meg knew well. It had remained unchanged since she first found the book. She never was sure whether Gerard left it behind at his campsite on purpose for her to find. Then, she thought he was just a peddler, travelling around in his wagon selling useful things and gewgaws at remote estates such as Springvale.

This page showed three women. One was Bethany, and the other two were Kathe and her mother, Ellen. Bethany had explained that the three of them together represent the stages of life. Obviously, Katherine was the embodiment of youth. Full of life and optimism, her strength is greater than the others', but she depends on their guidance. She still has much to learn, but Ellen has taught her well through her girlhood, and at the moment she appears in the book Kathe is ready to begin her work as a healer. Bethany represents maturity. She is the trusted counselor to both Kathe and Ellen. Bethany is physically stronger than most women her age, but her wisdom is her greatest treasure. Actually, Bethany is far older than she looks in the picture, for she taught not only Ellen, but Ellen's mother, the healing arts.

These three women represent an ideal, but the cycle can be broken by death or by the choices each of them makes. Meg wondered whether she and Kathe would ever become mothers like Ellen and where they would find help and advice with Bethany staying on the island. Meg wasn't in the picture, but Bethany might as well have been her grandmother. She taught her how to read and write, and how to tell a story. She also helped her to manage her gift, a special sensitivity to the talking animals. This sensitivity included some creatures others could not understand, like the lion, the dolphins and, for a while at least, the dragon.

Gerard turned the page. This one was also familiar. It showed Gerard and Bethany standing on the beach. Bethany is holding Patrick's hand. They all are waving, but Bethany is not looking ahead towards the longboat that has just left the beach. She is turned towards Patrick, and she is looking at him intently, as if she is trying to memorize his face.

This scene really happened. Meg knew because she watched it from a distance. A few minutes after the *Goshawk* raised its sails, Patrick gave Bethany a long hug, wiped tears from her cheek with his finger, and climbed onto the dragon's back where Meg was waiting for him. He tied himself to the harness, wrapped his arms around her waist, and they flew.

Meg realized Gerard was about to turn the page again. He looked at Bethany, as if asking for permission. She nodded.

And here was Meg making her first appearance in the book. She wasn't alone. She was riding a dragon and Gale was there too – just as he was now, very close, looking over her shoulder. It was as if the book was not only showing them the future but encouraging them to leave the island. Did this mean she was right about the North and the secret it might hold?

Meg knew the picture might change at any time, but for now it felt like a blessing.

Stormer was still wrapped in his blanket when Soren shook him awake and told him they had to report for inspection in Brethren's small public square. Most of the Claymon had demanded bunk space from the residents of Brethren, but Stormer had decided to sleep in a shed by the waterfront, where he could be alone and hear the sound of the waves. He reluctantly left a dream in which he was not afraid of bears, stretched, and plodded after Soren towards the center of town.

Now, still half asleep, he stood at attention with the rest of the soldiers. Two full days had passed since he climbed up the steps of the inn and reported to Honorus. During those days he did everything he could to go back to being a nobody, and it seemed he had succeeded. No one had asked him any more questions about finding Katherine Elder or how it happened that she escaped him. And no one seemed to think it was odd that he slept alone or skirted around the fringes of their conversations.

Strangely, the young recruit, who had gone with the commander to track Lady Katherine, had returned alone and reported that their leader was tracking the Lady on his own with the help of a Woods Runner. Everyone accepted the story, and Stormer had no reason to doubt it.

It still stung Stormer that he was stuck here playing soldier and spy instead of protecting, or at least following, Lady Katherine. He wasn't even a very good spy. There had been no opportunity to report to Abel who, as far as Stormer knew, was still recovering from his battle wounds in the house on the hill. It was even possible Abel had died. The one time Stormer saw him, it looked like he had lost a lot of blood.

Even though he knew it had all happened, Stormer's memories of events from just three days ago were becoming more and more dreamlike – finding Kathe, the appearance of a snarling panther who came to guide her; being sent back here to Brethren; and agreeing to become a spy for her friends. He had even reported to Honorus and somehow survived the experience even though he told the magician a mess of half-truths.

He and the other Claymon had begun packing up and preparing to return to Ostara. He risked a glance in the direction of the hill that rose steeply at the edge of the town. He was too far away to see the blue door from here. Before they left town the next day, he'd have to slip away and tell Abel what he knew, however little it was. Maybe after dark tonight.

"Soren." The Sergeant was calling someone forward.

Soren was next to Stormer. He startled, then quickly walked to the front of the formation. He probably didn't know why his name was being called, but Stormer had an idea, and his heart started to race.

The Claymon force could have been ready to march a few hours after the battle, even with one man gravely injured and on a litter. They had only lingered in Brethren because Honorus had been hiding in his room ever since retreating from his brother and the dragon on the beach. Everyone expected him to emerge sooner or later, but it still came as an unpleasant shock when he stepped out from the deep shadows of the inn's door.

Stormer wondered how long he had been lurking there. Honorus had found some clothes since the last time Stormer saw him, but they were ill fitting. He must have ordered someone to steal them from the tallest citizen of Brethren, and by the looks of them, that previous owner was a lazy fisherman. There was a gaping, unpatched hole in in the knee of the canvas trousers. Stormer kept his eyes on the magician's bony, white kneecap and tried to convince himself he was seeing an ordinary person.

Someone had retrieved the magician's cloak from the beach and dried it, but it was patterned with a moldy bloom of salt stains. The garment's deep hood concealed Honorus's face. Few of those present knew the face had remained skeletal while the rest of his body grew young and strong. Stormer could under-stand why he'd want to keep that a secret as long as he could.

As usual, when he was worried about something, Stormer al-lowed his mind to wander. It kept him from focusing on the source of his unease. He hadn't asked any questions of his com-rades since reporting to Honorus, but from careful listening he had learned more about what they saw on the beach – or thought they saw. He wondered whether the changes in Honorus started from the toes up, and maybe his brother, Patrick, broke the spell before the magic had a chance to reach his head. If Patrick had not broken the spell, would those blotchy spots on the magician's scaly scalp be hidden under a full head of hair? And what color would that hair be? Black, he decided. Definitely.

As this was going through his head, Stormer watched Soren walk toward Honorus. Although he couldn't hear what they were saying, it looked like the magician asked a question, and Soren responded. Stormer pictured the narrowing of the magician's sunken eyes, hidden from view in the deep tunnel of the hood. Soren had half-turned and had lifted his arm to point into the ranks when he stiffened to his full height and began to jerk his arms and legs. Everyone saw the fear on his wide-eyed face. His mouth gaped in a scream as he collapsed to the ground, but he had no breath to make the sound. The other Claymon were too well-trained, or too afraid of Honorus, to react.

Soren was as much a nobody as Stormer, but a far better soldier. Stormer had never heard him question an order, and lately Soren had started bragging that he would be up for a promotion soon. Stormer wasn't sure there was anything to that rumor, but he wasn't looking forward to having Soren bossing him around. In other words, Soren was very good at staying out of trouble and only attracting attention when he wanted it.

Stormer knew the truth. He was the one Honorus wanted. And he knew there was no way he could escape. Even though he was healthy, thanks to Katherine, many of his comrades were faster runners, and any one of them could tell the magician who had scouted along the beach and which of the two had come back and reported to him. Anyone who might have been inclined to help Stormer had already left town. He was completely on his own. He felt a pang of guilt about giving Honorus Soren's name instead of his own, especially since it would only buy him a few extra moments of anonymity.

He might as well get it over with. For the first time since he put on the Claymon uniform, Stormer left his position in the ranks without being ordered to do so. He had some fresh practice making dangerous decisions, but this one felt suicidal. From deep in his past, he heard his mother's voice telling him, 'Sometimes the only way out is through.'

His comrades continued to stand at attention, staring straight ahead as Stormer wove his way through them and stood in front of the magician, next to Soren's body. Now that Honorus's spine was straight, and he was able to stand erect, he was taller than Stormer. If Stormer looked straight ahead, he saw the shape of the magician's unshaven chin within the shadows of the cloak. It was a warm morning. Honorus must be getting hot in there.

Stormer looked down at Soren for a long time before turning his attention back to the chin. He couldn't tell if Soren was alive or dead. Dead, he thought. He was glad his comrade's eyes were closed.

Stormer made himself look up.

"I expect it's me you want."

"I expect it's me you want, Sir," Honorus parroted in a quivery whisper. Since the voice emerged from the magician's unimproved face, Stormer supposed it was only natural Honorus had retained his whispery, whiney voice.

"Yes." If he was about to join Soren lying like a broken scare crow in the dirt, Stormer didn't see the need to be too polite.

"Your friend paid the price for your lie," Honorus said.

Stormer's mouth was dry. "He wasn't my friend, and even Peter Greystone doesn't kill someone just because of a lie. Anyway, you're the one who killed him, not me," Stormer said, speaking loudly enough to be heard by the nearest soldiers.

He knew he was being impudent, if not insubordinate. He was afraid, but angry too. Soren might have been a bully when he'd had a few drinks, but he didn't deserve to die. Since Stormer had lost any control over his own fate, he simply waited. He wanted the last thing he saw to be something beautiful, and since coming to Brethren, the thing he liked best was the way the sun sparkled off the surface of the sea. He turned toward the water, which was just visible past the end of the street. The waves this morning were small, but lively, and a few clouds scudded into view. It would probably rain later, but he wouldn't be here to feel it.

Since Stormer had turned partly away from the magician, he could also see the face of the man standing beside Honorus, off to one side and a little behind him. It was the sergeant who had returned to Brethren with him from the headland. He was now the ranking officer in charge of the Claymon force. This officer should have reported to the magician after they returned to the town together that night. His impassive face revealed no regrets.

"What is your name?" Honorus asked

"Since I am a liar, why would you believe me?"

"This time I will be expecting a lie, and I will know."

"Don't be so sure. You didn't know last time, did you?" Stormer couldn't have explained why he was trying to provoke the magician. Honorus wasn't even a soldier, but for some reason all the Claymon were dancing to his tune, even waiting around in Brethren until he saw fit to come out of the inn.

"What difference does it make, anyway? You're just going to kill me." Stormer pointed at Soren's body.

"Believe me, I am tempted," Honorus said, "One of my personal guards was killed in the battle. You will replace him. I want to keep you close until I know what you are hiding. Then I will decide what to do with you."

"Depending on what you think I am hiding."

"Depending on what you think I am hiding, Sir." Honorus said.

The only sound was the wind blowing through the vines that twined up the inn's porch posts. They were loaded with pink buds, and Stormer thought they would bloom soon, but he wouldn't be in Brethren long enough to see the flowers.

"Get your kit and report to me," Honorus said, and when Stormer made no move to leave, he barked, "Go!"

Stormer thought, *Death might be better than this,* but he went, leaving his fellow soldiers standing at attention like toy soldiers.

Over his shoulder he called, "My name is Stormer."

8

THE MAGICIAN'S SERVANT

STORMER DROPPED HIS SMALL bedroll and pack onto the bench next to the inn door. He lowered himself down next to them and waited in the shade of the vines. Since everyone heard the magician's orders, he assumed he was released from his usual duties. He still felt shaky after his encounter with Honorus, so he closed his eyes and tried to appear unconcerned. He listened to footsteps entering and leaving the inn across the wooden floor of the porch, but he didn't peek to see whether they belonged to soldiers or citizens.

His comrades would be watching. None of them had said anything to him yet, but he knew they blamed him for what had happened that morning. They'd be muttering among themselves. Soren was well-liked among the other soldiers. Stormer doubted whether most of them even knew his name.

He expected retaliation, but for now he was in the service of the magician, and the Claymon would not do anything to anger Honorus, especially after he had demonstrated his displeasure on Soren.

Stormer knew himself to be a most ordinary, if inferior, Claymon soldier. This is the first time he had done anything to set himself apart. Anything besides deciding to desert and become a spy, that is. Honorus should have been able to steal the thoughts from his head as if he were squeezing the juice from an apple and then dispose of him as he had Soren, but for some reason, he couldn't.

While he was sitting there with his eyes closed, Stormer tried to figure out what the difference could be. It had to do with secrets – all the things he knew but was unwilling to tell. From what he had seen, Honorus knew how to get inside anyone's head, and those he interrogated soon gave up everything to him, no matter how deeply their secrets were buried. That's why Greystone used the counselor and why the Claymon did everything he demanded.

Almost anyone's head, Stormer corrected. It looked as if Honorus couldn't get inside his. For this reason, it was natural the magician would think Stormer was hiding something, and it happened he was right. Unfortunately, Stormer still didn't know what he was doing that kept the magician locked out. If he could figure that out, maybe he could keep doing it.

When Stormer opened his eyes, Honorus's other guard was standing in front of him. How long had he been there? This man was probably in his forties, a veteran by Claymon standards, but for some as-yet-unknown reason, he shared the bad luck of being assigned as one of Honorus's personal guards. He was small and skinny for a Northerner. Maybe that's why he had pulled the duty.

"You'll sleep on the floor outside his door tonight," the man said shortly. "Everything he has, those books and all, is already packed up, so there is nothing for you to do today."

"He told me to report for duty."

"I've just told you," the guard said with distaste before he went back into the inn, slamming the door behind him. Although he expected it, Stormer realized he had better get used to this reaction. While once they would not have noticed him, his fellow soldiers now positively disliked him. It didn't matter that any one of them would have done the same in his shoes.

Stormer picked up his kit and carried it into the inn and up the stairs to the hallway outside the magician's room. He leaned it against the wall at the end of the corridor. There was very little in his pack that he cared about, but he removed a square of folded leather that held a drawing his sister had made of their mother and father and the three letters his mother had written to him since he was conscripted. A scribe had read them to him back in Ostara, and Stormer had memorized their contents, but the scraps of parchment were precious to him. He put the letters inside the leather pouch, along with a small bag of coins he'd saved. Then he put the pouch inside the waistband of his pants and made sure his shirt covered it.

His fellow soldiers might not dare to attack him while he was under Honorus's protection, but that didn't mean they wouldn't destroy his belongings. The rest ought to be safe here at the end of the corridor. Anyone with a mind to disturb them would have to walk by the magician's door. He would shake the blanket out the window before he wrapped himself in it tonight just in case a spider or scorpion had somehow made its way into the folds.

Since it seemed he had the rest of the day to do anything he wanted to, and since the magician and the Claymon would be leaving Brethren the next day, Stormer went down to the sea with a mind to retrace the route he had taken when he was sent to look for Katherine. When he reached the water's edge, he looked back towards the inn. Someone was peering towards him through an upstairs window. As if he didn't care, he turned back around and walked along the shore with purpose.

Anyone watching him would think he had a destination in mind when he only wanted to be out of sight of the town and the other Claymon for a while. He had already played with the idea of finding the stream and picking up where he left off, following it to the headland, but it had been almost two days since he lost sight of Lady Katherine and became a spy for her friends. He wasn't a skilled tracker who could follow her after so much time had passed, especially with the panther leading her.

Besides, he had promised to be a spy, and though he had learned he could lie, it was a promise he planned to keep if he could.

He glanced over his shoulder in time to see somebody duck down behind one of the fishing boats that had been pulled onto the shore. He smiled for the first time that day. Honorus must have sent his other guard to follow him. Well, he would pretend he hadn't seen him, and he and Ratface would both take a nice, long walk on the beach. Since the man hadn't offered Stormer his name, he felt justified in giving him one.

When he reached the spot where he remembered Katherine coming ashore, Stormer stopped and watched a hawk circling lazily above the headland. Then he took his time climbing the low dune and sat for a time on top of the small rise, enjoying the breeze and the view of the water, imagining the man following him crouching in the sun that beat down like a blacksmith's hammer on the sand. Ratface was visible as a tiny dot in the distance. He probably hoped Stormer had mistaken him for a townsman, but just as people of the north rarely bother to slide on the ice, and as people near the forest struggle to tame the trees and keep them away from their dwellings, most of the people of Brethren seemed uninterested in the sea except as a means of livelihood.

After a time, Stormer rose, stretched and headed down the backside of the dune. He enjoyed imagining the panic Ratface would feel as he disappeared from sight. Though Stormer's tracks were obvious in the deep sand, Ratface wouldn't want to lose sight of his quarry. He couldn't know whether Stormer intended to escape by reaching the headland. He admitted it would be logical to expect him to run. His service to Honorus was likely to end badly. He wondered whether Ratface had been told to stop him.

It didn't matter. He had already made his decision. After finding the stream, drinking some water, and resting for a time in the cool shadiness by the streambank, Stormer retraced his steps, passing Ratface at the base of the steep cliff, where the surface still showed signs of his and Katherine's fall. He didn't say any-thing to the man, but simply allowed him to trail him back to the inn porch, closer this time. Stormer returned to his former place on the bench and pretended to fall asleep again.

He listened to the guard's footsteps drag as they climbed the two steps. He paused to look at Stormer sitting there, and then went inside. To report, no doubt.

Stormer hadn't eaten all day. When he was sure Ratface wasn't coming back, he opened his eyes, looked around and eased inside the door of the inn. The public room was empty in the middle of the afternoon, except for two old-timers drowsing over a game of cards under the window. They didn't look up as he walked quickly to the kitchen door and pushed it open, startling a young girl who was beginning to chop some kind of stringy-looking meat to put into the pie crust that waited at the ready. Her eyes widened, and she held up the knife in warning. Stormer held out his hands to show he wasn't there to hurt her.

That's the first thing Katherine did when he showed up. She pulled her knife. He didn't have any experience with women, and he hoped this wasn't going to happen whenever he met one of them.

"I am only looking for something to eat," he said, hoping she would understand. The people here spoke neither Claymon nor Ostaran, but most of them knew a few words of the common speech.

She pushed a portion of the cooked meat towards him with the blade of her knife and tore a chunk of bread from a nearby loaf. "You're the one who was so cheeky with the man upstairs," she accused. "I watched it through the window."

She went back to chopping, then added, "Why aren't you afraid of him?"

It was a fair question. Even though the Claymon had been in Brethren for what seemed like forever, this was his first conver-sation with anyone from the town. His superiors were the ones who made all the demands for lodging or supplies and ordered the people of Brethren to stay out of the way.

"I haven't got anything to lose, I guess, except my life, and everyone knows he'll take that when he wants it," Stormer answered. "It doesn't seem worth the effort to pretend I respect him. Thank you for the food."

She looked at him in surprise. "You are welcome."

The back door of the kitchen was standing open. "Can you pretend you haven't seen me?"

"Unless the old man asks me."

"Fair enough," Stormer said after he swallowed the last bite of bread and meat, which was tastier than it looked.

Once outside, he pressed his back to the side of the inn and eased his way to the corner. The magician's window looked out on the other side, towards the sea. Stormer dashed in the opposite direction and hid behind the shop next door.

He peered around the corner and watched a group of five soldiers walking an equal number of horses up the street towards the shed the Claymon had commandeered to be a stable. The men were talking among themselves, and the horses' hooves made a lot of noise, so he moved again, this time leaping over a fence and into a small back yard where a bored dog, rather than barking, ran circles of joy around him. He patted it and let himself out the other side through a gate. Then he walked in the alley without bothering to hide. No one was likely to question him in this part of the town. It would be more suspicious to skulk.

Starting up the hillside path, Stormer startled a hawk into flight. It had been sitting on a high branch of one of the last big trees of Brethren. From here on he would be visible and vulnerable until he reached the house with the blue door.

He rapped sharply, just as Ellen had. This time it took a little longer for the old lady to answer, and when she did, her eyes narrowed in suspicion.

"Why are you coming here in the middle of the day?" she hissed.

"I know. I'm sorry," he said. "It is the first chance I've had, and there won't be another one. Please, let me inside." He heard the desperation in his voice. The house was far enough up the hillside and away from the town that he wouldn't be recognized unless the watcher had a spyglass, but there were plenty of those in a sea-side town.

The last time he was here, he had agreed to work for Lady Katherine's friends, but what if they had changed their minds? And what good is a spy if he has no one to report to? Right now, Stormer wished he had followed the stream to the headland that morning after all, even if it meant being hunted down as a deserter.

"Let him in," someone said from deeper inside the house.

Without relaxing her disapproving glare, the old woman opened the door just wide enough for Stormer to squeeze through. When his eyes adjusted to the dimness inside the house, Stormer saw someone was sitting in a chair by the cold hearth, and going closer, he recognized the man who had been so badly injured, the one who was left behind.

"Here is our spy," said Abel.

"What I want to know is, when are you leaving?" the old woman said.

Stormer almost said, *I just got here,* but then he realized she was talking about the Claymon.

"Fischer will not come home until you are gone." She gestured towards a window. A wooden chair sat beside it, with a spyglass on the seat.

"The *Goshawk* is at anchor with plenty of supplies to wait out the Claymon," Abel explained. "You Northerners are no longer interested in the ship now that the People and Katherine Elder are gone. You don't even seem to care that the men sent to board the ship have not returned."

Since Abel was right about all that, Stormer didn't bother to answer him. The Claymon assumed the men who rowed out to the *Goshawk* had all been killed, and with their force so reduced, there didn't seem to be anything they could do to retaliate. The *Goshawk's* captain had the advantage over any small boat that might try to approach him. Too, the Claymon were anxious to be away from Brethren. They saw it as an evil place.

"Tomorrow. We march tomorrow," he said.

"And you have come here to report before you leave," Abel said. "I confess I was too hurt to take your measure when you came here last, but if I'd had to place a wager, I would have guessed I'd never see you again. Yet here you are."

Stormer squinted in the dim light to better see the white bandage on Abel's side. At least the wound no longer seemed to be seeping blood.

"Is that because you thought I was a liar, or because you thought you would die," Stormer asked.

"I can see why Katherine likes you," Abel said with a laugh. "You are as direct as she is."

"She doesn't like me," Stormer said, and Abel could see the boy thought he was telling the truth.

"Sit down and tell me everything."

Stormer had never been told to sit when reporting, let alone to pull a chair close or to be offered a glass of cool water. He told Abel everything that had happened, and as he did, the story swelled with importance. He had reported to Honorus…had seen him face to face, and the magician didn't get anything from him about Patrick or the others or what had happened to Katherine. That was something. And now he was going to become one of Honorus's personal guards. Who knew what he'd find out in the coming days? It might have been exciting if he wasn't so scared.

Stormer watched Abel's face the whole time he was giving this report, which was also unusual. Normally, he didn't care what his officer's reaction might be. He didn't have any control over their response, so his mouth said what was expected while he gave his mind freedom to roam. He realized he cared whether this man believed him. The whole time Stormer was speaking,

Abel's eyes were alive in his pale face, and they actually sparked when Stormer told about reporting to Honorus in his chamber and about the confrontation in the street that morning.

After he had told everything he could remember, Abel said, "It seems there is more to you than we thought."

"Do you know why Honorus can't read me as he does others?" Stormer asked.

"I wish I did. You are the first person I have met who has any defense against him. Even his brother has little control over Honorus's influence, and Patrick has been struggling against him all his life."

Now that he had finished talking, Stormer allowed his attention to wander to the window, where the old lady was standing with the spyglass in one hand. She held a small square of polished silver in the other hand, and she allowed it to catch the sun, showing and hiding it in a pattern Stormer didn't understand.

"She's sending a message to her son," Abel said. "You had better be going."

Abel had not asked whether anyone had followed him to the captain's house.

Now that the time had come, Stormer realized he didn't want to leave. He felt safe here and unprepared to return to Brethren to face the magician, especially since he still hadn't learned how he could continue to keep his secrets safe. He had enjoyed sitting here for this short time, talking with Abel. He couldn't remember the last time someone had been kind to him or had treated him as an equal, except for Lady Katherine.

At the same time, he knew he had to go. As a spy, he was doing something useful for the first time in a long while. He had one more question first.

"Once I leave, I won't be able to report to you again. How will you know if I learn something important?"

"Or maybe we will want to send a message to you." Abel smiled. "Believe it or not, I have thought of that. My shoulder is healing, but I won't be able to travel for a few more days. And you are about to leave Brethren. Patrick will want to know what you have told me today. It is time to call our messenger."

Abel picked up a thick leather glove from the small table next to his chair and rose painfully to his feet, waving off Stormer's offer to help. He hobbled to the window where the old lady had finished signaling her son and threw it open. And waited.

Stormer followed and stood to one side, next to the door. What messenger? The Claymon sometimes used doves to send messages, but even though they could fly long distances, it only worked if you were sending the bird to the place it considered its home, and half the time they never arrived there at all. Based on the glove Abel wore on his right hand and the way he was supporting himself, gripping the shutter with his left, he wasn't waiting for a dove.

The red-tailed hawk made no sound as it swept into the house, made a tight circle around the room, and landed on Abel's outstretched arm. It flapped its wings wildly for a few moments as it caught its balance, creating enough wind to ruffle Stormer's hair and flutter the pages of a book Abel had left on the table. The old lady had disappeared into a side chamber the moment Abel went to the window. This visitor had been here before.

Without realizing he had done so, Stormer retreated to the farthest corner of the room. Once the hawk had settled on Abel's arm, Stormer waited for him to hood the bird, but he made no move to do so. Some of the wealthy Claymon had taken up falconry, including Peter Greystone, so Stormer knew something of the sport, but he had never been so close to such a magnificent creature. It was many times the size of Greystone's kestrels.

He focused on the hawk's curved talons which were digging into the gauntlet. When he met its eyes, the bird's gaze bored through him, and he held his breath until it turned to Abel.

"This is the messenger?" Stormer squeaked. Was Abel expecting to teach him the basics of falconry in the minutes before he had to return to the town? There was no sign of a small case for carrying messages, which should have been strapped to the hawk's leg. This bird could probably carry the weight of a whole book if it had to, but Stormer couldn't see how it would be of any use to him. He could neither read nor write.

"I felt the same way the first time I met Lightning," Abel said in a soothing voice, as if he were talking to the bird, not Stormer. "Ellen and I discussed this problem before she left Brethren, and I sent a sparrow to look for him. It was very brave of the sparrow, don't you think?"

Stormer nodded, afraid he'd squeak again if he said anything. He cautiously moved closer. For the first time, he realized this might be one of the talking animals. Having already met Maraba, the panther, and having seen the way Kathe could communicate with her, he wasn't as surprised as he should have been.

"The next part of the plan Ellen and I made is based on a guess. She told me a healing is a kind of exchange. When Kathe healed you after you were attacked by the bear, she got to know you better than your own mother does…and I hope, better than Honorus ever will. But whether you understand it or not, you also know Kathe, and because of that, it is possible you'll be able to understand Lightning when he speaks to you. I think we had better see whether that's true before you go back to the town, don't you agree?"

Stormer reached for the door latch. "I'm Claymon, and we don't believe in talking animals. I owe the Lady Katherine my life, and that is our bond. There isn't anything else."

"Don't be foolish," Abel said. "Don't you realize the trouble you're in?"

Though he continued to speak in a low, soothing voice, Stormer could tell Abel was losing patience.

"As soon as you return to Brethren, you will enter Honorus's service. I wouldn't want to be in your shoes. From now on you are one of us, and we will help you if we can. But we won't be able to help if you can't get word to us."

The hawk continued to sit like a feathered statue. It had turned its eye back to Stormer. He felt like prey.

"We will want to know anything you can tell us about the movements of Honorus and the Claymon. The rebels outside Ostara and the refugees on their way back to Pallas are few. The information you collect may save their lives, but it will be useless if you cannot pass on what you learn, and quickly. If you have another idea, this is the time to tell me."

"I'm sorry. I have to go now," Stormer stammered.

The hair on the back of his neck lifted in what felt like a light breeze, though no breeze entered through the open window.

"*I will train him.*"

The hawk's voice entered Stormer's mind through his skin, as if he were reading the air before a storm. He forced himself to break away from Lightning's gaze and turned to Abel. He felt dizzy, and his mouth was gaping. His world, which had already shifted, rearranged itself again.

"Maybe this will work," Stormer said, "Except I can't walk around with a giant hawk on my arm. I'm still a private in the Claymon army, even if Honorus has set me apart."

"Ask him," Abel said. "But don't try too hard, he is very sensitive."

Stormer didn't know what Abel meant, but he tried to imitate Katherine when she spoke to the panther. She had whispered the words, but it looked to him as if she were considering every one of them before she spoke. Maybe Abel was right about the connection between the two of them. He realized he did know how to do it. He had to be careful and clear, and he had to think the words before he repeated them out loud.

"Greetings, feathered one." He began politely. "I will gladly be your student, but for the safety of us both, we cannot be seen together."

The hawk's answer came in a rush. "*When you need me, I will know. Go to a place with trees, or if there are no trees, be outside, away from other people. I do not have to sit on your arm or even be very close to you to hear you, and you do not have to use your human voice to talk to me.*"

"That's right," Abel said. "You only have to speak aloud if you are with someone who doesn't understand the animals and you want them to know what you are saying. Now go."

Stormer passed through the blue door once more, into a new world. He had only gone a little way before he sat down on a rock and put his head on his knees. He stayed there until his dizziness eased. Then he made his way down the hillside and towards the magician who had probably spent his day devising ways to pry open his skull, but Stormer barely noticed the rocks under his feet. He was no longer just a Claymon soldier who would serve until he was either killed in battle or released to make some kind of a life back in his northern homeland. As on the day of his healing, he felt changed. Anything was possible now. That beautiful bird had spoken to him, and it had promised to come to him again. Lightning would be watching over him from now on.

9

GOING HOME

GRIT CARRIED THE REFUGEES up the mountainside – grit and their trust in Patrick, who was never more than a few steps ahead of them. When they had climbed above the tree line, he knew they were watching where he planted his feet as he chose the route. When, long after midnight, the first of the party finally reached the ridge top, he stopped and gazed ahead over rank after rank of blue-black hills outlined by a trace of sunrise, but they could not rest here.

For the hundredth time, he counted the people of Pallas – those nearest to him anyway. In the dim light, they resembled grey stones leaning against one another. He was afraid they would be as immovable as stones when it was time to walk again. Below, the snowy escarpment looked like a trap, but that was because of what happened the last time he crossed it. Patchson and Ellen were still out of sight. He had not spoken with them since they left the cabin before midnight. They followed at the end of the ragged line of refugees to encourage and guide the weakest.

Patrick pressed his palms over his aching eyes; he didn't know how his people had kept themselves moving through this endless night. That was another sign of how tired he was. He had started to think of them as his people, and their faces were beginning to fall into place in his memories. Besides the baker, Marios, he had recognized a boy who used to work for his mother, doing simple chores and running errands after she was confined to her sick room. He didn't know their names, but he also had recognized the faces of two women, neighbors, who were almost always standing by their doorsteps talking and laughing when he walked through the streets of Pallas early in the morning in the old days. After all they had been through, and after the deaths of both their husbands, they were still inseparable.

Remembering Maraba's instructions from the first time he crossed the mountains, Patrick had prepared for the descent by carrying lengths of rope. Now he gave one to each of the strongest refugees, instructing them to tie one end around their own waist and the other to someone weaker. He told them not to think of anything when they were descending except themselves, their partners, and their footing. He instructed them to go slowly, but they could hardly go more slowly than they already were. The pair at the front of the line would watch Patrick's steps, the second pair would watch the first's, and in that way they would all make their way to the bottom of the slope safely. That was the plan. Once they were there, and only then, would they rest.

He swept his arm toward the blue hills lying ahead and below. "Once we make it down, walking will be easier. We should be home in three days. Or maybe four," he amended, considering their pace so far and reading the grey fatigue on their faces. Even the children had the pinched expressions of old men.

Although they had escaped the island of Niue and, he believed, would now begin to grow again, the children could never regain their innocence. It remained to be seen what kind of adults they might become. Patrick took the hand of the nearest boy, and as he tied the other end of his own rope around the child's waist, he vowed that, once they were all home again, these children would learn to play.

When Ellen caught up, she was carrying a baby, and the child's mother was leaning on her arm. Patrick heard Patchson's voice before he saw him. Although he was a Woods Runner and a quiet man, Patchson had been keeping up a constant stream of encouragement as he tried to get the oldest refugees to keep climbing. Patrick caught Ellen's eye, and she smiled faintly through her weariness.

"Ready?" he said. And without waiting for an answer, they began the descent. He wondered how long it would take before they realized going down is as hard as climbing up.

When Katherine woke up, she was lying on her side on wet leaves. She felt stiff and cold, and it took a few moments to remember how she had gotten there. The rain had stopped, and the air felt heavy. Wisps of mist floated among the trees. The last thing she remembered was falling asleep against Jasper's warm side, but now the bear was nowhere in sight.

"Oro, Maraba – Jasper," she called. The events of the previous night flooded back, and she jumped to her feet and looked around. Patch was the only one there, standing by the rim of the ravine, gazing off into the forest.

"They have gone," he said. "Oro to his owlets, Maraba to her solitude, and Jasper – well, who knows where Jasper goes?"

"I wanted to thank them."

"I said it for you," Patch said quickly, as if he were afraid she might start crying again.

Katherine's tears the night before had welled from shock and exhaustion. Now that she had slept, and in the light of day, she wouldn't succumb again. She went to the edge of the ravine and looked down at the Claymon commander sprawled at the bottom.

"Should we pile some stones over his body?" she asked.

"Who would we be doing that for? Not for him, and no one else is likely to come this way. The owl told me you want to go to Bethany's farm, and that suits me. Unless you have changed your mind."

"You mean you'll go with me?"

"I serve the sleeper, and he asked me to find you and look after you. I will lead you wherever you want to go," Patch said.

Beyond that promise to Patrick, the old Runner had no reason to help her. As a woman of Ostara, she was nothing to the forest people. Katherine noticed Patch was still looking off over the ravine, and intuitively, she knew what he was seeing – a cottage with smoke curling from the chimney, fruit trees, milk goats, chickens, a newly planted vegetable garden, and most important, the expression on Maron's face when she looked up from her work to see him walking up the path.

"I haven't changed my mind. I think going to Bethany's farm is best, don't you? It is peaceful there, and safe."

The Woods Runner finally smiled. "You're right about that, and we should make good time, just the two of us. You had better have something to eat."

He dug through his pack and pulled out the loaf the old woman had given him back in Brethren. He tore off a piece for Katherine, and she gnawed at it greedily. She had not eaten anything except a few leaves and some mushrooms she plucked along the way since before she dove off the *Goshawk* the day before, and she had vomited those up.

Patch tore off another chunk for her. She looked at him questioningly.

"We can find food along the way if we aren't trying to run from the Northerners, and we'll move more swiftly with full bellies," he explained, giving her the bread and passing her the water skin.

He had filled the bag from the stream the day before, and it was morning cool. It was one of the best things Katherine had ever tasted. She passed it back to him, and he took a long drink while she tightened her belt and checked her pocket to see whether the firestone was still there.

"Ready, Lady?" he said.

She couldn't imagine anyone less a lady than herself after everything she had seen and done in the past few days. "It's Kathe," she said. "Just Kathe."

The last time Patrick climbed this mountain, he was roped to Katherine. The panther paired them, but he was sure Maraba didn't do it because Katherine was weaker. He didn't know the man or the talking animal who would dare to tell Kathe she wasn't strong enough. It was as likely she would save him if they ran into trouble.

He remembered he was in one of his moods when they began to climb that morning. These had been coming upon him without warning ever since he woke up from his enchanted sleep in the cave behind the waterfall, though it didn't happen as often after he met Gerard. The old peddler and his quest to rescue the refugees from Niue had given Patrick a sense of purpose, but even that couldn't completely vanquish his feeling that he was out of place in this time. Like the children and elders he was leading home to their forest, he had lost something he could never regain. He mourned the future he might have lived if fate had allowed him to stay in his own time.

On the day when they were roped together, climbing, but not talking, Patrick's dark mood had a different cause. Even though he told himself not to, he had started to imagine a future with Katherine. In fact, he could hardly imagine life without her, but he had decided it was impossible for them to be together. He felt twice robbed.

On that day, he still believed he would have to stay on the Island of Niue forever. Now, with the refugees gingerly picking their way down the slope behind him, everything had changed again.

The refugees were moving slowly, without talking or complaining. They had already crossed from snow to rock before the sun cleared the horizon, and Patrick believed the danger of another avalanche was past. As they descended, the slope grew more gradual, though it hadn't seemed that way when he and Kathe were climbing it.

He began to think about what they would do when they got to the bottom of the mountain. There should still be plenty of daylight. He and Patchson would go hunting, and with a little luck, they would bring back some meat for the pots. It wouldn't be much, but it wouldn't take much to give the people some hope, especially since they would have just crossed the greatest obstacle between Brethren and home.

He was just about to call a halt so they could sit down for a moment, drink some water, and eat the rest of the food they had reserved for the crossing when he heard the sound of rocks breaking loose from the mountainside. Before he could spin around, several small stones stung his shins. He managed to dodge one that would have knocked him down. He pulled the boy who was at the other end of his rope closer and held him downslope, shielding him.

Marios, the baker, was next in line behind Patrick. He must have missed his footing. He had fallen onto his side and slid until he managed to brace himself against a boulder. Now he was struggling to hold the old man who was tied to him. He must have tripped over Marios when he fell, and now he was on his back, further downhill, too surprised to cry out.

Though it seemed much longer, the danger lasted only a few moments before the rope caught. The knot held, and Patrick could breathe again. The rest of the refugees had frozen in place. Patrick signaled them to sit down.

The old man's tunic was torn, and his back was scraped and bloody, but he didn't seem to have broken any bones. Patrick dug through his bundle to find something to use as a bandage and gave him his own flask. It held a measure of wine Fischer's mother had pressed on him when he left the house. She had told him he would likely need it before he reached the other side of the mountain.

Marios had caught himself quickly after he stumbled. He was sitting on the slope rubbing his shoulder by the time Ellen reached him. "Nearly pulled my arm out of the socket, but I'll be all right. Guess my mind went wandering after we got beyond the snow. It'll not happen again."

We don't have one of you to spare. Not one. Patrick thought as he turned back to the work of choosing a route down the mountainside.

10

Padraik's Secret

THIS TIME THE MAP was kind. Instead of a long, icy flight across the sea, it granted Gale and Meg softly glowing stars and a moon like a lighthouse beacon. It was cold, all right, but they warmed each other, and Gale's delight in flying was so fresh that Meg saw the experience anew through his eyes.

The night passed quickly, and when they saw the curve of the coast in the distance, sooner than she expected, Meg asked Padraik to land in the cove just north of Brethren where they had rested the last time, when they brought Patrick to the mainland. Even though it was easier for her and Gale to make the crossing this time, it was still a long way to the mountains of the north, and who knew when they would find a place to fish again.

The last thing Gale did before they left Niue was lash the fishing spear to the dragon's harness in case he needed to help feed Padraik. If it turned out the dragon could hunt for himself, then maybe Gale would catch a fish for the two of them to eat. And in that case, Meg would even dare a small fire.

Every time the dragon landed, he did it with greater finesse, and based on the way he leapt into the air when they left Niue, he was getting better at take-offs too. Provided they could find enough for him to eat, Meg thought he could continue to grow stronger and fly even farther, far enough to find the place where another dragon lived.

It was a breezy morning, and the waves broke with a bigger crash here in the cove than along the sheltered beach on Niue. From where she was sitting, the water looked murky. Gale wouldn't be able to see a fish, let alone spear one, but Padraik recovered quickly after the flight. He set to work soon after landing, and it looked as if he would catch enough fish for all three of them.

Meg thought about staying and resting in the sun for the rest of the day. It would be safer to fly only at night until they were away from human habitation. However, soon after mid-day Padraik roused himself from his nap and sun bath, and he did something she had never seen him do before. First he rolled around half in, half out of the water on his back, exactly like a dog, and then he shook the sand from his scales in a tornado of wings and tail, pelting her and Gale with water and grit. They covered their faces with their hands and shouted at him. The sand stung, but they had to laugh, especially when he came and sat in front of them, completely blocking the sun and looking like a hound eager for the hunt.

"We have to be careful," Meg told Gale, forgetting for a moment that Padraik understood everything she said and most of what she thought. "He's not harmless."

"No, I'm not," said the dragon. *"But I won't hurt you. Unless it's by accident."*

They told him he had to sit in the sun a little longer to dry his scales while they put out the fire and got the harness ready for another flight. He obeyed this time, but they suspected this would not always be the case. Rough ropes on wet skin would be a bad combination, no matter how armored the dragon's back might be.

"I wonder if he will miss Niue the way I miss Springvale," Gale said.

"If you are having second thoughts, this is the time to act," Meg said. "Brethren is just over that hill."

He grinned, mistaking her serious offer for a joke. "And miss being the one to find a lady dragon in the far north? I've no doubt I'll see Springvale again one day, but this will be my only chance to ride on a dragon's back with you, Lady Meg."

She snorted and bent to her work. Even if they were successful in this quest, she had vowed never to go back to Springvale.

When they were airborne again, Meg asked Padraik to circle over Brethren before he headed north. It was risky, but she wanted to see if the *Goshawk* had arrived yet. If they flew low enough, they might even see some of their friends. Surely it couldn't do any harm. Maybe no one would look up, and if someone did and told the tale, well, they would soon be gone, and who would believe it?

The settlement looked even smaller and more isolated from the air, just a few streets of houses clustered along dirt lanes straggling partway up the hillside. There was the inn at the edge of the town nearest the sea. There were no other villages or even lone dwellings in sight up or down the coast. A single thin line zig-zagged east before disappearing into the stunted trees. That must be the trail around the mountains that brought the Claymon to Brethren. She searched the hillside above the town for a spot of blue that marked the home of Captain Fischer's mother, but she couldn't find it. Then she turned her attention to the beach.

She gasped and tightened her grip on the ropes.

"Do you see? Swords flashing!" Gale had to shout to be heard over the sound of the wind.

It was the Claymon. She could tell by the red on their uniforms, but the people they were fighting looked like fishermen. They wore faded browns and greens, so there might be Woods Runners too. It was hard to tell in the melee of wrestling, slashing figures. If there were Runners down there, Meg knew who they had to be.

"Padraik!" she shouted aloud, but the dragon had already read her mind. He gathered speed and swept so low over the combatants on the beach that Meg could see their expressions change from fierce hatred to shock. The fighters on both sides staggered back and stared at the sky.

"You did it!" Gale crowed, slapping the dragon's side.

Not far away, closer to the water, a huddled group that could only be the refugees sat inside a shroud of darkness. From up here, it looked as if they were enveloped in a swarm of wasps, and in the imperfect and fleeting view from the dragon's back, they could see the swarm was emanating from a tall, hooded figure standing close to the waves.

As Padraik swept across the beach, Meg saw someone jump onto the cloaked figure from behind. Looking over her shoulder, she saw the two struggling and watched them fall back into the water. The black cloud melted away, turning a poisonous-looking orange before dissipating.

While the dragon flew towards the end of the beach, Meg couldn't look away from the conflict at the edge of the sea. It was hard to see what was happening from such a height, but she was almost sure only one man was standing there now. He seemed to be bent over a dark splotch that must have been the cloaked figure. By the way it floated, face down and with the cloak spreading like a dark blossom on the surface of the shallow water, Meg thought the man must have drowned.

Padraik had completed his turn at the edge of town and was about to make one final pass over the beach. The Claymon had scattered. It looked like they were all running towards the town except for two who were dead or too hurt to join them.

Over by the water's edge, the first man had turned away from the other, who was still floating in the sea. He waded ashore, towards the refugees. That meant he didn't see when the drowned man started to flounder in the waves and rise to his knees. Meg tried to make sense of the scene as she watched him stand and struggle free from the sodden cloak that was weighing him down.

The dragon recognized Patrick before Meg did. The refugees from Pallas had brought little with them when they fled to the island of Niue. Their most lasting treasure was a song. It was ancient and had been written as praise and prayer to the man now standing below, unaware of the threat rising behind him. The song was one of the few things the dragon could not strip from the people, but he had taken the hero's name.

The man Meg had thought drowned lurched towards shore with his arms raised. Patrick's attention was all on the beach, and on the bright haired woman standing between him and the refugees. It was Ellen.

This time Meg did not have time to shout.

Padraik hissed. It was a terrible sound, like oil spitting from an overheated skillet, but much louder. Without warning, the dragon went into a deep dive and swooped towards the water's edge. Other than that warning hiss, he had no thought to spare for the humans on his back. Even if Meg had tried to stop him, she couldn't have done it. He would not have heard her. All Meg and Gale could do was cling to the ropes and hook their feet under the harness, feeling they would surely be stripped from the dragon's back in his free fall. If they had known Padraik could fly like this, they never would have dared to climb onto his back.

When he reached the nadir of his dive, Padraik did something even he didn't know he could do. He opened his mouth wide, baring his needle-like teeth, and roared. It wasn't a roar like that of a bear or a mountain lion. The dragon's roar echoed like a storm elbowing its way through mountains. It seemed to reach them from another world, a world they only visited in their nightmares.

Everyone on the beach, whether standing and staring at the sky or running as fast as they could towards the town, stopped in that instant and clapped their hands over their ears, even the two men on the beach. Until then, the two had been engaged in a struggle without swords or fists. Meg didn't understand the nature of the conflict, but she could see it was deadly.

When the dragon rocketed down with his wings swept back like a Merlin about to seize an unsuspecting sparrow, the hold the assailant held over Patrick broke, causing both men to stumble forward, clutching their ears.

Meg could not let loose of the rope to protect her own hearing, and she was afraid she would never hear anything again after Padraik's shriek. She expected it to echo inside her skull for the rest of her life.

The struggle on the beach seemed to be over, but Padraik's anger was not yet spent. With his roar still vibrating, the dragon expelled a stream of fire as bright as a lightning strike. It scorched the sand at the water's edge and split the water near the shore, making a boiling arc where the two men had been standing moments earlier.

Before Meg or Gale could react, Padraik was climbing upward again and slowing his flight, resuming steady, level wingbeats. When she laid her hand on his side, Meg could feel the dragon's heart pounding. Now that she could once again think about something other than her fear, Meg again saw the man she had thought drowned, the one who had risen to attack Patrick. He was running faster than anyone should be able to run, heading straight towards the inn.

The only person she had ever heard of who could do the things this man had done was Patrick's brother, Honorus. Meg knew about him from Bethany's stories of her girlhood in Pallas, and she knew he was another of the Old Ones. She and her friends had tricked Honorus when they stole the *Goshawk*, but unlike Bethany and Gerard, Honorus was crippled by age. This must be some new enemy.

Gale risked releasing one hand and shook her shoulder. She looked back to see him mouthing words she could not hear.

"What?" She said.

Gale shook his head in frustration and pointed to his ears. He closed his eyes and thought, *"Can't hear anything. Ringing."*

"Me too," she thought.

Padraik made one more circle over the beach. The refugees were still there, but all the Claymon soldiers and any townspeople had disappeared to the inn and houses of Brethren. They must know stone and wood could not protect them from dragon fire.

Meg placed her palm on Padraik's side again, and she felt his blood pulsing as if it sought another way to vent his rage. She stroked him and made crooning sounds. His thoughts continued to be a mixture of angry colors, like a sky before a storm.

"It is a good thing we came to Brethren when we did, but we had better stay away from towns from now on," Meg thought. *"The next time might not work out so well."*

"I couldn't see what was happening down there, but it seems like he did what he had to do to save our friends – and maybe a little more than he had to." Gale thought. *"I guess he didn't have any reason to use fire as a weapon on the island. Now he'll have to learn to control it. But he's smart. He'll figure it out."*

Meg struggled to hear something, anything, beyond Gale's thoughts and the ringing in her ears. *"He'll have to, but the Claymon will carry the story of the dragon when they go back over the mountain to Ostara, or wherever it is they are going next."*

Gale continued her thought, *"And somebody will be bound to hear it and decide to become a dragon slayer."*

She felt a wave of protectiveness even though only a few minutes had passed since she was sure Padraik was going to kill her in his headlong flight. *How will we keep him safe?*

By then their deadly innocent had left Brethren behind, and with powerful, steady wings, flew towards the north.

11

STORMER'S DREAM

AFTER THE BLUE DOOR closed behind him, Stormer hurried back down the exposed hillside. Ratface was probably searching for him, and he allowed himself a moment of pleasure, imagining the other guard's frustration. When he reached the first cluster of houses at the edge of the town, he slowed down and walked in the middle of the street, no longer trying to hide. He wanted it to look as if he were just taking a walk around Brethren on this last afternoon before the Claymon began their journey back over the mountains to Ostara. Because he had been relieved of any other duties for the day, walking ought to seem a reasonable way to pass the time.

Stormer didn't see any locals. Except for those who relied on the sea for their livelihood, they had mostly stayed out of sight since the Claymon came to the town. One of the first things the Claymon did when they reached Brethren was commandeer many of the homes. For the first time, Stormer wondered where those residents had been sleeping. By now everyone probably knew the Northerners were about to leave, and they'd be getting their town back the next day. They wouldn't want to risk trouble before then.

He passed a few soldiers, but none spoke to him. One man hacked and spat into the street as he passed by. The phlegm just missed the toe of Stormer's boot, but he walked on as if he didn't notice.

When Stormer approached the inn, Ratface was standing on the steps with his arms crossed and an expression on his face someplace between anger and fear. No doubt he had been ordered to follow Stormer all day, but he lost him after they got back from the beach. Honorus wouldn't have been happy about that, especially since Stormer had now been missing for most of the afternoon.

Stormer slowed his steps as his exhilaration over meeting Lightning faded, and he realized he would soon be answering questions about his movements. He felt an itch of worry. He could make promises to himself and to Abel, but the truth was he didn't know what he might tell Honorus the next time he was questioned. His defense against the counselor's probing wasn't likely to last. The old man was clever. He'd find a way around it.

"Where've you been?" Ratface said. "The counselor has had me scouring the town."

"You told me there was nothing for me to do, so I went for a walk in the hills. I wouldn't have gone if I'd known I'd be wanted," Stormer said reasonably.

"You'll be doing plenty of walking starting tomorrow morning." Ratface jabbed his thumb over his shoulder and snarled, "There's a pot in the corridor outside his room. Empty it into the privy."

Stormer nodded. He jostled Ratface when he pushed past him through the doorway. Stormer knew he was supposed to show remorse about the trouble he had caused, but he didn't want to start any bad habits. He might have to work for Honorus, but he didn't have to treat Ratface as his superior. They shared the bad luck of being singled out to serve the counselor, and as far as Stormer was concerned, that meant they were equals.

Climbing the stairs, Stormer realized he had never pictured Honorus squatting over a chamber pot. Then again, he and his fellow soldiers had never seen the counselor eat or drink anything either. The Claymon tolerated Honorus because he was one of Greystone's pets, but soldiers have a hive mind when it comes to dealing with problems such as the enigmatic counselor. Without discussion, they decide when gossip is futile, or even dangerous.

Stormer considered the possibility that Honorus was an ordinary person who happened to have some unusual abilities. Even though he had seen these abilities used to deadly purpose, Stormer had also seen the magician at his most pitiful, as a feeble old man and later, with too small, borrowed clothes stretched over a young-looking, but very human body. With that naked skull wobbling on top of his skinny neck, Honorus didn't look so threatening, and he must know it. He had started wearing his hood again so that his face would always be in shadow.

After performing his odorous duty and rinsing out the pot, Stormer carried it back upstairs, knocked on the magician's door, and when there was no answer, opened it just wide enough to slide the chamber pot inside. Then he sat on the floor with his back against the wall of the corridor and waited. He wasn't in any hurry to go downstairs again, although he would eventually have to find something to eat. Soon the remnant of the Claymon force would return to the inn for one last night of drinking, assuming there was anything left in the town to drink.

Ratface came upstairs carrying a tray holding Honorus's evening meal and disappeared inside the bedchamber. He was in there for a long time. Maybe he had to taste what was on the plate, or maybe he was answering more questions. Stormer closed his eyes and tried not to see Soren's wide, blank eyes and gaping mouth when Honorus was rifling through his mind for the information he wanted – information Soren would have given eagerly if he were asked in the usual way.

To keep that image at bay, Stormer turned his thoughts back to food. He remembered the girl in the kitchen, and he wondered whether she would give him something. She must have known he was trying to sneak away when he surprised her at her work earlier in the day, but it didn't seem like she had told anyone. Now that Honorus had set him apart him from his comrades,

Stormer wanted to stay away from them. He couldn't eat in the taproom. Honorus was the one who killed Soren, but Stormer knew his Claymon comrades wouldn't see it that way.

When Ratface finally emerged, without the tray, he went downstairs without saying anything to Stormer and without looking to either side. The dirty window at the end of the corridor didn't admit much light, but as far as Stormer could tell, his fellow guard looked surly, but otherwise undamaged.

Stormer dozed and waited until the voices and clanking of dishes in the room below diminished. He walked quietly to the end of the corridor to look for a back stairway, but there wasn't one in this small inn. He waited still longer, pacing the corridor, until the sounds faded even more, stopping at the window now and then to watch soldiers straggling out in twos and threes, crossing the spill of light outside the inn door.

When he judged most of the soldiers must have left the inn, Stormer crept down the stairs. As the night before, there was a guard standing at the bottom, but he must have assumed Stormer was on some errand for the counselor. He didn't try to stop him. His fellow soldiers might despise him, but being the magician's servant also provided a kind of protection.

A few Claymon lingered in the taproom. There were no townspeople there. He felt their eyes following him as he crossed to the kitchen and resisted the temptation to meet them. Better to pretend he didn't notice. The innkeeper was standing at the bar with his head resting on his arms.

In the kitchen, the same girl was washing up. Stormer picked up a rag and began to dry the dishes. With a wry smile, she took it away, handed him a slightly cleaner one and said, "That's the one I use to wipe the tables."

They worked in silence until all the plates were neatly stacked on the scarred worktable in the middle of the room. After Stormer replaced the last clean pot on its hook, he hung the rag over the back of a chair and asked, "I don't suppose you've got any scraps?"

He eyed a bowl of gristly looking meat sitting on the end of the counter closest to the door.

"Sorry. My cousin will be coming by for that," she said. "I've been saving what I can to help him feed a big dog he's been keeping."

Stormer looked so disappointed that she laughed and relented. "Maybe there's a bowl of soup left. You can eat that and then scrub the soup pot if you have a mind to. Then I'll be done."

A memory tugged at Stormer, and while he ate the last soup from the pot, savoring the burnt bits, he realized where he had seen a big dog before. It might not be the same one, but most of the other dogs he had seen in Brethren were small brown mongrels that seemed to be related to one another. They were healthy enough, but they were left to scavenge what they could find at the back doors of the houses. They didn't seem to belong to any one person.

"Is this a wolfish looking dog?" Stormer asked. "A mix of brown and black, with pointed ears and a long tail?"

The girl glanced nervously towards the taproom door. "Yes, but nobody is supposed to know about it."

"Don't worry." Stormer said. "It's just that I think I've seen her before."

"How did you know it's a her?"

"That dog's person may be friend of mine," he said.

"Don't tell anyone you know where it is," the girl pleaded. Despite her kindness, she didn't completely trust Stormer. "It would cause trouble for my cousin, and there's a man who'll be taking her away soon."

"I won't," Stormer promised, wiping up the last of the soup with a heel of bread and carrying the pot to the wash tub.

When he crossed the taproom again to return upstairs, it was empty. The innkeeper must have gone to bed, and although there was still a guard at the bottom of the stairs, he was now sitting on the second step. He didn't bother getting up as Stormer passed. He might even have been asleep. Sitting down on duty was forbidden, but who could blame him? Keeping watch over the stairway up to Honorus's room was almost as bad a duty as being one of the old man's personal guards, though less dangerous. No one except Honorus, Ratface or Stormer was likely to pass that way. Since Honorus's transformation on the beach, the other bedchambers were kept empty, by his order.

The corridor at the top of the stairs was almost completely dark, but Stormer could make out a dark bundle lying to one side of the doorway. He assumed it was Ratface. No soldier stood outside the door tonight to protect Honorus from – what, exactly? Stormer wondered why he had not yet been given any instructions for morning. They would march early. They always did.

He shrugged and pulled open his pack. The window at the end of the corridor was stuck, but he managed to work it open and shook his blanket vigorously enough to dislodge any creature his comrades might have hidden in its folds. Making no effort to be quiet, he removed the rest of his possessions, turned the bag upside down and shook that outside too. Then he replaced everything, rolled his cloak, put it on top of the pack as a pillow, and curled up on the gritty floor under his blanket. He didn't bother to close the window on this mild night, not when a breeze might carry some freshness into the stale space.

Even though Stormer was bone tired, he couldn't fall asleep at first. His mind kept replaying Soren's murder, then being singled out and learning he'd have to serve Honorus, and finally climbing the hill where he talked to Abel. Most of all, he thought about Lightning and the moment he realized he could speak with the talking animals – or at least one of them. As Stormer grew sleepier, all these events started to spin behind his eyes as a jumble of images. He continued to lie with his eyes closed, waiting for his mind to quiet.

He shifted his shoulder blades, trying to find some comfort on the unforgiving floor. It was late, and he knew he would be assigned something to do as soon as he woke up, even if it was just to start walking. Honorus would go on horseback, but Stormer and Ratface would be expected to keep up with him on foot. At least they wouldn't be hauling the heavy chair this time.

Stormer was in the middle of a dream about hauling a sled full of books up a rocky trail when he noticed someone blocking the path ahead of him. Trees pressed closely on both sides. There was no way for the dreaming Stormer to get around the figure, so he stopped.

It didn't bother him that it was so dark or that he was alone. Ever since he was a little boy, Stormer had been a dreamer, and a part of him always knew he was dreaming. Even when his dreams were dark, full of irritated Claymon officers, or even bears, Stormer was in control. If the dream became too disturbing, he knew he could wake up, and when he dozed again, chances were the next dream would be sweeter.

The figure didn't come any closer and he couldn't yet see who it was. As Stormer waited, he felt the edge of dread, like the point of a sharp knife pressed against his throat. At the same time, his sleeping body grew heavier. He let go of the rope on the sled he had been hauling, and it slid a few steps down the hill before catching on a rock.

It was growing brighter on the path. He thought a cloud must be sliding off the moon, but there was no moon in this dream. With effort, Stormer turned away from the figure on the path and looked up into the blank sky. There weren't any stars in this dream world either, so what was the source of the light? It had formed itself into a faint globe, and it expanded to contain him. Now he could see its source. It was coming from whoever was blocking the path.

In the eerie half-light, Stormer could now see the figure was cloaked and hooded, and he knew he should be able to give it a name. It was too tall to be the commander, too thin to be a bear. A bear wouldn't be wearing a cloak anyway. If it was the man from the house on the hill, then why was Stormer afraid? This was someone else. He needed to remember.

The sleeper's legs twitched under his blanket, as if he were trying to run, and the man standing over him in the corridor smiled a thin, humorless smile.

In the dream, the phantom raised its arms and pushed the hood back from its face. In the corridor, the sleeper made a choking sound and tried to awaken. He rocked his body from side to side and banged his heels against the wooden floor. He brought his hands to his face and clawed at his eyes.

He was trapped by a web of light. The strands brightened and formed themselves around him like a cocoon, becoming glowing, sulfur-colored ropes that tightened and burned. Stormer lay with his arms crossed awkwardly over his chest, elbows plastered to his side. He gasped and moaned, though to anyone observing the scene in the corridor, there would have been no obvious reason for his distress.

Honorus stood outside the open door of his bedchamber and watched the struggle with grim pleasure. Back in Ostara, there would be many opportunities to test his abilities in Peter Greystone's prisons, but now that he had achieved his transformation, or most of it, he needed to understand how his powers had developed. The soldier died in the street this morning before he could extract any information from him. He would not allow that to happen this time.

This soldier, the one called Stormer, had already eluded him twice. At those times, the traps Honorus conjured to ensnare him failed. It was as if the boy's mind was slippery, like melting ice. He couldn't make his spells stick.

He still didn't understand why that happened. Perhaps there was some lingering weakness after his transformation. He had practiced on the other guard when he brought his supper, tightening the trap with precision and delicately searching until he was certain the man knew nothing about Stormer's movements. Honorus was certain the man never even sensed what was happening to him.

Now, in the dream, Stormer felt the coiling ropes and struggled to breathe. He knew exactly what had happened to Soren. Somehow, Stormer had avoided capture when he reported to Honorus and again that morning in the street, but he wouldn't escape a third time. It was too late to awaken.

The sleeper surrendered and waited. Now half-awake, but still unable to move, he realized he would receive no new orders before dawn from his master. That was never part of the plan. Honorus would take all his secrets, and the innkeeper would find his body lying on the corridor floor after the Claymon left the town.

In the unbearable knowledge that he was about to give up everything, including his life, Stormer shifted his attention. Earlier, he had turned his gaze towards the ever-changing surface of the sea, but today he had found something more beautiful. Without consciously choosing to do it, he filled his mind with that image.

In his dream, Stormer could almost see the shape of Honorus through the poisonous fog he had created between the two of them. The magician's arms were raised, and flickers of brightness, like heat Lightning, gathered in the air and probed in his direction.

Stormer closed his dreaming eyes and submitted to the crushing weight of the ropes. At the same time, he created a picture of Lightning in his mind. The bird had promised to teach him how to talk with his kind. That would never happen now, but at least he could see the hawk once more in his mind's eye. He tried to recreate every detail – its deadly, curving talons; shining feathers; bright and intelligent eyes. As he created the image, it obscured everything else, and with his eyes closed, he didn't see when the light sparking from Honorus's hands began to flicker and die as if his fingers were so many guttering candles.

The red-tailed hawk slept in a tree near the edge of Brethren. He knew he should already have been soaring over the mountains, and in his hawk dream, that is exactly what he was doing.

The man in the house, the one who was hurt, trusted him to take a message, but Lightning wanted to talk to the boy one more time, and he couldn't do that at night. In the morning he would find a way.

There was something he wanted to say to Stormer, but he didn't yet know what it was. Lightning's wings itched. As soon as he talked to the boy, and after the soldiers marched out of Brethren, he would fly, and he would find the one called Patrick.

Morning was still a long way off when Lightning startled awake and spread his wings. He was no creature of the night like Oro, but he flew anyway, sweeping towards the center of the town with powerful wingbeats. The summons had come too quickly for him to be surprised. There was no choice except to answer. Folding his wings, he dove through the open window at the end of the corridor and screamed. The sleeping boy did not hear the sound, but the hawk's slashing talons drove the magician back into his bedchamber. The door slammed, followed by the click of the lock.

The hawk landed awkwardly on the floor next to Stormer's head.

Lightning sat with his head cocked to one side, waiting for the boy to wake up. He wondered if he had come too late, but that couldn't be. If the boy had been dead, he couldn't have called. The hawk pulled at the blanket with his beak and poked at Stormer's shoulder with his talons. He didn't break the skin, but he pushed hard enough that Stormer started to wake up. The boy gasped and fought back. The ropes had burned away, but the ash had crossed over into the waking world and left grey marks on his arms and clothing. Stormer flailed in his panic.

"Stop! Stop at once!" Lightning thought in the tone he used with his nestlings when they were testing their wings too soon and might fall or push one another from the nest.

Stormer stopped. After a few moments his breathing quieted, and he opened his eyes. At first, he stared straight up at the ceiling, but then one hand began to feel along the wooden floor, and he gathered the rough wool of his blanket in the other. He turned his head. There was just enough light coming through the window to see it reflected in Lightning's eyes.

"You came," Stormer whispered. He wanted to sit up, but his body wouldn't cooperate. He and Lightning were alone. There was no sign of Honorus. Ratface was gone too.

"Of course I came, when you called like that," Lightning said.

"I called?" This time Stormer didn't use his voice. He thought the words as he had been taught that afternoon.

"Loud enough to get my attention, and I was half-way up the hill and sound asleep."

"You saved me," Stormer said.

"You saved yourself. The spell was already breaking when I got here, but the bad man didn't know it yet. I just got rid of him and kept him from killing you in some ordinary way while you were trying to wake up."

"Ordinary way?"

"Instead of squeezing the life out of you in your sleep. Like maybe holding your blanket over your face or slipping a knife between your ribs."

Now Stormer made himself sit up. *"He was here?"*

"Until I flew at him and made this sound." Lightning screamed.

"I would have run away too." Stormer said. He would have jumped to his feet when he heard it this time, but he didn't think his legs would hold him yet.

"Anyone would," Lightning said with satisfaction, preening the feathers on his shoulder.

The sky grew faintly grey as the world turned closer to sunrise.

"I have to go now, and you must decide what you will do," Lightning said.

"What do you think I should do?"

"I can't make the choice for you. But you knew it would be dangerous to serve him." The hawk tipped his head towards the Magician's door.

Stormer was already rolling his blanket to stow in his pack. He clumsily tied his cloak around his shoulders.

"Can he hear us?" he asked.

"No. He doesn't know how. He never has."

Stormer thought for a moment and said, *"I think I finally understand how I have been protecting myself from him. It seems like such a small thing, but when I'm bored my mind wanders, and when I'm scared, I guess I do it on purpose. Somehow, that makes it hard for Honorus to capture and empty me. He could do it when I was sleeping, though, until I thought of you."*

"Called me."

Stormer still had trouble believing he had called the hawk. *"What if I pretend I don't remember what happened? That I was asleep, and I didn't wake up through any of it? What if I say I had a bad dream? The worst I have ever had? Do you think he'd try again?"*

"He might, and next time I might not be close enough to help you."

"I bet he won't dare for a while, Stormer said. *I heard how he was with the dragon, and he must have been just about as scared when you flew at him."*

Lightning didn't answer. It was nothing but the plain truth.

Stormer's next words were hard to say. *"I'll stay here. I'll watch him. If I have to, I'll run away later."*

The corridor was brightening. *"I know you have to fly today, but will you visit me sometimes? I may have information to give you."* That was true, but it wasn't the main reason Stormer wanted to see the hawk again.

"I don't have any choice," Lightning said. *"There was something I wanted to tell you, and now I know what it is. I wondered when I met you up on the hill, but when you called me I was certain. Sometimes we animals are more than guides to humans. We are friends. You and I are friends now."*

Without waiting for Stormer to answer, Lightning walked along the corridor to the open window and jumped up onto the sill. Then, without looking back, he launched himself and flew in the direction of the mountains on steady wings.

12

A Guide and a Gift

PATRICK HAD LED THEM to the other side. The people of Pallas were starting to think their grandchildren might one day sit at their feet to hear stories of their return to the forest city.

To Patrick, keeping watch a distance away from the camp, the glow of the small fires looked like a kind of a celebration. The people sitting in circles soaking up the warmth were smiling and talking in a way they hadn't since leaving the *Goshawk* and beaching at Brethren. He wished he could feel as relieved as they did, but he was already looking ahead to reaching Pallas. He knew their troubles were far from over.

Honorus almost killed them back in Brethren. Patrick knew the refugees had not forgotten that terrible attack on the beach, and ever since then they had been tired and hungry. Limping along on bruised feet and climbing and descending the unmarked mountainsides had tapped reserves of strength they would have sworn they did not have. Only by leaning upon each other and by following in Patrick's footsteps had they come to this safe, green place.

They weren't home yet, not even close, but now that they had made a camp inside the edge of a forest, at least they were on familiar ground. Patrick had assured them walking would be easier from now on. Just being under gold-green spring leaves gave them new hope. White flowers carpeted the forest floor in every direction, and they glowed in the failing day, extending the fire-light.

In a way, the refugees' capacity for hope was as unexpected as their physical survival. That hope should have died on the beach when Honorus almost killed them – and did kill Meier Steele. It was hard to believe these were the same people who watched silently, with deadened eyes, as Patch and Patrick buried their old leader in a shallow grave, beyond the point where sand transitioned to deep-rooted grasses, out of the reach of storms and waves.

Other than collecting wood and lighting the fires, there was little to do to set up camp. And Patrick had decided there was no need to be careful about pursuit. Honorus and the Claymon must have followed the easier road toward Ostara. Otherwise they would have caught up with the refugees by now.

No matter what the Claymon might choose to do, that part of the story was out of his hands. Patrick guessed Honorus was still too frightened by his encounter with the dragon and too con-fused by his own transformation to have decided what he would do about the People. He seemed to believe they were his to lead or to destroy. Honorus was selfish and manipulative, and as far as anyone could tell, he had no conscience, but he was still Pat-rick's brother. The two of them might be estranged, but Patrick believed he could still guess what Honorus was thinking.

As soon as the camping place was chosen, Patchson broke away without a word and disappeared among the trees. It was urgent that he hunt, but that wasn't the reason he disappeared. After so much time among people, the solitary Woods Runner had a ferocious need to be alone. Patrick understood. He wanted to walk away himself. He wasn't sure they would see Patchson again that night, but he returned just before dark carrying two rabbits and a squirrel.

A few young refugees skinned and gutted the animals, and others ventured a short distance from the camp to find wild on-ion tops to add to the broth. Now the unlucky creatures were stewing in the cooking pots, and Patrick could smell the meat even from this distance. The first meal of what the refugees had already started to call their new life would seem a feast, even if there still wasn't enough to fill their bellies.

Ellen left the spill of firelight and joined Patrick where he sat on the ground under an ancient, twisted tree. "Holding yourself apart is becoming a habit. Why don't you come and sit by the fire?"

When he didn't answer at once, she said, "Maybe you still think you don't belong, but this is your time now, whether you like it or not. And these are your people – at least until another leader steps forward. Best get to know them."

He rose to his feet but made no move to follow her back to the camp. "How do they seem to you?" he asked. He wondered how she knew the reason behind his dark moods. Had Katherine told her?

She was not sure what he meant. "Bone tired. Marios wasn't much hurt when he fell. Just scrapes. It's a miracle, that they all made it across. The elders who stayed back with me wanted to stop many times. They sat down on the ground, and it looked as if they would never budge again, but somehow they kept each other moving. One of them told me, 'When we get back to Pallas, we'll sit in the sun and remember all this.'"

"That's what I mean," Patrick said. "They don't know how much Pallas has changed. They are so few, and the work will be hard. They don't understand."

"I have never been to Pallas, but Katherine has told me what she saw there." Ellen said, after a pause. "The way she described it, it is still beautiful. I think the people will pick up whatever traces they can find from their old lives, and that's where they will begin. Remember, by the time you came for them on Niue, they had given up hope of ever seeing it again."

"You'll see for yourself soon," Patrick said.

When Ellen did not answer, he took a step closer and tried to read her face in the gathering darkness.

She considered her next words carefully. It was not easy to give Patrick this news. "I will be parting from you in the morning. I have decided to return to my husband's camp."

Before Patrick could try to dissuade her, she said, "Don't you feel it? It may be the tide is changing. The Claymon have been advancing ever since they took Ostara last year. That conflict back on the beach in Brethren was small, but we won, and that's the first time the Claymon have been defeated, as far as I know. It doesn't hurt that we were aided by a dragon. And our little force was made up of Ostarans, refugees from Pallas, Woods Runners, even a few sailors from Brethren."

"So?"

"So if I know Greystone, he won't care that the battle, if you can call it that, was small. He counts any defeat as humiliation. He won't let it pass. That's why he's still looking for Katherine – because he cannot have her. She has eluded him again and again. We don't know yet whether he'll blame the folk of Brethren, the Ostarans, or you for the loss on the beach or for her escape, Patrick, but whenever and wherever he moves from now on, we have to prepare to face him together."

Patrick had assumed Ellen would be coming with him to Pallas and staying for a while – at least until the People had started new lives there. The refugees had come to trust and depend upon her, and to be honest, so had he. "I still don't understand why you are going back to the rebels," he said.

"My husband is stubborn, but he isn't stupid," she said thoughtfully. "If we are going to work together to defeat the Claymon, then we will need messengers, and who better to help us than the animal guides, who can move without notice between Devon's camp and Pallas? Blackie can help us too, carrying information between the rebels and Ostara."

They stood quietly for a few minutes, watching the flames of the distant campfires.

"Your husband is deaf to the animal guides," Patrick said, finally understanding.

"Yes, I need to make him understand they can help and are telling us the truth. He'll have to agree to let me be his interpreter. It won't be easy, but I think I can make him believe me, especially considering the new messenger the Lady has sent to us."

Patrick looked at her blankly. "The new messenger…"

Ellen pointed over his shoulder. Patrick turned around slowly and came face to face with an enormous, fierce-looking red-tailed hawk. It was sitting on a branch of the twisted tree at eye-level as if it had always been there.

"Patrick, meet Lightning."

Although Patch was a man of the forest, not the mountains, he had an instinct for choosing the best route no matter where he was. It was not a matter of pride, just simple fact, but he was ready to put this foreign landscape behind him. He couldn't see the sun, but he didn't have to. It was past time to get started.

They would move quickly – or as quickly as Katherine could manage. On the other side of these mountains, no more than two days' walk away, lay the beginnings of his forest home, and deep within that forest, Bethany's farm lay hidden. Patch had never been there, but he would find it. He was a patient man. It was one of the few qualifications necessary to guard the hero, but now he watched Kathe eating the breakfast he had given her, and it was all he could do not to hurry her.

Kathe had slept, not well but enough, and as soon as she finished eating, she too was ready. Like Patch, she was looking forward to reaching the farm. The past winter, spent there with Bethany and Meg, was the happiest of her life. The farm was a place of peace and safety and, she admitted, comfort.

By the time they reached it, she surely would have made a plan. There was nothing she could do to help Meg or Gale. They should have begun their quest to find a lady dragon by now.

Maybe one of the animal guides would bring her news of Patrick, though. She had to find out where he and Abel went after his father left Brethren to lead the refugees back to Pallas. Then she could decide what to do next.

Once Patch saw Kathe was ready, they left without looking down into the ravine again. First they retraced their steps from the night before, climbing over the fallen tree where Kathe hid before she was discovered, and then they continued to follow the faint animal trail she and the guides had been following before the Claymon caught up with them.

During that day of walking, and the next, the Woods Runner was kind enough, watching Kathe for signs she was faltering and sharing the food he had carried from Brethren, but they passed the time in near silence. Woods Runners need a good reason to strike up a conversation, though Patch and his son were more talkative than most.

He did not take time to hunt, but they both collected what they could along the way. Kathe had spent the winter studying Bethany's specimens of edible plants and had memorized their characteristics, but the fresh growth did not look much like Bethany's crumbling examples.

Each time she saw a growing thing she thought might be safe to eat, she called, "Patch," with a question in her voice before she picked it, and he paused to either nod or shake his head. He did not volunteer much other information, and when he did speak, his names for the plants were different than the ones she had learned. Patch wasn't sure if it was curiosity or just simple hunger that made Kathe keep questioning him this way.

Kathe told herself Bethany would help her to put all this knowledge in order the next time they were together. She knew her training as a healer was far from complete. Even though Bethany and Gerard remained in Niue, and even though it had been their choice to stay there, Kathe refused to believe she would never see her teacher again.

They had travelled together from Abel's cabin on the way to Brethren, but Patch had not gotten to know Kathe well. He and Patchson were often off hunting, not rejoining the others until evening. In the short time before they all fell asleep after supper, Patch remembered the girl smiling and talking with her mother, and with Meg and Patrick. If he had to describe her to someone, he would have said she was friendly and cheerful, but he had not seen her smile since they left the ravine.

The longer they walked together, the more Patch thought he ought to find something to say, but he couldn't think what it might be. He decided to wait until Kathe struck up a conversation, and just asking him which plants she could eat did not count. He knew he should already have told her what he knew: that there had been a battle on the beach; that Abel had been badly wounded; about the dragon; that Patrick was leading the refugees to the city of Pallas because his father had been killed; that her mother was with him; that Honorus was stronger than ever; and that Stormer had returned to the town and had become a spy.

He was not keeping this information secret, not really. He simply could not bring himself to do so much talking. He was not sure himself what happened back in Brethren. It was a confusing story, and some of it would be painful for her to hear. It looked as if Abel had lost too much blood to recover, and Patch did not want to give Kathe that news, especially after what happened back at the ravine.

She would have questions, and he would not be able to answer them. As far as Patch could see, there was nothing Kathe could do to help her friends. He convinced himself there would be no harm in saving his news until they reached Bethany's farm. That would be soon enough. After that, he and Maron would return to the forest near Pallas and take up their lives again. He had already decided he wouldn't travel any more, even if Patchson did. Even if Patrick did.

It would be easy for him and Maron to return and rebuild their old home, much easier than it would be for the city people returning to their roofless stone houses.

Patch glanced back over his shoulder. Kathe was still walking, and she took a few more steps before she realized he had stopped. She patiently waited for him to go on. She had been keeping her eyes on his back whenever she was not scanning the area for plants, but her thoughts seemed to have taken her far away. Patch was not even sure she noticed when they started to climb.

Once darkness started to shrink the world again, Patch stopped for the last time that day and gestured towards the dark space under the sweep of an evergreen's lowest branches. Katherine had spent enough nights in the forest to know what he meant, and she managed a small smile, her first, to thank him. She took the piece of bread he handed her, lay down on the thick layer of pine needles, and fell into a dreamless sleep with half of it still uneaten in her hand.

When she woke up, the darkness was complete. There was no breath of wind. The mountainside was completely silent. From where she lay under the branches, she could not see the sky. The pine needles were thick, and she was tired enough to have slept until morning. She lay there quietly, eating the rest of her portion of bread, waiting for sleep to return or for whatever had woken her to happen again.

Patch snored softly on the other side of the tree trunk. She wondered why he was not awake too.

When the owl hooted for the second time, it was soft and distant, but the sound had woven itself into her dreams on so many nights that she did not doubt it. She pushed aside the blanket Patch had given her and crawled out from under the tree. She stood and stretched, trying to decide which direction the sound had come from. She knew Oro was probably much closer than he seemed. If he wanted to speak to her, he would have to show himself.

Out under the sky it was a bit easier to see, and she walked farther from the pine where Patch slumbered, but not too far. She was not sure she would be able to find it again. She hoped she would not have to call out and wake him. Their tracking and hunting abilities made Woods Runners seem more than human, but she had followed Patch long enough to know that, while he was still a good guide, he was also a tired, old man. She hoped he knew how thankful she was for his help, but if they stumbled into more trouble, she would be just as likely to save him as the other way around.

Kathe stood in the open, within shouting range of the tree, and made herself still. She gazed up at the stars, and within a few moments, she saw the dark shape she had been expecting fly over her head. He landed on a branch a few feet off the ground. *"Patch told me you were taking care of your owlets,"* Katherine said. She did not speak aloud, and she hoped the Woods Runner was sleeping too deeply to be attuned to animal speech.

"I did, I was, but I promised I would bring you a mouse." Oro said.

Kathe heard a soft plop on the leaves at her feet as Oro released the tiny creature from his talons. She almost said, *Have you ever seen a human eat a mouse?* but then she realized he had seen her eat rabbits and squirrels. Was a mouse really so different? So as not to hurt his feelings, she picked it up and held the small, warm body in her hand.

"I thank you. I have eaten some bread. I will save this for the morning."

"They are better when they are fresh," Oro said.

"I am sure you are right, but I cannot swallow the bones and fur, as you can."

"You can't?" Oro said. He sounded surprised, as if he always thought humans must cough up those parts in pellets, as owls do.

It was time to change the subject. *"Is there anything else you want to tell me?"* she asked.

There was a time when Kathe thought the animal guides would help her to find her way home to Ostara. Now she knew

they always had a plan of their own, and she had come to trust
their choices. If she had insisted upon going to Ostara by herself
as she intended when she ran away from Springvale, she would
likely be married to Peter Greystone by now. Instead, she had
followed Oro and other guides to Patrick's cave, to the forest city
and to Bethany's farm.

If Kathe had ignored their guidance, she would have lost her
freedom, and Patrick would never have awakened. Over time,
she figured out she was supposed to travel to Niue with the others. The book showed her there, along with her mother and
Bethany. Now she wasn't certain where she should go, and she
hoped Oro had come to advise her.

"The Woods Man won't find Bethany's farm without my help," Oro
said.

"Are you saying I am right to be going there?"

*"Yes, and then we won't have to worry about you for a while. You will
be safe, like an owlet in a nest."*

Kathe wasn't sure he had answered her question. If she understood him correctly, then the farm would be a safe place for
her, but she would be outside any events he and the other animals were contriving. She wasn't sure what to think of that, but
she was too glad to see him to argue now. She could set off again
on her own later if she had to.

She would have to tell Patch they would both be following an
animal guide from now on. Maybe he would be able to turn some
of his attention to hunting. He had not said anything to her, but
she had noticed the food bag was getting lighter.

That reminded her of another urgent question. With Oro
hanging around, what would she do about his gift?

13

ON THE SWORD'S EDGE

MEG WATCHED THE WORLD unfold. From her perch on Padraik's back, gazing to the east, the mountains looked as if they rolled on forever. They turned gold, then blue, in the afternoon light, ridge after ridge stretching into the distance. To the west, the endless sea was patterned with the white crests of waves. Every day since they left Brethren the mountains had grown higher and more forbidding. Every night it was more difficult to find a place to land and rest.

When she, Gale and Padraik started this journey, the coastline was punctuated by the golden crescents of sandy coves where a dragon could hunt for fish, and where they could rest their aching hips in yielding sand. No longer. On the last two nights they were forced to camp on narrow ledges at the top of cliffs that plunged straight into the sea. And last night, when she crawled to the edge, Meg saw seabirds flying so far below they looked like snowflakes swirling in the wind.

It was a good thing Padraik was getting better at landing. Still, when they finally spotted last night's resting place, it had seemed as small as a handkerchief from above. Meg kept her eyes tightly closed until they were safely on the ground. As soon as they dismounted and removed the harness, Padraik lay down on the naked rock, too exhausted to speak. Meg stroked his neck and told him to fish only for himself this time. The effort would be too great to do any more, and in any case, there was no wood for making a fire. She and Gale would have to eat the dry biscuits from their bags.

Now, as darkness gathered again and as Meg scanned the landscape below for another place to rest, she thought about Padraik's gut-wrenching sweep over the beach in Brethren, when his shriek half deafened them. The dragon's attack was effective. Honorus ran, and Patrick was still alive.

As time passed, the ringing in Meg and Gale's ears gradually faded, but Meg believed a trace of the sound would always be there. She prepared small wads of cloth for herself and Gale so they could stuff their ears the next time, but she knew if Padraik became that angry again, there would be no time to react.

They outflew spring. Back home on Bethany's farm, and even in Brethren, winter had already released its grip, but as they traveled north, each night was colder than the last. When it was time to sleep, Meg spread a piece of canvas on the sand or rock on the sheltered side of the dragon, and she doubled the blankets over herself and Gale. They spent their nights as they did their days, spooned together. It was a practical decision, and there was no one to disapprove. Meg touched her hand to her cheek numbed by icy wind. She was glad for Gale's warmth where he leaned against her back.

Padraik was carrying them both and flying all day. Even though he never complained, they knew he tested his limits every time he took to the sky. That is why she and Gale did not complain to each other about the cold or about how their legs and backs ached after a day on the dragon's bony spine. After dismounting at the end of the day, they hobbled like a parody of old age.

Back on the Island of Niue, Meg and Gerard had decided the best place to look for another dragon would be in the wild mountains to the north, between the sea and the flat plains of the Claymon homeland. If a dragon lived anywhere near people, they reasoned, it would not be a secret for long – except on Niue, of course, and now that secret had been freed. The Claymon and the refugees from Pallas would carry the news with them back to the populated lands.

Now that they were well into those wild mountains, Meg was beginning to doubt the choice. She took a deep breath and tried to find the well of confidence that had been sustaining her.

"Nothing can live here," Padraik said.

Meg dragged herself away from her thoughts. The dragon almost never spoke when he was flying. The three of them spent their days following the coastline in silence. Now, as his words formed in her mind, they seemed to warm her.

"Look."

The ridgeline below was a sword's edge slicing the sky. Meg continued to search for a small plot of flat rock, but the passes between the mountains had become boulder fields. Snow and ice reached out into the sea like fingers.

Early that morning, soon after they took flight, Gale gripped Meg's arm and pointed. The wind made it impossible for them to hear each other, and it took too much effort to communicate by animal speech unless it was an emergency. Together, they watched a chunk of ice as big as a ship break off at the edge of the cliff and tumble into the water, where it submerged and bobbed to the surface, joining an archipelago of floating ice islands.

"There is nothing to eat." Padraik said. *"On my island there were fish or sometimes birds, and when my belly was full I slept in the sun. Now I am cold and there is nowhere to lie down. She doesn't live here."*

He was right. They had not even seen a mountain goat in days, and no birds soared above these heights. When Padraik lived on his island, he didn't know anything about the wide world until Meg showed him the little she had seen of it. Gale, who had been to Ostara, added to the dragon's store of knowledge. She did not know what Gerard and Bethany might have told Padraik once he figured out how to talk to them. Now he was flying over mountains that, a short time ago, didn't exist in any of their memories or imaginations. Still, she had learned to trust him, and she realized it was time to drop her façade of confidence. It didn't fool him anyway.

"Where do you think we should look?" she asked.

"Away from the water." Obviously, he had been thinking. His answer was precise. *"If we are going to find another of my kind, it will be in a warm place where she can find food. It doesn't have to be an island. It could be a fire mountain."*

"Like the one on Niue?" she asked, remembering a small, lazy cloud of smoke punctuating a perennially blue sky.

"Yes. My island has hot sun and a fire mountain." For the first time, Padraik sounded homesick.

"What if it is a he?" Gale interjected. Meg had not realized he was listening.

Neither of them answered him. The question should not have been asked. The dragon had to be a female. Padraik had never said so, but he would never share a territory with another male, no matter how lonely he might be.

As if Gale had not spoken, Padraik continued, *"We must fly away from the sea to get away from these mountains and to find a place to rest and to hunt – and I am too cold."*

Meg knew Patrick carried a fire within himself, and that it had sustained him through the journey. *"What will you eat until we find that place?"* Meg asked. *"There will be no more fish."*

"I will eat the food I am carrying."

Meg shivered. Even though it had only been because of a mis-understanding, she knew Padraik had killed, if not eaten, people. She knew he had brought her along as a companion and that he was carrying Gale because she asked him to, but she wondered whether he really needed her. He would be able to fly much faster and farther without riders. She had come to think of Padraik as a friend, but what is friendship to a dragon?

"The food I am carrying in the skin bags," he said. He sounded offended. She was afraid Padraik had read her thoughts.

Before leaving Niue, she and Gale had stuffed two large bags full of as many supplies from the *Goshawk* as they would hold, mostly hard biscuits because they would last. Meg believed the dragon only ate meat. His teeth were for biting and tearing. How would he eat the biscuits? They might make him sick.

"It's either that, or we go back to my island," Padraik said.

"I'm not sure we can go back," Gale said. *"We have gone too far."*

"It's settled then," Meg said, and as soon as she spoke the words, the Dragon turned inland, away from the lowering sun. Suddenly, Meg felt even colder, but it wasn't because of the wind. Padraik might grow too tired to fly before he found a place to land. The food would not last much more than a day if they were sharing it with a dragon, and the waterskins were almost empty. Gale must know it too. Neither of them said anything, but he squeezed her shoulder and together, they continued to look for a place to land.

14

AN UNEASY TRUCE

ELLEN CREPT OUT OF the refugees' camp before first light without saying any goodbyes. Patrick was sitting with his back against a tree next to last night's smoldering fire. His hood was pulled over his eyes. She thought he was asleep until he looked up and raised his hand in parting. She had to go, but she knew the People would not understand. She had been with them ever since they left the island, and they had come to depend on her. They thought Patrick's leadership and her encouragement had brought them over the mountains, and they would miss having a healer. Eventually they would have to recognize it was their own courage that had carried them this far. Besides, she would see them again, and it might be soon, depending on Devon's reaction to her news.

The Ostaran rebel encampment was not so far away. If she walked all day, she would be almost there by nightfall, and then she would have to decide whether to enter the camp right away, or to wait until morning. It probably wouldn't matter. Devon's scouts would tell him she was coming long before she arrived.

Ellen rehearsed the words she intended to say to her husband. She knew it would be up to her to begin the conversation. Devon would be too angry to say anything. She had wounded his pride when she ignored his wishes and went off on her own, and every day she was gone that wound must have festered. It had been little more than two weeks since she left her husband's camp to join her daughter at Bethany's farm, but when she tried to count the days she had been away, Ellen kept getting confused. It was the island, she thought.

No matter how long she had been away, Devon would expect her to kneel and lower her head as a sign of contrition, but that wouldn't happen. Not this time. She knew she shouldn't say anything until he forgave her, or at least showed some sign of softening. But Ellen wasn't sorry, and if she was going to return to this marriage, it would have to be on her terms. After all, she didn't expect an apology from Devon for sending their son to bring her and Katherine back to the rebel camp, by force if necessary.

This would be a new beginning, or it would be no beginning at all. When Ellen asked herself whether she still loved Devon Elder, the answer was yes. He could be kind, and no one had ever doubted his courage. They shared more than twenty years and two children. Once, that would have been enough to justify a lifetime of compromises, but no longer.

No, she wouldn't kneel. She would stand and say, "I know a way to drive the invaders from Ostara, but you must trust me."

That would not do. He would seize on the word 'trust' and begin to list all the ways she had proven herself to be untrustworthy. His voice would drown out anything else she hoped to say.

She tried, "I bring you news of new allies."

That was better, but then she would have to tell him who those allies were: talking animals, a man from a ruined city who had recently woken up from an enchanted sleep, some Woods Runners, and a small group of refugees. Devon would laugh at her, and that is if she were lucky.

As the day went on and Ellen drew closer to the camp, she gave up trying to picture her reunion with her husband and instead concentrated on moving cautiously. Even though she was coming to the camp from the mountains and was unlikely to meet Claymon patrols, she must not put her people at risk. She paused and gave a short whistle. It sounded exactly like the alarm note of a Robin, but Devon's scouts would recognize the sound. It was her own signal, the one she used back when she was Greystone's prisoner and slipped away to report what she had seen and heard.

The scouts must know she was coming by now. She wondered why they were not answering. The Ostarans were no Woods Runners, but during the year of the Claymon occupation, the rebels had learned how to stay hidden unless they wanted to be seen. By now one of them must surely be on his way back to the camp to tell Devon Elder that Lady Ellen would be there in time for a late supper.

Every time Ellen signaled, she held her breath, listening for a response. She didn't hear anything except the wind in the trees and the usual rustlings in the forest made by the claws of small creatures. The chipmunks and squirrels weren't talking animals, and she amused herself by watching them as they went about their lives – lives in which there were no invaders, no magicians, no angry husbands. She stopped herself as she drifted towards self-pity. These creatures might become dinner for an owl in the coming dusk. They weren't safe either.

Just as she was about to whistle again, Ellen sensed someone behind her. She was not sure what she had heard or scented, but she spun around, swinging her walking stick hard at knee level. If it had been a Claymon trying to ambush her, the blow would have brought him to the ground. If it was an Ostaran scout, he'd have received an important lesson about how to treat the Lady of Ostara. As it was, Maraba leapt neatly over the stick that whistled beneath her. Ellen staggered a few steps back in surprise.

The black panther sat down in front of her and stared. *"Why did you do that?"*

"Why were you sneaking up on me?"

"I wasn't sneaking. That's the way I always move," Maraba said sulkily.

Ellen had to admit Maraba was right. *"I am sorry I swung at you, but I didn't know who was behind me. If it had been an enemy, waiting to see could have cost me my freedom."*

Without acknowledging the apology, Maraba suddenly sat down and twisted herself backwards into an impossible shape. She started to clean one hind leg.

"Why have you come here?" Ellen asked.

The Panther paused her bath, then licked her paw and ran it over one silky ear. *"You are going to see your man."*

"Yes, that's right."

"You need to make him listen to you so that he will help us. You are afraid he will think you are lying when you tell him about us even though he has already seen plenty of proof. The black dog brought messages to you from the city, and the feathered ones came often when you lived in the camp."

"Yes." Ellen didn't bother asking how Maraba had come to know all this. *"It is partly my fault. He can't understand animal speech, and I never tried very hard to make him understand. Talking to him about it only makes him angry, and then life is more difficult for both of us. If Blackie gave me information I thought my husband ought to know, I passed it on. I never told him how I found out, and he never asked."* Ellen never challenged Devon's determined lack of curiosity.

"It will be easier for him to believe if I am with you," Maraba said.

This was true. Devon could hardly ignore a black panther standing by his wife's side. It was also impossible. Ellen shook her head. *"It might be easier for him, but it is too dangerous for you. The guards will kill you before we reach the camp. To them you are just a wild animal."*

"I know that," Maraba said, resuming her bath.

Knowing Maraba's sense of drama, Ellen waited to hear the rest of the panther's plan. She knew this guide well enough to accept that any human she decided to assist would have to adapt. The panther was stubborn and had a different way of reasoning than humans. There was no point in arguing with her. Besides, if she had listened more carefully to Maraba the last time she tried to help, Kathe and Patrick wouldn't have been caught by the avalanche.

While she waited, Ellen again wondered whether any of her husband's men were watching and if so, what they were thinking. It must be obvious to them that she wasn't afraid of the panther, but even so, Maraba already was in danger.

As if she had read Ellen's mind, Maraba abruptly stopped licking herself and took a step away. She moved towards the edge of the sunny clearing, where the undergrowth grew thickest.

"There is a man over there," Maraba said. *"But he only has a sword – no arrows. He knows he can't kill me, but he is beginning to think he will have to try. I'll go now, but when you meet your man, think of me. I'll be nearby, and I will come to you."*

Ellen silently vowed she would avoid all thoughts of the panther when she met Devon, even though this practically guaranteed Maraba would be on her mind. She watched the cat claw her way up a tree trunk and disappear among the branches. She wondered whether the coming reunion had just become harder or easier.

Now that she knew for certain that one of Devon's men was nearby, she saw no reason to continue the journey alone. She whistled a last time and sat down on a log, deliberately gazing away from the spot where Maraba had told her the scout was hidden.

It must have been obvious she wouldn't move until he showed himself. Only a few moments passed before she felt a hand on her shoulder. Her son Bard sat down next to her on the log, and she hugged him.

"I hoped it would be you," she said.

He sighed. "Nothing you do surprises me, Mother, but what were you up to just then? The panther was stalking you, and then it started acting like a house cat. I was ready to kill it if I had to."

"I'm glad you didn't try," she said.

She realized she had hurt his feelings. He felt guilty about hesitating when he thought she was in danger. "There is no shame in being afraid, you know, no matter what your father may say. Besides, she would have been gone long before you touched her with your sword. She was lucky you aren't carrying your bow."

"She? And how did you know I am without my bow? I always have it with me, but I broke the string and didn't have another to replace it. No. Don't tell me." Bard stood up and held out his hand. "You will have enough trouble explaining your behavior to Father."

"I do not intend to explain my behavior to anyone," Ellen snapped. "I did what had to be done, and now I must make him listen to me. The future of Ostara depends on it." After walking by Bard's side in silence for a few minutes, she continued calmly. "I'll practice by explaining everything to you. You might respect me enough to listen without twisting my words to start an argument."

"Of course I respect you, Mother. And so does Father. Do you blame him for being angry? Everyone knew he allowed you to go to bring Katherine back from the witch, but then you defied his order and refused to return, even when he sent me after you."

"Allowed. Order. Witch," she said evenly. "These are some of the words that might lead to sparks between your father and me. But I will not let that happen. I am not returning to quarrel with him."

"How can I help?"

Ellen stopped walking and glanced at her son in surprise.

"I know you wouldn't come back unless it was something serious," Bard said. "The last time we met, you told me it would be worse for us if you and Kathe came back with me to the camp, and I couldn't help but see you were right. Yet here you are."

"There is one thing," Ellen said. "Will you spread the message that the panther is not to be harmed? She is here to help, and she has a name. It is Maraba."

Maraba knew Bard was without his bow because she read his thoughts. And the panther could do that because Bard was

Ellen's son. Physically, he resembled his father, but he seemed to have inherited something from Ellen too. If the animals could read his thoughts, then he should be able to talk to them.

After Oro came and announced he would be leading Katherine and Patch to Bethany's farm, the rest of the journey was easy. When Katherine told the Runner about the Owl's midnight visit, Patch gave her one of his rare smiles. When she held out her hand and showed him Oro's gift, he actually laughed.

He picked the mouse up by its tail and looked at it closely. "That owl must think mighty highly of you," he said. He skinned the tiny creature, and she sharpened a twig so she could make a show of roasting it over the small fire they made for that purpose. When it was ready, she closed her eyes, told herself she was about to taste rabbit, and she made it disappear in two bites.

She expected Oro was watching. She hoped she had shown her appreciation. She also hoped he was too disgusted by her insistence on cooking the gift to waste any more of his precious mice on her.

Before two more days had passed, Kathe and Patch stood in front of the hedge that encircled Bethany's farm, delaying the moment when they would have to force their way through it. Even now, in early spring, it was too thick to see anything on the other side.

"I don't know how to open a passage, though I know Bethany and my mother can do it." Kathe said. "When we first came here, we crawled underneath, but it took weeks for all the scratches to heal, and the thorns ruined our clothes. Except for Patrick's," she remembered. "And that's only because he was wearing leather. When it was time for us to leave, Bethany made a real door for us."

Having accomplished his purpose, Oro had flown off again without giving any further advice. Kathe wished she'd asked him to fly across the hedge first to tell Maron they were there.

They walked around the border of the farm, but the whole hedge looked thick and healthy, even though no one ever tended or trimmed it. At this time of year it was covered with buds that would soon open to small, white flowers. By late summer it would be loaded with red berries. Then the hedge would be alive with songbirds. Even now, many flew in and out of the branches carrying nesting materials.

Kathe said, "I'm sorry. I guess there's nothing for us to do but to take our punishment."

The hedge was twice as tall as either of them, but Patch managed to throw their bags over the top, and then he dropped to his belly. "I'll go first and tell you how it is," he said.

"No, don't do that. I want it to be a surprise. If I know in advance it is going to be as hard as it was last time, it will be even worse."

The Woods Runner did not make any sound as he crossed through the hedge. That might be a good sign. Or maybe the barrier kept sounds from escaping the farm as it kept visitors from entering.

As soon as Patch's feet disappeared, she followed, and she knew at once they were expected. At least, it felt as if the hedge was welcoming her. The stems bent slightly, easing the way as she wormed her way through, and the thorns had become soft, like feathers, tickling instead of slicing.

When she emerged on the inside, Patch offered his hand. He pulled her to her feet, and they stood together looking up the slight rise, across the orchard and pasture to Bethany's cottage. The fruit trees were in bud, and smoke curled from the chimney of the house. It looked just as Katherine remembered it except that it now seemed to be the birthplace of spring. Outside the hedge, tiny miracles of leaves were unfolding all around, but here the intense green shocked Kathe's eyes. The sun flickered like firelight where it reflected from the house's glass windowpanes. They could just make out the figure of a woman standing in front of the door.

"You go on," Kathe said. "I'll collect the bags and follow you."

Patch didn't argue. He seemed to have been struck dumb, and he started towards the open door as if drawn there by an invisible thread. Kathe reminded herself this was the first time Patch had been to the farm, and she took a moment to see it through his eyes. From her winter with Bethany and Meg in the cottage, she knew it was a sanctuary, but today it seemed a kind of paradise.

For generations, the Woods Runners had watched over Patrick as he slowly recovered from terrible wounds after his first battle. After he fell, the Lady asked the Runners to carry his body to the cave behind the waterfall. From that day forward, while Patrick slept, he was never alone. A Woods Runner was always nearby. Patch's father passed the duty to his son, and in time, Patch shared the duty with Patchson.

Kathe knew guarding Patrick's resting place became more difficult after the Claymon came and after most of the Runners were recruited to track for the Northerners. It was harder still after Katherine, with the help of Meg and Gale, found Patrick's cave and woke him. Since that day, Patch and Patchson had wandered to places far from their beloved forest – to the mountains, the sea, even the City of Ostara. Patch once told her he thought they were the last two Woods Runners in service of the hero.

Patch believed his son was still following and watching over Patrick, wherever he was. Patch and Patchson also believed the Forest Lady was the only one who could release them from their duty to keep Patrick safe. Maybe now that they had reached the farm, the old Runner would be able to rest for a while.

When Katherine saw Patch take his wife's hand, and they walked towards her, she picked up the bags and the waterskins. She breathed in the scent of crushed thyme and walked through the orchard to meet them. She loved this place, but she was already preparing herself to leave.

15

THE GAME BEGINS

WHEN LIGHTNING LEFT HIM, Stormer dragged himself to the end of the corridor, but by the time he was able to pull himself to his feet and lean out the window, the hawk was out of sight. He took shallow breaths, testing his battered ribcage, and ran his fingers over his chest looking for remnants of the ropes that had seemed so real in his dream. Stormer managed to take a couple of deeper breaths before he vomited out the window. He watched listlessly as the meager contents of his stomach landed on the ground below, at the base of the steps leading to the door of the Inn.

Even though he had spent the night lying in his bedroll outside the magician's door, his body was as sore as it would have been after a hard training session. He slumped to the floor again, rested his back against the wall, and closed his eyes.

When the roiling in his guts had settled a little, Stormer crawled back to his blanket. He was shaking, but he wasn't cold. Sweat beaded on his forehead and soaked his armpits. He drew himself into a ball, pulled his blanket over his head and lay there with his eyes closed.

Too soon, he started hearing voices from the public room below and then the sound of footsteps on the stairs that could only be Ratface bringing Honorus his breakfast. Stormer kept his body turned towards the wall, feigning sleep, until he felt the sharp jab of a boot toe in the small of his back. It was all he could do to resist grabbing Ratface's ankle. It would have been easy to bring him crashing to the floor, along with the magician's food tray, but giving in to the impulse would only make his troubles worse. He had to pretend nothing unusual had happened during the night.

Stormer rolled onto his back and sat up.

"Why aren't you up yet?" Ratface snarled.

"There was no one here to wake me," Stormer said. "I woke up in the middle of the night, though, and you weren't here. Where'd you go?"

"None of your business!" Ratface said. Then, negating his own words, he reluctantly continued, "The counselor told me to find another place to sleep. Don't know why. Did you see anything?"

Stormer stretched gingerly and yawned. He shook out his blanket and began to roll it up again. "Not me. I slept like the dead."

"Go find something to eat and then get back here," Ratface said. "Make it quick. We have to carry all his belongings to the stables and get his horse saddled."

Stormer kept his back to Ratface as he forced himself to stand. He didn't want the man to see him grimace. "Shouldn't you be taking that tray to him? The food isn't getting any warmer while you're standing there."

He watched Ratface tap on Honorus's door. When it swung open a crack, he used his foot to push it wide enough to enter. Stormer was surprised to feel some sympathy for Ratface. How many times had the magician opened up that round head and sorted through what little was up there? It must have been easy for Honorus to read Ratface, and Stormer had no doubt that is why his fellow servant was still alive. Still, it couldn't be pleasant, and there was no hope Ratface would ever be given a change of duty. No one else was going to volunteer for his job, that's for sure.

Stormer, on the other hand, did not expect he would be in the magician's service for long. He tried not to imagine how it was likely to end.

Now, sitting at a table by himself in the public room, he might as well have already been a ghost for the attention anyone paid him. He was lucky the serving girl did not think he was invisible. It was his friend from the kitchen, and she even spared him a smile. He ordered eggs, toasted bread with jam, and a double portion of bacon.

She put her hands on her hips and stared at him until she realized he was joking.

"Porridge is all we've got, and that's more water than oats."

"Then that's what I'll have," he said. "We'll be leaving soon, and then you and the other people in this town can get back to living life the way it was before. Thanks for helping me yesterday," he added in an undertone.

"I didn't do anything," she said. "You just decided to leave the inn through the back door, and your supper, such as it was, was your pay for washing the pots."

When she brought him the porridge, she made sure no one was looking before she handed him a small package wrapped in cloth. "Early this morning, I did some baking from the last of the flour I kept hidden away. It's for the celebration we're planning for after we see the last of you. Not you…"

"I understand what you mean," Stormer said.

"Anyway, there's enough for me to give you a bit."

"I'll tuck it away and think of your kindness when I am in need," he said.

She was right about the porridge. It was thin and grey, with no sweetness. Stormer drank it from the bowl and slowly climbed back up the stairs. He was in no hurry to enter Honorus's room again, but at the same time, he was curious. Ever since he woke up, he had been trying to remember what had happened during the night. As the details of his dream came back to him, he was beginning to think that, as bad as the nightmare was for him, it must have been nasty for Honorus too.

Nobody was in the corridor, so Stormer made himself rap on the door with confidence. He was scared, but he was determined not to show it. It still wasn't latched, and it swung open at his touch. Ratface was by the window next to the desk, carefully stowing the last of the books. Honorus watched this process with his back to the door.

The magician turned as Stormer entered. His face might have been paler than usual, but that wasn't saying much. His papery skin seemed never to have been touched by sun, but it looked positively bloodless today. Stormer lowered his eyes towards Honorus's knees and exercised his peripheral vision.

A Claymon soldier is expected to travel with everything he needs in a pack on his shoulders, and since he must carry it, he keeps it as light as he can. Stormer had already stowed the serving maid's gift in the center of his bag, where it was less likely to be crushed, but first he broke off a corner of one of the small, round cakes. There were walnuts, and dark, sweet chunks of something he had never tasted before. It was all he could do not to eat all the cakes immediately, but he quickly stashed them away. He suspected a time would come when they would taste even better.

Honorus, in contrast, had not only brought his books to Brethren but also the ornate chair that was half buried in sand down by the sea. It might have been claimed by the tide by now. The counselor had brought other items he considered necessities – a silver mirror, a glass drinking cup so fragile that it must be packed in its own wooden box, and several changes of stiffly embroidered clothing that no longer fit the magician's restored body. Based on the bulging bags heaped on the floor, Honorus wasn't leaving anything behind even though he was still wearing the same stolen, worn-out clothes as the day before.

"You are lazy, and you will be punished," the counselor said tonelessly.

When Honorus spoke, Stormer was not surprised at his words, but he was startled again by the thin, reedy voice coming from a young man's throat. Stormer pictured him sitting at the table staring into the silver mirror and running his hand over his scalp to see whether any hair was starting to grow.

He risked a quick glimpse into the magician's face. He was staring straight ahead, but not directly at Stormer, and his eyes were narrowed. He didn't seem to be using any magic now. He didn't have to. The authority he had been given by Peter Greystone was enough. Stormer knew Honorus could treat his servants any way he wished, and no one would question him. Ratface was carefully tying the top of the canvas saddle bag over Honorus's precious books. He probably hoped Honorus had forgotten he was there.

The counselor tested the weight of the bag Ratface had finished packing and pointed one thin finger at the bed.

"When we leave, you will carry this bag and all my other baggage. The books will be your special responsibility."

Stormer did not respond. Everyone knew Honorus always carried his precious books in his own saddlebags.

As if Honorus could read his mind, he said, "These volumes are beyond price. If you damage one of them, you will first pay with your eyes, then your life. An ignorant slave like you never can read them, but you will protect them." His voice wavered with suppressed fury.

Stormer nodded as if he understood, and he did. They were about to cross the mountains again, and even by the easiest way, it would mean at least three days of rough travel. Honorus would sleep on cushions in a tent each night, a tent Stormer would carry, but everyone else would sleep rough. It was spring. There would be rain.

When the time came to open the bag that held the books, a corner would be bent. Some pages would be wavy with moisture. That is when he would die.

This was to be his punishment for humiliating the magician. It did not matter whether Stormer remembered what happened during the dream. Honorus remembered. At first Stormer thought Lightning had saved him, but as more and more of the dream came back to him, he realized the hawk was right. He had saved himself from the Magician's snare, and now he knew how he did it.

Stormer doubted Honorus would try the same trick again, but there was nothing to stop the magician from killing him in one of the more ordinary ways. And in the meantime, he would make sure Stormer suffered. Anticipation would make his eventual death that much sweeter for the counselor.

When Stormer completed his third trip to Brethren's stable with the last of Honorus's gear in his arms, he tried to convince himself the weakness he felt was only his imagination. The soreness that came from wrestling against the magician's invisible bonds was real enough, though. At least Stormer had learned how he was expected to carry everything. He gave the sledge an experimental shove.

When the Claymon came to Brethren, Stormer had felt sorry for the men who had to pull the sledge. Its tracks slid well enough over leaves, and even over rocks, but as soon as the ground became soft, which was often in this season, they dug into the ground. Back then, he never thought he would be one of those men, but the sledge that had made its way into his dream last night was now here in truth, loaded with Honorus's belongings.

As Stormer set about strapping everything down as tightly as he could, he was already picturing himself lifting the front of the sledge out of the muck and then running to the back to push it forward a few feet. None of his fellow soldiers would offer to help. They had already made that clear. To them, he might as well already be dead.

So far today Stormer had done only what needed to be done in the next moment. He was so frightened by the dream and so intent on safeguarding his thoughts that he just concentrated on the next task. Now he straightened from his work and allowed himself a moment of self-pity. In his imagination, the days ahead seemed to stretch on forever. And when they reached Ostara — well, he wasn't ready to think about that.

Then he remembered the cakes in his bag. He was the only Claymon leaving Brethren with a gift. That was something.

16

THE DRAGON'S HEART

PADRAIK FLEW THROUGH THAT whole night, long after Meg believed he should have reached the end of his strength and fallen from the sky. After the decision was made to fly inland across the mountains instead of up the ridgeline that ran parallel to the coast, he didn't speak again.

Gale's head was heavy against her shoulder. She reached back and tugged at the rope harness with frozen fingers. He couldn't sleep. It was too dangerous. Her own eyes had been drifting shut ever since darkness fell. She panicked every time it happened. She shook her head and forced herself to continue searching the moonlit range for any place to rest, but soon, she knew, sleep would come.

The ropes holding them onto Padraik's back offered an illusion of safety. If she or Gale slipped sideways, they would throw the dragon off balance. It would break the steady pattern of his wing beats and then? Padraik would not have enough strength to recover. There was nowhere to land. They would spiral and smash into a mountainside.

Meg reached back again and pinched Gale's leg. "Wake up!" she shouted above the wind.

"Wha? Huh?" he grumbled.

She felt him startle and pulled tighter on the harness to keep him from falling. Gale had been so deeply asleep that it took a few heart-stopping moments for him to remember where he was.

"*I need your help,*" she said, speaking mind to mind. "*I'm about to fall asleep myself, and I can't. I need you to help me stay awake. And your eyes are sharper than mine. If we don't find a place to rest before morning, it will be the end for us.*"

"*Sorry,*" Gale said. "*I didn't know I was sleeping.*"

"*I know. If someone told me back at Springvale that someday I'd be fighting sleep while I was riding on the back of a dragon, I would have laughed and told them to save their stories for winter.*"

Meg was not sure whether Padraik could feel her hand on his neck, but she stroked the frosted scales and murmured to him. The cold and the wind were constant, and the pain in her hips from riding for so long was a torment. Padraik was an ancient and fierce being, with quick intelligence and his own way of seeing this world, but now she spoke to him as she would to a child.

"*You are brave. You are strong. No matter what happens, I am glad I met you. I wouldn't have missed this for anything.*"

As Meg crooned the words over and over, the first rays of a sunrise broke over the curve of the world. The mountains below still looked as sharp as broken glass, and the snow on the peaks glittered in new light. She looked ahead and saw more mountains, but something else too.

Beyond the next ridgeline was a valley. From above, it looked as if it was almost the size of the cleared lands around Springvale. And instead of being a rock-filled chasm, this place seemed to be smooth and nearly flat. It was green, too, and even from so far above, she picked out trees and what might be fields or pastures. Gale pulled her sleeve and pointed to the north end of the valley, where two mountain ridges met. It was hard to tell from this distance, but it looked as if there was a cluster of buildings next to the rocks on both sides of a silver waterfall. It cascaded down the face of the mountain, creating a cloud of mist and spray and partly obscuring the settlement. Once it reached level ground, the stream sliced the valley in two, carrying with it the promise of sweet, fresh water.

Meg patted Padraik's neck again, harder. This time she almost lost her balance, and it was Gale's turn to steady her.

"We should land at the other end, away from the town, in case there are people," she yelled, forgetting to speak silently. She forced herself to calm down. She supposed her reaction meant she had given up hope of finding anyplace to land before Padraik's strength gave out or before she and Gale froze solid. And even when she still had hope, it was only for a ledge, something like the aeries where they had rested the past few nights. Her modest dream had been to huddle someplace out of the wind and eat the last of the dry cakes in their saddle bags. Tears ran down her cheeks as she looked over the expanse of green that was closer with every wingbeat.

"You haven't noticed the most important thing yet," Padraik said, as he turned slightly and glided toward the southern end of the valley.

Meg scanned the horizon all around, trying to see what Padraik was seeing, but it was Gale who spotted it first – a thin streak of smoke rising from a rather ordinary-looking mountain on the other side of the valley.

"Ah," Meg breathed.

When Padraik staggered to a halt, Meg slipped half-way down his side, still tethered to the dragon. Gale tore at the knots of his own waist rope and jumped, but his legs wouldn't bear his weight. He fell forward into the grass. As soon as he could stand, he untied Meg's rope and helped her to the ground. Then the three of them lay in soft grass until the sun fully cleared the mountain tops and started to warm them.

When Meg opened her eyes, she saw Padraik lying on his side. He was trying to lick dew from the stems of grass. She limped to the dragon and untied the skins dangling from the improvised harness. This was another sign they were all near the end of their strength. Removing the ropes from Padraik's back should have been their first chore after landing.

"Gale, will you finish taking off the harness and free Padraik?" she asked, "I'll go to the river and fill the skins. It can't be far. That way." she said, gesturing to the East.

"Wait. I'll go with you," he said. We don't know anything about this place."

"Padraik needs water now, and we can't leave him alone," she said. "If people saw us land, and if they come here, it will be up to us to defend him We may not be able to convince them he isn't dangerous. Remember how we felt the first time we saw him?"

She was right. Gale watched Meg wade through the knee-high grass toward a line of trees in the distance and then set to work removing and neatly piling the ropes. He dug through Meg's pack and found the jar of salve she had been using to sooth the sore places on the dragon's back. Padraik stopped licking the dew and closed his eyes as Gale dabbed the pale-yellow paste on the sores.

When he finished, Gale went to the dragon's head and hollowed a depression in the ground in front of the Dragon's head. He lined it with one of the waxed canvas bags so it would be ready to hold water when Meg returned.

Gale was used to seeing Padraik basking in the sun on the beach back on the island of Niue, but now the dragon's jewel-like colors had dulled, and his skin felt cold and dry. Even though reptiles are cold-blooded, that didn't seem right, especially since the sun was quickly warming the valley.

When Meg returned, she poured the contents of one whole water skin into the depression Gale had made and handed the other to him.

"I drank at the river," she said. "It looked pure, and even if it isn't, I don't see that we have any choice."

Gale drank as much as he could hold and then handed the skin back to her. She was sitting on the ground in front of Padraik, watching him lap the water from the depression like a dog. She took a travel cake out of a saddle bag and offered it to him as she would offer a carrot to a horse, on her flat palm.

"You said you would eat this. You have to eat," she said firmly.

Padraik stretched his neck forward, over the nearly empty puddle, and delicately took the round cake with his lips. Once it was in his mouth, he did not seem to know what to do with it, and he dropped it.

"It is hard. I tear my food, and then I swallow it," he said in disgust.

"This is all we have," Meg replied.

"You like it. You can have it," the dragon said, turning away and lowering his head to the grass again.

Just as after his long flight back to Niue after taking Patrick to the mainland, Meg knew Padraik would die if he did not eat meat soon, and as before, he was too weak to hunt. Meg scooped the rejected travel cake off the ground and dropped it into the pool to soften it. While it still held its shape, she offered it to him again. This time he did not just drop it. He spat it at her. She wiped a piece of the porridge-like substance, mingled with dragon saliva, off her cheek.

Worry made her voice sharp. "If you don't eat soon, you will die." Then, more calmly, she continued, speaking to Gale, "I didn't meet anyone on my way to the river, but there is a pasture on the other side."

Gale knew what she was thinking. "Let me go this time. I'll fill the water skins again and see what I can find." He grabbed two of the remaining travel cakes to eat on the way.

Meg dumped the rest of the water into Padraik's pool and handed the bag up to Gale. Neither of them had voiced their intention. If Gale didn't manage to shoot a wild animal, he would have to steal a domestic one. That wouldn't make them any friends in this valley, but they didn't see any other way.

17

THROUGH THE WATER GATE

AS THEY APPROACHED PALLAS, the shapes of the forested hills started to feel familiar to the refugees. Patrick reached the mother spring that supplied the city with water a few steps before the others and placed his hand on the sun-warmed stone of the last viaduct pier. He closed his eyes and listened to the trickle of water as it made its way down the hill through the channel overhead. As on the rainy day the summer before, when he passed this way with his friends, it seemed a miracle that the viaduct still stood and carried water to the city.

Last summer, from the evening Katherine discovered his resting place in the cave until a few days later, when they reached the forest city, Patrick had been more than half sleepwalking. At that time, Katherine and Meg still didn't know who he was or that they were taking him home. Kathe was simply following a stag, one of the oldest of the animal guides, and later, the traces of an old road. She and Meg had to urge and half-drag him along.

This second life he now was living didn't begin until the two women found his sword, Mabus, buried deep within the ruins of Pallas. By then he was so weak Katherine had to curl his fingers around the weapon's hilt. He owed his final awakening as much to their stubbornness as to the power of the blade.

Now he didn't know where his friends were. Except for Rowan. She was still with Abel back in Brethren – if Abel was still alive. Patrick wished he had brought the dog across the mountains with him. The hound should be here to greet Katherine when she came. If she came.

His sister, Bethany, was still with Gerard on the island of Niue. And Meg and Gale? The last time he saw them they were riding on a very angry dragon.

A few of the younger refugees recognized the spring as a landmark. They shouted and scrambled up the hill to dip their hands and splash each other.

"Almost there," Marios said, coming up beside Patrick. His voice sounded muffled. Patrick grasped the baker's arm but did not look into his face. He knew it would be twisted by emotion.

When the other refugees had caught up and were standing behind them, Patrick said, "It's not far now," even though they already knew exactly how many steps they were from the outer wall of their beloved city.

Unlike the wet summer day when he and Katherine, Meg and Gale last passed this way, the air this morning was soft, with only the slightest trace of lingering chill from the night before. Despite taking careful steps, Patrick could not help crushing some of the plants that formed a carpet of green underfoot. Some were beginning to flower, and sweet fragrance rose from the sun-warmed blossoms

As they made their way down the hill to the city, he wondered again at the endurance of the aqueduct. He knew leaks would have to be repaired, and the last section was broken. In that place the water emptied itself into a pool not far from the city gate. The People would not want for water, at least. It would be a lean summer, but they were arriving at the right time to begin collecting wild food.

Patrick's mental list of the work that would have to be done once they reached Pallas kept shifting and getting longer. He was finding it difficult to concentrate. There always were a lot of birds singing at this time of year as they defined their territories and tried to attract mates, but this morning their songs were an uproar, drowning out all other sounds. Not only that. In the branches above and on the ground at the edges of human sight, Patrick sensed movement. It seemed every fallen log had a chippie sitting on its highest point, and squirrels chattered up and down the tree trunks. The twitching noses of rabbits poked from the underbrush, and there were other creatures too – larger ones he could not quite make out.

The excitement the people of Pallas had been feeling became something more like reverence, and they walked this last, short distance in silence. There were so many singers in the forest, it was impossible to untangle a single voice, but the underlying message was unmistakable. It was a song of welcome. Welcome and joy.

When they reached the city gate, Patrick realized he was smiling for the first time since – well, he could not remember the last time he felt this happy. Even though many of the refugees died in the exodus from the city so long ago, and more were lost through the years on the island of Niue, not one person had died since they boarded the *Goshawk* and sailed for Brethren.

No, that was not right. Patrick pictured his father lying murdered on the beach, and his smile faded.

"Welcome," he said, turning around to face the refugees. "Don't be afraid. Your losses have been great, but so is your spirit."

Later they would find a place they could all sit together and talk. Patrick was Meier Steele's son, and the People treated him as their leader, even as their savior. Now that they were home, that would have to change. All the decisions about the city's future would be theirs. They would have to choose a council from among themselves. So many years of hiding together in their cave on Niue ought to have taught them how to cooperate.

Patrick had warned the People about the pack of wild dogs that roamed the town. With the dogs and unknown threats in mind, they entered the city through the water gate as a tight group. Patrick knew what he would see on the other side, but everyone else stopped short to stare at their city transformed –

the street barely a grassy path; doorways obscured by leaf litter and shrubs; the corner fountains, once gathering places, dry and full of small plants. Their mouths opened in a round, uniform, sigh. They looked like a choir tensed for a performance.

The moment passed. They started to explore, taking turns poking their heads through the doors of the closest houses, looking up through the open roofs to the sky. This was in the upper city, where the houses were built of stone rather than wood. They were beginning to understand what they might find in the lower, older part of the town.

For a few minutes the city was as silent as it must have been before their return, especially when compared to all the bird song and burgeoning life they had left behind outside the city walls, but then the people of Pallas began to speak among themselves, laying the groundwork for their future. This was the meeting Patrick had been imagining, but it was being held all around him in the street. No one had to call it.

Marios was the first to speak up. "The walls here are solid, and these houses are closest to the water. I say we choose the two closest to the gate and work together to repair them. There will be enough room for all of us, and we can build out and down from here."

A woman Patrick had mentally placed among the grandmothers said, "I agree. It will take time, but soon enough we will have our own homes again. For now, we should continue to stay together. None of us, not even the babies, will live to see this city straining at its walls as before we left, but we are home!"

At her words, a shout went up.

Marios spoke up again, talking just to Patrick this time. "We will have to do some trading before I can make you those cakes, boy, but my oven will still be there, down in my old shop. I'll bake for you soon."

For a moment, Patrick allowed himself to be that boy again, stealing away to the baker's shop and waiting impatiently for treats to emerge from a stone oven.

"Who is the woman who spoke just now?"

"That's Anna. She was my brother's wife."

The widow glanced in Patrick's direction and caught his eye. He nodded to her and watched her turn back to the refugees who were clustered around her. She held a small boy by the hand. Anna. Patrick wondered why it should make such a difference to know her name. His father had known the names of every person in Pallas. So few of them had returned from Niue. The least he could do was find out who they once were and who they had become. Their memories of the living city would guide the restoration of Pallas.

Now that the seed of a plan had sprouted among the People, they were eager to get to work. Patrick did not yet know whether any Woods Runners remained in the surrounding forest. Patch and Patchson seemed to think all the other Runners were in the service of the Claymon, but they might be wrong about that. Surely some of their families were still here. If he could find them, Patrick thought those old allies and trading partners would help.

On this sparkling morning, the City was infused with new life. Patrick glanced up and down the street, half expecting to see his old master in the distance, at the turning of the street. Leonides might even be with a Lady dressed in green, but there was no trace of either of them. Surely the Lady knew the People had returned. Patrick shrugged. She would welcome them in her own way.

Every person who had returned to Pallas with him today, and Patrick himself, was an Old One. Each had endured an interrupted life, and from all the activity Patrick saw, they were now anxious to move forward. From now on they would age, grow old, and eventually die.

Leonides was different. Patrick wasn't sure, but he thought his old master might be truly immortal. Back when Patrick was a boy, spending every day in the woodworking shop, Leonides seemed to be a perfectly ordinary middle-aged man. He was a kind, if strict, teacher. Remembering him made Patrick miss Gerard. And Bethany, too.

The People were already crawling in and out through the doorways of the houses and arguing over which should become their new homes. Patrick could hear them sharing stories about the prosperous residents who once lived in the ruins. It seemed no one from those families had survived the exile. Patrick listened to the muted voices as they chattered from room to room, talking about the work needed to make these shells into places where they could live.

The small pack of teenage boys separated themselves and volunteered to search for tools and materials in the lower city. Patrick knew they were hungry to explore. Two of the men volunteered to go along, and they all disappeared around the curve in the street.

The most important work, making certain nothing like the exodus could ever happen again, was up to him, and it would have to wait. Plan after plan had played through Patrick's mind, but he could not yet see any way to defend the city if Honorus returned, especially if he came with a Claymon force.

After a word to Marios, Patrick walked away from the people of Pallas and from playing the part of a hero. He followed the familiar streets to his family home. He wondered whether he would sense the ghosts of his parents, and he wanted to climb the tower. He wanted to be alone.

18

Gerard and Bethany

BETHANY WALKED ALONG THE shore of the harbor wiggling her toes in the sand, feeling for the shelled creatures hidden just under the surface. She wanted to make more of the thin, salty, soup that had become their daily meal here, but she had been looking all morning, and she had only found a few.

During their first days here on Niue, she and Gerard had explored the island. It took them two whole days from sun-up until after sundown to walk around the shoreline because they had to pick their way across rocks that plunged steeply into the sea. They slept under the stars, but that wasn't unusual. The weather on Niue was so mild that they slept outside the cave on the sand most nights. There were no predators, no biting insects. It had only rained twice since they arrived on the island. The showers came from small clouds that seemed to arise from the volcano, itself.

They had already seen most of the island of Niue when they climbed its mountain to look for the refuges. The cave on the high slopes where they found the people of Pallas was dry, but there was little food so far from the sea. Gerard and Bethany returned to it a few days after the ship sailed away, but they weren't tempted to stay there, despite its long view. The beach inside the harbor, in front of Padraik's cave, was the only stretch of sand and the only safe place to land a boat.

Toward the end of the second day, Gerard stopped Bethany before they finished crossing the last rocky section of shore. Another few minutes and they would be on the crescent of beach below the cliff-face.

It was almost dark by then, and Bethany was so intent on her footing that she wouldn't have noticed the small boat half hidden behind a rock outcropping if Gerard wasn't pointing at it. The vessel's peeling paint might have been blue or red. She couldn't tell in the fading light. At first Bethany didn't understand what it meant, but then she realized Captain Fischer must have left it behind.

"It has been troubling me – keeping this secret from you," Gerard said, as waves rolled in from the open ocean and crashed against the island, pluming up through blowholes in the rocks just behind them.

Gerard didn't say the captain or anyone else had insisted on leaving the boat here, so it must have been his own idea, and it must have taken some planning to find this safe place to bring it ashore when she wasn't looking.

The vessel was a little bigger than a rowing-boat – just big enough to carry the two of them. It was upside down, so she couldn't tell whether there was any way to rig a sail. She sat down on the hull and gazed at the waves for a few minutes before looking up into her husband's face. His expression was a mystery.

"Do you feel better now?" she asked.

Bethany was angry, but only because Gerard hadn't trusted her enough to tell her about his plans. She supposed he hadn't wanted to seem as if he were disagreeing with her choice, which was for the two of them to stay here on the island together. Why should it matter to him what she thought? He had gone his own way plenty of times in their long lives together.

Though she wouldn't admit it out loud yet, it was a relief to know the boat was here. Just in case. On the other hand, Gerard must know it would be impossible for the two of them ever to sail back into the stream of time and to the mainland in it. The vessel was too small for the open sea, and neither of them had any experience on open water except for the voyage from Brethren to Niue.

She sighed and shook her head, unable to imagine what might make them choose to climb into this boat and launch it into the sea. Together, they should be able to move it into the cave. They could take care of it there, and upside down it would make a place to sit, at least.

"I promised we would spend the rest of our years together," he said. "I guess I was afraid you would think I was regretting my promise."

"Old fool," she said. "You weren't planning to leave without me, were you?"

Bethany asked herself, was it the pictures in the book that convinced her to stay on the island, or did she make her choice so that Gerard would have to keep his promise?

Now, back on the beach with the boat safely stowed in the cave, Bethany was having trouble remembering how long they had been here. She supposed it was possible they had already eaten the entire population of small, succulent shellfish from the tiny beach. She sighed. Other edible creatures clung to rocks, but she wasn't fond of their gritty texture.

She glanced towards the shallows, where Gerard stood poised, holding the makeshift spear above his head. It was similar to the weapon Gale made and used when he was hunting fish for Padraik. Bethany was better than her husband when it came to spearing fish, but today he had insisted.

"How will I ever learn if I don't try," he said reasonably, not meeting her eyes.

She knew the truth. He was bored, and honestly, so was she. Not with each other. They still looked forward to sitting by their small fire every night, just outside the entrance of the cave, watching the ever-changing dance of the flames, but the days were very long, and Bethany had started to dream about her farm. She wondered what season it was there now. It should still be spring, but she couldn't be sure. She didn't know the content of Gerard's dreams. He claimed he didn't remember them.

He gave a shout, and Bethany turned in time to see him pull a small fish from the sea. It was still wriggling. She gave up her search for shellfish and hurried to meet him. They would have soup for supper, after all.

She'd throw the leavings from the meal to their three remaining chickens. The birds spent their days close together along the cliff top, pestered by the parrots, searching for nonexistent insects in the grasses growing there. Idly, Bethany wondered whether the chickens were now immortal too. If she and Gerard didn't eat them, would they live forever? They came into the cave to roost every night, lining themselves up along the keel of the boat. She had made nests of sea-weed next to the wall, but if the hens laid any eggs, Bethany never found them.

Captain Fischer had given them a few books. They read and re-read them in the heat of the afternoons while they rested in the shade of the cliff. They still had only one volume of their own, the changeable history that contained the map to this island and which might offer clues about their future. An image in this book had convinced Bethany it was right for her and Gerard to stay together on Niue while the refugees and the others reentered the stream of time. Gerard kept that book well wrapped in canvas and hidden away at the very back of the cave, among Padraik's stored treasures. Maybe it was time to look into it again.

Gerard smiled broadly as he splashed to shore. She took the fish, and before she could congratulate him, he turned back to try again. Over the years when they were apart, she would have traded everything for one of his smiles.

19

Shifting Vision

WHEN ELLEN STEPPED INTO her husband's camp, she might as well have been invisible. Even with Bard at her side, no one acknowledged her arrival. There should have been shouts of greeting and children running up to pull on her skirts, eager to tell her everything that had happened while she was away.

Elaine, who once was one of Ellen's companions in Ostara, glanced up from tending a small cooking fire and nodded encouragement before quickly turning away. It was an invitation to talk later. For now, it was as if everyone was waiting for a thunderstorm to burst and ease the tension – tension she had caused.

The exiled Ostarans busied themselves with tasks around the edges of the small clearing. There were others living and hiding farther up in the hills, but Devon himself was nowhere in sight. Was he away on a raid? She didn't see the horses that should be tethered around the perimeter of the camp. He must be waiting in his tent for her to come to him. She never expected him to meet her, but that didn't keep her from feeling disappointed.

Bard squeezed her shoulder and whispered, "We both know he doesn't bite," before moving away to speak with a few men who were squatting in a circle, sharpening their knives.

If they were all together in one place, which they never were these days, the rebels would number over two hundred, including many children and elders. They were few compared with the Claymon, but more than enough to be an annoyance to

Greystone when they ambushed the convoys of supplies destined for the city. Word had spread, and few were willing to trade with Ostara now, even when Greystone provided his own men as escorts.

While the rebels counted this as a victory, Devon knew raiding alone would not drive the Claymon out of Ostara. Some of his own men, whose families remained within the city walls enduring the siege, argued that the raids only intensified the suffering there. Others countered that Greystone could hardly pretend to be the legitimate ruler of the city when he was reduced to the same strategies as the rebels and had to steal supplies where he could find them. Ellen wondered if the Claymon leader knew that a share of the goods the rebels captured made their way into Ostara – just not to him. Devon wasn't going to let the people starve if he could help it.

There was no point in putting off this meeting any longer. Ellen made her way towards a tent on the opposite side of the clearing, exactly like every other except for the banner hanging across its entrance – it pictured a green dragon soaring above a river of stars. That was something – that their emblems were still combined. She pushed it aside and ducked inside.

Devon was there. He sat on the edge of his low bed, staring away from the door. He seemed to be pretending he was unaware of her arrival. He was fingering the edge of the blanket. It was one of his nervous habits. It was a blanket she wove herself, long ago, using wool she spun and dyed in bright colors one winter in Ostara.

If their positions had been reversed, she would have had some mending in her lap and avoided his eyes by paying close attention to her stitches. Not for the first time, she thought the ability to retreat into ever-present handwork was one of the few advantages of being a woman.

When their marriage was arranged, Ellen and Devon were both teenagers. Her parents would have allowed her to refuse, but she liked her groom as soon as she met him. He brought a bunch of wilting flowers he had picked along the way, and though Ellen sensed his shyness, he had a sweet smile. When she managed to coax a laugh from him at dinner that night, her decision was made. He didn't know what he was getting into.

Ellen had settled on the first words she would say to him. Instead, the words that came out of her mouth were, "Greetings, Husband. There is no time for this dance. I need your help."

She had his attention. Devon turned towards her. He didn't smile, but his face looked unguarded. Ellen sensed his relief at her safe return. She saw how he had aged during the last year. His hair was streaked with grey.

Ellen wanted to cross the few paces between them, to embrace him and to lay her head on his shoulder, but she was determined to present herself as, if not an equal, at least someone worth heeding, so she straightened her shoulders. She held her hands out to him and spoke formally.

"By helping me, you will be aiding us both, our city, and many others you have never met. Together we may even drive the Claymon from these lands. Will you listen?"

The moment of vulnerability passed. Ellen saw her husband's mouth tighten, and as the silence stretched on, she wondered whether he would answer her at all.

Finally he said, "This is not the first time you have made a fool of me, but I swear it will be the last."

This conversation was already slipping out of control, escalating into an argument. Next, Devon would tell her everything she had chosen to do, whether working as a healer back in Ostara or staying behind after the invasion as a spy – even going to find their daughter – had been only because he allowed it and that he bitterly regretted the freedom he had given her. It had made her ungrateful and wayward. Things were going to change. She had heard the speech many times.

Her role was to attempt a defense, to point out that she had always fulfilled all her duties in their house, that being a healer wasn't something he allowed, but simply who she was. It would be so easy to play the familiar parts until all the words were said and then to wait for the uneasy reconciliation, but Ellen was finished with saying "I'm sorry" even though Devon craved the words. She longed to be at peace with him, but she couldn't bear to ask for his forgiveness any longer.

Ellen had not been given leave to sit, but she was weary from walking, so she lowered herself onto a cushion and began to stroke the silky ears of one of the dogs lazing nearby. They hadn't gotten the message that she was in trouble, so another moved closer, lifted his head into her lap and gazed up adoringly.

She smiled down at the dog as if she hadn't heard Devon's words and said, "Abel should be bringing this news, but he is not yet well enough to travel. He sends his greetings. He will meet us as soon as he has recovered."

Devon couldn't help himself. "Abel, hurt?"

Ellen knew how much her husband had missed his advisor's steady guidance. "You thought he had abandoned you? That we both had abandoned you?"

Devon finally met her eyes, and she saw the truth. "Never," she said.

She took his continued silence as permission to continue. "I left him no more than four days ago in the town of Brethren, on the other side of the mountains, on the coast. He led me there along with Katherine and her friends from Springvale, Bethany and her husband Gerard, and Patrick."

"Those names are not familiar to me," Devon said. "Bethany, I think, is the witch who aims to ruin our daughter as she ruined you, but I do not know the others."

"And how would you know them?" Ellen asked in a reasonable voice, though it cost her something. "When did you last pass the boundaries of your own lands? The Claymon are here in Ostara, but they are in many other places too. Soon, they will be everywhere unless we act together."

"You are suggesting an alliance with men I do not know?"

"Men, and women, and – others. Leash the dogs."

"What? Why should I?" Devon said. "You think you can command me?"

"There is someone I want you to meet," Ellen said in the same even tone. "Leash them."

She began to tie the leather straps to the hounds' collars. When Devon saw she was serious, he helped her, and she handed him the other ends of the tethers.

"Hold tight. Wrap the straps around your fist and keep them close. Make them obey you." Ellen stood.

Devon's dogs were well trained, but she knew they were about to be tested.

"You have always had a way with the dogs, husband. You understand each other. You care for them, love them, and they do your will. Well, I understand animals too. In fact, I count them as friends, and I am able to talk with them."

Devon wasn't sure how to respond to her statement, presented as fact, that he loved his dogs, when everyone knew he only needed them for the hunt and to protect the camp. That was all.

He decided to start with her second point. He wasn't surprised when Ellen spoke of having animals as friends even though he had done his best to ignore his wife's odd behavior. He still felt uneasy when he remembered the hawk that swept through camp just above Ellen's upturned face. And then there was Blackie. He remembered coming upon Ellen kneeling in the corridor of the house in Ostara. She was looking into the dog's face so intently that she wasn't aware of him walking up behind her. She jumped to her feet and walked off with purpose, without saying a word to him — as if the animal told had her something important.

"No. Not the talking animals again," he snapped. "I should have had you locked away when you first began to speak of them. It would have been humiliating to admit my wife was insane, but I would have been spared a hundred other insults." The dogs were sitting on their haunches looking up at him. They didn't understand why they had been leashed, but they knew when their master was angry.

Ellen's face reddened, but again she managed to keep her temper. It was one thing to suspect her husband had had these thoughts. Another to hear them spoken. She kept her gaze steady and sent the summons. She hoped Maraba's promise was serious, that she was nearby, and that Bard would manage her safe passage through the camp.

As she waited, she couldn't help thinking that all these interactions — of friend to friend, of husband to wife, of man to wild animal were controlled by long established rules. Rules often are based upon realities, and they can make life simpler in a city or a rebel camp — or in a family — but rules also make people lazy. As she had told Devon, their usual dance would no longer serve them.

During her marriage, Ellen had made no secret of her connection to the talking animals, but she seldom spoke of it, and for her own safety, she communicated with them at the edges of the domestic world where she lived with her husband. It had been easy for Devon to ignore this side of her. Since he never said anything about it, Ellen even thought he might have blinded himself to it. She was about to forever change the way he thought about her, but she didn't know any other way. She could never be the wife he thought he wanted, but there was a chance she could become the partner he needed.

Ellen did not turn towards the door, but she saw Devon's eyes widen when the black panther nosed the pennant aside and slinked inside. His hand tightened on the leashes. Ellen held her hand close to her side until she felt velvety ears and rested her palm lightly on Maraba's head to emphasize their connection.

Far from lunging as she had feared they might, the dogs hid behind Devon and whined.

"Witch," her husband hissed, his eyes wide.

Ellen said firmly. "I am who I always have been. Your wife. Mother to Katherine and Bard. Healer. Talking animals are real.

I'm able to hear them, and so can Katherine. With practice, Bard will be able to hear them too. I pity your deafness, but I am willing to relay their messages."

Ellen could see the struggle play out on Devon's face as his pride and long-held beliefs warred against the reality standing in front of him. She searched for traces of the young man who had come to court her, and she waited.

Finally, Devon sighed, "What message?"

Ellen felt her knees almost give way. "Her name is Maraba. She and her kind are no happier about the Claymon being here than we are. They are willing to act as couriers between us and our allies, to help and protect us." Ellen paused and gentled her voice. "As they have been protecting and guiding me, husband. Can you trust me? I have sometimes had to make the choice between pleasing you and doing my duty. It has never been my purpose to hurt you."

For once Devon did not point out that her duty was, above all else, to please him. "How should I address this creature? Can she understand me even though I can't hear her?"

"As I said. Her name is Maraba, and yes, she can understand you."

Devon paused again before speaking. "It would have been better to have accepted this woman's gifts long ago. I have loved her from the first day I met her, and I thought I could make her into a proper wife, content to run my household and mother my children. My faults are those of any man. I am careless, abrupt, and sometimes I am stubborn, but her? She seemed to run towards every contagion rather than avoiding it. I thought she was putting our family at risk."

Although he still was speaking to Maraba, Devon had turned to Ellen. "Instead of turning away from blood, she dealt with every injury set before her. Her skill, and her courage, have been useful since we were driven from Ostara. Now she is asking me to talk to you. Everything I have been taught tells me you are an enemy of humankind. She wants me to send a message to those she assures me will become my friends. I will not go so far, but I will say this. Tell Abel to come to me as quickly as he can. I believe my wife, but I sorely need his counsel. I am willing to consider making new friends and forming a new plan. We cannot continue to simply sting the Claymon. The time has come to cut off their head."

As soon as Devon had finished speaking, without saying goodbye, Maraba slipped back outside. When Ellen pushed the pennant aside, she saw the tip of the panther's tail disappear into the forest. Bard and his companions were still sitting to one side of the clearing, and he had placed himself facing the tent so that the others, intent on whatever he was saying, wouldn't have seen Maraba arrive. In fact, looking around, Ellen wasn't sure anyone had seen the visitor except herself, Devon, and the hounds.

She felt her husband's hand on her shoulder and turned into his arms.

He stroked her hair. "Elaine has been cooking something over the fire. I had some luck hunting this morning. Will you sit and eat with me, wife?"

Kathe patted the goat's bony head and watched her trot off into the pasture. She stretched to unknot her back and shoulders from hunching to do the milking and carefully carried the bucket of fresh milk towards the house. This was the day she was going to show Maron how to make cheese. She used to watch the servants making it in the kitchen in Ostara, and she had helped with the process at Springvale. Now she was looking forward to trying to make it on her own. Kathe's mouth watered at the thought of fresh, creamy cheese blended with some of the herbs growing along the path. Spread on fresh bread, it would make a dinner fit for a lord, or a lady.

Ever since she and Patch arrived at Bethany's farm, there had been more than enough work to keep the three of them busy, but it wasn't enough to keep Kathe's mind off Patrick and what could be happening in Pallas, or in Ostara, where her father and brother continued to harass the Claymon.

Spring is the time for planting, for making the small repairs that were neglected over the winter and for caring for new life on the farm. Kathe loved it all, and she was not yet tired of sleeping in a bed every night or of having plenty of good food to eat, but she couldn't forget the tumult overtaking the world beyond the hedge. When they arrived here, she had been running for days and she desperately needed rest. Now, after little more than a week, she already felt she had stayed here too long.

The only other time she had met Maron was on the morning when she and Ellen, Meg and Bethany left the farm together. There were still traces of snow on the ground under the trees then, and ice coated the pond where ducks now paddled. That day the Woods Woman had been nearly mute as Bethany showed her the farm and told her what she would have to do in the coming months.

The last few days had revealed a different Maron. She was still quiet, but full of questions about farming Katherine and Patch could not answer. Bethany had a few books about gardening and caring for animals, and Kathe tried to help by reading passages aloud at night. In this way she added to all their knowledge. Marion worked from sunup to sundown, but Kathe sometimes saw her sitting in the pasture holding a lamb on her lap or standing in the orchard gently touching the swelling buds. It was easy to see how happy she was here.

Kathe walked into the cottage and put her bucket on the table in front of the hearth. It took a few moments for her eyes to adjust after the brightness outside. She checked to see whether the bowls and the sieve she had set aside for the cheese making were still on the table and began to rummage in a basket for a piece of cloth to use for straining. It was then she saw Patch sitting on the stairs, which was an odd place for him to sit considering there were cushions on the benches by the hearth. His wife was nowhere in sight.

"Where is Maron?" Kathe asked. "I think we have everything we'll need to make the cheese."

When he didn't answer she walked closer. It is always difficult to tell what a Woods Runner is thinking, but something in his expression made her ask, "What is wrong?"

She took his arm and led him to the bench. "Tell me."

"It's time for Maron and me to be getting back to the forest," he muttered. "That's our home. But she won't go. She likes it here, and she promised Bethany she would care for the place until she gets back."

"But Bethany isn't coming back," Kathe said. She didn't think she would ever finish mourning the loss of her friend who had stayed behind on Niue.

"That's right, and that's what I told her, but she said it doesn't matter. She's staying."

Kathe knew a little about the lives of the Woods Runners. They had always lived in the forest not far from Pallas, and maybe near other cities too. The men were hunters and trackers, and the women stayed at home, preparing the skins of the animals their husbands brought to them, caring for the children, and planting gardens. Their homes could be taken apart and moved every few years, and then the clearings where they had planted their crops were reclaimed by the forest. Kathe could see why Bethany's farm, with its snug cottage, orchard and pasture, would appeal to the Woods Woman, and Maron had spent more time waiting for her men to come home than most.

Patch was still talking. "I told her I wanted to go home, and that I was done with travelling. I told her I'd be staying with her from now on, only hunting for a day or two at a time. She said in that case, I can stay with her here."

"Well," Kathe said hesitantly, "Can't you?"

The Woods Runner was silent, as if she had asked a foolish question.

She went on, "Have you tried to leave? If the hedge will let you out and back in without harm, then maybe it's a sign. Maybe you're meant to stay here, for a while at least. Would the freedom to leave this place be enough for you to be happy? Pallas is only a few days' journey away, isn't it? You could even go there and return to be with Maron."

Kathe left Patch to continue thinking, or sulking, and went to look for Maron. She found her gathering eggs. She looked as serene as ever. Her disagreement with Patch seemed to have left her unaffected. Nevertheless, she stopped her work and came to stand by Katherine. Together they leaned against the wooden pasture fence and watched the lambs and kids playing.

"You have been talking to my husband," Maron said.

Kathe told her what Patch had said to her and how she had responded.

"I didn't think about that, that he could continue his travelling. I love him, but after so many years I am content with my own company. He seems to think his promise to stay at home will be enough to sway me," Maron said. "but I love this place."

"I think," Kathe said carefully, "he needs you more than you realize."

"He has me. Give him time," Maron said cheerfully. "He'll come around." She didn't seem to care whether he did or didn't. After a pause, she said, "I suppose you'll be leaving soon."

"What makes you say that?"

"After the life I've led, I can tell when a body is getting restless. You are, and so is Patch, whether he admits it or not. He has told me about you. It seems you have work to do. Why don't you ask him to take you to Pallas? If he is meant to come back to me, then he'll return."

20

THE SLEDGE

LESS THAN AN HOUR passed on the trail before Stormer had to roll his blanket and use it to pad his shoulder where it was being rubbed raw by the rope harness. Before mid-day, he lost count of the number of times he had lifted the front of the sledge and pulled it a few feet forward before it got stuck again. The addition of the magician's books to the load had made it too heavy to pull in this season, but Honorus refused to allow his unburdened pack animal to carry the saddlebags.

Stormer's struggle to keep the sledge moving had slowed the whole Claymon force and provided a kind of macabre entertainment for his fellow soldiers. None of them offered any assistance, even the few he might once have considered friends. He didn't blame them. To help him would lead to notice by Honorus. If their positions were reversed, he would have done the same.

They were taking the road back to Ostara, such as it was. It was not much travelled. The Claymon had been the last to pass this way when they came to Brethren. That's why Stormer knew the path would only become steeper and rougher as they travelled through the mountains.

Since the commander did not return in time to rejoin the Claymon before they left Brethren, the soldiers had assumed he was still tracking Katherine Elder. Stormer spared a moment of worry on her behalf. As much as the Claymon dreaded returning to

Ostara with bad news, they couldn't wait any longer. As soon as Honorus emerged from his room after the battle on the beach, he had ordered their departure.

Now it fell to the sergeant to reason with Honorus about Stormer, the sledge, and their lack of progress. At this rate, it would take over a week to reach Ostara instead of four or five days. Nobody wanted that. The only benefit of their slow pace was that it would delay the moment when they would have to stand in front of Peter Greystone and admit defeat.

The conversation between the sergeant and the magician took some time. Stormer couldn't hear what they were saying, so he took the chance to once again tighten the ropes that were holding the books onto the sledge.

If he were in charge, Stormer would argue they should divide the contents of the sledge among the pack animals, which were carrying less than they had on the way to Brethren. On that journey, the sledge was used to haul Honorus's chair, which was too bulky to carry any other way but light enough not to slow them too much. Since the chair had been lost to the tide back in Brethren, the Claymon didn't need the sledge at all, and it could be abandoned.

Watching from a distance, you wouldn't say the conversation was an argument. The officer spoke, no doubt stating the problem, and the magician stared ahead, seeming to ignore him. Eventually Honorus must have relented because the Officer ordered two of the lowest-ranking men to work with Stormer to keep the sledge moving at something close to a walking pace. The young recruits didn't have as much to lose as Stormer did, and they were unconcerned about protecting the precious books. Even though he believed he might as well already be dead, he winced every time one of them braced a shoulder against a bag and shoved.

As Stormer labored, he couldn't help wondering why, if books were so precious, Honorus didn't just carry them in the usual way and kill him back in Brethren. The makeshift harness bit into his shoulder again, and he moaned. At that moment, Honorus glanced back in his direction. His face was still shadowed by his hood, but Stormer was sure he saw a ghastly smile.

He understood why Honorus was making him pull the sledge. It was punishment for last night's humiliation. It might not make sense to risk damage to his books, but this was the plan the magician had come up with in his fury. They were the heaviest objects he possessed. And he wasn't the sort to change his mind once he'd given an order.

Honorus was more convinced than ever that Stormer carried secrets. He wanted him to suffer while he decided how to extract them.

In last night's dream, Stormer turned out to be more powerful than Honorus. Somehow, he even sent the counselor running back into his room, but which of them was stronger now? Honorus didn't need to use magic today. He was at the head of the column on horseback, and Stormer's new friend, the hawk, was nowhere in sight.

After the sergeant called a halt on the first night, and after Stormer and Ratface set up Honorus's tent, Stormer had just enough strength left to throw a square of canvas over the top of the sledge. Then he crawled under one edge of it and fell into a dead sleep on the ground.

He awoke after midnight in the silent camp because his back and legs were cramping. The last night and day had tested him to the limit of his endurance. He stretched his legs straight, winced, and touched his shoulders where the straps had cut into them. He was sure he could never pull the sledge for a second day, even with the other two men pushing. He wondered what would happen then.

He crawled out from under the canvas and leaned against the bags of books, accepting that it wouldn't make any difference if he were to bend one of the leather covers. Honorus might not be able to find the key that would unlock his mind, but in the end, his misery could only end one way.

Maybe now was the time to run, but Stormer hadn't yet learned what Honorus planned to do after he got back to Ostara, or what role the Claymon would play in those plans. He didn't want to give up until he had to.

"Can you hear me?" he said tentatively, in the silent way he used to communicate with Lightning. He could use some advice. The hawk had told him he'd be far away, carrying messages across the mountains for Abel, but Stormer was so lonely he had to try. He listened for an answer but heard only the wind in the trees and the snoring of his fellow soldiers.

The next time he woke up, the stars were circling towards morning. He had unconsciously drawn his knees up tightly for warmth. They ached, but this time he didn't move. He snugged his blanket closer around his shoulders. There should still be a couple more hours before he'd have to rise and harness himself to the sledge like a mule.

Stormer had almost dropped off again when he felt an alarm he couldn't ignore. Before he realized what had triggered the attack, his breath started to come fast and shallow. This is the feeling that made him fall down on the trail after the bear attacked him. He often had attacks like this in the years before Katherine healed him, but he hadn't had one since – until now.

He choked as he recognized the musky scent of a bear. This time the feeling of suffocation was caused by pure panic. He couldn't get enough air, and his fingers tingled as he started to lose consciousness. At the same moment, he felt a wetness on his cheek, as if someone were running a rough rag across his face.

He fell onto his side and opened his eyes to see a bulky shape lumbering away. As it disappeared among the trees, Stormer forced himself to breathe more slowly and touched his cheek. It was wet. Where were the guards?

"I heard you. It took me a while to get here," said a voice in his skull. *"And then I couldn't wake you up. I thought you were dead."*

One thing was certain. This wasn't Lightning. Stormer was proud that he could talk to the red-tailed hawk. It hadn't taken long for him to get used to the idea of having a bird as a friend, but he didn't know he'd be able to talk to other animals too – least of all the one he feared the most.

"*Who are you?*" he asked. Even though he didn't speak the words aloud, he was afraid his internal voice squeaked.

"*Name's Jasper.*" Stormer thought the creature chuckled, as if he knew what Stormer was thinking. "*You called?*"

"*I guess I shouldn't have done that. I wanted to talk to a hawk named Lightning even though I know he is far from here. I didn't think anyone else was listening.*"

"*Someone is always listening,*" the bear said from the shadows. "*Is there something I can do as long as I'm here?*" The bear yawned. Anyone who was lying awake in the camp could have heard that sound.

Stormer struggled to think. He didn't know the bear, and he wasn't about to go any closer to it, at least not yet. And he couldn't ask Jasper for advice, since they had just met. He wasn't even sure he should trust him or that he could believe a bear wanted to help. Anyone could see he was in trouble, but there wasn't anything the bear could do about it.

When Stormer didn't say anything, Jasper yawned again, even more loudly and said "*Well, in that case, I guess I'll go back to my den.*"

Stormer heard sticks cracking and brush rustling as Jasper moved away from the campsite. He wondered again why no one had sounded the alarm.

"*Wait,*" he said.

The noise stopped.

"*Do you think you could knock down the tent?*" There was only one.

"*I don't know that word, but I guess you mean the thing that looks like a cave.*" Without waiting for confirmation, Jasper said, "*Sure I can. It would be my pleasure.*"

The crashing intensified as Jasper ran back into the camp. It was still very dark, but Stormer was certain he saw the bear rear up and put his whole weight against the top of Honorus's tent. There was the sound of a pole snapping, and then the whole structure fell in on itself. A moment later, Honorus started to yell.

Jasper backed up and turned towards the sledge, where Stormer was still lying on his side. *"Is that what you had in mind?"* he asked. Then he was gone.

The Claymon had camped right on the trail, and the guards were posted some distance ahead and behind on the path. That might explain why they hadn't heard the sounds Jasper made, but there was no way they could ignore Honorus's yelling, a mixture of oaths and screams for help. Stormer struggled to his feet and hobbled to the collapsed tent, where the magician was struggling like a fish in a net.

Ratface was there too, and together they lifted the canvas so Honorus could crawl out from underneath it. He must have slept in his clothes. He was wrapped in a blanket, but his cloak was still somewhere under the ruined tent.

Now, in torchlight, everyone saw how Honorus's transformation had not reached his skull. Stormer knew Honorus had been trying to hide that fact, and seeing the skeletal head stitched to the top of a strong, young-looking body silenced the Claymon soldiers who had straggled over and gathered in a ring.

It's a pity, Stormer thought, when he realized Honorus was uninjured. At the same time, he knew the only thing worse than hauling the books on the sledge would be hauling Honorus himself if he couldn't ride his horse. It would have to be enough to see him confused and angry and to know there was no way he could possibly connect the collapse of his tent to Stormer.

Honorus stormed at the Claymon officer. "Greystone will hear of this. Your guards let a wild beast attack me. I could have been killed!"

The officer did not respond at once, and Stormer guessed he also regretted Greystone's pet magician was unhurt. Then he held up the side of the ruined tent to reveal five long gashes. "Looks like it must have been a bear," he said. "Probably smelled some food inside."

Dawn was still a long time off, but the officer turned to the rest of the soldiers and said, "We're all awake, so we might as well get moving. Maybe we can make up some time. Pack up and saddle the horses." He gestured at the tent. "And leave this behind."

Honorus started to sputter, and the officer said loudly enough for everyone to hear, "You're a lot stronger than the last time we passed this way. You'll have to sleep rough like the rest of us."

Even though the sledge was just as heavy as the day before, when Stormer took up the harness again it felt lighter. That must have been because knew he had a second friend among the animals.

21

Shepherd Boy

TALL TREES LINED BOTH banks of the river. Their tiny leaves were still more gold than green on the fresh spring morning, and they glimmered as they fluttered in the breeze. At Gale's feet, white flowers he could not name were starting to open in the warming day, releasing a sweet fragrance.

Gale's errand was urgent. He had to find meat for the hungry dragon, but he paused. He had never seen such a lovely place. Even Springvale couldn't compare to it. The pasture on the other side of the river was so green it almost hurt his eyes, and it was framed by high, snow crowned mountains. This juxtaposition of tamed and wild land was enchanting.

Gale could see the grass had been cropped short under the trees on the opposite bank of the river. It looked as if animals had been coming down to the water there. Maybe that meant the water wasn't so deep on that side. Gale worked his way along the bank until he was directly across from that spot and waded in.

This was a small river, but it rushed with snow melt, shockingly cold. At this season it was in flood, and Gale soon was in water up to his waist. By the time he reached the middle, it was up to his chest. He struggled to find his footing on the rocky bed in the strong current. He was more than half-way across when he stepped in a hole and went under. Fighting his way to the surface, he gasped for air. Somehow, he managed to grab the waterskins just before they slipped from his shoulder and vanished downstream. There was no point in trying to regain his footing, so he swam, allowing the current to carry him downstream while he angled towards the other side.

By the time he reached the opposite bank, he was as cold as when they were flying, and wet besides. He crawled out of the water and partway up the eroded bank, looking for the sun and shivering. From above, he and Meg had seen the river from above and saw how it snaked its way back and forth as it made its way through the valley. His crossing had carried him around one of the curves. He was lucky to have started across where he did. Not much farther downstream, the water churned around rocks.

Gale realized he wouldn't be able to bring a sheep back across the river for Padraik. He wasn't even sure he'd be able to cross again himself. He'd have to find a wild goat or a deer closer to where Padraik was hidden, back on the other side.

He had nearly convinced himself to cross before he lost his nerve, but he thought as long as he was here he might as well explore. Chances were, Meg was still trying to convince Padraik to try the travel cakes. He didn't have to like them. Gale was tired of them himself, but they'd keep the dragon alive until they found some meat for him.

Gale scrambled the rest of the way up the bank. There were no white flowers here. They had all been eaten by whatever had cropped the grass short. The pasture stretched ahead of him up the sides of low hills, and even farther away, partway up the mountainside. There were pens and walls built from the rocks that littered the ground. Pathways worn into the surface of the earth crisscrossed the pasture. This part of the valley was heavily grazed close to the river, which made sense. The shepherds wouldn't want to take their flocks farther from the water than they had to.

Gale studied a small structure in the distance. From where he was standing, it looked like it had three sides, and just beyond it a small group of sheep grazed.

If this part of the valley had inhabitants, they were nowhere in sight, and the town he and Meg had seen wasn't visible either. They had thought the valley was flat, but now Gale could see it was made up of gently rolling hills, with the bones of the mountains poking through at the edges.

There would be no cover once Gale left the trees by the river and no way to sneak across the pasture, so he started walking purposefully towards the shelter. He had already decided against stealing a sheep, and anyway, he had never been a thief. He just wanted to see what was in the shed.

Back at Springvale, when a wolf or a hungry cottager helped himself to any of the estate's livestock, even a chicken, Gale's father was implacable. When Gale was young, his father would track and shoot the wolf himself. Later, he sent Gale to do it. If the culprit was a cottager, he'd be publicly punished. If the offender was caught a second time, he'd likely be hanged as an example to others tempted by easy meat. It only happened twice during his lifetime, but Gale remembered the executions as if they happened yesterday. Lord Stefan required his son to be there, standing by his side and close enough see the thief's face contort and turn purple as the rope choked him. There was no reason to think the owner of the sheep would be more forgiving.

Gale hadn't stolen anything yet, and he probably wouldn't. But if he did, he knew he had better not get caught. As he came closer to the shed, he saw a ring of stones just outside the entrance and, even though there were no flames, Gale smelled wood-smoke. A brown cloak hung on a peg by the entrance, and a long shepherd's crook leaned against the corner of the shed, but nobody was in sight.

Gale could guess why the structure was open on one side. On cold nights, with snow swirling and wind sweeping down from the mountains through the open pasture, the sheep would crowd inside the shelter to stay warm, warming their shepherd at the same time.

Gale peeked around the edge of the doorway, and as he expected, there was a low platform built up against the wall, lined with sheepskin. A boy lay there, fast asleep. It was hard to tell how old he was, maybe thirteen or fourteen. The sheep baaed as Gale approached, but he knew that sound was mild compared to the racket they'd make if he tried to catch one of them. No matter how deeply a shepherd boy might be sleeping, he would be attuned to the sounds of his flock.

The boy stirred. Gale retreated ten steps and called, "Hello. Good Morning." He had no idea what language the boy might speak, but he knew they were at the very western edge of the Claymon homeland. He didn't speak any Claymon, so he called his greeting in the common speech, which most people seemed to understand. In his experience, it usually sounded something like the local language, only badly spoken.

Even if he couldn't get food for Padraik, maybe he'd learn something about this place. The town they had seen looked large, even prosperous. If its people were traders, maybe he could ask for help, especially if he and Meg could somehow keep Padraik out of sight. Gale fingered the bag at his waist where a few pieces of gold nested. It was a miracle he hadn't lost them while crossing the river. He wouldn't steal a sheep, but maybe he could buy one.

Before he finished this thought, the boy was standing in front of the fire ring brandishing his crook in two hands like a cudgel. He was barefoot, and a knife was tucked under his belt. His hair stuck up in every direction, and he had a deep crease on his cheek where his face had been resting on his blanket.

Gale held his hands in front of him so the shepherd could see he was unarmed, though that wasn't completely true. He had brought a coil of rope and a knife, but they were hidden from sight under his tunic. He had left the waterskins hanging in a tree back by the river.

"Who are you?" The boy said. At least, that's what Gale heard. It wasn't quite the common speech, so he made a guess.

"I am a traveler," Gale replied.

"Where did you come from."

Gale pointed up at the high mountains behind him, and he could already feel his story falling apart. The smallest child would know that was impossible, and this was no child, but a boy on the brink of manhood.

Gale held the shepherd boy's gaze as he reached under his tunic and pulled out the bag of coins. He shook it so the boy could hear it jingle. "Will you sell me a sheep?" he asked slowly, pointing at the flock with his other hand. He opened the bag and displayed the coins on his palm.

The boy shook his head vigorously.

These were not his sheep to sell. They were his father's, or they belonged to some rich man who had hired him to keep them safe.

He put the coins away again and patted his chest, "Gale."

The boy still looked wary, but at least he had lowered the shepherd's crook.

Gale still wasn't sure the boy understood him, so he repeated his greeting. "Hello. I am Gale."

"I am Brit," the boy said, tapping his own chest.

"Well met, Brit."

Gale knew he had to return to Meg and Padraik soon. Meg would be wondering what was taking him so long. He still needed to find a better place to cross the river, and once he reached the other side he'd have to fill the waterskins, but there was one more piece of information he needed before he left.

He and the boy stood silently watching each other. It seemed they had reached the end of their supply of words. Then Gale smiled. He made sure he had the boy's attention, and he pointed a little farther down the valley behind the boy, at the broken-off mountain with a lazy curl of smoke around the top.

The expression on the boy's face gave him the answer he was looking for, but he needed to know more. In frustration, Gale looked around for a stick, but there weren't any in this treeless place, so he quickly circled around to the bare dirt in front of the hut's door and crouched. Smoothing the dirt with the side of his hand, he pulled out his knife and used its point to begin drawing something.

Brit's curiosity overcame his distrust, and he squatted nearby to study the emerging image. As soon as he realized what it was, he began to speak rapidly, pointing back and forth between Gale's crude drawing and the mountain top.

"Slow down, slow down," Gale said, sheathing his knife and holding his hands out again. He wondered how many sheep this boy had lost to the dragon. If this one was like Padraik, it might avoid eating people, but it had to eat something. The shed would provide a measure of safety to a shepherd, and he could herd the sheep inside at night, but sheep had to graze, and there would be no way to keep the dragon from taking as many as it wanted. This explained why the flock was so small and why the land between the hut and the river was heavily grazed. This is the place Brit felt safest. A crook might rescue a sheep caught by the river's current, but it is no weapon at all against a dragon.

The boy pulled out his own knife and drew a row of stick men next to the dragon. Three, four, five. He glanced at Gale to make sure he had his attention and then drew a line through each of the figures. It was easy to interpret the message. Five men had tried to kill this dragon. All were dead.

Gale held out his hand for the boy's knife as he smoothed the dirt again. He drew two sheep, hoping they would look like an ewe and a ram. He pointed to the mountain again, and then to the dragon he had drawn.

"Is it male, or female?" he asked.

The boy looked confused, and he shrugged. He probably thought Gale was asking whether the dragon preferred to kill ewes or rams. Unless the people here knew this dragon as well as he and Meg knew Padraik, they probably didn't even know whether it was a male or female. Since Padraik had never met another dragon, even he might not be able to tell.

Gale held out his hand, and after a moment the boy grasped it. Speaking slowly, he said, "I am a friend. I will try to help."

He had walked half-way back to the river when he heard a shout. The boy was coming after him holding something in his arms. When he caught up, he handed Gale a heavy bundle wrapped in coarse cloth.

"You help," he said, nodding towards the volcano. Gale watched until the boy reached the shed and took up his crook again. When Brit went to his flock, Gale thought he was counting them. There couldn't be more than twenty. He wondered whether any were missing this morning.

He unwrapped a corner of the cloth and confirmed what his nose had been telling him. Brit had given him a large piece of smoked mutton. It wouldn't be what he was used to, but Padraik should like it better than the travel bread.

22

TO THE PLAIN OF OSTARA

ON THE SECOND DAY, with two men pushing and with Stormer pulling the sledge, the Claymon made better time. That night after supper, Honorus threw his bowl aside and announced that, since he no longer had a tent, he would sleep in the center of the camp next to the fire. It was obvious he expected to have the space to himself. He ordered Ratface and Stormer to keep the fire burning high all night. He wasn't going to risk a return visit from the bear, so they would take it in turns to feed the blaze. Ratface was never going to be Stormer's friend, but at least he had stopped bullying him. He now saw the two of them as partners in misfortune.

Since eating something warm at the end of the day and gathering around the fire was the only pleasure the Claymon could look forward to, there was some grumbling at Honorus's announcement, but it was all done out of the magician's earshot. The sergeant was not prepared to confront Honorus again. He might oversee the Claymon, but as Peter Greystone's counselor, Honorus still held power over all of them. As darkness fell, the Claymon retreated to the edge of the camp where they made a fire of their own.

When it was his turn to tend the fire, Stormer tried to ignore the pile of furs where Honorus lay. He felt the magician's eyes following him as he walked back and forth between the forest and the fire, dragging branches, dropping them and breaking them into pieces. Stormer made no effort to be quiet. He didn't sense anything like the weird light or the bonds that snared him in his dream. Everyone knew Honorus was afraid the bear would return, but Stormer believed he was uneasy about something else as well.

Ever since his conscription into the Claymon army, his superiors never missed a chance to tell Stormer he was nobody – ignorant, low-ranking, and disposable. That is why it took him so long to believe the counselor was afraid of him, even though there did not seem to be any other explanation.

During his dream back at the inn – the dream that turned into something else – Honorus had not expected a fight. When Stormer resisted and overcame him, it must have come as a jolt – so much so that Honorus gave up, retreated to his room, and slammed the door. Stormer thought Lightning had frightened the magician, but the hawk told Stormer the contest was already decided when he arrived.

When it was Ratface's turn to tend the fire, Stormer crept away and fell into a deep sleep on the far side of the sledge where Honorus couldn't see him, but when his turn came again, he sensed Honorus was still awake and watching.

The next two days followed the same pattern. In the distance, Stormer's eyes would land on a goal, which might be an oddly shaped tree or a turn in the road, and he set himself to the work of achieving it. He knew this was a game he was certain to lose, but if he was going to quit, he should have rebelled back in Brethren. Maybe continuing to try meant he was stupid, but he still hoped he would learn something useful for Abel and the others. He even hoped he would find a way to pass that information along. Memories of the day he went to the house with the blue door seemed to come from another part of his life even though he went there less than a week ago.

Also, Stormer knew if he quit and refused to continue pulling the sledge any farther, Honorus would have him killed immediately.

At the end of the fourth day, the Claymon reached the ridge-line. Then, instead of pulling the sledge uphill all day, Stormer's job suddenly became keeping it from sliding down too quickly. If it was moving too fast when it hit a muddy patch, it would stop with a jolt, and the bags of books would shift. They might break loose from the top of the load. He tried not to picture the precious volumes spilling out of the bags and lying in the muck with their pages fluttering.

The two men who had been assigned to share the duty held the back of the sledge on the steepest, smoothest sections of trail, while Stormer pushed on the front and guided it down the trail. At first he welcomed the change, but he soon found it almost as hard as pulling the sledge up hill.

Late in the afternoon of the fifth day, they reached the edge of the stunted forest close to the base of the mountain. The Plain of Ostara finally lay before them. If it had been up to the Claymon, they would have pushed on to reach the city that night, but with the accursed sledge slowing them, that wasn't possible. They couldn't leave the counselor, and he wouldn't leave his possessions, so the sergeant sent a rider to Ostara to announce they would be there the next morning.

As they prepared to camp one last time, there was more grumbling from the troops. Crossing the plain to the city in darkness might have invited a rebel attack, but even here, at the edge of the forest, there was danger. The Claymon set extra guards. It would be bad enough to return to Ostara to report the defeat they had suffered in Brethren without enduring an encounter with the rebels so close to the city.

The sergeant put himself into the guard rotation so that he would be watching at dawn. He positioned himself behind a rock outcropping a distance back up the hillside, where he could look out over the trees to the open plain beyond. That meant he was the first to see horses galloping toward the camp. He first thought it was a band of rebels, and he almost raised an alarm, but as he opened his mouth to shout, he realized Devon Elder's men would have attacked in the night. No. The horses were coming straight from Ostara. Greystone had risen early and was riding out to meet them.

The sergeant still didn't know who it was the Claymon fought back on the beach in Brethren. There were a couple of Woods Runners and a few other swordsmen who might have been citizens of the town. He was sure he had never seen any of them before. One was wearing a ragged sweater but carried a weapon fit for a prince. It was no more than a skirmish, really, but he knew Greystone wouldn't see it that way. His chest tightened.

Not only had the Claymon been vanquished from the beach in that battle, but Greystone surely would expect them to be returning to Pallas with Katherine Elder. Putting this worry aside, the sergeant tried to decide whether he should say anything about the dragon in his report. Not for the first time, he cursed his commander, who had abandoned his responsibilities to track the girl. The sergeant should not be the one making this report.

According to gossip that filtered down to the troops, Greystone was as repulsed by Honorus as everyone else, but he still kept him near. It was a strange dependency, one that made the others in Greystone's retinue nervous. It was rumored that Greystone relied on Honorus's advice when judging the loyalty of his inner circle, and there was no doubt his unique skills were useful during interrogations.

Before they left for Brethren, when Honorus asked for men to cross the mountains with him so he could seek refugees from a long-abandoned city, Greystone did not hesitate. He had not yet turned his attention to the forest, but he had heard stories of ruins hidden there. As soon as Ostara was secure he planned to see them for himself. When that time came, it wouldn't hurt to have his servant in control of Pallas. Too, Honorus had predicted Katherine Elder would be found among the refugees. He did not understand why that might be, but his counselor was usually right.

That is why Greystone assigned the commander, the sergeant, and the other soldiers to accompany Honorus. Before they left for Brethren, the two officers had to swear they would obey the magician. He even made them kneel and kiss his ring.

At the beginning of the expedition, the commander had privately complained to the sergeant that Honorus's tale of refugees surviving so long on an island was mad. Even though it turned out to be true, there was still much about the events back in Brethren that didn't make sense.

Now, as he raced back to the camp, the sergeant wished the bear had stayed a little longer that first night. Judging from the size of its tracks, it might have taken the magician's head off with one bite. As far as the sergeant was concerned, Honorus had brought nothing but bad luck to the Claymon since they found him crabbing his way across the plain towards the city.

He spared a glance towards the fire, where the pile of furs marked the magician's sleeping spot.

Greystone was about to see how his counselor had changed. How would the magician explain his transformation? More important, how would Honorus's report differ from his own? He pictured Honorus running across the beach, stumbling and falling onto his knees in the sand as the dragon screamed above them, and he decided to leave that part out.

Stormer heard the approaching horses, and he guessed what they meant. Instead of continuing to his doom in Ostara, the end of his story was coming out to meet him. He knew this would be his best chance to slip away, as the camp woke up and prepared to face Greystone.

Since it looked as if he weren't going to have to pull the sledge any farther, Stormer folded back the canvas he had been using as a cover each night and untied one of the bags that was still secured on top of the load. The books looked undamaged. It was a miracle considering all they had been through since he'd loaded them on the sledge in Brethren.

When Stormer was sure no one was looking, he paged through the top few volumes in the open bag before pocketing the smallest one. It held perfectly formed letters that marched across each page like ants. He had never learned how to read, and he never even held a book before he met the magician, but he wanted one now. He wasn't sure why he did it, but he told himself Honorus wouldn't miss it, at least not right away.

Then, since this might be his last morning, he ate the last crumbs of cake the serving girl had given him before he left Brethren. Her kindness and the bear's visit had sustained him during the hellish journey over rocks and mud. Then, even though the window for escape was closing, Stormer busied himself with camp chores.

As the party from Ostara drew nearer, Stormer saw Greystone had ridden his battle horse to this meeting. He whipped it to a gallop as he crossed the last of the plain. It would have been an impressive sight for Lady Katherine Elder. Unfortunately, she was not there to see it. The horse reared when Peter Greystone pulled back on the reins. Its sides heaved and it pranced in place to settle itself. When it shook its head, foam flew in every direction. A frothy gob landed on the sergeant's face. It trickled down his cheek and dripped onto the front of his uniform.

The camp was silent as Greystone surveyed the scene from his saddle. Well, not quite silent. Stormer might have been the only one who noticed small birds singing from the treetops as the sun rose into the clear sky. The birds were keeping their distance from the men arranged below them like actors awaiting their moment on stage, but their morning chorus was louder than ever.

There was no way to disguise the reduced Claymon numbers or that there were no women there. Honorus stood next to the sergeant. He was well-wrapped in his cloak, once again hiding his face from view. Back in Brethren, the commander had sent a pigeon to Ostara as soon as he was sure Katherine Elder was among the refugees. He couldn't wait to tell Greystone she would soon be under Claymon protection.

Obviously, the pigeon had survived its flight over the mountains. Greystone swung down from his saddle. He wore the bright red uniform of a Claymon officer and a short cape. The clothing was tight, which showed off his fine legs and his pudgy belly dissected by his sword belt. He even wore a feather in his hat. The sergeant started to sweat.

"Where is she? Where is my Katherine?" Greystone called, refusing to believe the evidence of his eyes.

"Sir, she escaped again," the sergeant said louder than he had wished, standing at attention and looking straight ahead. "She came to Brethren by ship with the refugees, but she swam to shore some distance from the town. When we left Brethren, the commander was still tracking her. No doubt he has found her by now, and he will soon return with her to Ostara."

Greystone did not comment but walked the short distance to the center of the encampment, with the sergeant and Honorus following him. He snapped his fingers at one of the men who had accompanied him from Ostara, and a folding stool materialized behind him. He sat down, leaving his subordinates, including Honorus, to stand.

The rest of the Claymon retreated to the perimeter of the camp, but Stormer stayed close. He was the magician's servant, after all. It was lucky no one had asked why he was wearing his pack. If they did, he would say he was ready to begin the last leg of the journey, but he wanted to be ready in case the moment came to bolt.

"I will hear your report first, Honorus." Greystone said. "And push back that hood. You know I need to see your face. And why are you suddenly so tall?" he added irritably.

Stormer thought Honorus hesitated before he uncovered his head. From where he was standing, he couldn't see the magician's face, but he saw Greystone's reaction. He didn't bother to hide it, and Honorus couldn't have missed seeing Greystone's repugnance.

Even though Stormer wasn't on the beach to see what happened, he knew Honorus's spell broke before it was complete. If it were not for the arrival of the dragon, Honorus's face might have been restored as well as his body. Instead, Honorus's skull was just a bony frame with skin like a poorly tanned hide stretched tightly over it. Where there should have been color in the man's cheeks and lips there was none, while his scalp was blotched by livid sores. Before the debacle on the beach, at least the body and head seemed to belong together. Now they were horribly mismatched, as if the magician had become a scarecrow to frighten anyone who saw him.

"I drew strength from my people," Honorus said stiffly. Stormer supposed this was an explanation of sorts, and true as far as it went. Maybe it would satisfy Greystone, but it revealed almost nothing about what had happened back in Brethren.

"Where are they? I lent you men so that you could claim them. You told me Katherine Elder would be with them. She should be here."

"They have been claimed," Honorus said.

It seemed he wasn't ready to explain that he hadn't actually sailed to find them himself. Everyone in the camp knew the entire plan had gone wrong almost from the beginning. As soon as the enemy stole the *Goshawk*, they – whoever they were – had the upper hand.

The sergeant listened intently while he waited for his turn to report. He had to know which details to include and which were to be forgotten. He thought one of them would have to say something about the dragon. The men who had been on the beach and who took part in the battle would not keep that secret. As soon as they were at liberty, the news would escape in some public house and from there it would burst out into the streets of Ostara. There would be no containing it.

Peter Greystone's companions looked nervous. They could read the signs. Greystone was angry. It started when he heard Katherine Elder had escaped again. From now on his responses would be more and more unpredictable.

"My counselor is speaking in riddles," Greystone said in a deceptively calm voice. "Sergeant. Your report."

The sergeant took two steps forward and squared his shoulders. At least the counselor was not conducting this interrogation. From the way Honorus was glaring at him, the less said about the events on the beach, the better.

He started at the beginning, with the provisioning of the *Goshawk* and its loss to the pirates. It was the first time he had used that word to describe them, but that's what they were. "I have come to believe your counselor knew the pirates. Some of them, at least. After they escaped with the ship, he told me they were also looking for the refugees, and he was content to wait for their return to Brethren. Honorus must have known these pirates were trailing us across the mountains, but he said nothing. If he had, the commander would have placed extra guards on the ship, and it would not have been stolen. Your counselor's silence had even more serious consequences after the ship returned."

Stormer noticed the sergeant's reluctance to use Honorus's name.

Honorus interrupted. "It is true. I did know some of them. My brother was one. I believed him long dead. My sister and her husband were a part of it, and they too have lived beyond their time. Katherine Elder was with them, and there were others who were strange to me. I suspected they would follow us and that they were also seeking the refugees, but I did not know they had reached Brethren." He looked accusingly at the sergeant. "How did you miss their arrival? Why was I not informed?"

"Enough," Greystone said. "If you both had been on the ship when it returned to Brethren with the refugees, my men would have been with you, and Katherine Elder would not have escaped."

Greystone still did not know about the creature from the island, the dragon Padraik. And neither Honorus nor any of the Claymon, including Stormer, knew about Meg. If she had not been there to calm the dragon, maybe no one would have returned.

"What happened after the ship returned?" Greystone snapped.

"It anchored a distance from shore, and we rowed out to meet it." The sergeant gestured at Honorus and said, "He made his servants bring his chair to the beach and sat there waiting. When we had almost reached the ship, longboats carrying the refugees and the pirates began to make their way to shore, and one of our boats gave chase. Though we didn't know it then, this must have been when Lady Katherine jumped into the sea and started to swim. Our other boat continued to the ship to search it. Six men were in that boat, and none of them returned to Brethren. Nor has the *Goshawk* returned to its berth. When we left the town, it was still anchored offshore."

He waited for a response from Greystone, and when there was none, he continued more hesitantly. "Two more were killed in the conflict on the beach, and one was wounded and died the next morning. We might have triumphed, but just as the fight started to turn in our favor, we heard the whistle that signaled the search party had picked up the Lady's trail. The commander immediately took on the duty of tracking her."

Silence swelled in the camp, except for the inappropriately cheerful birdsong.

"So, nine of my men are dead or missing. Ten if we count your leader, who so bravely went after the girl." Half to himself Greystone said, "I can only imagine how frightened she must have been, finding herself all alone on the shore. How brave she was to jump overboard to get away from the pirates."

Stormer thought everyone was meant to hear the remark. Greystone seemed to want them to think the only reason he wanted to find Katherine Elder was because he was concerned for her safety. Since everyone was used to pretending they agreed with him, his entire retinue nodded as one.

"Tell me more about the battle." Greystone demanded.

The sergeant glanced nervously at Honorus before continuing, "The men we fought were not soldiers, but two of them were good swordsmen. They were fighting for their lives, and even though they were few, their tactics were unpredictable. By then our numbers were reduced." He paused, aware he was making excuses. "And I must tell you, my Lord. Two of our opponents were Woods Runners."

Greystone weighed this news. If it turned out that he could no longer trust the men from the forest, his plans would have to change. His agreement with the Woods Runners was unspoken, but he had thought they understood. They tracked his enemies and brought him information. In return, he paid them well. Even though they were mercenaries, they had never before given him reason to mistrust them. For that reason, and because they were of use, he had not invaded the forest homeland where their families lived their primitive lives.

"There is something more you aren't telling me," Greystone barked, jumping up from the stool and knocking it backwards into the fire. One of his men scrambled to retrieve it.

This was the moment, Stormer thought. This was when Honorus, or maybe the sergeant, would tell Greystone the rest of the story. Stormer almost wished he had been there to see the dragon himself except that if he were there, Katherine Elder would surely have been captured soon after she swam to shore, and he might have been killed in the fight on the beach. Still, although his fellow soldiers had told him almost nothing about the dragon, he had eavesdropped on their conversations, and he knew it must have been amazing. He also knew, because the girl in the kitchen had told him, that by the time the dragon made its second pass over the beach, the Claymon had all raced for cover.

While Stormer's mind wandered over what might have been, Honorus had started to talk again.

"This one is hiding secrets," he spat, pointing a long, boney finger at Stormer. "I have done what I can to extract them, but he is not what he seems. He is protected. He knows what will happen if he doesn't give them up. By now my brother has led my people across the mountains and back to Pallas. Soon I will follow. My brother has allies. I must know who they are. He will also tell me who has laid a spell powerful enough to deny me entry to his mind."

The moment had passed. Stormer had delayed his escape too long. A sick dread started in his belly and spread through his whole body. Honorus, the sergeant, and even Peter Greystone were staring at him.

"As punishment, this creature pulled my sledge here over the mountains. His end might as well come here and now. If he tells what he knows, then perhaps his death will be merciful. Do you remember what I told you I was going to do?" Honorus put his face so close to Stormer's that he could smell his rancid breath. He turned away.

"Cut my eyes out," Stormer muttered. The other soldiers, drawn by the drama at the center of the camp, started to edge closer and circled around.

Honorus drew a thin blade from a scabbard hidden beneath his cloak and held it up, testing the edge. "Are you ready to talk now?"

Desperately looking for a way to gain a few more moments, Stormer said, "You said you'd cut out my eyes if the books were damaged. You haven't even looked at them. I kept them safe. See for yourself."

In his rage, Honorus had forgotten this part of the bargain. He nodded at the two soldiers closest to Stormer, and they moved in and held him by his arms. Honorus walked over to the sledge, opened one of the bags, and lifted the top volume. It had a red leather binding, and he held it up so that everyone could see the golden lettering on its spine. Then he opened the cover and ripped out the first few pages, tossing them into the wind.

Stormer gasped as he realized his mistake. He thought Honorus loved the books. The truth was, Honorus only loved power. Power and cruelty. Honorus had his own secrets. He did not want to talk about what happened back in Brethren, about the dragon, or about the refugees who were fewer and much weaker than he had expected. Tormenting Stormer was a distraction to keep Peter Greystone from asking any more questions about the failure of the mission.

Stormer had never expected to be so close to Peter Greystone, let alone enduring his stare. He always thought the Claymon leader would be bigger. He wasn't even as tall as Stormer. His splendid clothes could not make up for his wispy beard and sallow complexion. As Honorus approached again, knife in hand, Stormer blurted, "All right. I'll tell you secrets."

The magician did not sheath his knife, but it seemed to Stormer that Greystone leaned forward.

"If you lie, you will die," Greystone said.

This was a ridiculous threat, but Stormer was not about to point that out. He looked up into the canopy of the small trees here at the edge of the forest, looking for the birds that were still singing, or for a trace of blue sky. If he was going to die anyway, he might as well tell what he knew.

"These are the secrets you have not heard from the counselor or the sergeant," Stormer said. He forced himself to speak loudly enough so that everyone there could hear him. "I was not there because I was sent to look for Lady Katherine. I was the one who found her trail and ordered my companion to signal the soldiers on the beach. I heard about the events on the beach later that day from my fellow soldiers and from a friend I made in the town."

Honorus took a step towards Stormer. These were not the secrets he wanted.

Greystone ordered. "Give your knife to my man and stand behind me," he said. "I will listen to him, and I will decide his fate."

"He admits he wasn't there. He'll say anything. He knows he is about to die," Honorus whined.

"Nevertheless," Greystone said with an edge to his voice. "Continue."

Stormer's mouth was dry. "As I said, I sent the other soldier to signal that we had found Katherine Elder's trail, that is true, but that isn't what ended the battle. Something else happened before that."

"Well, what was it?" Greystone yelled. His patience was nearly gone.

"It was a dragon. A dragon flew low over the beach, faster than a hawk swooping down on its prey, and not only that, there were two people riding on its back. That is what ended the battle, and it happened before my partner signaled."

Greystone turned to the sergeant, who nodded miserably.

"You didn't think that was important?" he said. Then, to Stormer, "What then?"

"The commander chose one soldier to accompany him and at once went after Lady Katherine. The rest of our men ran to the town."

"They retreated," Greystone said flatly.

Since he still had Greystone's attention, Stormer decided he might as well tell the rest of it. "My friend from the town told me this next part of the story. The rest of us, of the Claymon, I mean, were too busy fighting to watch Honorus. Once the dragon appeared, well, that changed everything. It didn't hurt anyone, but it sure did scare them. Those who were there say they'll never forget it."

Surely everyone clustered in the center of the camp knew Stormer was desperate. He was trying to gain a few more minutes by stretching out the story. Still, Greystone had not yet interrupted him, and even the men who were there had their eyes riveted to his face. It was as if they were hungry to hear the story again.

He continued, "By then the people from the island had left the boats and were huddled together on the beach. There weren't very many of them, not enough to fill a city, and they were in very poor condition – thin and weak. My friend didn't understand what was happening."

"What did he tell you?" Greystone said.

"She. She told me it looked like a dark cloud formed around the people, and the next thing she noticed was your counselor changing. He looked stronger every minute, and the cloud was getting darker. That's when one of the enemies, the one Honorus says is his brother, I'd guess, came running down to the water's edge and attacked him. That broke the spell." Stormer didn't care if the magician was annoyed that he had used his name.

"So, this was going on at the same time as the battle," Greystone said thoughtfully. The sergeant looked as if he wished he could become invisible. Honorus glared at Stormer over Greystone's shoulder, and he felt familiar bands begin to tighten around his chest. He struggled against the men who were holding him.

Stormer kept talking as he fought Honorus's spell. His voice rasped, and his breath came in gasps. "Your counselor was winning. Everyone could see that. Then the dragon came. Everyone stopped fighting to look. The dragon came a second time. It flew even lower, right over the heads of Honorus and his brother. This time it screamed like nothing my friend had ever heard before. Some who were there said it breathed fire."

Stormer sagged between the two men holding him and croaked, "Honorus ran towards the town then, outpacing everyone, and so did my friend. That's all she saw."

Honorus would not have to use his knife to kill him after all. Stormer might keep his eyes, but the scraps of information he had been storing away to share with the rebels would die with him. Greystone had probably seen this happen during a hundred interrogations.

Now that the time had come, the secrets Stormer had gathered during his short time as a spy seemed trivial. Chances were Greystone didn't even know his counselor wasn't trying to extract information from Stormer any longer. He was simply executing him. When it was finished, the counselor would claim it had gone a little too far. That he didn't know the limits of his new strength. Stormer tried to remember how he had saved himself before and failed.

When shouting erupted around him, Stormer's vision was already dimming. He was too far gone to understand what was happening. When the soldiers who had been holding him let loose of his arms, he collapsed onto the ground. At the same time, the bands Honorus had conjured around his chest suddenly released. His hands groped for them as they had after his dream, even though he knew they weren't real. He heard shouts, oaths and, more distantly, someone shouting an order. "To Greystone! To Greystone!"

Stormer struggled to sit up and crawled away from the center of the camp on his elbows and knees. Horses reared and kicked around him. He wondered whether he had survived another contest with Honorus only to be brained by hooves.

He thought he was among the pack animals and horses of the Claymon, but he heard a woman shout, "That's him!" Someone caught hold of his pack and hauled him to his feet.

"Give me your hand!"

Someone clasped his wrist and hauled Stormer onto the back of a horse.

"Hang on," the stranger said, and then the chaos was behind them.

23

THE OTHER SIDE

THEY FLEW ACROSS THE plain at a gallop. Escaping Honorus in a dream had felt like a miracle. Escaping him in real life was even more bewildering. Stormer's ribs had been crushed again, and he didn't know whether he had just been saved or kidnapped. It was all he could do to breathe and stay on the horse's back. He wrapped his arms around the stranger's waist and clamped his legs to the horse's sides.

Trying to understand what had just happened, he squeezed his eyes shut. His mind carried him back to a long-ago summer, when he raced his friends across the endless grasslands of the North. They rode their own shaggy ponies, but never this fast.

Such a headlong run could not last long. As the rider slowed his mount, Stormer realized this was not a heavy battle steed like Greystone's, but a small, wiry horse bred for speed. It pranced in place as the rider bent forward and whispered something into one quivering ear. Stormer waited for his own heart to slow and looked around.

There were six horses in all, counting the one he and the stranger were riding. The other five were a distance behind but closing the gap quickly. Stormer had already guessed who they must be. These were the rebels from Ostara – the ones who hid in the hills and took every chance they could to harass Peter Greystone.

Their leader, Devon Elder, once ruled in Ostara, and he was Katherine's father. Though too few to overcome the Claymon, they had broken the supply chain heading to the city so that it was virtually under siege. They often harried Claymon patrols, delaying or preventing the arrival of reports, further isolating far-flung troops. From what he had heard, these rebels were the reason Greystone stayed in Ostara instead of leading his forces into new territory. Now Stormer was their prisoner.

He ought to have been afraid.

His rescuer waited silently for the others to catch up. When they did, Stormer saw there were four riders on horses of the same kind he and his rescuer were riding. One of them led a fifth horse that dwarfed the others. It was Peter Greystone's war horse.

"Taking him won't prevent Greystone from following us," said the one leading the horse, "But I couldn't resist. He'll just have to ride another."

"We have never been so close to him," the man who had saved Stormer said. "This would have been our chance to cut off their head."

"Perhaps," said a woman's voice.

Stormer had heard that voice before – shouting orders back in the Claymon encampment, and somewhere else.

"Don't let their appearance fool you, Bard. The men in his retinue look soft, but they are well-trained. They have too much leisure, and when I was in Ostara, I watched them practicing swordsmanship every day. We surprised them back there, but if we had lingered, and especially if we had tried to fight through to their master, we would soon have found ourselves outmatched as well as outnumbered. Besides, that wasn't our mission."

Stormer knew her now. This was Katherine's mother, Ellen, but he didn't understand how she had come to be here. The last time he spoke with her was back in Brethren, when she invited him to be a spy.

"What was your mission?" Stormer croaked.

"To rescue you," his savior said.

Ellen must have sensed other questions forming and rising to the surface in Stormer's mind like bubbles in a glass of ale, so she forestalled them by holding up one gloved hand.

"There is no time to explain now. We are not yet safe." She nodded to the rider who was holding Greystone's horse. He slapped its rump, and they watched it trot off across the plain.

"We couldn't have hidden or fed the brute," she said, shrugging. Stormer thought he heard a trace of regret in her voice.

"You are riding with Bard," she said. "My son."

Bard turned his head and nodded. Other introductions would have to wait. The horses were running again.

The next time they stopped, everyone dismounted. The riders led their horses through a cleft in a tumble of rocks and into a maze of steep ravines, some barely wide enough to allow their passage. When they emerged back into open country, they continued to follow a trail Stormer couldn't see.

Stormer followed Bard on foot. The Ostarans had left him unbound. That and Ellen's presence reassured him. He felt no urge to escape, and anyway, where would he go? He was lost. He didn't even know where the Claymon camp was any longer, not that he wanted to go back there. He could probably make his way downhill, back to the plain, and follow one of the many paths that led to Ostara, but it would have been madness to do that.

Behind Stormer, Ellen led two horses. The second rider had stayed behind at the cleft in the rock to watch for pursuers. Stormer was beginning to understand why the raiders had been so successful in outmaneuvering Peter Greystone, whose military actions were always bold rather than subtle.

Stormer glanced over his shoulder. Lady Ellen was lost in thought. She might even have forgotten his presence. He wondered how much farther they had to go and how much longer he could keep walking. He had not eaten anything the night before or that morning, and resisting Honorus's spell had taken the last of his strength.

When he stumbled, Ellen woke from her musings and whistled for Bard's attention. He helped Stormer back onto the horse and resumed leading it along at the same unhurried pace. With the sun on his shoulders and the beast's swaying walk, Stormer soon dropped into a half-doze.

Keeping one hand wrapped in the horse's mane and the other on the edge of the simple saddle, he once again was on his own pony, riding home from his family's pastureland. He saw his mother's house in the distance, with grass and flowers growing on the low sod roof. Smoke rose from the chimney and his mouth watered. She would be waiting for his return with a pot of soup bubbling over her cooking fire. He could almost smell the cooked meat and the edible bulbs that grew on the steppes.

Ellen shook his arm. Stormer left his dream behind and blinked, trying to understand what she was saying.

"We are almost there."

In a moment Stormer was alert, his daydream forgotten. Ellen's calm, friendly voice was reassuring, but as far as he knew, he would be the first Claymon soldier ever to enter this camp. The rebels had never taken prisoners, as far as he knew. Stormer still did not understand why they were bringing him here. They should have blindfolded him, at least.

Stormer wondered why Ellen had not yet asked him anything about the Claymon. After all, she was the one who suggested making him a spy in the first place. She had been walking a few paces behind him ever since they passed into rebel territory. Stormer was afraid he soon would have to make a formal report to her and maybe to others, too. Her husband, Devon, had become a legend among the Claymon. Stormer had learned so little in his short time as a spy. They would be disappointed. He swallowed and wished he could have a drink of water.

"How did you know I needed help?" he asked.

She smiled. "Your friends. Jasper sent word that you were with the Claymon, and he told us what he understood of your plight." She chuckled, "He told us how he helped you take revenge on Honorus."

Bard must have been listening. He called back, "I'd have liked to be there to see that."

Ellen continued, "From the time you started your descent to the plain, Lightning has been watching your progress. He told us where you camped last night, and we made our plans."

"Lightning?"

"Yes. That hawk seems to think keeping you safe is his special project."

"But the bear and the hawk didn't know Honorus was planning to kill me," Stormer said.

"Are you sure about that? After what happened back in Brethren, Lightning was sure it could end no other way," Ellen said. "There is more to you than I guessed. We were lucky all the Claymon were so focused on what Honorus was doing to you when we attacked."

"Yes, lucky," Stormer said. He was thinking that if they had come five minutes later he would not be here talking to her.

Ellen reached up and squeezed his arm. "Don't worry," she said.

The rebel camp was a tidy circle of small tents, much smaller than Stormer expected. It looked as if it had been there for many months, though the Claymon had believed the rebels must be moving from place to place or hiding higher up on the mountainside in caves. There was a lively fire inside a circle of stones, with logs pulled next to it for sitting. The rebels had been there long enough to wear tracks into the grass between the fire and the tents. Few people were in sight.

The fire burned cleanly. There was almost no smoke, and Stormer breathed deeply to calm himself. No matter what happened to him in this camp, he could never go back to the Claymon. Never mind that he'd been kidnapped. Even without Honorus's death sentence, Stormer would be considered a traitor or a deserter, and from now on, the order would be to kill him on sight.

He guessed that meant he had well and truly gone over to the other side. He waited for the guilt he ought to be feeling to set in. When it didn't rise, he wondered, *What is wrong with me?* The decision he made back in Brethren, to become a spy for Katherine's sake, had led him here. Now he was neither Claymon nor spy, and he wouldn't ever be going home again.

Stormer caught a whiff of something. It smelled delicious, and he saw a pot bubbling over the fire. When he tried to dismount, he almost fell, but Bard was ready and steadied him. Ellen led him close to the fire, made him sit on the log, and gave him a bowl of thick stew. It was the meal from his daydream and more food than he had seen in days.

"After you have eaten, you will tell us what you have learned," she said. She ducked inside a slightly larger tent that had a colorful banner covering its door. There were still two or three people lingering near the fire. They smiled but didn't speak to him.

With his eyes fixed on shreds of meat swimming in broth, Stormer forced away his worry. There would be time enough for that later. If they were feeding him, they must plan to let him keep living – at least for now.

24

STONE WALLS

PATRICK LEANED AGAINST WHAT was left of the wall around the tower. It was as if he were standing in a small boat riding on an ocean of treetops, but instead of waves, green leaves ruffled in the lively breeze. He gazed out over the forest, but he didn't see it. He didn't even hear when the birds started to return to their nests and sing their evening songs. His attention was all inward.

This tower was his father's folly, tacked onto one corner of the family home, and the house itself was the oldest in Pallas. Built almost entirely of stone, its walls and the tower had survived the years of abandonment. Patrick had been climbing up here early in the morning and just before dark every day since his return to the city.

Of course, he did not spend all his time up here. During the days, he hunted with Patch or helped the people in the work of repairing the homes they had chosen near the aqueduct gate.

The two houses were large enough to hold everyone, for now. They had already carried away the debris that had settled inside over so many years. The metal parts of their old picks and shovels had rusted away, and their wooden barrows had decayed, so they sharpened digging sticks and wove rough baskets. As a result, they now slept within walls once again. The houses' stone floors were well-crafted, even beautiful, but they were harder than the dirt floor of the cave on Niue. For the time being, heaps of pine boughs sufficed as mattresses.

Besides the work of clearing the rooms, they had almost finished making temporary roofs. These would not keep out spiders, snakes, or even a hard rain, but the interlaced branches were a start. Every day, the teenagers scoured the city for anything that had survived from the past and could be used again – planks, pieces of canvas protected from the elements in cupboards or chests, even pieces of interior walls or roof beams that had only partly rotted away.

Patrick had expected the people's optimism to fade quickly after their return to Pallas, but they continued to tackle each task with determination – even with cheerfulness. They were still frail, but with each day they regained more of the strength Honorus stole from them. Their faces were coming alive in a way they never did under Niue's sun.

When Marios caught Patrick inspecting one of the roofs they had cobbled together, he assured him they would be replaced as soon as proper tools were available. That wouldn't happen until trading was reestablished with other cities. Patrick thought, but did not say, he wanted to postpone contact with the rest of the world as long as possible.

A nightingale's call finally distracted him from his thoughts. It sounded as if it was singing from the very top of the big sycamore tree in the park across the street from his house. For a moment, the sweetness of the song brought him back into the present, but soon he turned back to shifting the pieces of the puzzle in which he found himself. He kept looking for a solution even though he was almost certain there wasn't one.

For the refugees, it was as if the pent-up energy of generations had all been loosed at one time. A short time earlier, after Patrick left them that afternoon, the new council had met again to discuss how they could divide the houses to create some privacy for families beginning new lives. Before he walked away, Anna told him one of the young women was pregnant.

"Don't you see," she said, when she saw his shocked face, "This means we really are free. From now on we can choose to live in mourning for all we have lost, or we can turn towards the future."

Patrick wondered whether she was only talking about the decision the refugees had to make. She might as well have been talking about him. He did not ask her, but he wondered whether Anna knew Honorus would be coming soon and that when he did, he would try to rule Pallas.

He did not know much about Anna except that her husband was dead. She must have had other friends and family who died during the years of exile, but he didn't ask her about them. No one talked about that. Not yet.

It took all their efforts to make just the two houses habitable, but that was only one of the reasons the people had chosen to stay together. Sometimes Patrick thought he heard voices from the old days echoing up and down the empty streets. The refugees who had returned to Pallas numbered forty-eight. During their exile on Niue, they had lived together in one small cave. It would have seemed strange to separate now to live in isolation, surrounded by the ghosts of their lost families and neighbors. Better to stay close to the living people they knew so well. Too, the wild dogs yipped and sang nearly every night. Even though their voices rose from the forest beyond the walls of Pallas, they gave the people another reason to stay close to one another.

A flock of small birds swirled close enough to ruffle Patrick's hair. They were small, brown and silent. He guessed he had been standing still so long they thought he was another tree.

The tower was not so high. Patrick might even survive a fall from the top. It was, however, the highest place in the city, and whenever he was not here, watching over the forest to the North, he felt uneasy. Spring was far advanced. When the invaders came, he wouldn't be able to see them through the leaves. He knew spending so many hours up here didn't make sense, but he couldn't seem to help himself.

Before they parted, after the mountains, Ellen gave him advice. She told him he had to get to know the people, to talk with them and to linger by their fires. He was trying. He now knew every name, and he had figured out who each of them used to be, back when Pallas was a living city. He worked next to them and shared their meals. He never asked whether any of them threw stones at his parents' windows that last winter in Pallas – before they left for their exile.

Nevertheless, he chose not to live with them in the houses by the gate. Each night, Patrick made his bed inside the hearth at the end of the great hall of his father's house. The room was open to the sky, but the fireplace was deep and dry, its chimney blocked by swallows' nests. That meant he was the only resident of Pallas with a roof that kept out the rain.

Each night, as he lay in the darkness, Patrick pictured the city as it was in his boyhood, and he tried to remember who he was before he went into battle and was nearly killed – before his long captivity in the cave behind the waterfall. He failed every time.

Twice, Patrick spoke with Marios about the fear that tainted his return to Pallas and made it impossible for him to fully share in the refugees' happiness. Honorus would return. Every day that certainty grew. Back in Brethren, his brother had survived the battle on the beach, and now he was stronger than ever.

"We have to prepare," Patrick said. "He's coming, and when he does, he'll be bringing soldiers with him."

"What can we do?" Marios asked, shrugging his shoulders.

"I don't know, but we have to be ready."

Marios laid his hand on Patrick's shoulder as if he were still the young boy who visited his bakery. "The joy of this homecoming must not be ruined by worry about the future."

When Patrick did not answer, Marios continued, "I will think on it and talk to the other council members. Together we will find a way."

Many days had passed since that conversation. Marios seemed to have forgotten about it, and Patrick still had no solution to the puzzle.

One of the sparrows landed on the wall next to his hand and tilted its head. Patrick was too lost in thought to notice.

The Woods Runners still made their homes in the forest. In his youth, Patrick had friends among those people. They helped him to find the right kind of tree for whatever he was making. He even visited one or two of their homes – snug, portable shelters they carried from clearing to clearing. In winter, those homes would be much warmer than the stone houses of Pallas, but he had decided not to ask the Woods Runners for help. They had problems of their own.

The only Runner who had returned to the city was Patchson. He lingered close to Pallas, hunting for the People and then retreating back into the trees. Although the young Woods Runner never said so, Patrick thought he stayed because he was continuing the tradition of watching over the one they called the Hero.

When Patrick asked Patchson whether there were other Woods Runners in the forest, he replied, "Some, but we are scattered. Nearly all the men still serve the Claymon. Even their wives don't know where they are."

The people of Pallas had a long relationship with the Woods Runners, but the People no longer had anything to trade. The council had not asked Patchson whether the Runners had deer hides to spare for their beds. The people did not want to start their new lives by asking for charity, but when the rains of fall arrived, if nothing had changed, they'd have to.

Although they never talked about it, Patrick knew Patchson must be worried about his father. There had been no word since Patch left Brethren to follow Katherine's trail. This wasn't unusual. Patch must have left his family for longer periods when Patchson was a boy. The Woods Runner families spent the cold months together, but during the summers the men roamed the forest.

Even so, Patch was an old man, and while he tracked Katherine, he was in turn being tracked by others. He had not seen his wife in more than a year. As far as Patrick knew, Maron was still taking care of Bethany's farm. What would the Woods Woman do when she learned Bethany wasn't ever coming back?

As Patrick stayed on the tower, wasting his time thinking about all the things he couldn't control, he avoided certain questions as long as he could. Was Katherine still alive? Had she been captured by the Claymon and taken back to Ostara?

This was why Patrick returned to the tower day after day. It's where he brought all his worries. It was too bad he couldn't leave them there.

The sparrow was joined by another. One of them hopped forward and pecked the back of his hand. Startled, he swung his arm and the birds flew away, but they didn't go far. His eyes followed their flight to the ancient sycamore in the park.

The light was failing. Patrick made his careful way down the stone steps and into what had once been the great hall of his family home.

The people of Ostara had trusted him to lead them home, but now that they had reclaimed Pallas, they had started to care for him in addition to all their other work. When they found out he intended to live in his family home, he found the hearth padded with what remained of last year's dry grasses, gathered from along the streets. When he protested, telling them to keep the material for themselves, they said there was not enough for all of them. They had already made beds for the old people, and later they could gather more.

If he did not turn up for breakfast, they sent the children to look for him. The young ones in their ash colored clothes stood in a row in front of the hearth and stared at him with their old eyes until he woke up. They wouldn't leave until he took a small hand and allowed himself to be led to where a meal was waiting. It was always the same meal, some kind of meat in a watery broth with whatever greens could be gathered in the forest. One day, with trade, variety would come, but for now no one was going hungry.

Patrick no longer thought of the children as old souls in young bodies. They threw themselves into every task their elders asked of them, but they also had started to skip and chase after one another. They climbed trees and the framework of the buildings.

Soon after they arrived in Pallas, one of the boys fell and broke an arm. Anna, who seemed to know how to do everything, set the break, but she did not tell him to stop climbing.

Now the wind whistled through the empty windows of his house. The currents sounded something like water, and it occurred to him that lying on his back in the deep hearth was not so different from lying on the stone bier in the cave behind the waterfall. Except now he could not seem to sleep.

An owl hooted from far away, and another answered. Patrick knew owl voices are deceptive. They might sound far away but be very close. He wouldn't have been surprised to be sharing this house with an owl. The floors of the rooms were as likely a hunting ground for mice as the forest floor.

When he heard a sound in the night that was not the wind or a great horned owl, Patrick rolled to his side and peered out into the darkness. There was just enough moonlight to see that the hall was deserted. The cry had sounded like one of the wild dogs, but it was close. He waited for it to come again. He had been using his cloak as a blanket, so he pulled it around his shoulders and took hold of the hilt of his sword, which was nested beside him in the grass. It didn't glow as it would have if an enemy was near, but he took Mabus with him anyway as he crossed the room to the door.

Until Patrick's return, his mother's old-fashioned roses had barred the main entrance. He had battled the thorns for a full day and paid in blood. Now the way was clear, so he followed the path to its end, where the shape of the sycamore tree loomed over the park across the street. He was not certain, but he thought someone was standing there.

Patrick walked part-way into the street and called, "Who is there? Patchson?" He thought the people must need him, but in that case, why didn't they come to him in the hall?

No one answered, and Mabus's hilt still felt cool in his hand, so Patrick crossed the street and entered the wilderness of the park. Once, this place had its own gardener, and the boys of the town gathered under the branches for their lessons. The sycamore was old even then. Now it was truly ancient.

The person, whoever it was, must have retreated deeper under the tree. The sweep of branches created a room larger than the great hall of the Steele mansion. If someone was hiding there, Patrick wouldn't find them unless they wanted to be found.

When he reached the outermost branches of the tree, where they almost touched the ground, Patrick called again. "Name yourself! What do you want?"

There was enough moonlight filtering through the branches to see a dark shape. Patrick thought it was a man, but there wasn't enough moonlight to illuminate his face. He wasn't wearing a hood, and he had his hand on the head of a large wolf.

"Don't be afraid."

The man had not said anything. It was the animal, and Patrick knew him. It was Lupe, one of the guardians of Pallas. This wolf had sired most of the wild dogs hereabouts, but as far as Patrick knew, none of his offspring were talking animals. Not even Rowan, the pup Kathe had adopted.

Patrick did not bother to tell Lupe he was not afraid of anything – except that Honorus would return before he had a plan.

"That is what he means," the man said. "You do not have to fear your brother's return. You aren't alone."

As soon as Patrick heard the voice, he knew who this was. More than his master, this man became his father after he left home. He taught him how to work with wood. He gave him his sword and showed him how to use it. The last time Patrick saw Leonides he was standing in the doorway of his shop. That was the day Patrick marched out with the city's militia to meet the Ostarans.

There should be someone else with him. Patrick peered deeper into the moon lit shadows.

"She is not here," said Leonides. "You still think you should have died in the battle, and you blame her for saving you."

Patrick did not have to ask who Leonides was talking about.

"Is she afraid to face me?" Patrick said.

Leonides laughed, "No, but she doesn't want to waste time talking about such things. This is where you are needed. When you understand why she saved you and you are ready to move forward, she will come."

"I already understand, and I have moved forward. All the way across the mountains and back again. I have brought the People home," Patrick said.

"Yes, you have done that, but even when you fought Honorus in Brethren, you continued to doubt yourself." Leonides paused and continued more gently. "The birds have told us how you stand on the tower, staring off over the trees."

"What else should I be doing?" Patrick said. "It is up to me to protect the People."

"Why do you think you are alone?" Leonides was impatient, as he was when Patrick was a boy, and sensed he was not listening. "Did you even notice the birds? They can tell you if danger is coming. You are spending too much time locked inside your own mind. Why haven't you called the animal guides?"

Leonides was right, but Patrick was not ready to admit it. The last time he spoke with one of the guides, he was still with Ellen, and it was the hawk, bringing a report from Abel.

"When have the animals ever hesitated to speak?" he said. "Why should I have to call them? Anyway, they can't help us."

"Are you sure about that?" Leonides said. "You are no longer a child, or even the young man who marched out from Pallas, but before you face your brother, you have to remember. Who were you before you were wounded? What have you learned since you awakened?"

Patrick knew Leonides wasn't just talking about the injuries from the battle now.

"Katherine woke you, but the tide that is pulling you back to sleep is still strong. For every step forward, you drift three into the past. There is nothing there for you," Leonides said.

"There is nothing here for me either, and you're wrong about sleep," Patrick said. His voice was bleak. "I long for just one dreamless night. I only bested Honorus back in Brethren because a dragon turned up. Honorus almost killed me. He is far stronger than me now. Did you know that?"

Leonides didn't answer.

Patrick went on, "I did not lose anyone on the journey over the mountains, but many of the people will die when Honorus gets here. This time they won't give up their freedom without a fight."

A second figure stepped forward out of the shadows and held out his hand. "It isn't just up to you," Marios said. "The council is making a plan. It is time for you to join our meetings."

Leonides said, "From now on you will find me in my old house whenever you want to talk to me. It is time for my hands to remember the shapes of my wood-working tools. The people need the things I can make. That is where I'll be until the danger has passed, and after that I intend to stay in Pallas and resume my old trade. Who knows? Maybe I'll even take a wife."

Patrick heard a smile in his voice.

Marios released Patrick's hand and disappeared into the shadows, heading uphill towards the water gate. Leonides gave Patrick an odd, formal salute and turned downhill in the direction of his workshop.

Only Lupe remained.

"You never have said very much," Patrick said. *"But maybe it's because I haven't been listening."*

A voice purred from the branches overhead. *"At least you are able to hear us if you try. What you need is practice. I will live here until you get rid of your deaf brother, and while we are waiting for him, I will tell you the story of my people."*

A black form dropped from the tree with a soft thud. Patrick managed not to flinch. He knew this panther well. And if he was honest with himself, he also knew why he had not tried to enlist the animal guides. They were the Lady's messengers, and he was still angry with her. This was why, in all his hours of thinking and worrying on top of the tower, he never thought of the many times they had helped him and his friends. At least, they tried to help.

"We honor the Lady, but we belong to ourselves," Maraba said.

The owl hooted again and dropped down onto a low branch of the Sycamore.

"Oro?" Patrick said.

"Good guess. It's Bijou. I'm Oro's Mate." She preened her feathers. *"When Leonides called this meeting, it was Oro's turn to feed our owlets. They are nearly ready to fly, and they are always so very hungry. I wasn't about to do it for him."*

"Greetings, Bijou." Patrick said. The night was growing brighter. It must be the rising moon.

"Oro and I will be nearby, and we will do what we can."

Clearly, this was the message she had come to deliver, but now that she had done so, Bijou seemed in no hurry to leave. She settled herself on the limb, and her head swiveled from side to side. Even though she was off duty, it seemed she could not keep herself from watching for mice in the leaf litter.

"Did he tell you there are three owlets? All big and healthy! They look just like me, but they have Oro's eyes." Bijou's own round eyes reflected gold in the moonlight. *"It is too soon to know if any of them will be able to talk, but we are watching for the signs."*

Patrick listened politely. Maraba and Lupe settled on their haunches as if this might be a long story.

"Oro and I never talk to each other around our owlets," she said, as if this was simply an example of good owl parenting. *"After they fly, we'll watch them, and if they show an interest in roosting near people or if they start to sing nonsense to themselves, we'll know."*

Patrick found he was curious about something that had never crossed his mind before, and it had nothing to do with the coming troubles. Leonides would have seen this as a good sign.

"Do you want them to be guides like you and Òro?"

"It doesn't matter what we want. They will be who they are. Still, we will be happy if one of them carries on the family tradition."

"No matter what, they will all be able to fly at night and to hunt with hardly any light. I have often envied the senses of owls," said Patrick.

He seemed to have said the right thing. Bijou preened herself again. *"Of course, we will love them all equally, no matter who they end up being. Who. Who. I guess that is a kind of joke."*

"How many owlets have you raised, in all, and of them, how many have had the gift?" he asked, chuckling politely.

She had to think. *"More than thirty, I'd say. Oro and I have been together a long time. Many birds stay with the same mate, and Oro and I are more faithful than most. And the answer to your other question is three."*

Three out of thirty. *"So, it is very rare,"* Patrick said.

"Yes. Well, I have enjoyed my little break from feeding this year's hatch. This meeting has been most stimulating. I will talk with Oro about sharing the duties more evenly so I can participate in events when they begin. It will all be so exciting."

She flew silently away over the Steele mansion and the forest beyond, a silhouette against the starlight.

Lupe spoke for the second time that night. *"I have told my children to stay in the forest now that the humans have returned to the city. They will obey. They will not harm you."*

The last time Patrick was in Pallas was a few days after he left the cave behind the waterfall. He might have died if Katherine and Meg had not found his sword buried in the chapel in Leonides's house. While he went to see what was left of his family's home, Meg and Katherine explored the city. When a pack of wild dogs attacked them, Meg escaped, but Katherine was badly bitten on her forearm. She would always bear the scar. If Gale had not returned and killed two of the dogs, she would probably have died that day. That wasn't quite right, Patrick remembered. Lupe was there too, and he was the one who called off the attack.

"They are not talking animals." Patrick said.

"No, but they are my children, and in time, some of them will sleep by your fires again."

Lupe continued to look up at him. He was waiting.

Patrick said, *"They are not our enemies. We will not hurt them."* Tomorrow he would talk to the council and make them understand that the wild dogs were not to be harmed.

That was the assurance Lupe needed. He slipped into the darkness.

"Well, shall we?" said Maraba.

That is when Patrick knew that, when Maraba said she would stay with him, she didn't just mean in the city, but in his house. The gaping roof and missing windows must have created this possibility, for she was no house cat. She trotted ahead of him up the path, through the front door, and settled herself in the hearth on one corner of the grasses the people had gathered for him.

Patrick pulled the rest of his makeshift mattress out of the fireplace. It wasn't going to rain tonight. He laid his sword by his side and settled under the sky to watch the movement of the stars.

She began, *"In the beginning the first panther was white. She was made from a cloud and played in the sky..."*

Patrick slept.

25

FIRE IN THE MOUNTAIN

GALE RETRIEVED THE WATER bags from the riverbank, slung them over his shoulder and carried the mutton upstream in his arms until he found a section where the river mazed through tumbled boulders. As the water rushed through the rocks, it threw up clouds of spray, but he thought he would be able to jump from one to the next. If he fell in, well, best not to think about that. It seemed like a better idea than trying to swim a second time. He knew he was lucky not to have drowned during his first crossing.

He watched the river for a few minutes. It looked powerful, and he already knew it was cold. Then, before he lost his nerve, he took off his shirt and tied the sleeves together to make it into a makeshift bag. He put the mutton inside and slung the bundle over one shoulder with the straps of the empty water bags over the other. He swung his arms and took a few practice jumps to see how the uneven weight would affect his balance.

As he started across, Gale looked only for the next boulder, not at the width of the whole river. He used to do this kind of thing for fun when he was a boy in Springvale, but now his life might depend on his agility. Back then, he was always ready to race, jump, climb, and balance when his friends challenged him.

The third rock wobbled. Gale almost fell, and he did a kind of dance as he struggled to regain his balance. The next gap was wider, but the boulder he aimed to reach was large and flat. He would have to jump up to reach it, and the top would be slippery.

He made it, barely, but the momentum carried him forward two steps. He had to make the next jump before he was ready, and he fell to his knees with one leg dangling into the water. He risked a look ahead. Three more rocks, and he'd be on the bank.

On his final leap, he landed in water up to his waist and groped for roots dangling along the bank while the current dragged at him, pulling him downstream into the rocks.

He caught one and used it to pull himself closer to the bank, where he grabbed a larger one. He still had the mutton. He could feel it pushing against his side, still secure in his shirt. It was all he could do to climb the slippery bank with the heavy meat dragging at him. One of the sleeves tore loose before he reached the top.

Back on the wild side of the river, Gale found a low place to fill the water bags. Then he crawled to the top of the bank again and fell onto his side among the white flowers. He wanted to stay there. The sun was warm, and the fragrance even sweeter now that he was lying on a level with the plants, but he had been gone too long. Padraik needed meat. Gale followed the river until he found the trail of crushed grasses that would lead him back to Meg and Padraik.

Padraik had been warming himself while Gale was away. He was sitting on his haunches and staring across the valley in the direction of the smoking mountain. The dragon did not say anything as Gale approached, and Gale reminded himself Padraik and Meg still did not know whether this was just an ordinary volcano. He could'nt wait to see their faces when he told them his news.

Meg had finished organizing the gear, and Gale could see she had started to make some snares from sticks and ropes, but right now she lay fast asleep in the grass. She didn't stir when Gale came close.

The improvised water hole was empty, but he did not know whether Padraik had drunk the water or if had drained away into the soil. He decided not to refill it right away. There were remnants of soggy travel cakes in the bottom.

"Welcome back, Gale," Gale said sarcastically. "You were gone a long time. We were starting to worry."

Meg sat up with a start and stared at him.

"So much for staying behind to keep him safe from the locals," Gale said, grinning and nodding towards the dragon.

"You were gone a long time," Meg said. "I watched for you. I guess I must have fallen asleep."

"I don't blame you, after what we've been through," Gale said. "But it was worth it. Crossing the river, I mean."

"Padraik, listen." Gale still spoke too loudly when he had something to tell the dragon.

Padraik shifted around until he was facing Meg and Gale. His scales still looked dry and dull, and his neck sagged wearily.

"First, this should help," Gale said, unwrapping the mutton flap. *"It isn't fresh, it's salty, and you haven't had this kind before, but I promise you'll like it better than travel cakes."*

He did not keep any of the meat back for himself or Meg. Padraik would need every bit.

Padraik would not be able to think about anything else until he finished eating the mutton, but the meat disappeared quickly. When nothing was left but bones, Padraik sighed with satisfaction. If a dragon can smack its lips, that is what he did. The mutton flap was equal to perhaps two large fish, so he was still hungry. Gale filled the hole with fresh water, and Padraik drained it.

"If you want more, you'll have to cross the river yourself," Gale said. *"The mutton should keep you alive until we can trap something else for you."*

"Mutton. Is that what you call it?" Padraik said. *"What a beautiful word!"*

"Where did you go?" Meg asked. "I can't wait any longer to hear what happened. You look half drowned."

Gale's hair lay wet and tangled over his shoulders. He had untied the knotted sleeves of his shirt and put it on while Patrick was eating, but it was torn, and covered in mud from the riverbank.

"I nearly drowned." Gale told the story from the beginning, starting with being swept off his feet by the river and crossing the pasture to the shelter. He had the feeling this was a story he would tell again and again, assuming he survived and returned to Springvale.

Gale kept his eyes glued to Padraik's face, and although he was certain he had the dragon's complete attention, he was disappointed Padraik didn't show more surprise when he came to the part where he described the pictures he and Brit drew in the dirt. His eyes might have brightened a little, but Gale couldn't even be sure of that.

After he finished, Meg jumped up and gave him a hug that almost knocked him off his feet. "Who knows how long it might have taken us to learn all this! And look. Padraik is already stronger!"

Gale wasn't sure he saw the change she was seeing in the dragon, but he hugged her back.

"Tell me again about the pictures the boy made," she said, more quietly.

After Gale repeated that part of the story, she said. "That's what I thought. It sounds as if the people here are trying to kill their dragon, and we still don't know whether it is a male or a female."

"Hey," Gale said, in protest. "I think I did pretty well for a first try."

"Yes, you did," Meg said, "but how are they going to react when a second dragon moves in, assuming they like each other, and Padraik decides he wants to stay.

"I have already decided. I am not going to stay here no matter how much mutton you give me," Padraik interrupted.

Meg and Gale stared at him.

"What do you mean you aren't going to stay?" Meg said. *"Getting to this valley almost killed you. We aren't likely to find another dragon."*

"I mean she is going to come home with me. I'm not going to always be killing people just because they want to fight me. I want to go back where it is always warm and there are plenty of fish to eat. And that's where it will be safe for our eggs."

"You are getting ahead of yourself, aren't you?" Meg said. *"You haven't even met her yet. She might even be a he. Anyway, maybe she likes this place as much as you like Niue."*

"She is a she." Padraik said.

"How do you know?"

"I just do," he said, sniffing the air. Meg doubted he knew anything of the sort, but there was no point in arguing with him.

She picked up the snares and headed off towards the river to set them. After a moment, Gale retrieved his bow and arrows from their gear and followed her.

"We'll be back soon," he told Padraik.

"Hey," he called. "Have you ever set a snare?"

Meg stopped and waited for him to catch up. He could tell from her face that she was still frustrated with Padraik, but she said, "I've watched you do it often enough, but I haven't seen any animals around here, have you?"

"Just the sheep on the other side of the river and a few birds, but there are trails and tracks on our side. It looks like wild sheep come down from the mountains, and there may be deer. We won't catch those with a snare, though."

Meg closed her eyes and listened. "I don't think there are any talking animals here. Except him, that is," she said, pointing back to where Padraik still sat like a statue. "So, I guess you can shoot a goat if you see one."

She pulled a travel cake from her pocket and handed it to him. "I saved this for you."

"It's the last one?"

She didn't bother to answer but bent to set one of the snares on a faint trail in the grass. "This isn't going to work, is it?"

"It hardly ever does," he admitted.

"What do you think we should do?" Meg asked.

The news Gale had brought, that there was a dragon here, was exciting, but a whole new set of problems had arisen, made worse by Padraik's announcement that he was going to go back to Niue and would be taking a lady dragon with him.

"She might not be a lady," Gale said.

"She might not be a talking dragon."

"There's only one way to find out," Gale said.

Meg knew what he meant. She had already thought of it. There was no time for a lengthy courtship. She would have to play matchmaker for the unlikely pair. The dragon in this valley would not know how to speak with humans. "I don't know if I can go through that again," she said, remembering her first encounter with Padraik. Images from that conversation were scorched into her mind. She still saw them sometimes when she was dreaming.

Gale took her hand. They stood together, gazing toward the volcano, but before they could begin to plan, he pulled away. In in a smooth motion, he sent an arrow flying towards the riverbank and ran.

When she caught up with him, he was standing over a creature that looked something like a deer, but it had two twisted, goat-like horns. It was still twitching. Gale drew his knife and plunged it into the animal's heart, finishing it off.

"What is it?" she said.

"Supper," Gale said. "And another piece of good luck."

Even though there was a risk someone might see the smoke, Meg built a small fire, Gale gutted and skinned the goat-deer, skewered pieces of meat, and quickly cooked them over the flames. It might have just been that they were so hungry, but they thought it was better than any meat they had ever tasted. Padraik ate his share raw, and he told them it was inferior to fish or salted mutton.

"I know you are trying your best," he said grudgingly. *"Tomorrow I will be strong enough to hunt for myself."*

"I'm not sure that's such a good idea," Gale said, picturing Padraik swooping down on Brit's flock and flying away with a sheep.

After Gale killed the animal, while he and Meg were carrying it slung between them back to the campsite, the two of them had started to make a plan. It grew out of the knowledge that they would not be able to hide Padraik for long and that there was nothing to be gained by waiting. Now that they had eaten, it was time to tell him.

Meg stood in front of Padraik. She put one hand on each side of his snout and made him look at her. That wasn't necessary when speaking mind to mind, but she believed he was sensitive to her touch, especially on his nose, and she wanted to make sure he was listening.

She said, *"We will sleep, and before morning you will fly again."* She glanced at the sky. *"There will be a moon tonight, and the fire in the mountain will guide us. Then we will see what we can do."*

Padraik hadn't interrupted. That was a good sign.

"The people here have attacked her. She will be angry and afraid. She may not be willing to talk to us," she continued. Somehow, she had taken on Padraik's certainty that they were soon to meet a lady dragon.

Now that the first step of the plan had been spoken, Meg sensed something new from Padraik.

"What if she doesn't like me?"

Meg took a step back. He was the only dragon she had ever met, so she did not know whether he was a big one or a small one. When he was happy and well fed, his scales shimmered. She thought he was beautiful, but there might be other dragons whose colors were more dazzling. Padraik could roar and breathe fire if he had to, but he didn't make a habit of it. He was stubborn and selfish, generous and strong. Most of all, he was brave.

"Why wouldn't she?" Meg said.

Now that the decision had been made, sleep was elusive. The three of them lay on their backs on the grass and stared up at the stars. Every so often one of them spoke.

"If only we had a gift for her."

"She might not understand us."

"What if she likes you, but you don't like her?"

When Padraik woke Meg and Gale, it took a few minutes for them to realize where they were. They had both fallen asleep towards midnight, and Gale was having a dream in which he was trying to cross the river again on the boulders, but he never could reach the other side. There was always one more tricky leap he had to make. He wanted to find Brit. He was going to ask the boy for a second piece of mutton so they would have a gift for the lady dragon.

In her dream, Meg was all alone in front of the gaping entrance of a cave. The red glow of the volcano illuminated the ledge where she stood, but it was so black inside the dragon's lair that it looked as if the opening had been painted on the rock.

"It is time," Padraik said, *"and I just remembered. Before we left my island, you told me I could bring one thing from my hoard, as long as it was very light and very small."*

Meg had forgotten. Even though she knew it was hard for Padraik to leave his hoard, she refused his request the first time he asked. She thought everything in the packs had to be useful. It would be hard enough for Padraik to carry her, Gale and the things they would need to keep them alive. She relented when he showed her what he wanted to bring. She had not seen it since that day. Maybe it had been lost along the way.

"I remember," she said.

Meg went to the pile of gear and pulled out the bags. The first one she opened was completely empty. The second still held some mittens and hats they wore when they were flying. There, in a corner at the bottom, she felt something small and hard. She held up a delicate, round shell. It glowed as white as the moon and just fit in the palm of her hand.

"I don't know anything about dragon courtship," she said, staring down at the shell.

"Neither do I," said Padraik.

"Do you still want me to be there?"

When they first met, back on the island of Niue, Meg was the only one who could understand Padraik. That made her precious to him. It is what saved her life and led to the bargain they had made – the same bargain that had carried them across the mountains and to this valley.

Since that day, Padraik had learned how to talk with humans. He had become as voluble and capricious as any of the other talking animals. It had been a long time since he filled her mind with the heat and swirling images that had left her weak and nauseous. Now that he was about to meet another of his own kind, maybe their bargain was complete.

"You will not need me. And she will wonder why people are with you."

"Now who is getting ahead of herself? How do we know if I can talk to her? I have never met another dragon, and she is a mountain dragon, not a water dragon. Until I met you, I had no one to hear my story. It may be the same for her. She might need you as much as I did. Besides. I am not ready to say goodbye to you. Not yet."

Meg slipped the shell into the pouch at her waist. She started to lay out the harness while Gale made one more trip to the river for water. She was no longer afraid of Padraik, but she tried not to think too much about the day they met. If one of the memories slipped through, it made her feel shaky and uncertain, and those emotions would not help her in the hours ahead.

They were about meet a dragon who had good reason to fear and hate people. There was a chance the lady dragon might incinerate Meg without bothering to find out who she was. Still, she was glad Padraik wanted her to be there.

She had almost finished fitting the harness on Padraik's back when Gale returned.

"Is this the last time we'll fly?" he asked.

She shrugged, not trusting her voice.

He put his arm around her shoulders. "Who knows? By bringing these two together, we may be saving the dragon race. That's worth dying for."

It would take more than one day of rest for Padraik to regain his strength after the long flight from Brethren, but he should be able to carry them to the other side of the valley. They had decided there wasn't enough time for Meg and Gale to ford the river and go by foot to meet him.

Padraik leapt into the air and headed east, straight towards the volcano. Once airborne, he flew slowly, gliding between wingbeats. The moon was about to set.

Gale would miss this. He gazed down on the shining river. He had long ago given up wondering about his role on this journey. At first he told himself he was Meg's protector, but that wasn't completely true. They kept each other safe. All that mattered was that he would be with her at the end. The closer they came to the other side of the valley, the more likely it seemed that they were flying towards that hour.

"This has been an adventure," he said. "I wouldn't have missed it for anything."

"It isn't over," she replied.

As Meg had hoped, once they left the pasture behind, they flew over wild lands again. In the darkness, they could see the glow from the volcano's broken cone. They flew towards the faint, ruddy light. It wasn't surprising no one wanted to live or pasture their beasts close to the mountain, which would have been forbidding even if it wasn't a dragon's abode. No plants grew high on the slope of the volcano, but the foothills were punctuated by patches of woodland. Moonlight reflected from small streams rushing down to meet the river. As they came closer, they saw smooth, black courses where molten rock had flowed down the slope.

They reached the mountain before dawn, with the sky barely beginning to lighten in the East. Padraik landed next to a small grove of pine trees, close to the base of the volcano. There, at the dragon's insistence, Meg and Gale removed the saddle bags and most of the ropes. By now the bags were nearly empty and weighed little, but Padraik wanted to be rid of them. When he met another dragon for the first time, he must not appear to be tame.

Meg wanted Gale to wait with the gear, but she couldn't find the words to tell him. If he stayed behind, and if she did not return, then he could make his way to the town at the end of the valley. Maybe he would find a way back to Ostara and from there to Springvale.

It cost Meg something to hold her tongue. If she asked him to stay, he would certainly refuse. She did not want their last conversation to be an argument. She reminded herself Gale had earned the right to be present. He knew he had the choice. He could wait here if he wanted to. She did not have to tell him.

Padraik leapt again and began flying back and forth close to the face of the volcano, searching for signs of a dragon. By now Meg and Gale were so used to riding on his back that the remaining rope was enough to steady them. Meg's dream was still vivid in her mind, and without consciously choosing, she focused her attention on the middle third of the mountain, looking for an oval of inky blackness.

"Take me down, please. I want to get off," she said, when Padraik had flown almost to the top of the cone. Her eyes teared and her lungs burned as they flew near the maw of the mountain. They had flown close to some big cracks in the mountainside, but they had found no opening large enough to lead to a dragon's lair. *"I can't explain it, but I think she lives nearer to the base. I'll search there while you and Gale keep flying. We must have missed something."*

Now it was Gale's turn to hold his tongue. From his expression, she could tell he thought separating was a bad idea. Padraik landed on a scree covered slope close to the base. She slid off his back, forced a smile, and held her hand up to Gale.

"Don't worry. It's because of my dream, you see."

"No, I don't see," Gale said. He held her hand too tightly.

"It is no stranger than taking guidance from a book," she said, pulling free. "If I find any sign of her, I'll wait for you."

Padraik launched himself again, and he and Gale resumed their search of the mountainside. Meg crawled and slid her way across the loose stones and began to work her way around the base of the mountain. You couldn't call it walking. She was climbing, scrambling up, and stopping often to scan the hillside around and above her.

She reminded herself that a dream is often just a dream. Still, it was the only clue she had, and it made sense to search here, away from the noxious gasses spurting from the vents in the upper slopes. She might find something they couldn't see from Padraik's back. The opening might be hidden behind one of the rock-falls or deep inside a cleft in the mountainside.

The sun was now half-way above the ridgeline. She was so intent on seeking dragon-sign and on finding her way over the stones that she did not at first notice when the way started to be a little easier. First there were fewer rocks, then almost none. She realized she was on a narrow path that sloped gradually upward, following the curve of the mountainside. Lava had flowed across the path in places and hardened to rock. Each time she came to a flow, the path continued on the other side.

She wondered what it could mean. Dragons were clever, but they were not builders. They did not make this. It must have been here before the dragon, but that did not seem likely either, considering this was a living, changing mountain.

While the cave in her dream had been so real, and its inky opening had seemed to be drawing her to it, Meg was starting to think she was wrong to have thought she would find her dreamscape. She had better call Padraik. She stopped on a smooth, flat place on the path where he should be able to land. She studied the path ahead and behind one more time before turning her attention to the sky.

That is when Meg saw the bones. She must have mistaken them for rocks and stepped right over them. She back tracked and stared down, holding her breath. Her mind went blank. She felt her blood turn to ice despite the warming morning. These bones once belonged to a sheep, and they still had some flesh between the ribs.

If she were to call Padraik, the creature who had left the carcass would surely hear her. The dragon might already know Meg was here. It probably did, in fact. Meg's heart raced. She had been a fool to think she was ready to meet a second dragon. She sat down on a rock and whispered, *"Padraik."*

When there was no answer after a few minutes, she stood and spread her arms. *"Padraik, I need you. Padraik. Padraik!"*

She kept her eyes glued to the sky until he appeared from the other side of the mountain. He was so far away and so high that he looked as small as a bird. She jumped and waved to get his attention.

She was still watching Padraik when she heard something move on the ledge behind her. Even though she knew what it must be, she forced herself to keep her eyes on Padraik. Only Padraik.

26

TIME TO CHOOSE

"MY WIFE TELLS ME you are to be trusted." Devon Elder's face revealed his doubt, and Stormer couldn't blame him. Looking at himself through the Ostaran leader's eyes, he saw only a low-ranking Claymon soldier in a filthy uniform. If it weren't for Ellen's assurance, Devon wouldn't be giving him this chance.

"She told me what our daughter did for you and how you tried to help her escape the Claymon."

This was at least the fourth time in the past week Stormer had found himself reporting to someone who usually wouldn't even have noticed him. It wasn't getting any easier. Ellen stood by her husband's side with a serene expression that completely hid whatever she was thinking. Nevertheless, Katherine's mother had a way of making Stormer feel everything would turn out right, even when he knew it couldn't.

Stormer remembered tracking Katherine across the beach on the day she swam ashore. If only he had delayed sending his partner to signal the Claymon! Everything would have been different. He was over-confident – too sure they would both reach the top of the headland and get away in time. And, if he was honest, he was still half controlled by his Claymon training that day. It had taught him to just follow orders and not to think about them too much.

Ellen said, "You were a spy for only a few days. Did you learn anything?"

Well, had he? Again, Stormer thought about all that had happened since he turned back toward Brethren after his first visit to the house with the blue door. He had found ways to stay close to Honorus and even to Greystone. He had climbed the hill and spoken with Abel, who seemed to think he was worth listening to. Stormer put up with the contempt of his fellow soldiers, and he eavesdropped on their conversations. He also had discovered he could understand the talking animals and had made two friends among their kind, the bear Jasper, and Lightning, the hawk.

Stormer straightened his back and forced himself to meet Devon Elder's eyes. The rebel leader's face was brown and windburned from living outdoors, and there were deep lines at the corners of his mouth. His expression was grim, almost scowling. He was a little shorter than Stormer, and strongly built. Stormer looked for traces of Katherine in Devon and found them in his blue eyes and red hair, though Devon's was streaked with grey. Her stubbornness might also be there. He couldn't be sure about that yet.

"Greystone is growing restless," Stormer began, in the common speech. He knew some Ostaran, but not enough to express everything that had happened. "You have trapped him in Ostara. He wants to ride South with his troops, but he fears the city will fall if he leaves. He is determined to crush you." Surely Ellen and Devon already knew all this, but so far Greystone had not turned his complete attention their way. His forces were still scattered.

He continued, "Honorus, has displeased him. There was a conflict back in Brethren. It wasn't much of a battle, but the Claymon were defeated there, well and truly, and it was mostly the magician's fault. No question about it." Stormer paused, organizing his thoughts. "Greystone was even more angry when he found out your Katherine had escaped again. That was Honorus's fault too. Yet the magician is still of use to him. I don't know whether it is because he can empty peoples' minds as easily as pouring water from a bucket, or for some other reason."

"Some people's minds," Ellen said. "Lightning told me."

Stormer was surprised. "That's right. For some reason he can't get into my head. His brother..."

"Patrick," she said.

"Yes. His brother left Brethren with the refugees. He is leading them to the forest city. Honorus plans to go there as soon as he can. He calls himself the Prince of Pallas. The refugees are few and weak. Honorus almost killed them back on the beach in Brethren. The counselor will take Claymon soldiers with him. He can't go back to the forest by himself because he has lost confidence in his powers."

"That's what you think," said Devon Elder. "You don't know that."

"You're right. But if I am guessing, it's because I am partly the cause of his doubt," Stormer said. "He has tried to read me. I was asleep the last time it happened. He must have thought his chances would be better if he came to me then. When it didn't work, he decided to punish me by making me pull a wooden sledge across the mountains." Here Stormer paused and at a nod from Ellen, he pulled open his shirt so that Devon could see the livid bruises on his shoulders. "This morning he would have killed me if you hadn't arrived when you did. Honorus wasn't about to let Peter Greystone know there is a limit to his abilities. Least of all that he found it in a nobody like me."

The wrinkle in Devon's forehead had deepened, and he was no longer looking at Stormer's face, but off into the distance.

"Greystone didn't say it to Honorus, but we know he plans to add the forest and the city of Pallas to his domain. He told Honorus he will want to trade with him once he is in charge there, but that isn't the way he works," Stormer said.

Devon said, "He will help Honorus to return to the forest. He may even let him call himself a prince, but the trees and anything else of value will belong to the Claymon."

"But before that, he will make a final push to get rid of us," Ellen said.

It would be easy for Greystone to destroy the resistance. He had held off this long because he knew that, if he pushed too hard, the Ostarans still living within the city's walls would turn against him. He knew they were waiting for their moment to rise, but it now seemed he might no longer care.

Outside the tent, the camp was quiet. They heard faint voices. A pony whinnied. Most of the rebels were on patrol or hiding in caves higher in the hills. The three people in the tent stood quietly, thinking. As when he reported to Abel, Stormer felt he was being treated as an equal. Despite Devon's doubts, the Ostaran leader had listened carefully, and he seemed to think the information in Stormer's report was important.

On the other hand, most of the information Stormer had given Devon wasn't new. There weren't any surprises, only restated truths Devon Elder must already know, but it made facing them more urgent.

Even before today, the rebels had known their position was becoming more dangerous. They did not know about Greystone's increased restlessness, but they must have guessed it. Devon had been having more and more trouble sleeping. The rebels had diverted too many supplies destined for Ostara; harried too many patrols; given the residents of the city too much reason for hope.

Devon had done what he could, and it was working. Everyone knew the Claymon in Ostara were hungry. And the Claymon must suspect Devon had been softening the embargo's effects on the Ostarans by smuggling food to them. Greystone would not allow it to continue indefinitely, and now the day had come. Greystone would gather his forces, crush the rebels, and leave a garrison in Ostara to maintain order.

"A bully like Greystone is even more dangerous when he is thwarted," Ellen said, breaking the silence. "It is time to add another voice to this conversation."

She swept aside the flag that hung over the tent door and held it open so that Stormer and Devon could follow her outside. She walked purposefully to the edge of the camp, stopping for a moment by the cooking fire where Bard was gutting a rabbit. She untied the straps of a leather gauntlet from her waist and slipped the glove over one hand. It was too big for her and reached past her elbow.

Stormer realized who was coming, so he was ready when Lightning swept down and landed on her wrist.

Devon took an involuntary step back. "I will never get used to this," he muttered.

Ellen looked at him and smiled slightly. "You can get used to anything, my dear. Think of all you have done and seen. It has not even been two years since the Claymon came, yet it seems as if we have been hiding and fighting all our lives." She stroked the feathers on Lightning's throat with her finger and offered him a bit of rabbit.

Stormer discovered he could not stop smiling.

"At least hood him," Devon said.

"This is not one of your falcons," she said. "He chooses to sit on my arm, and he prefers to be on the same level as us when he speaks, but I would no sooner hood him than I would hood Stormer."

Like Ellen, Stormer was shocked by Devon's suggestion, and his surprise must have shown on his face.

Devon said gruffly, "Don't tell me you can understand them too!"

"I don't know about understanding them, but I have met one." Stormer said.

Ellen sensed Devon's growing uneasiness and turned her attention to Lightning. Her husband would have to deal with his doubts as best he could. She spoke aloud so Devon would know what she was saying. "Welcome, Lightning. What have you come to tell us?"

There were only a few people in the camp at this time of day, but they had stopped whatever they were doing and formed a ring, staying well back as they stared at the regal-looking hawk on Ellen's arm. Stormer could see Devon was not the only one getting used to the idea of talking animals. If the Claymon had chosen to attack at that moment, they would have faced no resistance at all.

Only Ellen, Stormer and maybe Bard could understand the hawk when he described what he had seen back at the Claymon camp, where only a few hours before the drama played out that nearly ended in Stormer's death. It seemed whenever Lightning was not carrying messages, he had tracked the Claymon progress over the mountains – watching over Stormer. Stormer caught Ellen's eye, and she seemed to understand what he was thinking.

"He told us where you would be," she said. "But we didn't know we would find you in so much trouble."

"I circled the sky above the enemy. It was easy to see. There are not many trees there, so close to the open lands. After you snatched this one," Lightning said, meaning Stormer, *"you rode away on your ponies. Then no one moved until the one with the shiny clothing started to scream like a rabbit."*

They knew he meant Greystone.

"The old man stood there with his face in his hands. I saw the leader and the others who came with him from the city draw their swords. They waved them around, and they pushed everyone else aside. They didn't seem to care if they hurt someone. Greystone and his men jumped onto horses and made them run after you, but by then you were far away."

The old man was Honorus. His body was strong and young looking, but all Lightning would have been able to see was the magician's bald skull. To Devon it must look as if Ellen and the hawk were just gazing at each other, but by the way she was concentrating, he had to know there was more to it than that. She seemed to sense her husband's impatience because she broke the hawk's gaze for a moment and shook her head at her husband.

"I continued to fly above them as they rode along the edge of the plain following your trail. With so many ponies, it was easy to see which way you had gone, even from high above. After a while, they came to a place where a big horse was eating grass. The leader jumped down from the horse he was riding and pulled the big one's head up – hard."

Ellen said, aloud so that Devon could hear, "You could see his anger."

"Yes, and then they took the big horse by the rope it was trailing and led it back towards their camp."

"How far did you follow them?" Devon asked. He was tired of being a bystander to a conversation he could not hear or understand.

Ellen relayed his question to Lightning.

"I watched them until they returned to the camp. The leader said something to the men who were waiting there. Then he and those who were riding with him started toward Ostara. Soon the ones who had crossed the mountains left too, and when I was sure they were going to the city, I came here."

Ellen repeated everything the hawk had said, being careful to be exact. She glanced at Bard. He was still over by the fire, but he was staring at the hawk with wide eyes.

Devon said, "Tell him I thank him. And tell him how glad we are to have a friend in the sky." After a pause, he added, "Ask him to tell us when he sees Greystone riding out from the city again. He won't have to wait long."

Stormer had put a little distance between himself and Ellen, but he watched Lightning closely. The hawk had come to Stormer's rescue again, telling the rebels where to find him when he was in danger. Lightning couldn't have known they would come at exactly the right time, could he? On the other hand, the last time he saw the hawk, back in Brethren, he said the two of them were connected somehow. There had been no time to explain. It was simply something Lightning could feel, and Stormer could feel it too, even though he was not any closer to understanding it.

Another question was even more puzzling. Of thousands of Claymon soldiers, why was he the one to be healed by Katherine Elder, to understand animal speech, to evade the probing of Honorus – and to escape? Of all these miracles, the most surprising might be that his service to the North had ended.

Ellen was talking to him. "Lightning is going to hunt now. Come here just before darkness falls, and he will be waiting for you. You may use my gauntlet."

Stormer was too surprised to answer.

"I want to talk to you," Lightning said. *"I need to find out who you are."*

"When you figure that out, let me know," Stormer said.

Ellen gave the hawk another piece of meat. Then she held out her arm, and Stormer felt the breeze ruffle his hair as Lightning took flight. Devon had already returned to the center of the camp and was talking to his son, their heads close together. A moment later Bard handed the rabbit he had been skinning to one of the other men and walked quickly away into the woods.

"He is going to warn our people who are in the caves and to call in the patrols, or as many as he can," Ellen said. "Most Ostarans who left the city when the Claymon came were young and ready to fight, but some of their families followed them. There are old people and children. They have supplies, and they are well hidden. They will be safe." Her voice became less certain the longer she talked.

Stormer wondered why she was telling him this.

"There is little time. We have only two choices, to stand and fight here, or to choose our ground somewhere else and fight Greystone there." She fell silent, still looking off in the direction Lightning had flown.

"In the forest," Stormer guessed.

"You feel it too. It is almost as if we are being led there. Bard has gone to tell the others to come. We will gather here tonight, and then we will decide."

"How?" Stormer was used to Greystone making the decisions and relaying them down through the chain of command. In fact, back in Brethren, most of the soldiers seemed to blame their defeat on a break in that chain – on Greystone giving the counselor too much authority.

"I have told Devon everything Lightning said, and I believe he will reach the conclusion I have reached, but I'd rather he did it on his own," Ellen said. "Tonight you will repeat what you know, and I will relay the hawk's words. Then my husband will tell the people of Ostara what he thinks we should do, and they will either agree or disagree."

She looked him up and down. "You need a bath. I think Bard has an old tunic you can wear. You are a little taller, but close enough in size."

He would have to report again, this time to a gathering of all the rebels. The last of Stormer's excitement at seeing Lightning again dissipated like smoke, and he felt all the effects from the weary days of pulling the sledge and the sleepless nights spent collecting firewood. He felt himself sway on his feet.

Ellen must have seen his fatigue. She gave him a gentle push towards a path that led away from the edge of the clearing. He heard flowing water before he took ten steps. She called after him, promising to send someone with clothing. He had not worn anything except a Claymon uniform since his conscription. He stopped and looked back at her.

"There is nothing else you have to do now," she said, "You will fall asleep, but I will make sure you awaken in time."

"How do you know I won't run away?" Stormer said.

"You have a meeting with Lightning. You won't miss that. Anyway, where would you go?" she replied.

She was right, but that was not why he would stay. The rebels had saved Stormer's life. Ellen had given him food, and she and Devon had listened to him. They even treated him with something like respect. He would be afraid to talk in front of so many strangers, but he wasn't going to leave just as a new life was beginning.

Stormer left his uniform on the bank. He stepped into the stream and washed off as much grime as he could, then sank into a deep pool and let the water flow over and around his body. He ran his fingers through his hair and rubbed his scalp. When he first waded into the water, it felt too cold, but soon it was like silk, not that he had ever felt silk against his skin.

He closed his eyes and let his mind drift back again to the day he returned to Brethren and let Katherine go on to the headland alone. He wondered where she was now. And where was the commander?

His eyes flew open as he realized that Ellen and Devon, worried as they were about a Claymon attack, did not look like two people whose only daughter was lost in a forest and fleeing from the enemy. That meant they knew exactly where she was. And why wouldn't they? The animals would have carried the news to Ellen. That is why she looked so serene.

Stormer felt lighter as he made his way to the stream bank, and it wasn't just all the dirt he had washed off. He had left most of his guilt over abandoning Katherine in the pool. He stood knee deep and pictured his regrets flowing through the rocks and disappearing downstream. Katherine must be safe; there was no other explanation. Her parents had not spoken one word of blame.

He found the trousers and tunic Ellen had promised hanging on a branch a few steps from the water. He had not seen whoever brought them, and he hoped whoever it was had not seen him either.

Ellen was wrong about one thing. Stormer did not go to sleep. He put on the clean clothes. They were soft from use and warm from hanging in the sun. Then he leaned back against a tree and waited for the light to change to dusk, the hour when Lightning would land on his outstretched arm for the first time.

27

LAMBING SEASON

PATCH AND KATHERINE STAYED on Bethany's farm long enough to help Maron plant lettuce and peas. Bethany had saved the seeds from the year before, dried them, and stored them away in jars in a cupboard. It was bittersweet for Katherine to see Bethany's neat script labeling the containers. She knew she was unlikely to ever meet her teacher again. Bethany's books were still here, lined up on their high shelf, and when Katherine wasn't helping Maron on the farm, she continued to study the healing arts.

At this time of year, there were plenty of chores to do every day. Together, she and Maron cut back last year's growth from the herb plants and helped Patch to repair the fence around the pasture. Every day it grew harder to think about leaving. It was the nature of the place. It was so utterly peaceful, yet there always was something that needed to be done. It was easy to put aside the troubles that were waiting outside the hedge.

For one thing, it was lambing season. Maron didn't know much about caring for livestock. The Woods Runners relied on wild game, but between her and Katherine's instincts and Bethany's books, they managed. There were two sets of twin lambs, and one of them was very small. It might have died if Maron hadn't carried it up to the cottage. When she found it could suck on her fingers, she made a bottle from a jar and a piece of cloth and fed it milk. After that, Katherine decided to stay until she was sure the little creature would live. She and Maron shared the duty of feeding the lamb at night and whenever it cried. Katherine held the small, warm body on her lap and watched it greedily empty the bottle before gently settling it back onto a blanket in its basket next to the fire.

During that time, which seemed to stretch far into the past but amounted to only a week or so, the buds swelled on the fruit trees, the hens laid more and more eggs each day, and every night Katherine laid her tired body in the same bed Bethany had given her when she first came to the farm with Meg and Rowan, Gale and Patrick. Last winter this was her room, hers and Meg's. Now, even though it was still early spring, she slept alone with the window propped open so she could hear the rain.

Finally, one evening when the light was rosy and they had eaten another omelet with herbs and cheese, Katherine turned to Patch and said, "Do you still plan to go with me to Pallas?"

The lamb was snuggled on her lap. If Katherine had to, she would go on to the forest city on her own. The hedge had given Patch the freedom to come and go at will. Once he went away overnight, but his restlessness had dissipated. Now he was sitting on the low wall in front of the cottage, holding Maron's hand.

He didn't answer right away, but Katherine had learned to be patient when it came to the Woods Runners.

"I am content here," he said. "and Maron is happy. I have come to understand why she feels that way."

He hadn't answered her question yet, so Kathe continued to wait.

"At the same time, I have a longing to see it finished."

Katherine didn't have to ask what he meant. All his life, Patch had been one of the Runners who guarded the wounded boy, Patrick. Most of them had turned from that duty. They chose to serve the Claymon instead. As far as Patch knew, he and Patchson, were the last two still fulfilling the old promise. Even though Patrick's wounds had healed and he now walked in the world again, and even though he had now brought the refugees home, the story wasn't quite done. Katherine and Patch didn't have to hear news from the animal guides to know more trouble was on the way for the people of Pallas.

Maron gently pulled her hand away and rose to her feet. It was getting too dark to see her face, but Kathe thought she heard a smile in her voice when she said, "I know better than to ask for promises, but I will be waiting here when you return. Send a message if you have a chance. In the meantime, there will be plenty to keep me busy. Summer is coming, and the days will pass quickly."

Once the decision was made, it took little time to prepare. By the time Katherine climbed the stairs to bed that night, the packs were ready and leaning against the wall by the door. Maron had set aside far more goat cheese, nutmeats and dried fruit than they would need for the journey.

Katherine had covered the ground before, so she knew it would take less than two days to reach the city. She was looking forward to the walk in this soft season, with plenty of food and no one chasing her.

She had not spoken to any of the animal guides since Oro led her and Patch to the farm, but by now she expected the owl would have carried or sent word to her parents that she was safe, and no doubt the small animals, the birds and squirrels, would notice and spread word of their departure in the morning.

Patrick was helping three other men haul a wooden beam up the hill from the lower town. This was a real find, and it was the last one they would need, for now. Once it was in place, they could finally begin to lay the boards for a floor and restore the upper story in the larger of the two houses by the gate. Combing the city for usable wood was a daily treasure hunt. Once the people knew the wild dogs would keep their promise, the refugees allowed the children to spend their days exploring the city after their lessons. Life in Pallas was beginning to follow predictable patterns.

Nearly every day, the children returned with things that had mysteriously survived – empty bottles; cooking pots that had spent the years protected from the elements inside brick ovens; even a few small chests that hid warm blankets mice had failed to discover.

These storage chests were all made in Leonides's workshop long ago. One of them looked familiar, and Patrick turned it over to find his own mark on the bottom. They were crafted from cedar and impervious to damp and insects.

As he had promised, Leonides had moved back into his house. After he had excavated some of his tools that were buried in the accumulated debris in his workshop and had repaired and sharpened them, he invited a teenager to move in to learn the wood working trade. Patrick visited the workshop almost every morning, watching the progress as Leonides and the boy made simple furniture for the two houses. But that wasn't all his old master was doing.

Somehow, Leonides had conjured a few large pieces of vellum. Early this morning he hardly noticed when Patrick came into the workshop. He was busy drawing something. Patrick wasn't sure what it was. It looked like a map of the city, except most of the streets were missing. When Leonides noticed Patrick looking over his shoulder, he didn't try to hide his work, but he didn't explain what he was doing either.

"It's just an idea I am working on. I'll present it to the council when it's finished."

Patrick wondered whether the drawing had anything to do with the mysterious structure Leonides was building in the yard behind the workshop. It had taken shape over the past few days, and it now seemed to be complete – but only because Leonides and the boy had stopped working on it.

Patrick studied it once more through the workshop window. It was the shape of a child's snowman, but many times the size, and it was made of woven branches. It stood in the center of the yard on a simple cart Leonides had improvised using wooden wheels cut from a log and more salvaged wood.

As with the drawing, Leonides was evasive about the purpose of the twig structure, but it must be important because he had spent so much time making it when there was other important work to be done.

Ever since the night in the park, Patrick had been watching and listening for the animal guides. He still wanted to talk to the Lady one day, but he discovered he was no longer angry with her for hiding him away in the cave. He was living outside his own time, but so were all the people he led back to Pallas from Brethren, and not one of them was moping about it. If they could make a new life, then so could he.

Sharing his house with the garrulous panther helped to keep him from retreating into himself. After a few nights telling the history of her kind, Maraba had finally reached the time of her great-great-great grandparents. It was quite a story, and Patrick had come to look forward to falling asleep to the sound of her voice each night.

Since Patrick was seeing Leonides every day, and since he had started to take part in the council meetings, he didn't spend as much time on top of his tower, though he still liked to watch dawn break over the forest from above. He continued to sleep in what was left of Steele hall, because Maraba was there, but Patrick felt a part of this newly reborn community in a way he hadn't before the midnight meeting with his allies in the park.

These days he even sought out Marios and the other refugees simply because he enjoyed their company. When they first returned to Pallas, the refugees had been like ghosts of the people who once lived here. Patrick had felt little towards them except a responsibility to protect them, but that wasn't true any longer.

A stranger coming to Pallas today might not notice anything unusual about the People beyond their clothes, which were still ragged and faded to no color at all, and their eyes, which were ageless. And the visitor would wonder why they were all living together in two houses with an entire city spread out below them.

Once Patrick started to listen, and even to seek out the animal guides, the world became less lonely. It didn't matter that he couldn't see what was going on under the forest canopy. No invader would be able to surprise the city. He still didn't know how they were going to repel Honorus or the Claymon, but at least a warning would allow them time to hide and delay, if nothing else. And there were plenty of places to hide in the ruined City of Pallas and outside its walls.

One of the first messages, brought to him by swallows swooping around the tower, told him that Katherine had reached Bethany's farm. She was that close. She had escaped across the mountains and was safe. He knew firsthand that no one could enter that place without the hedge's consent.

Patrick shifted the weight of the beam to his other shoulder. He was still pondering what Leonides was making and planning when a raven landed on the top of a wall just up the street and cocked its head to one side.

"Hey," Patrick said. "Let's rest."

The man who was carrying the other end of the beam had noticed the bird too. He nodded at the man who was holding up the middle. "The two of us can carry it from here. It isn't far."

"Wait for me when you get there. I won't be long. I'll help lift it into place."

Patrick watched the men and the beam disappear up the street and waited for the messenger to speak. When the bird remained silent, he took a few steps closer and looked up at it. It seemed to be a perfectly ordinary raven, which is to say, not ordinary at all. Ravens are completely black, from their curving claws to their strong-looking beaks. They have bright black eyes and glossy feathers.

Patrick supposed he might be mistaken. Maybe this was not one of the talking animals. You never know with a raven. They are all tricksters, and they are very intelligent.

"Do you bring news?" Patrick tried speaking in the usual way – mind to mind.

The bird said nothing.

Maybe he should try being more polite. He said, *"Greetings, faithful one."* This was a reference to the ravens' practice of mating for life, a piece of information he had picked up from the Woods Runners.

Still, the bird said nothing, but it didn't fly away either. Patrick was transfixed by its gaze like an insect on a thorn. The raven's eyes were windows into a different kind of intelligence. Patrick felt something of this foreignness every time he spoke to one of the talking animals, but with the Raven it was different. With the others, even though he valued their advice, there was a sense of separation.

Without breaking the gaze, Patrick felt in his bag, looking for a piece of cooked squirrel wrapped in cloth. It had been left over from breakfast, and Sylvie gave it to him. He didn't want to take it. None of the refugees, except the children, were granted the luxury of lunch, and he certainly wasn't going to eat it in front of men who had nothing.

He held the meat up so that the raven could see it and placed it on the highest stone step of the nearest building. That way, if the bird flew down to it, they would be on a level. *"You have flown far, and you must be hungry. Please accept this small gift, Sir Raven."*

After waiting a little longer, Patrick decided this was only an ordinary raven that had chosen to roost on the housetop. He had half turned to follow the other men up the street when the bird drifted down and landed next to the gift. He swallowed it in one gulp.

"Is this how it's done, then?" Raven asked, cocking its head to one side again. *"Is there always a gift first? I have not spoken to a person. In my life, I have listened to words, but that I can speak has always been a*

secret. My mother taught me it was something to be ashamed of. She couldn't talk, and she only figured out I could when some people camped under her nest one night. I was almost ready to fledge, and she found me teetering on the edge, straining to hear words from down below. I hadn't even turned away to fight my nest mates for the grasshopper she brought. That's when she knew."

"How did you know it was something you had to hide?" Patrick asked. He was again captivated by the bird's depthless eyes.

"She gave me a shove, that's how! And I never saw her or my nest mates again."

Patrick believed someone had sent Raven to him, but he was willing to wait for that information. Since he had been spending so much time with Maraba, Patrick had come to think of the talking animals as more than just messengers. Some of them could tell stories to make you forget your troubles. He waited for more.

"I couldn't fly, not yet. And so I tumbled down through the branches, screaming, and I landed right in the humans' cooking pot. Lucky for me, it wasn't boiling yet, and landing in the water is what saved me. A woman heard me. She saw me fall and snatched me out of the pot. My arrival caused some excitement in the camp, I'll tell you."

"I'll bet it did."

Raven went on, *"It turned out I had fallen out of a tree and into a family. They were on their way to sell their woven goods at the fair in Ostara. At first the woman was angry when I fell into their pot, and the father joked that they should cook me for supper."*

"But here you are," Patrick said.

"Yes. There was a girl, not quite a child and not quite a grown-up woman. When her father joked about cooking me, she started to cry. She felt sorry for me because I had fallen, as she thought, from the nest, and she begged her parents to let her keep me as her pet."

"That is quite a story," Patrick said. "But now you are fully grown, and you are a pet no longer."

"Is there something wrong with being a pet?" Raven said worriedly. *"The girl is kind to me, and I love her. She gives me food and strokes my*

feathers. I sit on top of her loom when she is weaving, and I squawk if she has made a mistake in the pattern."

"Why don't you just tell her if she makes a mistake?"

"My girl does not know how to speak to me, and I do not know how to teach her. I am here because spring has come, and she has been leaving the window next to the loom open every day. I have been feeling such restlessness! I hear other voices – other birds telling me a battle is coming. I want to protect my human family, and I want to protect my raven family even though they pushed me out." Raven broke the connection between himself and Patrick by looking up at the sky. *"My girl stood at the window and watched me when I flew away. We both know I will return to her."*

Patrick didn't know what to say. He realized Raven had been saving this story. He was the first human who could understand it.

"An owl was going to bring you this message, but his mate called him back to their nest. Their owlets have grown so much that they both have to hunt all night. He gave the message to a squirrel to take to you, but you know how they are. The owl saw the squirrel playing in the forest the next day, and when he asked him about the message, the squirrel had forgotten all about it.

I was flying by just then, wondering how I could protect my families from the bad thing that is coming. Usually owls try to chase ravens away. Apparently, we eat their nestlings. Oro swooped at me, but I have never killed anything in all my life. My girl knows what I like, and she feeds me every day. Once Oro realized I could talk and that I was no threat to his owlets, he decided to give me my very first message."

Patrick thought this was the longest story he had ever heard from one of the talking animals, except for Maraba's tale. He had not yet heard the news Oro had entrusted to Raven.

"This is it. This is what the owl asked me to tell you. The Flame-Child is coming. She has left the farm, and one of the green men is coming with her. Watch for her. This happened – let's see – two days ago. And then there is the time it took for me to fly here, and to find you. So, she will arrive…"

Patrick finished for him. *"Just about now."* He began to trot up the street, towards the water gate. *"You can come,"* he called back to Raven.

28

RUBY

EVEN THOUGH HE HAD not recovered from the long flight to reach this valley, Padraik dove towards the ledge. He flew even faster than when he swooped over the battle in Brethren. When he was close enough that Meg could see Gale's wide eyes and open mouth, and even his white hands gripping the rope, she bolted back down the trail. She was afraid Padraik was flying too fast to land in the narrow space. She had only taken three steps when she caught her toe and fell forward onto her forearms, bouncing onto the side of her face and sliding farther down the hill.

After she came to a stop, Meg tested her bones and carefully pulled herself to her knees. She felt her nose. Her hand came away covered with blood, but it didn't feel broken. Her face and arms were scraped, and there would be bruises, but the fall could have been worse. She forced herself to her feet.

She had been thinking of it as a road, but the path that spiraled up the mountainside was rarely wide enough for two people to walk side by side. Padraik had landed in smaller spaces during their long flight, but she knew how nervous he must be this time. If the other dragon distracted him, it would lead to disaster. Silently, she begged him not to show off.

She looked back up the trail towards the narrow ledge outside the new dragon's cave, squinted and shielded her eyes. The dragon of this mountain seemed to be made from fire. It was so brilliant that, at first, Meg couldn't see anything else. When he was well fed and rested, Padraik's scales were as green as the sea on a cloudy day, but this new dragon was as pure red as the volcano's glow. It was the same color as the blood oozing from the scrapes on Meg's arms. The new dragon was larger than Padraik, and it was sitting so still that, if Meg hadn't known better, she might have thought it was a statue carved from a giant ruby.

In the time it had taken Meg to fall and to regain her feet, Padraik had already landed, and she watched Gale slide from his back, pulling the remaining harness off with him. Now he was making his way to her, coiling the last length of rope as he came.

Meg allowed him to take her hand and winced. She must have sprained some fingers when she fell. She felt shaky and sick, but she didn't know whether it was because of shock or fear of what was to come. She was no longer the girl on the beach back in Niue, meeting a dragon for the first time. Now she knew what lay ahead.

Meg limped up the trail until she was a few paces behind Padraik and waited for him to give her a sign. Gale would have joined her, but she motioned for him to wait farther downhill. He'd still be in sight, but she hoped the distance would make his presence less threatening. In his drawing, the shepherd boy had shown men attacking this dragon. Even though its glittering scales seemed unblemished by scars, it would surely be wary, or worse.

Was this dragon a female? Meg couldn't tell. It had the same shape as Padraik, and its deceptively fragile-looking wings were furled. Did Padraik know? She wanted to ask but she knew she must not hurry this introduction.

The sun had fully cleared the mountain. The wind teased Meg's hair.

When Padraik spoke to Meg, he did so in the way of a talking animal. *"Isn't she terrible?"* he whispered.

Meg didn't understand what he meant. *"I feel terror at the sight of her if that's what you mean. Don't you like her?"* At least he had answered her other question. This was a she dragon.

"I mean, she is beautiful. Terribly beautiful. What should I do?"

It was a good question. As the silence stretched on, Meg reached into her pocket and found the moon shell, Padraik's gift. She edged between the two dragons and placed it on top of a flat rock. Even though it was so small, it shimmered like a fragment of the full moon reflected in water.

She returned to her place without turning her back on the red dragon, who still sat in front of the entrance to her cave. She was partly turned away and seemed to be gazing off toward the end of the valley.

"Aren't you going to show her who you are?" she asked Padraik.

He had to break the silence, but this was the moment Meg had been dreading. He would have to speak to this dragon in the same way he used to communicate with Meg when they first met. Then the red dragon would reply, but she would not know how to gentle her voice. The images she sent exploding into the air would not hurt Padraik. Gale would be blind and deaf to them. Meg steeled herself.

She had recovered from her first meetings with Padraik back on Niue, and she had come to this place by choice, but she never would forget how it felt to hear him for the first time. Meg thought the story of a fire dragon, especially one that had been in battle, like this female, would burn even hotter than the story of a water dragon like Padraik. Padraik never meant to hurt her, and neither would this dragon, but that wouldn't make any difference.

Meg thought she might as well sit down. This was likely to take a while, and she knew if she didn't sit, there was a good chance she would fall.

Padraik hesitated. Meg sensed his shyness. His whole future depended upon this encounter, but before he could begin, a new voice broke the silence. The lady dragon spoke in the bursts of colors and images Meg had been expecting. It was as if she had been waiting for them to arrive so that she could tell her story.

Meg rocked forward and backward, pressing her hands to the sides of her head. The dragon was hungry. So hungry. She was flying, cruising low over the valley, clutching a dead sheep in her talons. She struggled to carry the heavy animal as she slowly made her way back to her cave.

She had survived by hunting at night, snatching up a sheep or a goat that had strayed before the shepherd herded the flock into the shelter for the night. It had been many days since her last kill. The shepherd boys were vigilant. She had flown out on the last three nights without success. She tried to catch one of the wild deer, but they ran too quickly for a weakened dragon to catch them. She had to find something to eat or she wouldn't have enough strength to hunt again.

At last she caught and killed a sheep she found grazing all by itself near the shepherd's hut. She did not hesitate to consider how strange that was. If she was going to survive, she had to take it. She was flying back towards the mountain's glow and the safety of her cave before she understood it had been a trap.

She could see them coming. Some of the men had been hiding in the hut, and now they were signaling to others across the plain, lighting torch after torch. More men, many more, were gathered on the path below her cave. They would be waiting when she returned to the mountain, and then, she knew, she would have to fight.

Meg moaned as she felt the dragon's despair. The men of the valley had banded together to destroy the predator that was killing their livestock. This wasn't like the other times, when fools came up the mountain one by one to prove their courage. This time the red dragon would be fighting for her life.

The dragon and Meg both shrieked in fear as the men raised their swords. There were so many! The dragon had not yet landed on the ledge in front of her cave. She flew back and forth, postponing the moment when she would have to face them. Men stood shoulder to shoulder, blocking the cave's entrance. She knew she should fly away, but where could she go? The cave was her home. She had to reclaim it.

She dropped the sheep. It hit the ground with a thud, and she watched it tumble down the mountainside. She circled once more, desperately seeking a weakness in her enemy. Exhaustion warred with anger. She couldn't think! Waves of red radiated from the she dragon, and Meg shuddered, fearing the images to come.

Padraik had moved close enough to Meg that she could reach out and touch his side. His scales were brightening, but they felt cool. He was countering the red dragon's frantic rage with images of his own – of a blue-green mountain jutting from the sea. In the picture he showed the female dragon, the black semi-circle of his cave was even more perfectly centered than it was in reality, and the soft sand of his beach was completely deserted. It was an image of peace. The darkness of Padraik's cave beckoned, offering refuge from the sun and the arching, cloudless sky.

Meg could almost hear the waves lapping against the shore, and she thought she felt Bethany's gentle touch soothing her scraped cheek. Padraik's image seemed to be calming the lady dragon. He had silenced her, at least.

The red dragon turned towards Meg, and for the first time, Meg saw her whole face. One eye glowed golden, like Padraik's. The other eye socket was a ragged, gaping void. Meg gasped. She didn't have to hear the rest of this dragon's story to know what had happened. The dragon had somehow vanquished the men who would have killed her, but she was sorely wounded, and even without examining her closely, Meg knew she never would regain her sight in that eye.

"Can she speak mind to mind?" Meg asked.

"I am Ruby." The dragon said, answering for herself.

I already knew that, Meg realized. Her name couldn't have been anything else. She risked a glance at Gale, who was creeping very slowly up the road towards them.

"Make the man stay back!"

Gale stopped at once. That meant he could hear Ruby, but Padraik also ordered. *"Stop! Her heart is racing. Ruby…"*

Meg retreated down the trail and stood next to Gale. Together, they watched the two dragons circling each other on the ledge. It looked like a dance, and Meg whispered, "They should be flying."

"They are doing the best they can," Gale said.

"Come with me." Padraik showed her his island again, this time from above, as it would look when they were almost there.

Ruby stumbled and backed up against the mountainside. Meg could sense her confusion. She was still afraid, but not of Padraik. What was it?

"Come with me." Padraik said again.

"I can't."

Padraik waited for an explanation.

Ruby tried. *"It is not our way. Dragons do not stay together. If we mate, and I make an egg, I will hide it deep inside this mountain. Someday, the volcano might carry it out and it might hatch. If that happens, our hatchling will never know us. It will spend its life alone, as you and I have. The race of dragons must die. I will not join with you to create a dragon child that will be tormented by mankind."*

Meg's heart sank. Ruby was right. There were no stories about two dragons living in one place. They were always alone. Except for their ability to talk, these two dragons were like lizards, or snakes. Like other reptiles, they would mate, and then the female would lay her egg. The baby dragon would be on its own, assuming it ever hatched at all. Its survival would depend upon luck.

It had been a mistake to come here, and judging from Padraik's silence, he was trying to come to terms with the impossibility of his proposal. Maybe he hadn't thought about it until Ruby laid it out for him. Padraik's ideas had always been a mix of wisdom and naiveté.

Meg's mind raced. She tried to decide what they should do next, but her disappointment was so great she couldn't concentrate. They would never find another lady dragon, and even if they could, the same barrier would arise. Anyway, Padraik had chosen this one. His dragon heart was breaking, and there was nothing Meg could do for him. They would have to find a place to hide until he regained his strength and then? They couldn't just leave and abandon Ruby. Meg had no doubt the men of this valley were planning their next attack. When they came again they would surely kill her.

Gale released her hand and strode the rest of the way up the hill to stand between the two dragons. She had seen him walk that way before, back at Springvale when he had to solve some problem between workers on the farm. His back was straight, and he held his hands out in front of him so Ruby could see he wasn't carrying a weapon.

What did he think he could do? This was between the two dragons, and they were at an impasse. Neither of them had spoken since Ruby's declaration, and the longer the silence stretched, the less likely it seemed that it would be broken.

Sensing Ruby's rising panic, Padraik said, *"Do not hurt him. He is not like the others."*

"Do you know how far we've come to find you?" Gale spoke with authority, and Meg remembered, for the first time in a very long time, that this scruffy-looking man was brought up to take charge of a large manor with wide holdings.

"Well, do you?" He repeated.

"I do not know where you came from." Ruby said.

"Do you see a lot of other dragons in these parts?"

"Never until today." The sadness and longing in Ruby's voice made Meg weep. She wiped the tears from her cheeks with the backs of her hands.

"You can talk. You can think. That means you can change." When Ruby didn't reply, Gale continued. *"I have been to his island,"* he inclined his head towards Padraik. *"It's a real place, and there is no one there who will hurt you, or your baby. But,"* Gale paused. *"Maybe you don't like him?"*

Ruby exclaimed. *"Not like him! But I do like him. I have just met him, but I can see he is strong, and he is kind."*

Her words, made of a combination of thought, noise and dragon images carried a lot of heat. Gale's eyes widened and he took several steps back. He glanced at Meg as if seeking advice. Meg still couldn't see where this was heading, but she nodded encouragement anyway.

"Then since I have already said you will be safe with Padraik, what is the problem?"

When she didn't answer immediately, Padraik said, *"Even if you choose not to return to my island with me, you have to let us help you. Otherwise, when the men come back, they will kill you."*

"I haven't flown since they hurt me," she said. *"I don't know if I can. I hid in my cave and they did not follow me there, but it hurts so much."*

Meg could believe it. It pained her just to look at Ruby's ruined face. Even if the dragon could fly, the wind over the wound would be torture.

"I have an idea, Gale said. I have an ointment that will soothe the wound, and if you will let me cover it, then it will be protected from the wind when you are flying."

What ointment? All they had was the little jar of salve they had been using to soothe the sore spots on Padraik's sides where the ropes chafed him. That must be what Gale was talking about, but it wasn't meant for such a serious injury. Meg's mind raced back to her winter at Bethany's cottage, and she struggled to remember what she had overheard from Kathe's lessons in the healing arts. Was there a plant growing in this valley that might soothe Ruby's injury or strengthen the ointment? Making a patch was a good idea, and it would be easy to contrive.

Meg turned away from the dragons and looked out over the valley. She shielded her eyes, already planning a short flight away from the ledge. Surely they could glide back to the wild, grassy area on the other side of the river, to where they landed when they first came to this valley. It wasn't so far. Both dragons were very hungry. For that matter, so was she! The meat she had eaten yesterday was a distant memory. Just thinking about it made her stomach growl. Until the dragons were strong again, she and Gale would have to hunt for them.

But first, and this was urgent, they would have to clean and dress Ruby's wound even though that would mean hurting her even more.

Meg's eyes followed the course of the river back towards the town at the end of the valley. Something wasn't right. She shaded her eyes.

"*Padraik!*" Meg said. Her thought was more urgent than a shout. A moment ago, nothing had been more important than the negotiations happening on the ledge behind her, but now she needed the green dragon's sharp eyes.

"*What do you see? There. On the river?*"

Meg glanced over her shoulder. Both dragons and Gale stared in shock at the black shapes moving down the valley, riding on the water. They were still little more than dots, but Padraik answered at once.

"*Ships,*" he said, confirming Meg's guess.

"*Not ships,*" Gale said, "*but many small boats. They'll have to come ashore before they reach the worst of the rocks, but the river is carrying them swiftly. They plan to surprise Ruby while she is hurt. They'll kill her.*"

"*Do they know about us, I wonder?*" Meg said. *Maybe your shepherd boy told them about you. Maybe we can talk to them. They might give us a little time if we promise to leave.*"

"*A little time to ensure the race of dragons will live on?*" Gale asked skeptically. "*It isn't worth the risk. A mob of angry men is on its way, and they aren't going to change course.*"

"*Did you kill any of them?*" Gale asked Ruby.

"*When a swarm of bees is stinging you, do you crush any of them?*" the red dragon replied.

"*So, the men will come, and they will not change their minds,*" Meg said bleakly. "*Any other ideas?*"

29

A CITY WAITS

THE CITY HAD ALREADY waited longer than it could remember. Pallas had been waiting so long that trees had breached its walls and crept out from its parklands into the streets. It had waited so long that vines shrouded its stone walls. All that time, it held its breath and listened for returning voices. As wooden rooftops sagged and collapsed and as the houses and shops filled with decaying leaves and birds' nests, it waited for the People to return.

This was a different kind of waiting. Now the People had returned, and the preparations for winter and for a potential attack occupied everyone from dawn until dark. The empty city spread out behind and below the houses the refugees had claimed near the water gate, but Pallas was once again alive. The people had repaired every leak in the aqueduct, and it again carried plenty of water to the pool outside the gate. The two fine stone houses the refugees had chosen as their bulwark had been made weather tight.

The people were relearning their city. The children roamed the streets in a tight pack, discovering secret places and jostling for dominance. Now they raced past Patrick, chattering excitedly. Somehow, they already knew about the visitors. Patrick shook his head and smiled, glancing up at Raven who was hopping and flying along the rooftops, making his way to the gate at Patrick's pace. It seemed the message, which the bird considered so important, had not been necessary at all, but Patrick wasn't about to tell him that.

When Patrick turned the corner and could see the first of the refugees' two houses, he broke into a run. Two Woods Runners standing in the middle of the street broke off their conversation and turned to greet him. They were Patch and Patchson. Father and son hadn't seen each other since Brethren. Now it was full summer. That wouldn't usually be a long separation for Woods Runners, but these were not ordinary times. The circumstances were so changed from the day when they parted from each other that it would take a full night of conversation before these two taciturn Runners made sense of everything that had happened.

Where was she? Patrick didn't see anyone else in the street. Patch wouldn't have returned without Katherine, would he? Maybe Raven was mistaken. Something must have happened in the time since Oro gave him the message. Patrick felt a seed of worry take root, but Patch didn't look like the bearer of bad news.

Just as he reached the Runners, Patrick looked beyond them and saw Anna, the council leader, in the doorway of the first house. She stepped outside and beckoned to someone. Without realizing he was doing it, Patrick held his breath.

Katherine stepped from the shadowed doorway into the sunshine. Time stopped for one breath, and then she ran to Patrick with her hands outstretched. Instead of taking her hands, he caught her shoulders and held her at arm's length, studying her face. He hadn't seen her since Niue, before he flew off on the dragon Padraik and she boarded the *Goshawk* headed for Brethren.

She looked – he searched for the word. Older? More serious? Her face was certainly thinner, but she seemed uninjured. There was color in her face. Her hair was as bright as ever, and her step was light. The uncertain expression in her eyes grew.

Patrick didn't trust his voice, so he pulled her into an embrace and relaxed as he felt her head on his shoulder. Until now, he had not realized just how worried he had been. After he sent Patch to find her and to help her escape the Claymon, he had turned his energy to bringing the refugees home, but she was always there, haunting the edges of his mind no matter what he was doing. He felt that specter rise and float away like a cloud lifted by a summer breeze. No matter what might happen, they would be together from now on.

"So," Katherine said, leaning away and smiling at him. "Are you glad to see me?"

As answer, he hugged her more tightly before releasing her and taking her hand.

"I have already given Katherine a tour of both houses and shown her the repairs we made to the gate and the aqueduct," Anna said. "I have offered her something to eat, but she told me she isn't hungry." Anna's voice sounded skeptical. Everyone in her life was constantly hungry. She spent most of her time trying to make sure there was something in the pot to fill their bellies.

"I am too excited to eat," Katherine said. "Patch and I camped near the Mother Spring last night. We didn't want to arrive here after you had all gone to sleep or too early in the morning. If you have the time, Patrick, will you please show me the rest of the city? I can eat later."

She opened her pack, which was bulging, and pulled out bags of extra food. "Patch has more in his pack," she said. "I hope it helps."

Anna was already on her knees sorting through the supplies. "Nuts!" she exclaimed. "Cheese!" She looked up at Kathe, her face glowing. "Thank you!"

"There's more where that came from," Patch said. "Bethany's farm isn't so far from here. My Maron is planting enough seeds to keep us all in vegetables through the summer and into winter too."

Patrick held up his hand. "There are a few matters we have to settle before we plan a feast," he said, "And we all have to stay close to Pallas for now."

The council had agreed to talk about the Claymon threat without actually naming it. They didn't want to frighten the children.

"You can tell me everything as we walk," Katherine said, starting down the street.

Patrick had to trot again to catch up with her. When he did, she took his arm and did a little dance step, no longer the strained, serious girl who had first greeted him. Then she stopped suddenly and put her hands on her hips, shifting her attention from Patrick to the raven, who was following them back down the street.

"Aren't you going to introduce me to your friend," she asked.

"Raven. Katherine. Katherine. Raven," Patrick said.

"I am pleased to know you," Katherine said, giving a slight bow.

"I just met him today myself," Patrick said. "And I'm afraid I made a mistake. He's new to this. Bringing messages, I mean. I gave him a piece of cooked rabbit, and he might think he has to have another one before he talks."

"Well, I don't have any food for him, and anyway, I have never met an animal guide who can keep quiet for very long, gift or no gift." Katherine said.

They continued on their way with the silent Raven trailing behind.

"Actually," Katherine said, "I remember the city well enough. So much has happened, I have to remind myself I was here only last spring. I just want you all to myself for a while."

Patrick was suddenly tongue-tied. He had come a long way in the year since he and Katherine met and came together to the ruined city. He was no longer a sleepwalker with one foot in the past. Having Katherine beside him in the sun-filled street almost made him forget he didn't belong in these times. He could even forget the danger that was coming to threaten the peaceful lives the refugees were creating. Almost.

"There's something I want to show you," he said. "It's something you haven't seen."

They walked in companionable silence all the way down the hill, stopping just before the main gate.

"Isn't this the house where we found your sword?" Katherine said. Someone had been working here. Except for the houses by the water gate, it was the only building that showed any signs of care. Someone had cleared the shrubs and vines from the doorway and had put a new bench next to the wall. She recognized the stairway that ran up the outside to the second story. It was the one Meg climbed to escape the wild dogs.

"Mabus. Yes," Patrick said. "You might not remember, but it is the house of my master. He's the one who taught me to work wood.

"I remember."

"Yes, well, as it turns out, Leonides is a great friend to the Lady who has been pulling my strings since the beginning. Maybe he is more than her friend. Now he is back, and he has taken a new apprentice." Patrick paused. "Leonides is no older than when I worked with him as a boy."

Katherine nodded. She wondered whether she would ever feel surprised again. Her girlhood in Ostara, running wild with Bard and learning her letters from her mother, might have been chapters from someone else's story. Ever since the owl Oro first spoke to her, she had stopped thinking of herself as an ordinary girl living an ordinary life.

Meeting people who had lived far beyond their time had become commonplace. She stole a glance at Patrick and wondered if he knew what she was thinking. When Patrick was wounded and the Lady told the Woods Runners to carry him to the cave where he would sleep and heal through the years, he was still young. He appeared older now, but it was mostly because the ordeal had left its mark – mostly in his eyes and in a deep melancholy that he couldn't quite shake off. She sensed sadness not far away and took his hand again. The darkness wouldn't claim him again while she was here.

Patrick led her straight through the house to the back yard. The area had been taken over for a construction project. Katherine looked at Patrick questioningly, but he didn't say anything, so she walked all the way around the crude wagon.

Just then Leonides' young apprentice came into the yard through the back gate carrying an armload of long, thin branches. He nodded shyly and dumped them on the ground next to the conveyance, then started to weave them into the structure, making it denser, closing the gaps.

"I give up. What is it?" Katherine said after looking at it from all sides.

Patrick and the apprentice shrugged.

The apprentice stopped working and turned to face her. "There will be no more making of beds or tables until this is done, the master says. And it won't be done until he says so. I don't know what it is, so I can't tell you when that will be."

The shape on the wagon bed had grown until it towered above the wall around the yard. That wall was at least as high as a tall man with his arms outstretched. Patrick thought it now looked like a crude statue of a bear standing on its hind legs. The boy would have to climb onto the wall to continue working on the top of it.

"You know what I think?" it was Raven chiming in.

Katherine decided to pretend he had been talking all along. *"No, what do you think it is?"*

"I think it is a nest. It's a nest big enough to hide everyone when the trouble comes."

Katherine tilted her head and looked again at the structure. It did look something like a nest, the kind the weaver birds make. It even had a small opening near the bottom. And it was big enough to hide several people, though not all the refugees.

"You're right about one thing," Patrick said. *"Leonides thinks this thing will help when Honorus comes back. He just isn't saying how."*

The apprentice was listening intently to this silent conversation between the humans and the raven. He was able to understand a part of what the raven was saying because the council had decided the people of Pallas would never again forget the talking animals. Learning to listen formed a part of morning lessons.

"The master says I am not to talk to anyone about this thing," the apprentice said slowly and very softly. This might have been the first time he ever had spoken to an animal guide.

"Is Leonides here?" Patrick asked."

"He has gone into the forest. He went yesterday, and he told me he will be away until tomorrow. In the meantime, I'm to keep making this bigger and tighter."

"He told me he has a plan," Patrick told Katherine, as they left the yard on their way back to the street, and he said he'll explain it to the council. That had better happen soon."

Patrick and Katherine made their way to the Steele mansion. It was in a part of the city Katherine and Meg didn't explore when they first came to Pallas, and she was anxious to see the house where Patrick spent his childhood.

Raven followed them.

"You brought me the message, and Katherine is here," Patrick said. *"Why are you still following me?"*

"The owl didn't tell me what to do after I brought the message," Raven said, *"and I can't go home until the trouble has come here and gone away again. Do you have a message I can take to someone else?"*

Patrick thought and shook his head. He'd like to know what Honorus and the Claymon were up to, and he wondered whether Ellen had had any luck convincing her husband to help, but there were other animals in the forest waiting to serve as messengers as soon as there was any movement.

"Don't worry," Katherine said kindly. *"You can stay with us. Sooner or later we will have need of your wings and your voice."*

30

FIGHT, OR FLIGHT?

WHILE MEG AND GALE stared across the valley, trying to come up with a way off the ledge, the two dragons conducted mysterious negotiations of their own. The two humans watched the force of would-be dragon slayers move relentlessly closer. Meg and Gale no longer needed the dragons' vision to clearly see the boats. There were five, and each held eight oarsmen, all straining to control their course around jutting rocks, propelling themselves forward as if the rush of a river in flood didn't give them enough speed on their deadly errand.

"Maybe they won't be able to stop, and they'll break themselves on the rocks in the rapids," Meg said.

"This is their valley," Gale replied sarcastically. "Do you think they'll forget that danger?"

Of course they wouldn't. It had been a stupid suggestion, but Meg didn't have any other ideas, and the closer the militia came, the more alarmed she felt. When the oarsmen beached the boats, and that would happen soon, the men would still have to cross the plain and climb the path to the cave, but that wouldn't take long. If Gale didn't have anything helpful to say, then why didn't he just hold his tongue?

"Don't argue," Padraik commanded silently so that Ruby would be able to hear him. *"You are wasting time."*

Meg wouldn't have called what she and Gale were having an argument. Not yet.

"You're right," Meg said. *"I'm sorry. It's just that there is nothing we can do. The men will be here soon, and we won't be able to protect you."*

"It is not up to you to protect us!" Padraik said. *"You only promised you would find a mate for me, and here she is. She is perfect. Now it is up to me to protect you."*

"Up to us," Ruby said.

Meg stared at her in surprise.

"The man is right," Ruby said. *"I can learn. Maybe I will die today, but if I live, I choose to go away from this place with my green dragon."*

"What about your hoard?" Meg asked. Padraik must have been very convincing. She had not been in the cave yet, so she hadn't seen Ruby's treasures, but Meg knew how difficult it was for Padraik to leave his hoard behind on the island even though he had some time to come to terms with the idea. His hoard was made up of shells, shiny bits of broken glass, and the metal things the refugees gave him when they were trying to appease him. None of it was valuable, though Meg would never tell him that.

"Padraik has told me I can take the moon shell and my smallest gems, and he will share his hoard with me. The choice is easy. I can stay here, try to protect my cave, and either starve or die in battle, or I can try to reach the island he has shown me. If we go there, we will be the first dragons ever to bury an egg in warm sand and to watch our baby grow," Ruby said. *"What is a hoard compared to that?"*

She was right, but that didn't change their predicament. In a way, it made it even worse.

Padraik was flexing his wings as he always did when he was about to fly. *"Take the rope from Loudmouth,"* he told Meg. *"You are better at flying, and we have to get the rest of the ropes and the supplies before the men climb out of their boats."*

It had been a long time since Padraik had called Gale Loudmouth. Meg realized the dragon was trying to lighten the mood.

"And if we retrieve the packs? What then?" Meg said.

"While we are gone, Loudmouth will make the bandage for Ruby's eye, and she will choose from her treasures." Padraik paused and made sure Gale was listening. *"When we return, we will put some of the salve on the*

wound. I never told you how good it felt when you smoothed it onto my sore places. I hope it will help her until we are safe."

Padraik had never said anything to Meg about the salve before, and she was glad to know it had helped him. Bethany had made it from beeswax and some of the herbs that grew around her cottage. Meg didn't even know which ones she had used.

When Ruby saw Meg looking at the raw wound where her eye should have been, she turned her head away. Padraik twined his neck around hers and whispered something. The red dragon glowed more brightly.

After that, they moved quickly. Meg tore a sleeve from her shirt so that Gale could use it to make the bandage. She wished there was something softer and cleaner to use. Then she looped the rope around Padraik's chest and climbed onto his back.

He leapt from the ledge before she had a good grip on the rope, but Meg had spent so many hours flying she almost felt like a part of the dragon. She lay forward until her chest was against his backbone and wrapped her arms around his neck, or as much of it as she could reach. There was nothing else to do except hang on.

As childlike as Padraik might seem at times, at his core was ancient wisdom. Now that Padraik had found Ruby and had imagined their lives on Niue, he would do anything to make it happen.

Within moments, they reached the narrow band of woodland at the base of the mountain. Meg wasn't certain she would recognize the clearing where the ropes and supplies were hidden, but Padraik did. As soon as he landed, Meg slid onto the ground, sprawling onto her hands and knees and losing more skin in the process. With her face six inches from the ground, she recognized the plants that were growing among the pebbles and tore off some of their leaves, stuffing them into one of the bags.

"We need these," she told Padraik, to explain the delay.

Meg crawled madly around the clearing, collecting the soft, thick leaves until the bag was bulging. Only then did she pull the other bags and the rest of the ropes from the cache. Without bothering to coil them, she stuffed the ropes into the nearly empty bags, setting a few aside. She dragged everything over to Padraik and quickly improvised a harness that would secure the packs.

As she raced to finish the task, she forced herself to test each knot. She and Gale always spent extra time before each flight adjusting the rope harness so that they would be safe and, as important, so that Padraik would have the freedom to fly and would not be rubbed raw by the ropes. They had learned where to place scraps of cloth and leather to pad the troublesome places where the ropes rubbed and chafed, but there was no time for any of that now.

"Hurry!" Padraik urged, as if he sensed her hesitation. *"The men in the boats must have seen us fly to this place, and when they start walking, they will come here first, even when they see me fly away and return to the mountain."*

"Why would they do that?" Meg asked. Her fingers were working without conscious thought as they remembered the knots she needed to tie.

"Think." He demanded.

Of course. As far as the men knew, there was only one dragon in the valley. Even if someone looked up and saw Padraik when he made his short flight, why would anyone think there were two dragons? Except Padraik was green, and the dragon the men had fought on the mountain was blood red. The men must know they had badly wounded Ruby. They probably believed she couldn't fly. They would want to know how and why a dragon had gone to the woods.

The detour to the clearing would slow the men down, but not for long. As soon as the packs were secure, Meg climbed onto Padraik's back again. This time she took an extra moment to settle herself and wrapped the ropes around her hands, tucking her feet under the harness she had tightened along his sides. On the way down to the clearing, Padraik only had to leap off the ledge and glide. The return would be more difficult. She wondered whether she should dismount and run up the path to the ledge. Maybe her weight would be too much for him.

"There is no time for that," Padraik said as the trees around the edges of the clearing began to sway as if in a sudden storm. His powerful wings were beating again, and once more Meg leaned over his neck, hoping to make it easier for him to take to the air.

It took a few extra steps, but Padraik leapt up, crossed the space between the clearing and the mountain, and started to climb in a series of shallow passes back and forth across the rock face. At first Meg thought he was flying so slowly because he lacked the strength for a steep ascent, but then she realized he was looking for something.

Like Padraik, Meg had seen Ruby's story. It was seared into her mind, so she knew at once what Padraik was searching for. It had to be the carcass of the sheep Ruby dropped when the men surprised her at her cave. Ruby's wound was still so fresh that the attack must have happened just before they arrived in the valley.

Dragons are not scavengers, but this was a special situation. To escape the men, the dragons would have to eat the sheep even if it had been lying on the mountainside for a few days.

Meg and Padraik spotted it at the same moment on their third pass across the mountain's base. In her excitement, Meg released one hand from the harness, shouted and pointed towards the hillside even though Padraik was already flying towards the patch of white among the dark rocks. The animal had caught on a rock outcropping just below the point where the mountainside began to rise more steeply.

Even as they dove towards the sheep and her breath was torn away by the wind, Meg appreciated this piece of luck. If the sheep had caught higher up, on the steeper slope closer to the ledge, Padraik wouldn't have been able to swoop close enough to grab the carcass. As it was, he had to judge his speed very carefully. If he wasn't flying fast enough when he caught the sheep in his claws, he would never be able to carry it.

On his first attempt, Padraik wasn't quite low enough. His claws barely brushed the sheep's back, and it shifted. Meg was sure it was going to slide farther down the hillside, but it settled with its front legs hooked around the outcropping. That would make it harder for Padraik to pull it loose.

When Padraik dove a second time, Meg couldn't bear to watch the rocks rushing towards her. She closed her eyes, and when she opened them again, they were already flying up, still making shallow climbs towards the ledge. Risking a look, she saw the wooly back of the sheep dangling below.

As soon as he cleared the ledge, he dropped the sheep carcass in the middle of the open space in front of Ruby's cave. Before Meg's feet had even touched the ground, Padraik and Ruby were tearing at the animal. Meg wanted to untie the packs so that she could start untangling the harness, and she needed to find the jar of salve for Ruby's eye, but she knew better than to approach the ravenous dragons.

Instead, she hurried to the cave entrance, where Gale had just finished making the bandage for Ruby's eye. He hugged her. Meg had already forgotten why she was annoyed with him.

"You were gone longer than I expected," he said. "Now I see why."

Meg watched the feasting dragons. It was horrifying, yet she couldn't turn away. It was already difficult to recognize the meal as a sheep.

"Our chances just got a little better, I think," she said.

"The men have grounded the boats," Gale said.

Meg went to the edge of the ledge and gazed down at the woods and plain stretching towards the river. She couldn't see the militia now. They must already be under the trees.

"Did they go towards the clearing?" she asked.

"Yes, but they must have reached it and left it by now. I assume there wasn't anything to see there."

"Just my footprints and some very suggestive claw marks," Meg said.

Meg pulled the leaves from the bag she had slung over her shoulder. With the side of her hand, she brushed loose stones and sand away from the flat top of one of the boulders. She carefully felt the sun-warmed rock with her fingertips, and when she was sure no grit remained, she heaped the plantain leaves on top.

"Good thinking." Gale said. "How did you know this is a good plant for Ruby's eye?"

Meg looked around until she found a smooth, round stone just the size of her hand and started to crush the leaves so that they would be ready when it was time to bandage the wound. The grinding stone started to turn green.

"It was a long winter," she said, "and I'm a good listener. It looks like they're already finished."

The dragons had turned away from the pitiful remains of the sheep, which now was only shreds of wool and bones. Gale and Meg pulled the remaining ropes from the packs, and Gale started to untangle them while Meg searched for the jar of salve.

"If you come here, I will see what I can do about your eye." She told Ruby.

Meg had never treated such a serious injury. The most she had ever done was clean and bandage her brothers' skinned knees. This was much the same, wasn't it, even if it looked so much worse?

Gale had some experience treating serious wounds from his work on the farm, but he was also faster when it came to dealing with the rope harnesses, and time was running out. There was nothing to do but get on with it. Meg laid the bandage on the rock next to the pile of mashed plantain leaves and opened the jar of salve. She dipped a corner of her former sleeve, now a bandage, in the oily mixture and dabbed it around the edges of the wound. She had hoped to be somewhere else when she did this, with time to work slowly and thoroughly. She should have washed Ruby's eye with clean water before she bandaged it, but there was not a drop of water for that or any other purpose so high on the mountain.

Meg grimaced. *"I am so sorry to be hurting you,"* she said.

Ruby let out a sigh that passed over Meg like a scorching breeze. The heat on the ledge suddenly felt nearly volcanic and sweat trickled down her back. Gale glanced her way and raised his eyebrows.

"At least it doesn't seem infected," Meg said, trying to be encouraging. She wondered how she would know if she was right. How does one tell if a dragon is suffering from an infection? Ruby's other eye looked bright, and her scales were shining. They seemed to be changing color, like coals under a fire. Was that a sign she was running a fever?

Meg gingerly dabbed more salve on the wound, nestled a handful of crushed plantain leaves over it, and tied the patch Gale had made around Ruby's head.

She stood back to look at her work. *"Does it feel any better? Does it feel like the bandage will stay on when you fly?"*

Ruby had not spoken while Meg was working, but now the red dragon moved her head back and forth, trying to get used to having a bandage and rope tied around her head. *"It does feel a little better,"* she said. *"When it is time to fly we will see."*

Gale had finished sorting the ropes and had reharnessed Padraik, working swiftly but taking time to carefully adjust the knots. Who knew how long they would have to fly before they could rest again?

"I will carry one of you," Ruby said.

"No." Padraik said. *"You don't even know if you can fly."*

"There's nothing wrong with my wings." Ruby's voice had taken on a stubborn tone, and she flexed her wings to show their impressive span. They were broader than Padraik's.

Meg almost smiled. Anyone could see Ruby was injured and afraid, but she was still a force to be respected. Padraik was going to have to learn to be diplomatic. No one would be ordering this lady dragon around.

"*I think Ruby is right,*" Meg said, aiming for a practical tone. "*Until you rest and eat again, neither of you will be strong enough to carry us both. If there are enough ropes to rig a simple harness, I'll ride Ruby. You can carry Gale and the packs, Padraik.*"

Meg looked at Ruby for agreement. This was a dragon of few words compared to Padraik, who enjoyed showing off his cleverness.

Padraik must have realized it would take too long to win this argument because he decided to move on, reasserting his leadership. "*We will not fly unless we have to,*" he said. "*We will make ourselves ready, but we will wait to see what the men do.*"

"*That makes sense,*" Gale said. "*Flight is a dangerous option. Maybe the men will turn back when they find out they have to fight two dragons.*"

"*We will not fight them,*" Padraik said. "*If it comes to that, and only then, we will fly. We have the advantage. We are above them.*"

"*The men will have bows,*" Gale said. "*They will attack from a distance.*" They all stopped what they were doing to look for signs of movement on the path below the ledge. This was the first time any of them had imagined men sending arrows flying towards Padraik and Ruby as they tried to fly away. A dragon is most vulnerable just after it has taken to the air, when it is possible to see its heart beating in the smooth place at the base of its throat.

"*If we do fly, do you know where we will go?*" Meg asked, trying not to think about the arrows.

"*We flew over mountains, so many mountains, to reach this valley. We flew all the way from the sea. If we have to fly, we will cross over Ruby's mountain, and we will keep going until the mountains are behind us and we can turn south. They can't go on forever.*" Padraik said.

"*Are you sure about that?*" Meg thought, but Padraik didn't answer.

Now that they had a plan, they worked feverishly to prepare for the flight they hoped they wouldn't have to make. As they worked, Padraik tried to explain to Ruby about harnesses and how it would feel to carry a human on her back, Meg wondered what the men of the valley would do when they saw a green dragon next to the red one. Ruby's eye patch somehow made her look more fierce. Meg had counted five boats on the river, so if each of them carried eight, that meant forty armed men were now on their way up to the ledge.

Ruby had chosen four green gems from her hoard plus one faceted stone that had no color of its own but sparked every hue of the rainbow. Together they all fit into the palm of Meg's hand. She held them to the light for a moment before she added them to the pouch that already held the moon shell while Ruby watched closely.

Meg put the pouch into the very bottom of one of the bags. It looked as if Gale was just about finished with the ropes.

"I'm just going to see where they are," Meg said, starting down the path before anyone could argue.

31

THE HEART OF THE FOREST

PETER GREYSTONE MOODILY KICKED at the remnants of the rebels' fire, sending ash into the air. There was nothing in the clearing except these dead coals and flattened places in the grass to show where tents had been. His courtiers kept their distance. They were familiar with this mood. After Honorus and the soldiers returned from Brethren and were attacked by the rebels, they knew Greystone would crush Devon Elder and anyone following him. The Claymon leader was itching for this fight.

He might have needed to vent his anger, but when he and his force crowded into the clearing, it was empty. A careless trail showed the rebels had left their encampment. Not only were the Ostarans gone, but it looked as if they had left at least two days ago. No live embers appeared when he angrily prodded the black ashes with a stick. Not a scrap of debris had been left behind

The Claymon leader had already sent his soldiers back towards the plain, to the carefully hidden turning through the rocks. One hundred of his most experienced infantrymen waited for him there — many more than he would have needed to defeat the rebels if the cowards had stayed to fight. Greystone was hungry to ride at the head of a real army again, but with his forces still scattered, he didn't dare to leave Ostara unprotected.

"Where are they?" he snarled.

His two courtiers knew Greystone meant Devon Elder, and they locked eyes in a silent duel to see which of them would take on the task of trying to soothe their commander.

The younger of the two men broke the gaze first. "Our scouts are determining his direction," he said. "All we know so far is that the rebels left this place together and all at once. Perhaps they learned of your plan to attack them and feared your wrath, my lord. You have long suspected there are spies in your court."

He stopped himself before speaking the name of Ellen, Devon Elder's wife and Katherine's mother. Even after all this time, just thinking about the woman was enough to send Greystone into a rage. He thought she was his prisoner in the months after his takeover of Ostara, and it took far too long to figure out she was really a spy. The night she escaped, taking the prisoners from the cellars with her, was the most humiliating of his life. Greystone was looking forward to capturing her again – and he would punish her. He had not decided what form that punishment would take yet, but he entertained himself by thinking about the possibilities.

Greystone walked the perimeter of the clearing. His face was bright red, and his mouth was pursed. It twisted as if he had tasted something that had gone bad. He should never have let the rebellion go on so long! He had believed his position in Ostara would be weaker if he attacked Elder's raiders, but instead the rebels acted like a disease, weakening him over time.

When Greystone took control of Ostara, more than a year before, there had been no need to fight or to lay siege to the city. Devon's foolish brother had all but handed it to him, and ever since then the rebels had done nothing but sting his patrols and supply trains and fly away back into the hills. Now he saw it would have been better to decisively crush his enemies in the beginning. Elder had stolen all the sweetness from his triumph. That would end now.

One of the scouts slipped into the clearing and slowly approached Greystone. He knelt and bent and touched his forehead to the ground. It was a Woods Runner. They still dressed in brown and green, but always with a touch of red to show their allegiance to the Claymon. Greystone continued to use the Runners even though the men who returned from Brethren had warned him they were no longer to be trusted. He still needed them.

"Speak!" the Claymon ordered, without allowing the man to rise.

"The trail is easy to follow," the scout said in an even voice into the ground at Greystone's feet. Either he wasn't afraid, or he was covering it well. "There are at least twelve horses, and more men and women are following on foot. They left this place in a hurry two nights ago."

"I could have guessed that myself! Where are they going?" Greystone shouted. It didn't matter where the rebels planned to hide themselves. Now that he had decided to deal with them, they would find no refuge.

"They are headed south and moving fast, or as fast as they can considering some of them are walking. I'd say they must be well along the forest road by now."

Greystone had never travelled the forest road himself – not yet. It was ancient. No one in Ostara had been able to tell him how long the road had been there or who built it. Sometimes Greystone even told the magician to ask those questions during interrogations, just because he was curious, but Honorus had no better success in getting answers. That could only mean the prisoners didn't know.

What he did know is the road was the only way to travel through the forest. He had already sent patrols to the South. They followed the rough track all the way to the other side and easily subdued small, rich holdings there, sending back reports after each victory. He should have been the one to lead the Claymon farther south! What lands lay beyond those his force controlled? No Claymon had yet searched within the forest for the city of Pallas which, legend said, lay at the forest's heart. It was a

city of marvels, and its treasure awaited anyone bold enough to
go there.

Greystone reminded himself it wasn't legend. After the magician returned from Brethren in disgrace and more a freak than
ever, Greystone discovered he could no longer bear to have
Honorus in his presence. Even though the counselor always
wore his hood, his eyes flickered like candles from its shadows,
and Greystone couldn't keep himself from picturing the old
man's skull.

Greystone had assigned ten men to Honorus and sent him
home toward Pallas the very same day, only a few hours after he
returned to Ostara. The magician had asked for a few days to rest
before beginning the journey, but Greystone didn't want to
spend a single night in the same house with him. Honorus didn't
argue after the Claymon made it clear he would have no escort
unless he left immediately.

When Greystone stood atop the city wall and watched Honorus ride away, he felt nothing but relief. His men had told him
about the part the magician played in their defeat back in Brethren. Honorus seemed unsettled after the debacle at the edge of
the plain. The magician had his talents, but Greystone now realized he had come to depend on him too much. He would be
more useful as the governor of Pallas, harvesting the forest's
riches for the Claymon. Greystone would allow Honorus to style
himself a prince for as long as it suited him.

Honorus expected to easily take his place as leader of the weak
refugees, assuming they had made it home to the forest city. Ten
men should be plenty. This was despite the problem of his
brother, who had rescued them in Brethren and caused trouble
for the Claymon there.

Greystone left the Woods Runner lying prostrate and joined
his courtiers in the center of the clearing. The tracker glanced up,
and when he saw the Claymon leader was no longer paying attention, he rose and disappeared back into the forest. There were
other questions he could have answered, and more information

he could have given to the Claymon leader, but Greystone had not asked.

"Yes, they are afraid of me," Greystone said, finally reining in his anger. "As they should be. We will follow them. If they are moving fast, we will move faster. We will find them. We will not rest until the rebels of Ostara are dead."

"All of them, my Lord?" said the older of the companions, thinking of Devon and Ellen Elder. They were father and mother to the woman Greystone still intended, so far as they knew, to make his bride. He had not been able to capture her, though he had come close once or twice. The memory of his tantrum after the men returned from Brethren without Katherine was fresh and raw.

"Yes, all of them," Devon spat. "It will be a lesson for Katherine. She and her family have toyed with me for too long. Her happiness is not essential to our union."

Greystone suddenly felt more cheerful. The mice had fled their nest, but he would stalk them and pounce. The soldiers who guarded the supply trains meant for Ostara had more than once reported the rebels laughing as they rode away, driving the pack animals ahead of them. By all the gods, he would come down on them like a boot, and they would not laugh then.

The man at the end of the file of ponies was indistinguishable from all the others, though he seemed to occupy a larger space. No one rode close to him. He wore the same deerskin tunic over sturdy brown trousers as everyone else, and he sat on his pony as if he had been riding his whole life. The expression on his face was the same as all the others' too, and if his brows slanted over darker eyes, anyone observing him would conclude his features had simply been passed down from adventuresome grandparents.

As he rode, Stormer thought about all that had happened in the days since he met Abel and Lightning in the house on the hill back in Brethren. No, it went farther back than that, to the day Katherine healed him. And if Lightning was to be believed, it went all the way back to the day Stormer was born. He was the youngest of five children. Even his own mother, who loved him, had seen nothing special about him, yet there surely must have been some signs that he would grow up to be different.

Stormer closed his eyes to recreate his most recent meeting with Lightning, back at the rebel camp. It took place just before darkness on the day Ellen, Bard, and the others rescued him. As he had been instructed, he stood at the edge of the clearing in the chosen place and waited, wearing Ellen's leather gauntlet. Stormer stretched out his arm, as she had and held it steady as the hawk landed and settled himself.

Stormer still couldn't believe this powerful bird was his friend, even his protector, so he stood as silent as a tree while Lightning flapped his wings. My arm is the branch where Lightning can rest, he thought. The powerful-looking hawk was lighter than he expected.

"That's the way I always think about it," Lightning said. *"Except that when I land in a tree, it doesn't give me meat."*

There was a pouch at Stormer's waist holding a fresh dove breast. He held it up between two fingers and felt a pinch when the hawk snatched it from him.

"Ow!"

"That's not the way to hold it," Lightning said. *"Didn't the Lady show you?"*

Stormer thought it was enough that Ellen had remembered to give him the treat for Lightning, considering all that was happening.

"Thank you," Stormer said, wanting to say those words first, knowing this friend could fly away at any moment.

"I think I am supposed to say 'You are welcome,'" Lightning said. He seemed to already understand the reason for Stormer's gratitude. *"Except it is as I told you. I do not choose. You call. I come."*

"I know that's what you said, but I still don't understand."

After a long period of silence, when Stormer heard nothing but the sounds of the people moving about the clearing behind him, Lightning said, *"When I was flying and watching, I had time to think."*

Stormer held his breath. He had the feeling Lightning was about to tell him something important.

"I have decided there is no reason."

"What?" Stormer said.

"No reason you can talk to me. No reason I can understand you. No reason I care whether you live or die. It just is."

Stormer felt deflated. *"Then I am not special."*

Lightning gently mocked him. *"You are no more special than I am. You are just a boy who can talk to animals and who can put up fences inside himself to keep the bad man away. That's all."*

When Lightning put it that way, Stormer stood up straighter, although he was already standing so stiffly his shoulders ached. When Lightning flew off without saying goodbye, it didn't matter. Stormer knew he would see him again.

When Stormer's turn came to speak to the rebels that night, he simply repeated everything he knew, using almost the same words he used when he reported to Devon Elder. When his hands started to shake, he clasped them together behind his back.

After that, Devon talked to his people, they talked to him, and before long they had reached a decision. They would play mouse to Greystone's cat, leading him to the forest city. After that there was nothing more to be said. The men started to collapse the tents while the women gathered every scrap of food and cooked a parting feast. A few Ostarans touched Stormer on his arm as they went about their work. Although the news of Greystone's restlessness was not surprising, everyone seemed to think

Stormer had done them a favor, and stranger still, they did not seem to hold his Claymon past against him.

When no one volunteered for the duty, Devon Elder chose two young men to lead those who would not be making the journey higher up the mountainside to the caves. They were to stay there with the most vulnerable Ostarans until he returned.

When they left, the Ostarans would carry little with them, so a few other men and women were chosen to carry the tents and other possessions to the caves and then return to the clearing. Since they could imagine no other future than Devon Elder's return, the old ones walked off into the dusk without argument, carrying the babies and leading little children by their hands.

"You are the best of us," Devon told the two men who would be staying behind, seeing their disappointment. "That's why I am asking you to protect them."

"It breaks my heart to leave so many in hiding here," he said, joining Ellen by the ponies after the children and elders had disappeared from view. She was holding up a saddle bag, judging its weight. They were preparing to travel through the night and would leave as soon as the last few Ostarans had returned from the caves.

"When I was in Ostara, in Greystone's court, I heard no talk of the caves," she said. "Not even the old magician said anything, and if anyone should have known about them, it was him. He was the one who interrogated all the prisoners."

She shuddered, remembering the broken people she failed to save after they were questioned by Honorus.

Devon put his arm around her. "I didn't tell you, but just before you returned, I learned the magician has left Ostara. He rode across the plain before dusk with ten of Greystone's soldiers, and he was heading towards the forest."

"It has begun, then. It will be just as Stormer predicted. Now that Honorus is returning to Pallas, Greystone will not delay to attack us. Where are your saddle bags? Are you ready?" Ellen said, her voice betraying her panic.

"Before the Claymon reach this place, our trail will be clear to the south," Devon said.

"But it must not be too clear," she said. "Greystone isn't stupid, and neither are the Woods Runners he employs. We have camped here too long. The Runners will easily follow the trail to the caves, and then our people will be in danger."

Bard was close by, listening, and he interrupted his parents. "I think not. Greystone will be in a fever to find us. If he must choose, he will follow the horses," he said. "And he will want to take his full force with him."

The two men Devon had chosen to stay behind were Bard's close friends. They weren't happy, but Bard knew they would do everything they could to protect the vulnerable Ostarans. That would include hiding and guarding the route to the caves. They wouldn't kill a Runner or even a Claymon unless they had to, but if it came to that, they wouldn't hesitate.

It was fully dark before they were ready to ride away, and when they did, Stormer was given his own pony, a strong, young mare that belonged to one of the men who was staying behind. She danced uneasily when he took the saddle. He soothed her with a gentle hand on the side of her neck. She quieted, recognizing an experienced rider.

The Ostarans crossed the plain and reached the beginning of the Forest Road just as the sun rose. After that, the novelty of riding beneath arching, spring-garbed branches made Stormer forget his exhaustion for a while. This forest had never seen an axe.

Even in this new and enchanting environment, his tired body craved rest. By afternoon, in the perpetual dusk under the roof of branches, and with his pony quietly following the pony in front of him, Stormer couldn't keep his chin from drooping to his chest.

He startled awake to the pressure of a hand on his arm and discovered he was just about to fall out of the saddle. The hand was Ellen's.

"I saw you swaying," she said.

Stormer tried to remember when he had last rested for more than an hour or two and decided it must have been before leaving Brethren, the night before Honorus made him a servant. No wonder he was having trouble staying awake.

He shook his head, trying to clear it and said. "Sorry. You have enough to worry about without keeping me awake. I will be more careful."

"You can't," she said. "Sleep will come. Not just for you, but for all of us. It won't be long now. Devon will call the first halt soon."

Stormer squinted into the forest on either side of the road and wondered how Devon would know where to stop. There wasn't much undergrowth, but the forest floor was pock-marked by the rootholes of fallen trees, and it was uneven and rocky. He didn't see any likely spot to make camp. Besides, despite the gloom, sunset was still hours away.

"In the meantime, I'll ride next to you, and we can keep each other awake. You're not the only one who is weary, you know."

They rode in silence for a time, until Stormer felt his eyelids growing heavy again. He shook his head and pinched his arm. "The forest city isn't along the road, is it?" he said. Stormer thought he already knew the answer, but Ellen's voice might help to keep him awake.

Instead of answering, she said, "Honorus has left Ostara? He went with ten soldiers given to him by Greystone, but he doesn't have any Woods Runners, and he will have to find Pallas without the help of animal guides. He cannot speak with them, and none of the Runners were on hand when he rode out from Ostara. That is significant, don't you think?"

Stormer forced his tired brain to explore the meaning of her words. "You mean, the Woods Runners don't want to help Honorus?" he said.

"Exactly," Ellen said, approval in her voice as for a clever student. "I was in Ostara when the Claymon first found Honorus and brought him to the city. He was in bad shape then. It must have taken him a long time to find his way from Pallas to the plain."

"So it might take him a while to get back to Pallas, even if he has soldiers with him. He doesn't know the way to his own city," Stormer said.

"That's what I believe," Ellen said. "On the other hand, Greystone will certainly have Runners with him when he leaves Ostara and comes after us. They don't care about protecting us, but they used to live in the forest around Pallas, and their families still do. They won't be eager to lead Greystone there."

They plodded along in silence for a few more minutes.

Stormer carried her thought forward. "They won't have to lead him there. He'll be able to follow us without their help." He indicated the line of ponies and people stretching ahead and behind. There was no way to hide such a trail.

It was too dark to see Ellen's face, but Stormer thought he heard a smile. "We have a surprise for Peter Greystone."

An early dusk was falling in the ancient forest when Stormer's pony stopped with its nose resting on the haunches of the horse in front of it. Devon walked back alongside the line of horses and walkers, clasping a hand here, touching a shoulder there. Without a word, ten of the Ostarans, including Bard, followed him forward to the head of the column. When Devon spoke to them, his voice was too soft for Stormer to hear. He embraced his son, and in the next moment, Bard and the others disappeared among the trees.

Some of the Ostarans who had been walking mounted the ponies left by those who had been chosen. Then Devon was back on his horse and they were moving again.

"What just happened?" Stormer said. Ellen still rode at his side.

"There is more than one path to Pallas if you have the help of animal guides," she said. "We have just reached the first of those paths, and some of us are following one of the guides on foot. The rest of us will continue on the road, riding the ponies. When we reach the second path…"

Stormer was beginning to understand. "More of us will follow, but the ponies will continue on."

"You have it. In the end, there will be only a few of us remaining. One or two men and an animal guide will lead the ponies in a wide circle around Pallas. The Claymon will follow, but by the time they arrive, the rest of us will already be in the forest city, and I hope, we will be ready for them."

"I thought most of you Ostarans can't understand the talking animals," Stormer said.

"That's why Bard went with the first group," Ellen said. "He has just learned that he can hear them, though their voices have been disturbing his dreams for many years. He has denied his gift for a long time. He will have to learn fast. The stag is leading the first group because he is steadiest and most silent. I trust he will not let the people fall too far behind him."

While Stormer digested this information, Ellen continued. "When we stop again, and I expect that to happen before morning, I will go. And the third time…"

Stormer already knew what she was going to say.

"You will go into the forest with Devon. You will follow the animal guide and tell my husband what to do."

Before she rode off to rejoin Devon at the front of the column, Ellen said, "As soon as each group leaves the road, the first thing they will do is rest. Your turn to sleep will come long before morning. And when you awaken, you will help my husband to find the city at the heart of the forest."

Stormer wasn't sleepy any longer. He had been chosen to lead the third group of Ostarans through the forest to Pallas, and that group would include Devon Elder. Even though he had some experience communicating with the talking animals, Stormer was worried. Who would it be? Not Lightning. He couldn't fly among the trees. Would it be Jasper? Stormer had only spoken with him one time, on the night the bear destroyed Honorus's tent.

Ellen had told him a stag would be leading the first group of rebels to Pallas. What if Stormer's group ended up being led by an animal he hadn't met yet? He might not be able to understand what it was telling him. With so much to worry about, Stormer slid from the pony and walked by her head, holding the reins loosely in his hand. She nuzzled his neck.

32

Parley

MEG PICKED HER WAY down the mountain trail, stopping to listen after every few steps. She ought to hear the men approaching soon. Even if they weren't talking to each other, there would be the sound of their feet scuffing up the path. These wouldn't be trained soldiers They'd be townsmen and farmers, but that didn't make them less dangerous. The last time they climbed to Ruby's ledge they badly wounded her. From Ruby's telling, Meg knew the men had taken some losses of their own. That would make her task more difficult, but she had to try. If only she could talk to the leaders, she might be able to convince them to turn back.

Meg didn't have a plan when she abruptly dashed back down the mountain. She left before Gale or Padraik could try to talk her out of making the attempt. If the militia made it to the ledge and saw Padraik next to Ruby, violence was sure to follow.

She and Gale had done everything they could to prepare and were ready to take to the sky if it came to that. Ruby seemed certain that she could still fly, but what if she was wrong? Even with the patch covering her eye, the pain would be severe. High above the mountains, the wind was sharp and cold.

Meg was a farm girl. That helped her to see this conflict from the men's point of view. They had lost sheep to the hungry dragon for many years. It had taken them this long to decide it was time to do something about it. She didn't know whether the people of the valley were usually peaceful or warlike, but either way, it wouldn't be easy to dissuade them now that they had worked themselves up to take this action.

When she heard them, they were still out of sight around the curve of the mountain. The footsteps sounded muffled, as if the men were barefooted or wearing soft shoes, and to her surprise, they were singing. It sounded like a marching song, probably meant to keep their courage up, but she couldn't understand the words. They were as muffled as the footsteps.

Before the men rounded the curve of the mountain, Meg scrambled partway up the rock face and perched above the trail. She didn't want them to see her right away.

When the improvised army came into view, she waited until they were a few steps away, then whistled loudly through two fingers held to her lips. It was the same shrill signal she used to call her brothers from their play long ago, and it worked just as well to get the attention of the would-be dragon slayers. Until that moment, their attention had been entirely on the path and, she guessed, on the dragon waiting above.

They stopped sharply at the unexpected order to halt. A few of the men towards the back of the column took an extra step and stumbled into the ones in front of them. Any misstep could lead to catastrophe on the narrow path. Meg watched as they regained their balance and gaped down over the dizzying drop to the valley. Only then did they look up to where she was sitting, knees tucked up, like a mountain lion on a rock. At least, that is what she wanted to look like.

The silence of the mountain enveloped the militia as they tried to make sense of what they were seeing. She guessed their thoughts. How could anyone be waiting for them where no creatures but goats or the dragon should be? And what's more, anyone could see this stranger was from outside the valley. Meg looked at herself through their eyes, and she knew she made an unimpressive emissary. She waited while they took in her torn clothes, and skinned arms. She touched her face. The scrape on her forehead must be livid.

What was going on behind all those blank faces? Did the men think she was a madwoman who was wandering alone in the mountains? Maybe they thought she was another victim of the red dragon.

During the few moments they stared up at her, Meg also studied the men. They were of all ages, from beardless teenagers to farmers so aged they must have had to insist on coming along. One of them was likely the shepherd boy who had given Gale that piece of mutton. Most seemed to be wearing their everyday clothing, and they carried an assortment of improvised weapons. There were a few short swords, but most bore knives, pitchforks and other farm tools, all sharpened to lethal brightness. The first time they made this climb, hunting a dragon probably felt like an adventure. What were they feeling now?

These weren't soldiers, but they did look like Claymon. Padraik had flown north and then inland. It was likely they had reached the Claymon borderlands. Except for those who were greying, all the would-be warriors were black-haired, with very blue eyes. She felt her courage waver like the flame of a candle as forty pairs of those eyes studied her.

She slid down from her perch. She needed to be on the same level if she was going to negotiate. Also, she thought she had better be ready to run.

"Does anyone here speak the common tongue?" she said loudly, walking towards the front of the militia with false bravado. She spoke clearly and held her hands open and forward even though anyone could see she was unarmed.

She had already picked out the two men who were leaders. They stood together a few paces ahead of the others on the narrow path. They didn't answer at once but turned their backs, whispering to each other. She had surprised them, but they didn't see her as a threat. In the silence on the mountain, she could make out some of what they were saying, but she still could not understand the words.

One of the men stepped forward. He was nearly as broad as he was tall, and his face was flushed from the climb. Sweat trickled down his neck, under his collar, and pooled in dark patches under his arms. He was one of those with a sword, and he held it out in front of him now.

"I speak the common tongue," he said.

"Then tell the others. You must return to your town and to your farms. You will not kill the dragon today, but if you leave the mountain now, she will trouble you no more."

He frowned and turned to confer with the second man. This time he didn't bother to lower his voice. She noticed the man who had spoken was better dressed than any of the others, in clothing that might be mistaken for a uniform, though it was pulled together from mismatched, ill-fitting pieces, especially the trousers, which were too short, exposing an expanse of hairy shin. He wore a short cape over his tunic, and whenever he moved, its lining flashed scarlet. From the air, she and Gale had been able to see only one large settlement in the valley. Maybe this was the mayor of the town. He might have once served in the Claymon army.

The two came to an agreement. The leader nodded and took two steps toward Meg. He was very close. Uncomfortably close. He drew his sword and held its tip to the hollow at the base of her throat.

"That is not needed! I am not armed!" Meg said, her throat suddenly even dryer, if possible. She forced herself to stand taller, as if that might make an impression on this red-faced man.

"You have no authority here. Get out of our way!"

Meg kept her eyes on the man's face and took a step back. It made her feel a little better even though he was still one lunge away from cutting her throat.

Strangely, this was one thing she had not been worried about when she started down the path to intercept the militia. She was only afraid she wouldn't be able to convince them to turn back. She had thought she could predict their actions, but she had been naive. She expected them to listen to reason, but people are often unreasonable. Especially men. Especially men with weapons.

"I said, move away," the man barked. "Unless the dragon is already dead, we will kill it today, and I will stand upon its body before the sun goes down. It will take no more of our livestock." He paused, his face almost purple as he tried to control his rage. "The last time we came here, it killed my brother and three other men. This time, it will not escape."

Meg understood now. No amount of reason could counterbalance the desire for vengeance. She stalled.

"If you want to kill the dragon, then go around me. There's enough room." Meg said. She raised her voice so that everyone there could hear, in the hope that some of the other men might understand what she was saying. "If you continue up to the dragon's ledge, more of you will die!"

If only she didn't have to rely on the scowling leader's translation.

"Two dragons are waiting there. Two!" Meg shouted, hoping to make them understand she was telling the truth. She jabbed two fingers towards the men. Meg had not forgotten Padraik's decision. He and Ruby would take to the sky before the men reached the ledge, despite the danger of flying. Her anger flared as she realized there would be no reprieve.

Her next words were not strictly truthful. With luck, the man with the sword would not be able to detect which were lies. "You thought you wounded the red dragon? She is as strong as she was before – and even stronger because she is angry. Her mate is here. He is a mighty green dragon from across the sea. A warrior. He has defeated armies. He has flown over the sea and the mountains to fight by her side. Do you count your lives as worthless? Are you really ready to die today?"

The men who made up the militia understood her tone, if not her words. They looked at each other uneasily. If the leader chose not to translate Meg's message, and if they didn't understand the common tongue, they couldn't know their mission was doomed. They probably thought she was a madwoman.

The leader's expressionless face showed her he was unmoved. He lowered his sword and shoved Meg hard, sending her sprawling toward the outer edge of the path and the sheer drop to the rocks below. She rolled twice before she caught herself, finally stopping with one leg and her hip dangling over the edge. She scrambled back to safety, launched herself forward and caught the leader's leg with both arms as he passed.

The militia leader fell hard, letting loose an "Oof" that needed no translation. He hadn't been expecting anything more from her. Meg sprang to her feet and dashed up the trail, trying to put space between herself and the militia. There was no time to be cautious. The leader's fall would slow them, but only for a few moments. She didn't know whether any of the men, other than the leader, had understood her warning. She had to reach the ledge so she could warn Padraik and Ruby to fly before the militia was within arrow range. Meg jumped over rocks and the eroded places in the trail and tried not to think about what would happen if she were to fall again.

She was just below Ruby's cave when she heard a rumble behind her. The path shifted violently, almost knocking her off her feet. Was the volcano erupting? Meg hugged the side of the mountain and tried to see the ledge above. Rocks bounded down the mountainside, crashing on the path below her. One bounced off the cliff face and ricocheted over the path directly above her head. Meg made herself as small as she could. Two more boulders shattered on the rocky path not ten steps away. She felt shards of sharp rock hit her back. The roar of rocks rolling and raining down the mountainside drowned all other noises. This army of stone was more dangerous and relentless than the militia.

Meg raised her head. As far as she could see, the entire path below was blocked. As she watched, another large chunk of fragile ledge broke off and sailed towards the valley far below, triggering another rockslide farther down the mountainside.

Meg scrambled up, gasping dust, desperate to put more space between herself and so much destruction. She spared a thought for the men she had left on the path below. Had they been caught and crushed by the rocks?

She heard a shout, but it seemed to come from far away. Her ears rang as they did after she rode Padraik into battle. A hand touched her shoulder. She jerked away and spun around with her fists flailing, pommeling whoever was trying to stop her.

"Meg! It's me!"

She landed one more blow before the words made sense. Gale was trying to catch and hold her arms. A trickle of blood dripped from his nose and ran over his lip.

She grabbed his hand, and they dragged each other the rest of the way up to the ledge. The dragons were nowhere to be seen. For one awful moment, Meg thought Ruby and Padraik must have abandoned them – had chosen to fly away together without waiting for two troublesome humans.

Then Padraik stuck his head out from the entrance to the cave. *"Is it safe to come out yet?"*

Relief made Meg laugh, and she discovered she couldn't answer right away. Then she said, *"Depends on what you mean by safe."*

She was still holding Gale's hand too tightly. She realized he was trying to get her to let it go.

"The men from the valley," Meg said, looking down over the mountainside. There was no one there.

"They are alive, or at least I think they are," Gale said. "There's no way to control a rockslide once you start it."

"You started that?" she said, sweeping her arm in the direction of the ruined path. She was having trouble believing one man could cause so much destruction. He was holding the hem of his shirt to his nose, trying to staunch the blood.

"That's just one of the differences between you and me," Gale said. He didn't seem to be holding the blow against her. "You talk, and I act."

"If you were going to talk to someone, it should have been me," he continued. "When you took off down the path, it was easy to guess what you were up to, so I followed you. I'll grant you, you're brave. It was like the first time you met Padraik. I saw the trouble you were in, but I didn't know how to help. Then, when you ran, I angled up the mountain as fast as I could, and when you had put some space between you and them, I gave a big rock a little nudge."

"I could have told you that you wouldn't be able to stop them with words," said Padraik as he left the cave. Ruby followed him, and they sat shoulder to shoulder on the ledge in front of the entrance. From now on Meg would never see one without the other. The sun was high, and their scales shone so brightly that it hurt Meg's eyes to look at them. Despite their hunger, which the single sheep carcass could not quell, and despite Ruby's injury, they glowed like faceted jewels, if jewels could be larger than the largest work horses back at Springvale.

"I had to try," Meg said.

"Words carry power, but they work too slowly," Padraik said. *"Rocks are better."*

Gale gazed out over the beautiful green valley and said, "They'll have turned back."

Meg thought of the leader's red face and the way he snarled when he lunged forward to push her towards the abyss. Yesterday, the men following him might have been farmers and merchants, blacksmiths, shepherds, or grandfathers. On this day, not one of them had been willing to cross their leader, not even to keep him from killing her.

She put her hands on her hips and faced Padraik. "It will take them some time to descend, and then they will have to cross the river again. They'll have a long walk back to the town, unless they intend to paddle upstream. What do you say?"

Gale knew what she was thinking. "I say they can spare another sheep, or even two." To the dragons he said, "You two can leave us in the woodland to gather a bundle of firewood. Humans don't eat raw meat."

33

GATHERING

THE DOVE GREY STONE of the Steele mansion was as beautiful as ever. Smooth and so pale it was almost white, the wall facing the street glowed through the vines that veiled its surface. As Katherine followed Patrick up the walk and through the wide doorway, she couldn't help feeling the house was welcoming her.

The last time she was here, she was asleep. Bethany chose to show Katherine what had happened to the Steeles, to Pallas and to its people in a dream. When Katherine wandered through this house then, as insubstantial as a ghost, it was the cold and the darkness she noticed – and the anguish of the people who were living here. Some of them were now dead. Others were so far away they might be lost forever.

Today, open to the sky, Patrick's family home seemed to have been cleansed by the wind and rain and refilled with light and possibility. Even more light poured through the single large window arching above the main door to the house. Only its graceful shape still remained. When Katherine pushed away the leaves on the floor around her feet and looked closely, she could still see shards of colored glass littering the floor.

She remembered that dream better than most of the real events in her life. While her body was lying in soft grass under a pear tree in Bethany's orchard, Katherine eavesdropped as Patrick's father complained about the people of the town. Once, the citizens of Pallas had chosen him to be their leader, but in the

end they turned against him. On the day Kathe dreamed her way
here, Meier Steele was about to leave his beloved city to become
a refugee. He was angry, and he did not yet know all the sorrow
that lay ahead.

Is a dream really a dream if everything in it turns out to be
truth? Bethany sent Katherine to Pallas. Her teacher wouldn't
have shown her lies. Now Katherine noted each clue confirming
the disaster that had befallen this city. She bent and picked up a
small piece of glass the color of the ocean, turning it over in her
hand before slipping it into her pocket. Only the wealthiest
householders in Pallas would have been able to buy enough glass
to fill the frame of the window above her head or to hire an artist
to design it. The colored shards reinforced her understanding of
this family's importance. That the window had been smashed
confirmed their fall from power.

Patrick had already crossed to the other side of the hall. Kathe
recognized his old pack leaning against the wall at the back of the
cave-like hearth. He had spread a blanket over a thick layer of
dry leaves and grasses in the place where a fire once would have
blazed. It looked strangely cozy, and it was deep enough to protect him from weather. She caught his eye and pointed up at the
roofline where Raven had settled himself on top of the wall. It
looked as if the bird was asleep.

"This is your house now," Katherine said. "Will you stay
here?" Her mind was already making a list of work that would
have to be done to make any part of this structure winter-ready.
At the same time, she knew it was none of her business.

"It's not quite mine," Patrick said. "I'm the younger son, remember. And as far as I know, my brother is still alive."

While they were walking in the forest, between Bethany's
farm and Pallas, Patch reluctantly gave Katherine a bare account
of what had happened in Brethren when the refugees came back
from Niue. He reeled out the story at unexpected moments, a
few sentences at a time when they stopped to eat or rest. She
wanted more, but there seemed to be no connection between

Patch's willingness to talk about that terrible day and Katherine's many questions.

One thing he did tell her was that her father's advisor, Abel, was badly hurt in the battle on the beach. On the day Patrick sent Patch to find her, neither of them was sure he would survive his wound. By now, he might have died. She didn't blame anyone for leaving her dog, Rowan, in Brethren with him, but Abel was supposed to bring her with him across the mountains when he was well enough to travel. Now Katherine knew she might not see either of them again.

Katherine closed her eyes and tried to reclaim the happiness she had been feeling just moments before. Thinking too much about the past or the future was a mistake. She didn't want to talk about any of it right now.

"Come with me," Patrick said. "There's something I want to show you."

Katherine followed him through a doorway in the corner of the hall. A stairway spiraled upwards in the narrow space. Made completely of stone, this tower had survived the city's long emptiness, and it would be easy to repair the hatch that must once have covered the opening at the top. Ironically, while weathertight, it was the one space in the house where no one could actually live. The tower was too slender, and the steps were treacherous, tapering to a point at the center of the structure. Her shoulder traced the outer wall as she followed Patrick up.

Katherine didn't yet know how many hours Patrick had spent at the top of the tower since returning to Pallas with the refugees. All she knew was, if he was showing it to her, it must be important. Also, if truth be told, she could never resist a stairway. Even if he weren't there, she would have had to climb it.

Patrick held out his hand as she emerged through the hatch and onto the top. There were higher towers in Katherine's home city, Ostara, but this was the highest in Pallas. After so many days spent walking faint trails in the closeness of the forest, the view made her dizzy. The space was just big enough for the two of them to stand, and a part of the wall around the top had fallen away. When Patrick slipped his arm around her waist, Katherine did not pull away.

She found it hard to believe there was a world beyond the green sea of trees that stretched to the horizon in all directions. Somewhere out there, Peter Greystone schemed. Even farther away lay Brethren, the wide ocean, and the island where Bethany and Gerard stayed behind when everyone else left. According to Patch, the dragon Padraik, the ones the refugees called Man Killer, was the one who saved them when they were about to lose the fight on the beach. And on that day he carried two riders.

Katherine felt herself spiraling into sadness again. She forced herself to turn her attention from the forest to the city, Pallas itself. It looked just as abandoned as on the day she and Meg explored its streets, except there was a thread of smoke in the distance.

Patrick frowned. "Why didn't I think of that? I'll ask Anna to cook as much as she can today and then put the fires out. We don't know when the trouble is coming." Like the refugees, Patrick had trained himself to avoid using the words Claymon or Honorus. They told themselves it was to protect the children but avoiding the words had become a superstition. The refugees seemed to think they could keep danger at bay if they didn't name it.

"It is so peaceful here," Katherine said, sensing Patrick's shifting mood.

"This was my father's retreat," Patrick finally said. "And now I come here whenever I need to think." He wasn't going to tell Katherine that he also came to the tower when he needed to brood. He still felt pulled towards the darkness, but he was determined not to go there – especially now that Kathe was standing next to him.

Katherine already knew Patrick's father died in the battle on the beach back in Brethren. Meier Steele had lived a long life here and through all the years on Niue, but when he arrived in

Brethren, he lived just long enough to pass the responsibility for the refugees to Patrick. That was something else Patrick and Katherine would talk about later, but not on this brilliant spring afternoon, with the leaves still more gold than green.

"What is happening over there?" Katherine asked, pointing into the distance.

There was subtle movement above the tree-tops, so far away that it might have been her imagination. Whatever was out there seemed to be isolated in one shape-shifting area, but as Katherine squinted, she could see it was slowly moving closer.

Patrick's distance vision was very good, one benefit of his long sleep in the cave behind the waterfall, but the movement was still too far away for him to see what was causing it. A few days before, with trouble on the way, and knowing Patrick's habit of climbing the tower, Leonides had offered to lend him his spyglass. Then something distracted them both, and Patrick forgot to take it away with him.

"More carelessness," he said, neglecting to offer Katherine any context for the remark.

Ignoring him, Kathe said, "If I had to guess, I'd say it looks like an eruption of birds. I mean, I can tell there's more than one kind. They're popping up above the trees and fluttering around before they dive back under the leaves."

"An eruption?" Patrick said, smiling. The word seemed too forceful for anything having to do with songbirds. He could see she was right, though. There certainly were birds, many of them, and they were excited about something under the canopy of leaves.

"If it's important, why doesn't one of the guides come to tell us?" Katherine asked.

It was a good question. One of the reasons Patrick felt he could spend a holiday in the city with Kathe was because he knew the city was well protected by animal guides.

"Raven!" Patrick called, looking down over the wall. "Hey, there!"

When the bird didn't answer at once, Patrick dropped a pebble-sized piece of broken masonry over the edge of the tower. It clattered against the stone next to Raven, startling him awake and almost caused him to lose his balance. He flapped his wings and tried to regain his dignity.

"Hey, messenger. I need you to do some scouting," Patrick said aloud.

That got Raven's attention.

"You really need me?" he said, sounding surprised and pleased. He launched himself, flew in a tight circle above the house and landed on the tower wall next to Katherine. *"What do you want me to do?"*

"Two things," Patrick said, smiling at the bird's eagerness. He noticed Katherine was smiling too.

"One. Go to the gate where the people live and tell anyone you find there that someone may be coming. We don't know if it's trouble yet, but they should bring everyone together. And Two. As quick as you can, fly over there and find out why those birds are so excited." Patrick pointed at the birds that were still – well maybe erupting was the right word after all. *"Then come back to the gate and report to us. We're going there now. We'll be waiting for you."*

If the raven had a hand, Patrick was sure he would have saluted. He took flight at once and flew like a black arrow towards the water gate.

"We thought we had a few more days," Patrick worried as he and Katherine raced down the stairs. "Leonides hasn't explained his plan. We don't know what that pile of sticks in his yard is for. He isn't even here!"

Half running back to the gate, Katherine struggled to match Patrick's long strides. She tried to understand exactly how he had changed since the last time she saw him. On that day, she was standing on the beach in Niue, and he was flying away on the back of the dragon Padraik, heading back into the stream of time and an unknown future. Now, it seemed he had found purpose. And she had never seen him smile twice in a single day.

Anna was kneeling in the street, adding sticks to the fire when Raven landed on the ground close by. He usually preferred to perch higher up and avoided the ground unless there was something there to eat, but Raven wanted Anna to notice him right away. As soon as he gave her Patrick's message, Raven flew over the city wall without waiting for her to react or answer him. He was as curious as Patrick and Katherine to know why the songbirds were behaving so strangely.

As Raven drew close to the disruption, he slowed. His mission was urgent, but he knew the best way to be a complete failure would be to get himself killed. As exciting as Raven found his role of messenger and spy, he was already looking forward to flying back through his girl's window and perching on her loom again.

Raven didn't see any talking birds here, but he saw there were sparrows and thrushes, warblers, vireos, and maybe more kinds. They were moving too quickly to name them. Close up, they almost looked like a swarm, as if whatever was below them had caused enough excitement to pull them away from the important business of mating and nest-building. Raven knew the birds' inability to speak to humans didn't mean they were unintelligent. Far from it.

Raven still didn't know what he would see when he worked up the courage to fly under the leaves, but he was beginning to understand it would be something unexpected.

He dropped into the treetops much as a swimmer will jump into unknown waters, cautiously, aware of the danger that might lurk below. The branches were thick, so he dropped down from one to the next, trying to remain inconspicuous even though none of the other birds were as large as he was.

When he finally reached a low limb, he was just behind a big group of people who were heading towards the city. Raven's heart began to pound, which is dangerous for a bird whose heart beats very quickly even when he is calm. He didn't know how to count them, but he had never seen so many people all in one place.

"It is the Claymon," he shouted, in the way he used to speak to humans, even though he had no reason to think anyone could hear him.

Then he noticed there were women. Women weren't usually soldiers, were they? Also, even though all the men and women wore similar clothing, those clothes didn't look like uniforms. If they were soldiers, then they all should have dressed the same way. Raven knew his understanding of the world was incomplete, gleaned as it was only from conversations overheard in the home of his girl and her family.

While he was still processing this information, Raven saw the people had stopped moving. He had carefully stayed some distance behind them, but four people had detached themselves from the mass of travelers and were walking back toward him. He hopped to a higher branch and made himself very still.

"We are not Claymon." The speaker was a woman. Her blond hair had been gathered into a long braid that hung almost to her waist. She had reached his tree ahead of the others and was staring straight up at him. Since there seemed to be no chance of fooling her into thinking he was an ordinary raven, he dropped lower again.

"I have been sent to see who you are, but I only know who you are not," Raven said. He was still afraid, but not as much as when he thought these people were the invaders Patrick so obviously feared.

The woman nodded and swept her hand back to indicate the others, who had stopped and turned to watch the interaction. *"We are the people of Ostara, come to ally ourselves with the people of Pallas. Together we will put an end to the blight the Claymon and Honorus have brought, both here and in Ostara. Our two cities have ancient ties, and our troubles arise from the same source. Tell those who sent you that Katherine's mother and father are coming, along with other friends."*

34

The Calm

EVEN THOUGH LEONIDES HAD warned his apprentice not to talk about it, everyone in Pallas knew he was building something in the yard behind the workshop. Some of last year's oak leaves still clung to the branches that had been woven into it, and it was so tall anyone could see the top and hear the dry leaves rustling from the opposite side of the wall enclosing the yard.

Even the boy who was helping to build it didn't know what it was. The people theorized it must be hollow. Otherwise, it would be too heavy for the rickety-looking cart. To them, Leonides' big idea looked like nothing more than an oversized pile of brush. It had no purpose any of them could guess.

Nevertheless, everyone in Pallas also knew Leonides was much more than just a skilled carpenter, so maybe the thing he was building was more than a pile of sticks. Leonides had somehow lived through the long years of their exile in the forest and seemed unchanged. He might look perfectly ordinary, but he was the Forest Lady's companion.

The Lady was a mystery too, but she was too solemn a topic for gossip. Except for Leonides, no one had ever seen her, not even Patrick, who had more reason than anyone else to know she was real. Still, now that Leonides had returned and resumed his place in his workshop, anything seemed possible. The Forest Lady seemed more present. The refugees caught themselves looking for her out of the corners of their eyes when they went to get water from the aqueduct pool. If a few of them thought they might have seen a flash of silken green, more iridescent than the new leaves, they kept it to themselves.

The sky was bright blue, but Patrick knew dark days were close. It had been a shock to learn that Leonides was away on one of his errands. His apprentice couldn't say where he had gone, but he told Patrick and Katherine his master expected to return by the next morning. That knowledge soothed Patrick's worry as the two of them hurried back up the hill from the Steele mansion to the gate. Surely Leonides wouldn't have chosen to go away if an enemy was close, but Patrick had to find out what had caused so much excitement among the bird-folk.

The street in front of the gate was empty, though the hastily doused fire still smoked, and there were other signs – a forgotten shawl hanging over a bush at the edge of the street, a pan of water set on a step, and bright gold glinting from the shield above a door where someone had rubbed away the grime of years.

At the direction of the council, everyone had been practicing for the day they knew was coming soon. Every evening, they sat in a circle and talked about ways to stay safe or, and this was more difficult, fight back. By now the people were hiding in scattered crannies in the city – far enough away that no intruder would hear a child's cry or a whispered conversation.

"Shouldn't we hide too?" Katherine said.

"Is that what you think?"

"Well," she hesitated, holding her position, but taking his hand. "The animals should have told us if it's danger that's coming."

"They should have," he agreed. "But they should have told us if anyone was coming – friend or foe."

Katherine and Patrick could see a little way into the brush that crowded up against the city walls. The water gate was rarely closed in the old days because it was used by the people from dawn until dark. Visitors almost always used the main gate to Pallas, at the bottom of the long street that bisected the town.

The water gate's wooden panels had long ago crumbled away, and though the council had brought up the idea of building new ones, repairing the houses was more urgent. Besides, a gate wouldn't keep the Claymon out – or Honorus either.

Raven made an abrupt landing on the stone arch above the opening and croaked raucously, as if excitement had made him momentarily forget how to speak to humans. It didn't matter. There was no time for him to report before the strangers arrived. Katherine and Patrick could already see glimpses of people walking among the trees.

Katherine squinted and stared. She cried out in surprise as the first of the newcomers came into view and held her hands over her mouth. Her mother and father were the first to pass through the gateway into Pallas. Her brother Bard was there, just behind them, and someone else.

It looked like Stormer, but how could he be here with her family? For that matter, why had any of them come here? Since Katherine was too stunned to move, Ellen wrapped her daughter in an embrace while the rest of the Ostarans streamed through the gateway and milled in the street, dropping their bundles against the walls of the houses.

Patrick ducked into the nearest house and emerged with a skin drum. He ran a short way down the street and beat it with a padded stick until the sound echoed from the walls.

When he returned, Patrick bowed to Devon Elder, but his words were for Ellen, "When you said you were going to talk to your husband, I thought it was about the animal guides. You never said anything about coming here."

"It had not been decided," she said.

"Peter Greystone and a force of Claymon are on their way," Ellen said. "They'll be at the lower gate within a day or a little longer. They still have Woods Runner guides."

"Greystone is tracking you?" Patrick said, sounding confused. He glanced in the direction of the water gate. "Then why are you sure he will come into the city through the main gate?"

"He thinks he is tracking us, but he really is following our ponies. A few of us are leading the animals here by a longer way. They plan to make a big circle and come to the city from that direction," Ellen said. "The Runners won't be fooled, but we believe they are reluctant to lead Greystone to their forest homeland. We believe they will do what they can to slow him."

Katherine's father was listening to Ellen just like everyone else, not as if he were waiting for a chance to interrupt or take over. Something had shifted between her mother and father since the last time Katherine had seen them together. When they entered Pallas just now, it was side by side. Devon looked solemn, even worried, but he no longer carried the undercurrent of anger that always made him so unapproachable.

When Ellen finished speaking, as if he knew Katherine was thinking about him, Devon pulled her into a rough hug. It was the first she could remember since she was small enough to sit on his lap. Over her father's shoulder, Katherine caught Stormer's eye. He no longer wore Claymon red, and he was holding himself a little apart. She promised herself she would talk with him soon. Obviously, she wasn't the only one having adventures since the two of them parted back on the beach.

The citizens of Pallas had left their hiding places and were returning by cautious twos and threes. The newcomers weren't wearing uniforms. They didn't look like a threat, but it took a few minutes to understand that these exhausted travelers were actually their old enemies, the Ostarans. As soon as they did, they discovered that all traces of animosity had burned away over the years under Niue's intense sun.

As soon as she understood the Ostarans had come to help, Anna and the other council members did what they could to welcome the travelers. Their two houses were the only roofed structures in the entire city. Leonides had already made a few beds for the old people and the children. They had been sleeping double, but tonight they would sleep triple. Everyone else would have to lie shoulder to shoulder on the floor.

Devon spoke up above the chatter of explanations and greetings, "We have been hunting since we left the forest road." He nodded towards three men whose bulging bags suggested the shapes of rabbits. One of them carried a small deer across his shoulders.

Patrick climbed partway up the exterior stairs that led up to the roof of one of the houses and looked out over the unexpected crowd. He wondered whether anything had really changed. There were a few more experienced fighters here, Devon and some of the young Ostaran men, but it was hard to see how that improved their chances against the Claymon. Greystone was coming with soldiers. He would ask the guides to find out how many, but the talking animals didn't understand counting or numbers. And according to their new allies, Honorus was also on his way with an escort of Claymon. Patrick did not know what wiles or magic his brother intended to use once he got here. More people in the city meant more lives at risk.

Patrick held the drum over his head and beat it again until silence settled in the street. Raven watched from his perch above the gate, head cocked to one side. Katherine had left her parents to stand at the base of the steps. When he caught her eye, she smiled up at him. He hoped she would sleep tonight. It would be her only chance to rest before the trouble that was coming to Pallas. He would offer her his hearth and keep watch from the rooftop.

The hilt of his sword felt warm in his hand as if it sensed the coming danger, or maybe Mabus was just reflecting his mood.

"With all our hearts, we welcome the people of Ostara," Patrick said. "You have come here to stand with us against the Claymon. We thank you. At the same time, we know you are here to drive the Northerners from your own city."

There were mutters of agreement. Some people shouted, "We fight together!" before quieting again.

"Our friends from the plains have told us we have only a little time. The Claymon will likely reach the lower gate by the end of the day tomorrow. We have much to do, but first we will share what we have and feast together. We will tell our Ostaran friends what we have done to prepare, and we will talk about what more may be done. Then, at dawn tomorrow morning, the council will meet here, whether Leonides has returned or not."

Some of the people stamped their feet in agreement, and there were a few cheers, but what Patrick mostly saw in the faces below was determination. For those who were so recently refugees, memories of the battle on the beach and of Honorus's attack were still raw. The Ostarans, too, had been exiled from their home. Everyone standing below, whether of the forest or the plain, had suffered great loss.

The children of Pallas sat cross-legged, staring up with wide eyes. They had known all along. Even though they were now growing, and learning to play, they had lived through the same dark times as everyone else. There were no innocents in Pallas.

In two days' time, Patrick feared, many of these people would be dead. Their city would be in the hands of his brother Honorus, and he would be controlled by the Claymon. Patrick had never voiced the thought to the council, but Patrick wondered why they didn't just leave – make a new home somewhere else?

As always, he answered the question himself before the thought could become words. This was their home. They would not abandon it again.

Patrick returned to the street, where he found Devon and Ellen Elder speaking with Anna and a few other members of the council.

Anna said, "All the houses except these two are still missing their roofs, but the walls are sound in other parts of the city. We've had the children carrying stones up there, as heavy as they can carry, lining them up along the tops to throw down on the invaders when the time comes. It has become a game for them. They have practiced dropping the stones onto targets in the streets, and then they carry them up again."

"The children..." Ellen began.

"I know what you are going to say," Anna said, "and I agree. The children must be safe, and I would like nothing more than to hide them. That's why we hid when Patrick warned us someone was coming. We didn't know it was going to be you."

"What would you have done if it had been them instead of us?" Ellen asked.

"We would have waited until night and attacked them by the light of torches. We have sharpened every weapon and tool we have. Every one of us will have something, even if it is just a club." Anna hesitated. "If you had been the Claymon, we would have tried to make our numbers seem greater by attacking from different directions, but even now that you have come, defeating them will be difficult."

Anna glanced at the men and women preparing the meat the Ostarans had brought, at the ones building up the fire, and at the children running down the street and out of sight.

Something in her voice told Patrick that, like him, Anna believed their cause was hopeless. He thought if she said anything more, her voice might break, so he continued for her, "If you had been the enemy, I would have given a different signal, and the children would have taken to the rooftops."

Ellen noticed no one was saying anything about Honorus. She understood. She didn't want to talk about him either. She had told Devon as little as possible about all she had seen and felt in the magician's presence in Ostara and in Brethren. Stones hurled from the tops of walls might stop some Claymon soldiers, but when Honorus came, he would wield magic.

Her stomach clenched. It was as if she were on the beach again, and Honorus was conjuring a black cloud like a writhing swarm. He hurt his own people to restore his youth. He killed his father. What might he do here?

Katherine had found Stormer. It wasn't difficult. He was standing exactly where he was when she first saw him, just inside and to the left of the gate. There were plenty of hands to prepare the food and to do the other chores, so she went to talk with him.

"I don't know how you have come to be here, but I'm glad to see you," Katherine said, by way of greeting.

They stood awkwardly, frozen in place, the only two unmoving bees in a busy hive.

"I'm glad I'm here too," Stormer said. "But I don't know why yet."

Katherine glanced at Patrick, who had his head bent toward her father's. "It probably doesn't help to know you aren't the only one who feels that way, does it? What happened after we parted on the beach? It feels like a long time ago."

Stormer's laugh was genuine. "Sorry. It's just that the story is so wild you'll have trouble believing it. I'll save it for later, after all this is settled."

He swept his arm in front of him, indicating everything happening in the street, but Katherine knew he was talking about the battle.

"I'll tell you one thing, though…"

Katherine's shocked silence was her reply.

"It turns out I might have understood that panther if I hadn't been so afraid of it."

"And here's something else," he said, squatting down to untie his pack. He pulled out a small book and handed it up to her, almost reluctantly. "Will you read this and tell me what is in it? It cost me something to get it."

Still speechless, Katherine nodded and slipped the book into her pocket.

Bard came up to them and put a casual arm around Katherine's shoulder. "Stormer, can you help us? We're trying to rig spits to roast some of this meat."

Stormer looked grateful to have been given something to do. Katherine wondered whether her brother was including the Claymon to be kind, or if he only wanted to put an end to their conversation.

Instead of sleeping, Patrick and Katherine climbed up onto the roof and talked into the night. Their whispered conversation mingled with distant owl calls, but they were unaware of them. While the stars circled towards morning, they told each other everything that had happened while they were apart. When the breeze shifted and brought them the green scent of the forest, they didn't notice. Their time together was too precious to waste on sleep. When they finally grew silent, they continued to sit side by side, gazing over the moonlit trees.

Long after midnight, when Katherine was settling her head on Patrick's shoulder and might have nodded off, the messenger came.

"I have been calling to you," Oro said, flapping his wings and turning his bright gold eyes like lanterns on the two of them. *"Calling and calling. You made me come here."* The great horned owl always looked as if he were frowning, His expression was naturally fierce, but this time Katherine could tell he was annoyed.

"We heard you, but you were talking to the other owls," Katherine said.

"No. You weren't listening."

"Honest. I heard owls hooting, or whatever you call it. There must have been at least three of you."

"You heard my wife gossiping with the neighbors." Oro said. *"They are asking about all the travelers in the forest. You weren't listening the right way."*

He was right. They should have been listening for messages from the animal guides through the night. That's how the warning would arrive. The rooftop was a perfect place for paying attention. It was quiet and private, but she and Patrick had chosen it only because they wanted someplace under the stars and above the coming danger where they could be alone.

They could have gone to the Steele mansion, but Patrick had told Katherine that Maraba came there almost every night. The panther sat by the hearth and talked non-stop. Patrick often fell asleep to the sound of her voice. As much as Katherine loved Maraba, and as safe as she felt around the big cat, being alone with Patrick had been more important to her.

Katherine felt ashamed, and with that feeling came the beginnings of panic. It had been selfish to think she could pretend the Claymon weren't coming, even for a few hours. Just because she wanted a time of peace didn't mean she could have one.

"Forgive us," Patrick said, balancing on the wall and bowing slightly to show his respect to the Owl. Katherine did the same, but more slowly. Her feet tingled from sitting so long. She held onto Patrick's arm until the sensation passed.

Oro picked at the feathers on his shoulders. Now that he had their attention, it looked like he was going to make them wait.

During their hours on the roof, the whole world had seemed quiet and peaceful, but morning was coming. Katherine's heart began to pound, and she thought she might have to sit down again.

Last night everyone feasted. They ate every scrap of meat the Ostarans had brought with them and all the food Katherine had carried from Bethany's farm.

They shouldn't have done that. They should have saved something for after the battle. The only way it made sense to leave no supplies was if they knew they wouldn't need them. After the meal, they clustered around the edges of the street, quietly talking about how they could oppose the Claymon. She didn't hear anyone talk about how many were going to die.

When he decided Patrick and Katherine had waited long enough, Oro spoke. *"The soldiers are encamped in the Hills now. They plan to come close to the city today. Then they will wait. They plan to surprise you tonight, after it is dark. Their leader was very angry when the Runners left him and went to be with their own people. He says he doesn't need them. He says the agreement between them is broken, and he will slaughter them with the rest of you."* After a moment, Oro continued. *"You didn't hear me, but you must have heard him shouting, even from so far away."*

Katherine assumed Oro was talking about Greystone. The Ostaran plan had worked. The Claymon had followed the ponies in a big circle.

The hills Oro was talking about were the Celadrian Hills, a range of low mountains she crossed when she and her friends came to the forest city the first time. The hills weren't far away, but they weren't within shouting distance for human ears – no matter how angry Greystone might be.

Oro went on. *"I sat in a tree above him. He is a man who talks, but he never listens. He suspects the Ostarans tricked him, but he doesn't know how. The Runners said nothing even though they saw every place where the people left the road and took the old paths.*

The men with the ponies kept walking last night. Even though they cannot understand our words, they have learned to trust us, and they have learned how to watch for us. One of my fledglings from two nestings ago is leading the men and the ponies to the big gate at the bottom of the hill. Maybe they are already here." It was easy to hear his pride.

Patrick said, *"Once it is night again, the Claymon will follow the trail the rest of the way to the city."*

"That is your plan, is it not? To lead them here and into the trap you have laid for them?" Oro said.

Patrick didn't answer. He was thinking about the sharpened tools, the rocks lined up along the tops of walls, and their few trained fighters. Devon Elder, Bard, and a few of the other Ostarans had been raiders. They had annoyed Greystone, and stolen his supplies, but they had never been in a real battle against him. Patrick himself had fought only twice – the first when he was terribly wounded, and then on the beach in Brethren. Both times he was saved by miracles in the forms of the Forest Lady and the green dragon. He couldn't count on a third rescue.

Oro said the Ostarans planned to attack tonight. The Woods Runners had led them this close, but it seemed they didn't tell Peter Greystone about the animal guides or about the movements of the Ostaran rebels. The Claymon thought they were going to surprise the city. They wouldn't be expecting much resistance. Now Patrick, his people, and the Ostarans had a single day in which to prepare a surprise for Greystone.

Oro cleared his throat. At least, that's what that rasping, squawking sound must have been. *"The consort has returned. The council is gathering."*

Patrick was already halfway down the stairs when Katherine knelt in front of Oro, who remained sitting on the edge of the wall. She reached out tentatively to gently stroke his feathers. He twitched his wing, but he didn't tell her to stop.

"I really am sorry I didn't listen," she said. *"Can you forgive me? I have never understood why you and all the others care what happens to us, but I thank you for coming."*

"Flame Child," Oro said. *"Look."*

Katherine stood up again and turned around. The city lay behind her, but in every other direction, there was nothing but forest. To the east, the sky had turned pearly grey, with a bloom of rosiness along the treetops.

Oro said, *"This city has been here longer than owls can remember. Since the beginning, people have made their homes within its walls, and it has never grown any larger. You can't see from here, but the Woods Runners and their children are planting gardens in every sunny clearing. There is room in the forest for people and animals."* He paused, to give her a chance to think about his words. *"We would miss you if you were gone."*

"There will always be people," Katherine said sadly. She thought of the villages and manors carving away at the edge of the forest to the south.

"Some people are greedy," Oro said. *"And most of them do not know us."*

"*Can I ask you a question?*" Kathe said. She took his silence for permission and said, "*What about Patrick's brother? Where is Honorus?*"

"*He is lost,*" Oro said unhelpfully.

"*Even if we somehow win today, people will still be greedy,*" Katherine said, when she realized Oro wasn't going to say anything else.

"*I know,*" Oro huffed. "*But we have to try.*"

35

THE DAY BEFORE

A S SOON AS THE council dispersed, Patrick returned to the ruined shell of the Steele mansion. He sat on the floor in front
of the hearth and polished his sword until it gleamed. Not
that anyone would notice the difference. Ever since Katherine
and Meg returned Mabus to him, he had always kept the blade
honed to perfect sharpness, and every night he wiped away fin-
germarks from the stones and metal of the hilt. It was a ritual,
almost a compulsion, that made him spend time doing this daily
task, but if he didn't do it, he found he couldn't sleep.

Patrick never used his sword for any purpose except battle
even though there were many times when it would have been
useful as a tool. He could have used Mabus to strip branches off
saplings when they were repairing the houses, or to cut back the
rose-bushes that constantly threatened to invade his house, but
he used an old knife of some soft metal that refused to hold an
edge instead.

Patrick knew he would rest his hand on the sword's hilt
through this day, and he would feel it growing ever warmer in
anticipation of the coming danger.

He wondered whether Maraba had come to tell more of her
story last night when he and Katherine stayed on the roof by the
water gate. Patrick felt a pang of guilt. Just as he and Katherine
had been deaf to Oro's calls, he had taken Maraba's presence for

granted. He should have tried to tell her he wouldn't be there, at least.

Raven was still following Patrick wherever he went.

"There's nothing happening here," Patrick told him. *"And there won't be until tonight. You should fly into the forest, see what you can find out. Oro said the Claymon will be making camp close to the city today. If you see any of them, tell me."*

Raven was intelligent. Even though he had lived his life isolated from other talking animals, Patrick had no doubt he would make an excellent spy.

"And keep your distance." If the bird had a fault, it was that he could be too trusting. Patrick didn't want some idle soldier to use his new friend for target practice.

As soon as the bird flew away, Patrick made his way to the top of the tower. Soon he would have to assume the role of leader. It already lay on his shoulders like a too-heavy cloak, but there was still a little time.

This morning, when Patrick leapt down the stairway from the roof where he and Katherine spent the night, he discovered the street in front of the repaired houses was already full of the allies. Everyone was gathering to hear what Leonides' might say. The council had made its decisions and had taken some steps to defend Pallas, but they knew the old man with the big ears and rough hands had his own ideas. This morning they finally would find out what those ideas were.

Leonides had slipped into the city before dawn and now stood with his back against the city wall with the council members, plus Devon and Ellen Elder, in a half-circle around him. They were crowded by the rest of the soon-to-be defenders of Pallas who huddled close. Those closest to the front whispered over their shoulders to those behind until Leonides's words reached the back. From above, where Kathe was watching, the mass of people looked like a swarm of bees reshaping itself. She couldn't see what was happening in the middle.

Almost as soon as Leonides had finished speaking, and after Patrick climbed back up the steps again to repeat Oro's message, the street emptied quickly. The People had been preparing for this day since before they arrived back in Pallas. From the beginning, they knew Honorus and Peter Greystone would come to threaten the peace they had created here.

The citizens were few, but their safe return to Pallas had given them a sense of invulnerability. It was enough of a miracle to maintain a feeble flame of hope. They would hold their newly reclaimed city or die in the attempt. That much had been agreed without any discussion at all.

They would meet again at mid-day, when they would form themselves into groups, with Patrick assigning an experienced fighter to each.

The children scoured the city for more rocks. They treated it as a game, awarding each other praise for the biggest or the roundest ones. Anna had told the children they must stay on the rooftops and out of the fight, but Patrick knew they would disobey. These weren't ordinary children. They might be learning how to play, but the game they were playing today was rooted in blood and death.

Leonides didn't say where he had been or explain his plan beyond telling the people of Pallas and the Ostarans what he wanted them to do. He didn't explain why they had to do it, and nobody argued or contradicted him. They set off to do as he asked because they didn't have better ideas. Also, his orders were beginning to make hazy sense.

Two large groups set off through the lower city and into the edge of the forest to find branches to barricade the first of the lanes that angled off the single main street that led, straight as an arrow, from the lower to the upper gate. This wasn't as difficult as it seemed. Two of these streets had already been closed by brush and fallen walls. Anyone could climb over or through the barriers, but as they worked, the people realized the Claymon were likely to choose the easiest way into the city. That had to be the route that would take them past the buildings where the children would be waiting with their improvised missiles.

Eight Ostarans volunteered to move the twig contraption Leonides had been building from his workshop to the street in front of the water gate. No one could tell whether it was finished. He had refused to explain its purpose, only saying it would be a surprise. It looked like nothing more than an enormous, misshapen cone sitting on the flat bed of a cart. The people of Pallas thought it looked like a woven bee skep, while the Ostarans thought it looked more like a wooden version of the stone cairns the Claymon had been erecting at every crossroads around Ostara. It didn't make any sense to them, but they pushed it up the hill anyway.

The cart was easier to move than they thought it would be. The wheels were perfectly round, and the axles moved freely. When they looked underneath, they could see the whole thing had been crafted from wood, and the pieces were pegged together. There was no metal, but the axles had been liberally smeared with some kind of fat. A big pot of the stuff nestled in one of the front corners of the cart. Leonides had made no provision for a driver to sit on the front edge, or for any animals to pull it.

The Ostarans found that four of them could push the cart, even though it was all up hill. The others walked ahead with Leonides, clearing the street of brush and rubble while the apprentice walked behind them with a stiff broom, sweeping away smaller stones and twigs. When they reached the top of the street, Leonides directed them to turn it around, even though it looked exactly the same to them from both directions. Turning it was a much harder task. It took a dozen Ostarans to lift the cart off the ground and to shuffle in a circle until it was facing in what Leonides said was the correct direction. Finally, when it stood in the exact center of the street where they could see all the way down the hill to the opposite gate, Leonides blocked the wheels with wedges of wood and told the Ostarans to go and help with the other preparations.

The Ostarans scratched their heads and muttered. The old woodworker obviously had designed this cart and whatever was on top of it to be a weapon in the coming fight. Their hosts, seemed to believe it was important and agreed to everything Leonides asked, but the Ostarans felt as if they were just humoring an old man.

Patrick, who had returned from his tower in time to help turn the cart, saw their faces and decided it was time to ask Leonides for an explanation, but before he could open his mouth, Katherine came out of the nearest house carrying an armload of torches. The people of Pallas already had a supply, but now that the Ostarans had arrived, more were needed.

"The trouble is," she said. "We don't have much to work with. There isn't another scrap of cloth in this town for wrapping, and we don't have any fuel. These won't burn for long."

An Ostaran spoke up. It was one of her brother's friends. "How about that pot of grease?"

He pointed at the big pot of fat in the corner of the cart. "Can't you dip the ends of the torches in that?"

Katherine's face brightened, but Leonides said, "No, you can't!" Then, as if he realized how abrupt he'd been, he said, "I've been saving that. I'll need it tonight. The layer of grease I put on the axles this morning will have soaked into the wood by then."

Kathe blinked. She was starting to see the outline of Leonides' plan, but she still didn't understand how he expected to stop the trained Claymon fighters. And the grease in the pot would solve her urgent problem.

"Surely you won't need it all," she said. "Tonight, darkness will be our friend at first, but the time will come when we will have to have light."

In a way, darkness would be an advantage for the defenders. The citizens and Ostarans would wait for the Claymon within the cloak of night, behind the barricades closest to the main gate, but the council had agreed torches must be ready when needed. Anna had already supervised the placement of torches along the street where the children would be waiting, but they planned to light them only if the Claymon reached that far into the city. The unfinished torches in Katherines arms would be used as weapons, to clear a space around a fighter, and help to tell a friend from an enemy in the darkness.

Leonides partly relented, "Leave them here. There will surely be some grease left after we finish our work, and my boy will coat them."

The apprentice had been walking slowly around the cart, jumping up now and then to tuck in a twig or make some other mysterious adjustment. Patrick wondered whether this boy was privy to the secrets Leonides was keeping. His old master used to refer to him as 'my boy' with the same tone of ownership long ago.

When the sun was directly overhead, the people made their way back to the street from the houses where they had been resting and eating the small meal Anna had conjured. She had spent the early morning hours scouring the forest for edible greens and spring mushrooms. One of the Ostarans disappeared just after sun-up, and he came back after an hour with three rabbits. All this had gone into the communal pot along with dried herbs Katherine brought from Bethany's.

Patrick pulled aside the men and women he had chosen to lead small groups of citizens and Ostarans. Long ago Patrick had agreed to be the city's general. Someone had to be in charge. It was no secret that the council had asked Leonides first. His connection with the Lady made him the logical choice. It was also no secret that he had refused.

Patrick wanted to avoid confronting the Claymon directly. He planned to use the Ostaran raiders' strategy of suddenly attacking from unexpected directions. They would strike and retreat, using their knowledge of the warren of side-streets to their advantage. Each time they struck the Claymon, he hoped to pick off a few of the soldiers, then move quickly to surprise them again farther up the street.

Patrick wished he had thought of barricading the lanes that branched off the main street as it crossed the older, lower part of Pallas. They could have been working to do it over the past weeks, but at least the task had given everyone something to do today besides worry. Before the mid-day meeting, Patrick had walked down to the main gate and found that the townspeople and the Ostarans had managed to completely block the first few lanes branching from the main thoroughfare on both sides. There wasn't time to block every side street and alley, but maybe that wouldn't matter. There was now only one clear route into the city for the Claymon.

Patrick placed his chosen leaders around the open space in front of the restored houses. Devon and Ellen Elder would be responsible for a group. Patch and Patchson would lead another one. He, himself, would oversee a group just inside the gate, on the opposite side of the street from Bard, who would be next to his parents. Anna had chosen two women to help her supervise the children on the roof. She had asked that Patrick treat the children as he did the other groups, and now, seeing them clustered around her, he understood that they knew their role.

That would make four groups on the ground and one on the rooftops. The young woman who was pregnant would go up to the rooftop with Anna and the children. Two old men had come to stand with Patrick's group even though he had asked them to stay behind at the top of the street. They were already old when they left Pallas to go to Niue, and they weren't growing any younger now that they had returned.

"After we win, then you can baby us," one of them said, in a tone that allowed no argument.

Patrick had told the members of his improvised army they could join any group they wished, as long as each group ended up having about the same number of members, and after some milling around, the groups formed. They looked to him standing above them on the steps, seeking direction, and Patrick felt sweat trickle down his spine. The people of Pallas and the Ostarans were so few, and so unready. He fought the urge to order them into the forest to hide.

The Claymon boy Katherine had healed was standing with Ellen Elder. The last time Patrick had spoken with Stormer was back in Brethren, when he volunteered to help. Ellen trusted him, and he was a trained soldier. Now that he no longer wore a Claymon uniform, he looked just like everyone else.

Katherine had joined Patch and Patchson's group. Once Patrick had approved the groups, he caught her eye and went over to her.

She knew what he was going to say, so she spoke first, "There's more at stake here than these lives." She swept her arm around the street, where the groups had circled their leaders. Each group had shut everyone else out as they made their final plans.

"My people came here because it's their last hope to weaken Greystone's hold on Ostara," Katherine said. "To the refugees, keeping their freedom and their home is more important than anything else. If they have to leave a second time…"

"I know," Patrick said. He paused as if he couldn't remember how to form words. "It would be better for them to die tonight."

"I should listen to what Patch is saying to my group," Katherine said.

"Patch and Patchson have ten. Why not move over and join mine?"

"You know why."

And Patrick did know. Katherine wouldn't join his group because she didn't want to distract him. The truth was, they would distract each other. In a skirmish with the Claymon, they would be too concerned about keeping each other safe.

"Meet me after your group has laid its plans," he said.

"You have got to make your rounds of the city and choose our positions. I am going to help Sylvie with the children, and there are more torches to finish wrapping and to place. You and I will spend the whole day together tomorrow." She gently kissed his cheek, noticing but not caring that her father was watching. Then she turned away and bent her head so she could hear what Patch was saying.

36

THEY ARE COMING

KATHERINE SHIVERED. SHE WAS alone again, but this time others were nearby, or at least close enough to hear if she called. Together, Patch's group had practiced the signal until he was satisfied it would fool a Claymon. When he decided everyone sounded enough like a tree frog, the old Woods Runner led them down the hill to the gate. They slipped out one by one and crept along the city wall, spacing themselves well apart before hiding inside the edge of the forest. In this way, they formed a half ring extending along the wall on both sides of the gate. When the Claymon came, someone from Patch's group would sound the alarm, giving those inside the city a few minutes warning.

The animal guides hadn't brought any more messages since early that day when Oro came to chastise Patrick and Katherine for ignoring him. Even Raven, who seemed determined to stay as close as he could to human friends, had not returned from his scouting mission. Patrick and his captains thought the dearth of information must mean Oro and the other guides were staying near the Claymon camp, watching the Northerners and waiting for movement, but with the animal guides, no news meant just that. The people waiting in Pallas would have to draw their own conclusions, and they might be wrong.

Katherine wished she knew how far away the Claymon were, at least. The animals' warning might come too late to do any good. Maybe the Woods Runners were no longer serving

Greystone, but Patch said the Claymon had grown better at tracking and moving silently.

Greystone might send spies before he ordered the attack. If Katherine or one of her group members were to notice a single Claymon passing by, there was a different, shorter call to use. That would let the group closest to the gate, her father's group, know a spy was heading their way.

Her brother Bard had wanted to leave Pallas to seek out the enemy camp himself, but Patrick decided against it. For one thing, Bard was in charge of one of the fighting groups, and he needed to stay in the city to prepare. For another, if he were caught, it would make their odds even worse. Right now, there were a lot of things Greystone didn't know. Claymon ignorance was one of the townspeople's few advantages.

Because he had followed the ponies, Greystone ought to be thinking the Ostarans would have barely arrived in Pallas. He couldn't know they had cut through the forest and arrived in time to make a swift alliance with the forest people. He wouldn't expect Pallas to be ready.

Chances were, Greystone believed he would be attacking a sleeping city with only a few, weak citizens, the refugees who had returned from Niue. Katherine's chin touched her chest. She thought she might fall asleep herself if she had to wait much longer. All this speculation was worth exactly nothing. Her eyes drifted shut, and she shifted on the log where she was sitting. It had a bush growing up next to and over it, and she was concealed by branches, but after several hours, her chosen seat had become very hard.

She tried to wake herself up by identifying every sound she heard. She didn't hear anything from her fellow watchers, not even a cough or a sneeze. Was the snapping of a twig an enemy's footstep or the movement of a deer? A light wind had come up, masking sounds and making her feel even more uneasy. The creaking of a tree swaying in the breeze could have been the creak of the Claymons' leather armor. She rolled her shoulder and arched her back.

It was after midnight when she said, in the way she used to speak to the animal guides, *"Are you here? Anyone?"*

She didn't intend to do that. It's just that she had been remembering another night, near the beginning of her journey more than a year ago, when she was alone and just learning to trust the animals. Tonight humans and animals each had their own duties. It was selfish to act from loneliness.

There was no answer. The longer she waited, the harder it was to push certain thoughts away. It was possible, maybe even likely, that she and Patrick wouldn't both survive the night. She told herself she was just being realistic. Most of the people she loved were gathered behind the walls of Pallas, and if they were right about what was coming, every one of them was in danger.

Katherine put her elbows on her knees and rested her head in her hands, massaging her forehead. The moon was in and out of clouds. She couldn't see anything under the trees' thick shadows. Closing her eyes didn't matter. Katherine continued to listen, but even though she had called out to the guides, she still swallowed a yelp of surprise when she felt something soft against her knee.

She put out a hand and felt the silky smoothness that could only be Maraba. The panther walked back and forth in front of her, rubbing her sides against Katherine's skirt and purring too loudly.

"Shhh. Someone might hear you," Katherine said.

"Is that any way to greet an old friend?" Maraba said. *"I can't help it. No cat can."*

Katherine felt for the panther's head in the darkness and wrapped her arms around her neck.

"Anyway, it doesn't matter. The men who are coming are making so much noise that they can't hear anything else."

"They're coming?" Katherine gasped, her throat tight.

There had been no spies. That's how confident Peter Greystone was that the city would be his by morning.

"You should make the signal," Maraba said.

There was no time to wonder how Maraba knew about the signal, but as she puffed out her cheeks to call the warning, Katherine saw the flaw in Patch's plan. This springtime forest was full of desperately trilling tree frogs. Patch might know the difference between her signal and a frog, but no one else would, including her newly trained comrades.

She took a drink from her water bag to moisten her mouth and trilled as loudly as she could, but a pitch higher and with a pulsing rhythm quite different from that of a real frog. It sounded like a bird call or maybe a ghost's wailed lament. No one would mistake that sound for a tree frog's mating call, except, she hoped, the Claymon.

When Stormer was helping to build the barricade, he was careful to leave a place to squeeze through when it was time to fight. As twilight deepened, he kept searching the neighborhood for sticks and other debris to make the barrier higher and stronger until Ellen came and told him it was enough.

"My husband wants all of us to stay still now," she whispered.

Devon Elder might have given this order to keep their location secret if an enemy scout managed to slip past Patch's team in the forest, but Stormer thought it more likely Devon was stretched to his limit. Through the day, Stormer had noticed Katherine's father was beginning to stand apart from everyone else. He had stopped talking, and his expression became more and more unreadable.

Too much depended on this night. If the townspeople and the Ostarans prevailed, Devon would no longer be the leader of rebels. He would return to Ostara through the main gate and ride across the square. He would climb the steep hill and reclaim his home. If the rebels prevailed, the people here in the forest city, the refugees, could continue to rebuild their lives in peace.

But if they were defeated? Everyone was thinking about that, but no one was saying anything, not even in whispers.

Towards nightfall, Devon had started to relay his messages to the team through Ellen. It was as if he feared his voice would reveal his feelings. Stormer trusted both Devon and Ellen. Devon had kept the rebels safe ever since the Claymon seized Ostara, but Ellen was stronger in many ways. Everyone knew it, including her husband.

It took a few repetitions of Katherine's call for Stormer to recognize he was hearing something unusual. By then the others in his group were already moving into position in front of the barrier. Because Devon Elder had more experience than the other group leaders, his team would be the first to attack from inside the entrance to the first lane that branched off from the main road. Even in near darkness, they could easily see the lower gate, where the Claymon would enter Pallas. Patrick and his group were ready inside the second street on the opposite side. This pattern continued up the hill until just before the buildings where the children were waiting next to their supply of rocks.

Now that the signal had been given, the news traveled through the town, carried on the wind that whistled around the buildings. The Claymon were almost here.

Stormer had no way to know which member of Patch's group had made the strange call in the forest. Nevertheless, he thought of Katherine. She was out there. Everything had happened so quickly. She probably hadn't had a chance to read the book he had given her yet. He saw her come down from the roof with Patrick in the morning. He guessed it hadn't mattered after all, that he had to abandon her back there below the headlands to return to Brethren. She had made it here on her own. She was fine.

Stormer tightened his grip on his knife's hilt. It was the same weapon he was given on the day he finished training, after he left his home village in the North to join the Claymon army. Before long, he would be using this knife against other Claymon.

It no longer mattered that his Claymon comrades hadn't liked or trusted him, especially at the end. And before that, most didn't even notice him. They wouldn't recognize him among the rebels and townspeople tonight. It was more than just discarding a uniform. Stormer didn't know himself any longer. He had his own reasons to fight – new reasons. If Pallas lost, and if he wasn't killed in battle…

He didn't allow the thought to go any further. Word came hissing down the line to his team to find their positions in front of the barricade. Stormer looked to the left and right at the others. In near darkness, he had to squint to see their shapes. They were as still as the trees in the forest, each clutching some weapon, even if it was just a sturdy branch. Three more members of the team remained behind the barricade, waiting to light torches next to the sheltering wall of a ruined shop, waiting for the final signal.

The crunch of boots echoed against the pavers in front of the gate. The Claymon weren't trying to be quiet. Two men in front of the mass of soldiers carried torches, but the light didn't penetrate down the lane as far as the barricade. Flames flickered gold from the clothing of the men just behind the torchbearers. Those would be Peter Greystone and his personal guards, Stormer thought. If the Claymon glanced into the entrance of the street, they must surely see the rebels, but they seemed not to notice anything amiss, only a dark, quiet city.

Devon stood at the center of his team with one arm raised. They kept their eyes on his hand. He dropped it sharply as the last of the Claymon passed through the gate and into the street. That's when Stormer's team attacked from one side, screaming threats and insults to make themselves seem more numerous and to give themselves courage. Now the scene was lit from above by their own torchbearers, who were clambering over the top of the barricade, handing the torches down to their comrades who had already crossed.

There was barely a breath of hesitation when the Claymon realized they would not take this town without a fight after all. Then their shouts and oaths joined those of the rebels, forming a toxic cacophony.

The Claymon continued to march up the street, leaving the men in the rear to deal with the rabble. Some of the rebels managed to jump onto the backs of the last rank of the Claymon from behind. Stormer slit the throat of his chosen victim before the man had time to realize he had already taken his last breath. He couldn't be sure, but from the single glance he allowed himself, Stormer thought this one was a stranger.

He turned to face another Claymon soldier. Stormer ducked what would have been a killing blow and flung himself low enough to grab the Claymon around the knees, stinging the man in the calf with his knife. As they both fell, Stormer began to pommel the soldier with his free fist and kept slashing with his knife. If he could only win the man's sword for himself, he might have a chance.

It took a few more blows before Stormer realized his opponent was still. The sword lay on the pavers, his for the taking. As he reached for it, he raised his eyes and was nearly blinded. Just in front of him, one of Bard's friends was thrusting a torch into the face of a snarling Claymon who was about to stab Stormer. He threw up his arm and felt the hairs singe as the Claymon cut the Ostaran torchbearer down instead.

With his free hand, Stormer caught the torch before it guttered, then rolled to one side, anticipating a blow. Swinging the captured sword wildly, with his back against the wall, he heard new sounds of battle from ahead. Patrick's team had attacked.

Patch's team joined the fray at the same time, flowing up through the gate, carrying branches ahead of them and yelling like banshees. It was hard to see, but Stormer thought Kathe was running just behind Patch, and there seemed to be an animal by her side. The confused Claymon retreated, backing up the hill with the surviving members of Devon's and Patch's teams pushing them as the other teams attacked from the side streets.

Stormer thought more Claymon were lying dead in the street than townspeople, but as he raced after them, he was afraid too many of his former comrades still survived. He had always known the Ostarans and the townspeople would be too few to prevail against Greystone, but they continued to harry the enemy, herding the Northerners deeper into the city.

Stormer held the torch high. It was beginning to run out of fuel, but he spared a glance behind, searching for Ellen. He couldn't see her, but he knew she must be there. By now she and Katherine would be searching for the wounded.

The Northerners formed an ever-tighter phalanx as the remaining teams attacked. The attacks always began with screamed threats, and then the voices changed to grunts and cries of anger and pain.

Just as the torch went out, Stormer flung it towards the center of the knot of Claymon and engaged another soldier. This time it was someone he knew. It was the man who spat on him back in Brethren. He lunged and struck the man's sword arm, knocked the weapon from his hand, and tossed it to a townsman who was trying to fight off an attacker with a wooden pike.

37

The Turning

Peter Greystone was arrogant. He was selfish, cruel, greedy and stubborn. One thing he was not was stupid. He allowed the townsfolk to drive him deeper into the city only because that's where he wanted to go anyway, but when the Claymon reached the place where the buildings bordering the street were taller, he ordered his men to stand and fight. The darkness under the walls felt ominous. It was too enclosed. He sensed the trap.

So far, no rebel Ostaran or refugee of Pallas had come within a sword's length of Greystone. His personal guards, their numbers swollen by the addition of extra men, formed a shield in front of him and to each side. Behind him, the Claymon had closed in upon themselves so tightly it was easier than usual to think of them as just a single weapon at his disposal, but as he surveyed the battle, he could see the edges of the formation were fraying, spooling out towards the black mouths of side streets as his men responded to the rebel attacks.

From where Greystone was standing, slightly above the fray, he couldn't tell exactly what was happening farther down the hill, but some of the curses ringing in the street were Claymon.

Though outwardly calm, as Greystone always was in battle, anger simmered just below the surface. He had come here to claim the rich resources of the forest. Greystone had denied Honorus Woods Runner guides so he would reach Pallas before the magician. The scum who were hindering him, especially the

Ostaran rebels who had somehow arrived so much sooner than he expected, meant less than nothing to him. They were only a swarm of biting flies. He would crush them.

Still, the sounds he was hearing from farther down the hill were troubling. Since the last cross-street, the fighting had come so close that Greystone had drawn his own sword. There was little room to move in the street, so it had fallen to the soldiers at the rear and at the sides to fight off the rebels. The neat ranks of Claymon who had entered the city had dissolved into a confused knot. The attackers were few, but they knew the ground, and there seemed to be some trained fighters among them.

If only he had chosen to ride into Pallas instead of marching at the head of his troops tonight. When he mounted his horse back in the camp, it flared its nostrils, and its eyes rolled back until only the whites shone like those of a demon in the darkness. It reared at the torchbearers, and he barely brought it back under control. The beast had not been right since the raiders stole it from him. They must have bewitched it somehow. Rather than risk looking foolish, Peter Greystone had chosen to march the short distance to the city tonight, and he ordered everyone else to do the same.

If he were on horseback now, he would get their attention. He would stamp out the embers of panic that were flaring. The rebels were pathetic, but they had boxed him and his men into this street that felt more and more like a cattle pen. The darkness was to their advantage, not his.

Greystone's nostrils flared. By the time he was finished with Pallas, there would be no city in the forest, not even a ruined one. When the mad freak Honorus returned, it would be to rule an empty, scorched place. And not only that. Greystone would keep his former counselor here, under guard forever. Honorus would never again escape the blighted wasteland that had once been Pallas.

His bearers pulled new torches from their packs and lit them from the nearly spent ones. The light bearers were protected, as he was, by others, much as the queen of a hive is protected by her drones. On some primitive level, the Claymon soldiers believed their survival depended on the well-being of their leader. Squinting into the distance, Greystone saw nothing but darkness. The enemies' torches had all gone out.

What Greystone couldn't know was that, down there in the darkness, his soldiers were falling and dying in greater numbers than the rebels. The Claymon had more real weapons and more experience, but they lacked the rebels' desperation. Also, the rebels could fall back and disappear into the side streets when they had to. There was nowhere for the Claymon to move except inch-by-inch up the street. The rebels were like waves slowly eroding a cliff face. And as the Claymon fell, more of the rebels and townsfolk gained swords.

Greystone bellowed in frustration, ordering his men to cease their advance and to stand and fight. A roar built among the Claymon. It was their battle cry. Even though their numbers were reduced, the sound was terrifying. At once the tide of battle began to turn. The Claymon were hungry to crush the rebels who had been treating them like easy pickings. They turned like a wave that curls and crashes on a shore. They surged forward and mowed down the closest Ostarans and townspeople before they understood that the rules had changed.

Patch was among the nearest to the Claymon when they turned. He had been harassing the soldiers as they climbed the hill, stabbing at them and retreating, and he had his sights on a man whose hunched shoulders made him seem to be the next easy target.

When Greystone's squire blew his horn, that same Claymon turned and yelled, thrusting his pike into the Woods Runner's side.

The soldier would have pulled out his pike and finished Patch with the knife he held in his other hand, but Patchson was fighting by his father's side. He leapt between the two and grappled with the Claymon. They fell, and the Northerner hit his head on the stone pavement and was still.

Patchson clasped his father under his arms and scrambled back – half dragging, half carrying Patch through the tangled legs of desperate rebels and avenging Claymon.

When Patch reached the open street beyond the fight, Kathe was there. She had been helping Ellen to care for the wounded, and her skirt and sleeves were sticky with blood. Claymon soldiers moaned and grabbed at her ankles as she searched for hurt townspeople and Ostarans. Her heart froze each time she pulled herself away from those grasping hands and moved on. She was searching for a beloved face. Her father, Bard – or Patrick. It was too much to hope they would all have been spared.

The baker, Marios, was the first townsman to call out to her. As soon as she knelt beside him, she saw he was beyond saving. Blood trickled from the corner of his mouth, and his eyes were already dimming. All she could do was hold his hands until he was gone. Only a few days ago, Marios had been working to repair his oven, and Katherine had heard him ask Patch when he'd be bringing butter and eggs from Bethany's farm. The refugees would have known their lives were returning to normal when Marios's first batch of cakes came out of that earthen oven. Now it would never happen.

She had just released his hands when she saw two hunched forms moving down the hill toward her. The moon peeked in and out from behind high clouds, illuminating their white faces. She stumbled over a dead Claymon as she ran to where Patchson had collapsed with his father in his arms.

"Here, let me," Kathe said. She pulled away the hand Patchson held pressed onto his father's belly. As soon as he released it, the blood began to flow again. It had already soaked Patch's tunic. Too much blood.

"My mother is in the wood-working shop," Katherine said, trying to keep her voice calm, but failing. She pulled a cloth from her bag and pressed it onto the wound. "Get her."

Patchson leapt to his feet and ran, using the night vision of the Woods Runners to keep himself from falling, but Katherine already knew he and Ellen wouldn't return in time.

She bent close to Patch's ear and whispered, "I never thanked you for coming to me that night, you stubborn, silent old man. Well, we will both have to be stubborn now."

She pressed more firmly and closed her eyes.

Farther up the street, Patrick heard the Claymon battle cry and knew what it meant. He gave his opponent a shove that toppled not only that man, but the one behind him. Then he darted through the doorway of the nearest building and leapt up the inside stairway. He balanced on the wall high above the fight. He was vulnerable to arrows there, but down in the street, where Greystone's neat phalanx of soldiers had divided into deadly fragments, no one was paying any attention to what was happening above them. Not yet.

"Fall back," he cried. "Fall back!"

Fearing the townspeople and Ostarans wouldn't hear his voice above the noise in time to save themselves, he placed two fingers to his mouth and whistled. That got their attention. He watched the townspeople melt away down the side-streets of the lower town.

The Claymon were shocked into stillness. They did not pursue those who, moments ago, had been fighting so fiercely. The soldiers stared into the sudden emptiness around them, as if they thought they might have been fighting ghosts before gazing up at Patrick like so many open-mouthed carp waiting for bread-crumbs.

"Shoot him, you idiots," Greystone yelled.

Silhouetted in the moonlight, Patrick pointed down the hill towards the gate through which the Claymon had entered Pallas.

Then he was gone, ducking below the wall to avoid a hail of arrows wasted against the stones.

"Hold your torches higher!!" Greystone ordered his bearers.

Up above, heading straight toward Greystone, was a creature from a nightmare. The dream had come to him every night since Honorus and the others returned from Brethren. Always, afterwards, he woke twisted in his sheets and drenched in sweat. It happened again last night, in camp, but this time the nightmare was vivid enough that he called out to the guard standing outside his tent. When the man entered, sword drawn, Greystone claimed he had heard a strange sound. He could not admit he had been frightened by a dream, but what he was seeing now was real. Too frightened to scream, Greystone unconsciously made a sign to ward off evil while his men fled on each side of him, up into the street ahead, mindlessly trying to escape.

It was just as his men had described, except back on the beach in Brethren there had been only one. Now there were two dragons. As they flew nearer, their wings spread an even deeper darkness over the channel of the street, and when they reached the Claymon, they screamed. The otherworldly sound echoed back and forth between the high stone walls. Torchlight reflected first green, then blood red, but only in the moment before the torchbearers ran.

Greystone's guard had already abandoned him, taking to their heels with the others. He knew he should be running too, but he was still frozen in place when the screaming started behind him, farther up the street. This wasn't the dragons. It was his own men screaming in terror, and there was something else. Since Greystone had just seen dragons, it was easy for him to believe there were giants in the darkness ahead, stamping their feet hard enough to shake the pavement.

A few men staggered back towards him from the darkness of the block ahead. Just then, a stone as big as a man's head fell from the top corner of the nearest wall. It shattered on the pavers close to Greystone's feet, and one of the shards struck the back of his right hand. He stared at the blood welling from the wound and tried to make sense of another sound. It sounded like laughter. That made no sense, but at the same time it couldn't be anything else. Children were laughing.

The dragons were still in sight, but they didn't make a second pass over the city. They had become nothing more than dark, silent shapes flying beyond the upper city, but whatever deadly game the children were playing was still unfinished.

"To me," Greystone screamed, almost sobbing.

He repeated his call until perhaps twenty of his men stood around him, including two of his guards. Where were all the others? He had come here with a hundred men. They couldn't all be dead! They must be hiding, as the rebels were, in the side-streets and houses. Or more likely they had made it through the gauntlet of rocks. Maybe they were still fighting somewhere up ahead of him in this accursed city.

The block ahead was quiet now, except for moaning. One of his guards knelt to relight a torch that lay fallen on the pavers.

"What do we do now?" the guard asked.

"My Lord," Greystone barked.

"What do we do now?" the guard repeated, not looking up, still trying to make a spark.

Greystone decided to forget about correcting the man for now and considered the question. If they retreated to the gate, the rebels would surely attack again. He could try to circle the dangerous part of the street ahead by the way of side-streets and alleys, but he didn't know Pallas, and there were likely other dangers lying in the darkness.

The disturbing laughter had stopped. The street was eerily quiet after the clashing sounds of battle, the screaming of the dragons, and the barrage of rocks. Even the moaning had quieted. Were the children waiting for new targets, or were they out of missiles?

"We have to get past this stretch of street to the next crossing," Greystone decided. "We will run for it."

His heart had been pounding ever since the appearance of the dragons. His terror was fading, but he knew he would see the monsters whenever he closed his eyes. "If we turn back, we will surely face attack again," he said. "We are few, maybe fewer than the rebels now, though we must have killed many of them.

The guard looked full into Greystone's face. By the light of the torch, his sneer was obvious.

"We?" he said. "I didn't see you fighting."

The other soldiers muttered among themselves, and Greystone pretended he didn't hear. There would be time to punish their insolence later.

"Stay in the very center. It's children up there. Even if they still have rocks, they won't be strong enough to throw them far.

His men had formed a circle around him.

"Seemed to us they were dropping them where they pleased." Which one said that?

Greystone could not allow himself to be questioned, especially by a man who shouldn't even have dared to speak in his presence unless ordered to do so. At the same time, there was nothing he could do about it. His fists clenched in frustration.

"Stay or leave, it's your choice," he spat. "But if you stay behind here, you'll be easy pickings for the demons who attacked us. If we stay together, at least we'll have a chance."

There was nothing the men could say to that and no point in waiting any longer for more courage. The surviving Claymon raced up the hill again as if the dragons were still chasing them. Greystone stayed a few paces behind, partly because he was slower and partly because he thought the children would use their remaining rocks on those who entered the street first.

He was wrong. The children did have more rocks, but they seemed to have saved them just for him. As soon as he entered the shadows of the tall buildings, stones rained around him, bouncing off the pavement or shattering into pieces. Maybe the brats were running out of big ones, but these small rocks were easier to throw and big enough to kill.

A fist-sized missile grazed Greystone's shoulder, knocking him to one side. He yelped, almost tripping over a soldier who had fallen in the first stampede up this street of death. He had no time to realize or appreciate that, if he hadn't stumbled just at that moment, he would surely have taken a second rock to his skull.

Greystone's breath came in sobs as he regained his balance and kept running. Then he was at the end of the gauntlet, swearing between gasps. The other survivors were waiting for him. He wasn't sure what he had expected, but seeing them there, he stood a little taller. They were just sheep without him to lead them.

"Something's going on up there," the guard said, pointing towards the upper end of the street. "Looks like they're making a bonfire."

Greystone's anger flared, fueled by the adrenaline of the dash through the street, by cheating death, and by his relief at the disappearance of the dragons. "It's too soon for them to be celebrating," he growled. "It's time for us to show them what happens when you take on the Claymon."

This time no one argued. The Claymon pictured rebels celebrating up ahead around their fire, and they were eager to avenge the humiliation they had suffered. Greystone took his usual place ahead of his much reduced force. His confidence returned, even surged. He reminded himself of what he had always known. One Claymon soldier was worth three of a rabble such as the rebels.

They had gone less than half a block farther when the men behind him suddenly stopped. Greystone hadn't ordered a halt, but before he could berate them, someone pointed and said. "The fire. It's moving!"

38

PATCH

KATHERINE DIDN'T HEAR PATRICK whistle the retreat or notice when the rebels obeyed him. As the townspeople and Ostarans dashed back down the hill and disappeared into side streets, a few paused to touch her shoulder or her hair. Others simply stopped and looked down at Patch for a moment, paying their final respects to the Woods Runner. They could see he was gone, or soon would be.

She didn't notice their concern, and soon the two of them were alone again. It was just Patch and her – and the dead.

In the weeks since she healed Stormer, Katherine had often thought about the morning she found him lying on the trail. There were still patches of snow under the pines then, and though swollen buds promised leaves and flowers, their blooming was still some time off. She thought it was important to remember everything about that day. Then maybe she could understand what she had done to help Stormer. How had she mended him?

Rowan had been the one who first found the young Claymon lying on the animal trail, nearly dead of shock. Her mother and Bethany had left the work of healing him to Katherine. They stood a short distance from her, ready to help if they were needed. Each time Katherine tried to remember what she had done, her mind refused to follow that path. It was as if she had briefly opened a door when she healed Stormer, and now it was firmly locked again. Finally, she simply accepted that it had happened.

Now she had to make it happen again.

Ellen couldn't leave the woodworker's shop at once. There were too many wounded who needed her immediate attention. As soon as she thought it safe to go out for a few minutes, she snatched up a bag of supplies and hurried the short distance up the street with Patchson leading the way. He hadn't given her much information – just that Patch had been badly hurt and she was needed. Well, that was the case for everyone who was lying on the floor in the shop. The sawdust was soaked with blood.

They had crossed half the distance to Patch when Ellen saw Katherine sitting on the ground. Somehow, she had pulled the Runner up until his head rested against her shoulder. Her arms were around him, and her hand was pressed to his side. That must be where he was hurt. Ellen ran a few steps to catch up with Patchson and grabbed his arm. He was so intent on reaching his father that he tried to pull away.

"Shhh. Stop here. We must leave her to it," Ellen whispered, though she thought Katherine was probably beyond hearing their voices.

"But she sent me for you. She must think you can help him," Patchson said. He had taken hold of Ellen's hand and was pulling her forward.

With difficulty, Ellen pulled free. "She doesn't trust herself. That's why she wanted me, but Katherine is your father's best chance." She paused, and when Patchson would have continued arguing, she said, "Please believe me."

Patchson turned back towards Ellen, "But she isn't doing anything!"

"She is," Ellen said, "And I will help her if she needs me. We can move a little closer if we are careful not to disturb her."

Patch was growing heavier against Katherine's shoulder, and he was cold. She could feel him going. Without consciously choosing to do it, she followed. She saw him almost at once, a short distance ahead. He was moving quickly, with light footsteps, following a trail in the deep forest. He didn't seem to know Katherine was trailing him. If this had not been a dream, she would surely have lost him.

Katherine knew where Patch must be going, but Bethany had never told her what to do if this happened. Beneath her hands, back in the conscious world, Patch's blood was clotting. It still flowed, but ever slower. Sweat trickled down Katherine's back. Back in the street, the breeze picked up, and Ellen placed her shawl around her daughter's shoulders.

In the dream world, Patch looked calm and happy. There was no conflict in this springtime forest. He simply had to follow the trail until he reached his destination. Even though she couldn't see where he was heading, she knew he could see the end of this path clearly. Should she try to stop him?

In the street Katherine shuddered. Ellen laid a hand on Patchson's arm.

Katherine turned away from the dream and returned to the street. She was taking a chance. She might not be able to find Patch again. She released the pressure on the Runner's wound and traced the place where the pike had entered his body with the tip of her finger. Under that single puncture lay injury after injury. How could one thrust do so much damage?

Still, she knew right away she could repair it. Some of it, at least. She finally remembered what she did when she healed Stormer, when she conjured the needle and thread from her sewing kit and mended his lungs with tiny stitches.

Except this time she would have to do two things at once. Was that possible? She would have to begin her work here but also keep following Patch deeper into the forest. She had to show him he had a choice – that he didn't have to leave yet.

It was risky. Back in Ostara, Katherine had spent many afternoons sewing and chatting with the ladies gathered in Ellen's room – followed by many evenings unpicking her mistakes by candlelight. Fine work requires close attention.

"Oro, Maraba, can you help?" Katherine cried.

While she waited for an answer, she started mending at the deepest place, where the Claymon pike had nicked an artery. That was where most of the blood had come from. After a few stitches, that bleeding stopped, but Patch had already lost so much! Katherine sighed and kindled a fire, raising her own body temperature, risking everything to warm the Woods Runner.

Ellen's eyes widened when Oro landed in the street in front of Katherine. She should have heard Katherine call the owl, and she should have been able to hear what they were saying to each other. So should Patchson. Oro was here for a reason, but what was it?

"You know why I called you. You know what I need you to do," Katherine said.

"Why not let him go? He is free. He is happy." Oro said.

"He may go, but only after he sees what he is leaving. He thinks he was given his death wound, and he has accepted that. I can repair the wound, but I want you can show him he has a choice."

"And you promise to accept his decision?" Oro asked.

"I will."

"Then I will help you." Oro did not close his eyes, but he hopped closer, so that his wing brushed the side of Patch's knee.

Katherine turned to Patch's intestines. The spear's razor edge had sliced them almost in half, and even more damage was done when the soldier withdrew the weapon. Katherine turned to repairing the delicate coil.

To Ellen and Patchson, it seemed nothing was happening, but they kept their eyes glued to the strange tableau. Ellen gripped Patchson's arm harder. Steam had started to rise from Katherine's head and shoulders, and there was a faint glow, like an aura, that encompassed both her daughter and the inert form of the Woods Runner who lay sprawled across her lap.

Katherine knew Oro would keep his promise, so she turned her attention to her work. She must not close the surface wound until she was certain all the internal damage had been mended. Her hair was soaked in sweat, and her hands, still held lightly over Patch's wound, trembled slightly. Ellen took an unconscious step forward, but this time it was Patchson who stopped her.

"Something's going on here. I don't know what it is, but maybe you're right. We had better let her finish," he said.

Meanwhile, in the dream world, Oro flew ahead of Patch, who turned from the path he had been following and followed the owl trustingly. Patch wasn't surprised a guide had come to lead him. He was certain they were going to the place in the forest where the trees had never been cut and where flowers bloomed all year round. It couldn't be far.

Patch kept his eyes on the owl until he was forced to an abrupt stop. A thick hedge blocked his path. Something about it was familiar. He must have been here before, though 'before' was becoming harder to remember. He didn't like the looks of it. The stems were dense and covered with wicked thorns. Oro had disappeared over the top of the hedge. This must be a test. If he wanted to reach the most ancient place, he would have to follow.

It would be worth a few scratches to reach the place he longed to see, the grove where a clear stream flowed from the earth, where he could finally rest. As Patch plunged ahead, the hedge parted for him, and he tumbled out onto his hands and knees on the other side.

He had crossed into an orderly landscape of orchard and pasture. Sheep and lambs grazed nearby, oblivious to his arrival. Patch stood up and brushed off his knees. In the distance, close to a house, somebody was working in a garden. It was a woman, and she was wielding a hoe. Chickens followed her down the rows, ready to snap up worms and insects from the turned soil. She stopped and stretched her back, wiping an arm across her forehead. She seemed to be looking right at Patch, but she showed no sign that she had seen him.

The great horned owl was sitting close by on a low branch of an apple tree.

"Who is she?" Patch said, but even as he asked the question, he was beginning to remember. He had been to this farm, had mended its fences and had sat by the fire in that cottage with smoke curling from its chimney. He had slept under the strange roof of that house, listening to the rain against the windows and the breathing of this woman. He had slept curled against her. Patch was a man of the forest, but he remembered being happy here.

"I have kept my promise" Oro said. *"I have shown you your choice. If it is your will, you may retrace your steps and follow the forest trail to its end. Or you may return to a world that is full of pain, but a world that includes this."* The owl lifted his wing to encompass the whole farm. *"You must choose."*

Before Patch could ask any questions, Oro took off and glided out of sight over the hedge.

39

ABLAZE

THE REMAINING CLAYMON CLUSTERED in a tight group behind Greystone. They stared at the monster hurtling down the hill towards them. When they first spotted it, the fire had been stationary, as a bonfire ought to be, but now it was moving. They didn't recognize the danger until it started to pick up speed. As it raced closer, they saw it wasn't a bonfire at all, but a living being cloaked in flames. Two eyes blazed red above golden tongues that licked out in every direction. As the monster swiftly closed the distance between them, the fire grew until it was nearly as tall as the buildings lining the street.

For the Claymon, time had slowed down, but really no time at all passed before the fire creature was close enough that they saw men running beside a wagon. The men poked at the monster with long poles, goading it to greater rage. They darted close to the wagon and shoved it to correct its course, but the wagon was soon hurtling downhill so fast that the runners fell behind. The fire creature swayed on top of the wagon, bouncing and teetering whenever it hit a rough place in the street, but always righting itself. Greystone thought he heard words coming from inside the roar of the fire. They were threats of doom in some strange language.

Greystone glanced over his shoulder into the darkness in the block below, where so many Claymon bodies had been crushed by rocks. Whoever threw the missiles down from the rooftops might have more. This fire creature wanted to drive them back into that blackness.

"Down the alley. Follow me!" Greystone cried.

He had taken only a few steps when he realized the entrance to the side street to his left was blocked by rebels. Their faces were veiled by darkness, but he could make out their shapes standing shoulder to shoulder, closing off the way. He ran towards the street on the right. It was the same there.

Turning around to face his remaining men, he snarled, "We'll fight our way through," but they were already gone, fleeing back down the hill. Their screams and the clatter of more rocks smashing against pavement echoed behind him. He shouted into the darkness, but there was no one to hear.

These sounds were almost drowned out by the sound of the fire itself. Greystone felt it in his chest, like thunder and hammers, and when he spun around, the beast spat red and blue sparks that caught at his coat.

It was nearly upon him. He squeezed his eyes tight against the broiling heat and threw himself against the wall of the nearest building, pressing his face against the stones. Flames reached out to singe his hair, and he beat at his collar and sleeve. He was sure the monster would leap off the wagon and burn him alive.

Then the wagon passed and was beyond him. Greystone watched it illuminate the block below, bumping over the bodies that lay there. It hadn't gone very far when a wheel hit a rock, and the wagon finally overturned. As it did, the fire collapsed, and Greystone finally saw it for what it was. This was no monster, but a trick built of wood by human hands.

There was no way to know whether any of his men had made it through the gauntlet for the second time, but even if they had, they were useless. Any survivors were probably through the gate and half-way back to the Claymon camp. He had left a few men there to guard the horses, but they too were out of reach.

Peter Greystone was alone. It was a strange situation, one he had never experienced, even as a young boy. There had always been someone to come running when he called. He wasn't yet ready to admit that his men wouldn't have returned this time even if they could hear him call.

Greystone listened to the crackling of the fire. The wind moaning through the street was keeping it alive, and the flames were now consuming the wagon that had carried it. Otherwise, Pallas was completely silent. Ignoring the rebels, who still blocked the side streets, Greystone walked closer to the beginning of the deadly block, where so many of his men lay injured and dead, and he looked up. Faces peered down at him over the edge of the roof. They were illuminated by the firelight, and they looked like... No. It was impossible.

As he had thought when he heard their laughter, these were children.

In the flickering light, Greystone could make out the mixture of men and women blocking his escape. They were as expressionless and still as if they had been carved from wood. What did they expect him to do? Greystone's anger at the Ostaran raiders was reduced to a simmer. His desire to possess the forest city had lost its urgency. In fact, Greystone was having trouble remembering why he had chosen to come to Pallas at all. He spared a thought for his bed chamber back in Ostara, with its goose down stuffed bed coverings and bell pull within easy reach.

Time stretched on, stretching Greystone's nerves with it. Then one man stepped out from among those blocking the street to his left. The others shuffled to fill the gap as the stranger approached Greystone.

The sky was pearling moment by moment. It was now light enough to see the man's features and even the strands of grey silvering his dark hair. Greystone was almost certain he had never met him, and yet...

He glanced over his shoulder at the rooftops, but the faces were gone. As he watched, a raven flew from the direction of the forest and landed on the corner of the nearest building. Peter Greystone shuddered. Ravens were bad luck.

"Name your terms," Greystone said, assuming he was talking to the rebel leader. He realized he didn't have any option except surrender. The rebels had won – for now. Subduing the Ostarans and taking Pallas would have to wait for another day. It would be enough to put this nightmare behind him.

"Terms?" The man spoke in the common tongue, but with a strange accent Greystone had only heard from one other person.

"What is it you want?" Greystone said, unable to keep the impatience from his voice. Now that he was no longer in immediate danger, he was beginning to feel the sting of being beaten by this rabble, and his usual haughty tone returned. "Tell me what you want as ransom. You have won the day."

"Not quite," Patrick said, drawing Mabus. Light burst from the stones in the sword's hilt and escaped between his fingers like the spokes of a wheel.

Greystone touched his face, where an old cut had faded to an almost invisible scar. Now he remembered. He had fought this man before. It was in Ostara on the night the prisoners escaped. The same night Katherine's mother Ellen disappeared. Greystone started to sweat.

He had gone through the events of that night plenty of times, both in his waking mind and in his dreams, from the instant he startled awake when the guards sounded the alarm to standing alone in the garden with blood dripping from his chin. He had grabbed his sword on the way out of the house, but he fought this man in his nightshirt. A dog had snapped at his ankles and clung to the hem, throwing him off balance. That's when this man cut his cheek.

He would have killed his attacker if the coward hadn't run away. Until the dog showed up, he had been winning. When his men found him there, Greystone raged that he had driven the intruders away, but privately he remembered his last encounter with this man as the most humiliating of his life.

That's why he knew the accent. This was Honorus's brother.

"Draw your sword," Patrick said. "Finish this."

Patrick had kept this part of the plan secret until just before Leonides' wooden contraption had been set afire and sent into motion. He wasn't certain whether he'd have to face Greystone on his own, but he wasn't in any mood for the argument he knew he'd get when he explained what he intended to do. As he expected, Anna did her best to dissuade him.

"What are you thinking?" she hissed. "Suppose it happens just as you suggest, and Greystone survives? I agree he cannot be allowed to leave Pallas, but why do you have to be the one to kill him? What if he kills you instead? Why can't we imprison him?"

"There is no time to talk about this now. If we imprison him, this will not be finished," Patrick said, swinging his arm to encompass the whole city. "He will poison everything. Greystone has hundreds of men in other places. No matter what, some will remain loyal. They will try to free him. He chose his fate when he came to Pallas."

"As head of the council, I forbid it," she said.

Patrick took her hand to soften his words, "I am so proud of you and all our people. Our friends from Ostara fought bravely too. The truth is, I am the one who must finish this. My brother is the one who set it all in motion. And I need you to be my witnesses."

Anna stopped arguing then even though she would never agree. She knew she couldn't change his mind. There was no time. By then the flames were already blooming in the dry wood at the center of Leonides' creation, and it would burn quickly.

She knew Patrick was right. Greystone would be a lightning rod for trouble. She forced herself to nod and tried not to imagine a Pallas without Patrick striding through its streets or brooding at the top of his tower.

As the woodworker's boy stepped back from the wagon with his bucket of grease in his hand, the fire roared as if alive. Anna and Patrick raced side-by-side down the hill to take their places in the human barricades. She squeezed into a place next to Patrick in the middle of the left-hand line and told herself she wouldn't close her eyes no matter what happened.

Everyone was here except those who were too hurt. The wounded had been carried to Leonides' house to be tended by Ellen and Katherine. That was another thing Anna wasn't ready to think about – the dead who hadn't yet been counted.

Some of the people who were standing shoulder to shoulder with her had been bloodied, and everyone was bone tired. The people of Pallas and the Ostarans held themselves under control now, but Anna couldn't predict what they would do if Greystone killed Patrick.

And she knew it could happen. Even though he had admitted defeat, Greystone had been leading his men into battle ever since he was old enough to climb onto a horse, and from what Anna had heard, he won every time. Maybe he had been living a soft life since he took the city of Ostara, and he might be getting pudgy around his middle, but he knew how to wield a sword. On the other hand, Patrick had fought in only two battles before last night. The first time he was nearly killed, and the second time he was only saved by the appearance of a dragon.

Anna reminded herself that the Lady of the Forest must have saved Patrick for a reason. He seemed to think he had lived on for this moment. Anna's stomach clenched as she waited to see whether he was right. From the corner of her eye, she caught movement above and watched a great-horned owl sweep down and take its place next to the raven on the edge of the roof.

At first, Greystone didn't seem to understand Patrick's demand. "Draw my sword? According to the rules of war, I am your prisoner. I've told you I am prepared to pay for my freedom."

"You cannot pay for it," Patrick replied, "But you can fight me for it."

"Are you without honor?" Greystone said, as if he were trying to explain something to a child. "I am at your mercy. You cannot kill me."

"I can," Patrick said. "Take off your coat."

"I will not."

Patrick nodded to the line of people on the right, and Bard and one of the other Ostarans started forward. "Help him out of his coat," Patrick said.

Greystone tore at the buttons and threw his coat onto the street, revealing the dull shine of the chain mail he was wearing underneath.

"Take that off too. It's mine, and I reclaim it." Patrick said. "You spoke of honor? You attacked this city in the night. I will not make you into a martyr for the Claymon by executing you or draw them here by imprisoning you. We will not send you away to make more trouble. We did not make the rules, and we will not follow them. This will end now."

"Kill me then," Greystone said, holding his arms wide. "You're going to do it anyway."

Patrick advanced with Mabus held low in front of him.

"This makes no sense," Greystone whined. Then, when Patrick didn't answer, he spat, "I'll kill you."

As Greystone drew his sword and rushed forward, Patrick blocked the first blow. The two men grappled, trying to knock each other off balance.

Patrick broke free first, giving Greystone a shove that sent him stumbling back, but the Claymon recovered quickly. When he stayed low and slashed upward, Patrick danced away.

The ringing of metal on metal filled the street. The dragons might have returned, and none of the witnesses would have noticed, so intent were they on watching the struggle. As the fight went on, first Patrick, then Greystone seemed to have the advantage. At first the two seemed evenly matched, but when both men began to tire, Greystone's experience gave him an advantage. He drew first blood with a deep slice to Patrick's thigh.

Patrick didn't fall, but he staggered back. As they had been ordered, the witnesses did not interfere, but they held their breath. The younger ones thought Patrick would rally. He would win because he was in the right. The old ones, Anna included, knew being right had very little to do with winning.

She tried to think. If Greystone should prevail, what then? They hadn't talked about what to do if the unthinkable happened.

The two swordsmen circled each other. Everyone could see Patrick was limping, but they couldn't tell how badly he was hurt. Even though Greystone's face was dripping sweat, he wore a sneer.

Greystone crouched with his back to the lower street, ready to counter Patrick's next blow or move in for the kill. The children had come down from the rooftop to stand with the others. They all had their eyes on Patrick, willing him to surprise the Claymon with a sudden blow. Maybe he was faking, and his wound wasn't as bad as it looked.

Only a few of the townspeople were watching Greystone when his eyes widened in shock. They unconsciously followed his gaze to see the big panther sitting in the street behind Patrick. She seemed to have appeared from nowhere, but they had been so intent on watching the fight that she could have been sitting there for some time.

Once she was sure she had Greystone's attention, she started to stalk slowly forward, her tail twitching. She stopped just beyond his sword's reach.

The blood had drained from Greystone's face. The street was so silent that everyone could hear his breath coming in short gasps. Patrick still held Mabus, but he pressed his other hand to his thigh.

"Why are you here, Maraba? This is my duty," Patrick said. She was a guide, a trickster, a storyteller. As far as he knew, she had never been a man killer.

"Don't be stupid," she said. *"This one and his kind have been carving away the edges of the forest for too long. If he gains Pallas, we soon will have no place to live, except the dream lands."* She spoke to Patrick, but her whole attention was on the Claymon leader. The end of her tail twitched again. Greystone was holding his sword in front of him, but he hadn't yet worked up enough courage to use it.

"You say it is your duty, but I say it is the duty of the guides to stop him. Besides, do you really want the children to see? They'll never be able to forget."

"They have already seen too much," Patrick said. Those who could understand animal speech heard the anguish in his voice.

"That may be, but a new world starts with this dawn," she said. *"Give the man a message for me."* She bared her fangs.

"What message?"

"Tell him to run."

39

SPRINGVALE

THE GATES SLAMMED SHUT soon after Padraik appeared in the sky over Springvale Manor and long before the green dragon landed in the meadow. The number of people peering over the top of the wall multiplied while Gale sat quietly astride the dragon, gazing toward his home and waiting for Ruby.

Even though it was barely dawn, workers had already gone out to begin their labor when the dragons appeared from the North. Some were swift enough to race back to the manor and squeeze through the gates before they closed. The rest melted away in other directions, abandoning their tools in the gardens.

The night before, in the forest city on the other side of the Celadrian Hills, Padraik and Ruby had flown low over the streets with predictable results. Their appearance caused the Claymon to stampede deep into the city. That's all the owl had asked them to do. The dragons were tempted to make another pass because they wanted to see the soldiers run again, but when Meg asked them to fly on, they accepted her decision.

Gale had asked the dragons for a last favor. That's why they had come here. When he told Padraik what he wanted, the green dragon was silent for a long time, and then he had a private conversation with his mate. Gale knew how eager Padraik was to show Ruby the island, and he had resigned himself to a refusal when Padraik relented.

"I believed I would never see my island again, he said. I know how it feels to lose your home. We will help you – as long as it doesn't take very long."

Flight makes the world small. Last summer it took days to walk from Springvale to Pallas with Meg, Katherine and Patrick. Now he and Meg were back here before he had been able to come up with a plan.

Gale had been away for almost a year. Now, over the pungent scent of dragon, he smelled plowed earth and wood smoke.

Ruby chose not to land right away. She circled the edge of the forest studying the manor and its encircling fields with her one good eye. Ever since the red dragon discovered she could still fly, she was never in a hurry to be earthbound.

To be honest, Meg wasn't eager for Ruby to land next to Padraik either. When Meg left Springvale she was a runaway kitchen girl, and as far as anyone here knew, that's still what she was. Back then she was quiet, obedient – and as skittish as a mouse. Back then she accepted that she belonged to Lord Stefan because she had been standing right there and listening when her father gave her away.

No doubt Stefan and her father would dispute her understanding of that transaction, but what else could she call it except a transfer of ownership? From the day Meg came to the manor she did Cook's bidding from the moment she opened her eyes in the morning until she closed them at night.

Lord Stefan gave her a blanket and enough to eat, and Meg found new clothes folded on top of her blanket at mid-winter each year. Younger girls than her were already married, and looking back, Meg was surprised she hadn't been married off before she left. Maybe Cook couldn't spare her. Or maybe there didn't happen to be any man needing a wife.

If she had stayed at Springvale, Meg would surely be married to a man chosen by Lord Stefan by now, and her husband would have been granted some land to work along the forest edge. Most of their crops would go to the manor to be used or sold as Lord

Stefan decided, and if they had children, one of them would go to serve in the manor as she had.

That was life at Springvale. The old Meg would have kept to the traditions without asking questions. She wouldn't have been able to imagine another choice and she would have been too afraid of what lay outside the well-ordered fields ever to leave. That time was long past. Meg understood why Gale had to come back, but she hadn't been able to find the right words to explain why she was so reluctant to accompany him. She felt she was returning to a prison

This was Gale's home, and someday the manor might be his, but as far as they knew, Lord Stefan was still firmly under the thumb of a governor appointed by Peter Greystone. She and Gale hadn't stayed in Pallas long enough to find out whether the Claymon had been defeated, but even if the townspeople and Ostarans won, it didn't mean the Claymon in Springvale would leave without a fight.

That's why they were arriving this way, and it's the reason she came back with him. She couldn't send Gale alone to face the Claymon who were standing between him and his birthright. If Padraik had not agreed to Gale's request, they would have said farewell to Padraik and Ruby back in the forest and finished the journey to Springvale by foot, but riding here on the back of a dragon was a lot more impressive. Honestly, when it came to evicting the invaders, they didn't have much else in their arsenal.

When Ruby had finally cruised over the manor and all its holdings, she gracefully drifted down and settled in the thick green grass next to Padraik. Her eye-patch gave her a rakish look, and she no longer seemed to be in pain. The curious cows that had been grazing in the meadow ambled a short distance away. They turned around and stared at the dragons with expressions similar to those of the people who were standing on the wall.

Padraik and Ruby shared a thought, *"Meat?"* Neither of them had ever seen or tasted a cow, but they looked delicious.

"It is little enough to ask," Gale said. *"When you leave here, your bellies will be full."*

"What are you waiting for?" Meg asked aloud. Nervousness made her voice too harsh. "By now, somebody must have recognized you." Her eyes skimmed the faces peeking over the edge of the manor wall. "There is your father, Gale. On the right-hand side of the gate. He is alive, at least. And that must be one of the Claymon standing next to him, that big man in red."

"I am waiting for someone to come out to parley," Gale said.

"Who will dare?" she asked.

Gale slid off Padraik's back and walked a few paces towards the gate, hoping to give the Claymon a nudge. After more waiting, the gate opened a crack, and a slight figure stumbled out in a hurry, as if it had been shoved. Whoever it was held on to the edge of the gate and tried to pull it open, but the gatekeepers were too strong and too fast. The doors shut again, and the bar clanked into position. The boy, for Meg and Gale could now see the person was too short to be full grown, stood with his back pressed against the wooden barricade. He must be trying to gather his courage while the people on top of the wall shouted threats and encouragement.

"Oh, for goodness sake," Meg said in exasperation. She slid off Ruby's back, gave her a kiss on the nose to reassure her, and set off across the meadow towards the child.

"Wait here," Gale told the dragons over his shoulder as he trotted to catch up.

"Don't forget about the meat," Padraik called after him.

"All right," Meg said, when she heard Gale behind her. She stopped for a moment so he could catch his breath. "You don't have a plan, and we don't have any weapons except two short knives and your bow."

They were already through the meadow and passing into the vegetable gardens. She detoured to pick up a discarded hoe, and a hand trowel. She handed the hoe to Gale. "It's better than nothing," she explained.

When they were almost within arrow's reach of the manor walls, Gale grabbed Meg's arm.

She stopped and knelt. "Come here," she called.

The child, who looked to be eight or nine years old, turned a tear-streaked face towards them. He wasn't anyone Meg knew, which meant he had been working at the manor for a short time. Maybe he had come here as she did, from a family on one of the outlying farms that had been stretched beyond its limits. Stefan, or more likely the Claymon, had decided they could spare him, and so here he was outside the walls.

The child inched slowly forward. Meg risked taking a few more steps to meet him and clasped his hand, leading him back to Gale.

"Do you bring a message from the manor?" Gale demanded. Meg glanced up at this man she had come to see as her equal and predicted their hard-won balance would soon be upset. The laughing young heir to Springvale was gone, or temporarily absent at least. He had been replaced by this wind-burnt and wild-looking dragon rider. Maybe his father hadn't yet recognized him after all. Gale's voice sounded grim, even angry.

The boy shook his head. He seemed to have been struck dumb. Meg thought about how she would have felt if she were sent on such an errand at his age. She would have fainted on the spot. She squeezed his shoulder in what she hoped was a reassuring way. The boy had glanced at Gale when he asked his question, but otherwise he had not taken his eyes off the dragons. Padraik and Ruby looked small from here, but even at a distance the sunlight sparking and glittering from their scales was mesmerizing.

"They are beautiful, aren't they?" She lifted a finger to her lips and lowered her voice. "We don't want anyone up at the Manor to know it, but I know you won't tell. This is just between us. The dragons are our friends."

"They do what you ask them to do?" the boy whispered. He moved closer to Meg, sensing an ally.

"Yes, that's right," Meg said, stretching the truth.

"They let you ride on them?" The boy asked. He seemed to need Meg to confirm what he had seen with his own eyes.

"Yes," she said, "and if you help us, maybe they will let you ride too."

Meg wasn't going to ask the dragons to fulfil such a frivolous request. They had come here by way of Pallas because Gale had asked them to do it, but Padraik and Ruby didn't owe them anything more. They had been very brave, but Meg knew the dragons were tired, and they still had a long way to go.

Now that she had taken a good look at the boy, Meg thought he was probably a little older than she first thought, but small for his age. She saw how his eyes had brightened, and she knew he was imagining himself in the sky on a dragon's back.

"Who is your master?" Gale asked abruptly.

Whether or not he ever was given the opportunity to ride one of the dragons, the boy seemed to have decided to view this encounter as an adventure instead of a death sentence, at least for now.

"The head gardener gives me my work every day. I heard Lord Stefan used to be the master of everyone, but he isn't any more. He still tells the overseer what to do, but he has his own master now."

"How many other outsiders are here with Stefan's master?" Gale didn't bother asking who that man might be. It had to be the Claymon he remembered from his last dinner at home, the one who had been sent here to find Katherine and to take control of Springvale.

"I heard most of the strangers rode away half a year ago, before I came here." The boy seemed unused to anyone asking him questions and listening to his answers, especially questions where the answers mattered. He thought and held out his hand to count on his fingers.

"Take your time," Meg said.

"There are five," he finally said. "They all live together in what used to be Lord Stefan's rooms, but I don't clean in there, and I don't serve at table either. We try to stay away from them. They are always angry."

Meg and Gale looked at each other. The Claymon probably had expected to be replaced by others by now, or at least to have received news from their faraway leaders, but that hadn't happened. Maybe they were worried. Maybe they thought they had been forgotten.

"Tell them this," Gale said.

The boy's eyes widened. Meg held her tongue. It was necessary that the child believe the threat in Gale's message. Gale made him repeat it twice. Then he released the child, who raced back to the gate. It opened just wide enough to drag him inside.

"You've given them something to think about," Meg said.

"I hope so."

"Is it time to give the dragons their breakfast?" She gazed at the cows placidly chewing their cuds on the opposite side of the pasture.

"I have an idea about that," Gale said. "We always used to keep beef hanging in the spring house down by the stream. I hope that's still true. I don't want to take the time to slaughter a cow right now, and I don't want Ruby and Padraik to get into the habit of doing that either. There's an old man whose job used to be to sit by the doorway to make sure nobody tampered with the meat. He might have died, but if he's living then…"

"Then we will have an ally, and the dragons will have their beef," Meg concluded. "I take back what I said. You do have a plan, and it just might work."

41

MENDING WALLS

MEG AND GALE REMOUNTED the dragons and flew a short distance, landing behind a fringe of trees near a farm at the north edge of the manor's holdings.

When the harness had been removed, Gale said, *"No matter what happens today, the two of you will be on your way by dawn tomorrow. If we don't vanquish them, the Claymon will be my problem, and I'll handle them alone."*

Meg noticed how he left her out of the conversation and nodded to herself. It was a small thing, but it confirmed something. The separation she had been expecting was already beginning.

Padraik said, *"I like one thing about your plan, and I like that it is the first thing."*

"Meat," Ruby and Padraik said in unison.

It was essential to find food for the dragons as soon as possible. Not only were they ravenous after flight, but they had already seen the herd of grazing cattle. It would be easy for them to kill one, but a cow is much heavier than a sheep – far too heavy for a dragon to carry. If they were to hunt near the manor, they would be vulnerable to attack.

That was one reason Gale wanted to avoid a kill. The other was that it would set a bad pattern. If the dragons could easily kill cows in Springvale, they might not choose to return to an island where the only food was small, slippery fish.

As usual, Padraik sensed Gale's thoughts. *"Don't worry. We don't want to stay where people are afraid of us. Soon they would come after us and try to kill us, like the men in Ruby's valley. We are going to a place where our dragon child will be safe."*

Dragons can't blush, but Ruby's red scales glowed more brightly.

"I'll be back as soon as I can," Gale said.

Meg didn't bother to answer him. She knew he would come back as quickly as he could. It was just something to say to take the place of all the other things he could have and should have, said. She watched Gale skirt the edge of the trees and disappear into the gully where the stream flowed back towards the manor

Meg shrugged off her irritation. She knew she was being unfair. Gale wanted to restore life in Springvale to the way it was before the Claymon came. But the truth was, Springvale had been forever changed – and so had she.

"Wait here," she told the dragons, but they were already dozing in a patch of sunshine, necks twined together.

Smiling, she shrugged off her worries and walked the short distance through the trees and into the small dirt yard in front of her father's barn. Her family had built a new house after the fire, but it was much smaller than the old one, and it looked as if it had been made of whatever scraps they could find. It didn't have any windows. One of her mother's woven blankets was nailed over the doorway. It must have been a long winter in there.

The last time Meg was here, when she was on the run from Springvale and the Claymon, she spent a day hiding in the byre loft. This time she went straight to the well and drew a pail of water. This was a poor farm in many ways, but the water from their well was as fresh and cold as she remembered. She drank her fill before anyone saw her. Her parents' and brothers' days were so full of work that they had no time to look up to see dragons in the sky.

The little girl, the one who was the image of Meg in miniature, was the first to notice her arrival. Meg watched her creep around the edge of the courtyard until she was standing on the opposite side of the well.

"Hello," Meg said.

The girl took another step forward, one finger in her mouth.

"Where is your Mum?"

The child removed the finger and pointed towards the house.

How strange not to know her own sister's name.

Her father and brothers would be in the fields by now, or at least Meg guessed that's where they were. She'd have to face them eventually. They would blame her for the fire. The Claymon hadn't cared that her father didn't know that she and her friends were hiding in his hayloft. And it didn't matter that he would have turned them over if he had known.

"I know who you are." The child had seemed so shy that Meg was surprised by her loud voice.

"Who am I then?" Meg asked, circling the well and dropping down onto her heels to be on a level with the girl.

"You are my sister Margaret, and I am Betty. Mum tol' me 'bout you"

Meg's chest ached. She couldn't speak. She wanted to hear everything Betty had to tell her – all the things her mother had said.

Meg heard her mother's gasp when she lifted the blanket and saw her two daughters together by the well.

"Once she starts talking, you won't be able to get her to stop." Sofie crossed the yard in a few steps and swept both girls into her arms.

Meg was still wiping tears from her face when her mother led her to the bench under the oak tree at the corner of the garden. Betty skipped ahead. The tree was close to where the old house had stood, and its bark was blackened on one side. Nevertheless, it lived. Its branches were covered with tiny leaves the size of squirrels' ears.

She wondered about the damage her mother was hiding. Meg couldn't see any obvious injury, but Sofie looked too thin. Her eyes were deep-set and smudged with bruise-like circles, and her smile was hiding secrets.

"It's easy to see you have been adventuring, my girl," Sofie said. She stroked Meg's hair as if she were a ghost who might disappear. "I can't believe you are really here."

It had been a long time since Meg had seen herself through someone else's eyes. Her last bath had been a quick, breath-snatching swim in a mountain river. The strong scent of smoke from their cooking fires followed her everywhere. She looked down at her legs. They were wrapped below the knee in strips of cloth torn from the bottom of her skirt to keep them warm in flight. She hadn't bothered to braid her hair since she left Bethany's farm, and it hadn't felt a comb since the voyage to Niue.

Her mother was right. She did look as if she had tales to tell, but there was no time for them now.

"Everything is about to change, Mum." Meg didn't know how to start. There was too much to say in very little time. "Gale and I have returned together, and we are going to make the Claymon leave."

"The young master is here?" Sofie's eyes widened, and her arms tightened around Betty.

"Yes. It is all going to happen tonight, but before that we need to eat. Can you spare any food?"

Her mother half rose, holding the child, and Meg realized she thought Gale was nearby. Meg didn't understand why hearing his name made her mother anxious, but Sofie clearly didn't want him to visit the farm.

"Don't worry," Meg reassured her, "He won't be back for a while. He has gone to find meat for the dragons."

Her mother sat down heavily. Sensing the shift in mood, Betty whimpered.

Hoping to give her mother time to recover from the news that there were dragons, Meg swept her hand to encompass the farm buildings.

"Tell me what has happened since that night you crept out to meet me in the forest."

Her mother closed her eyes. Betty's finger was back in her mouth. The little girl rested her head against Sofie's shoulder.

Sofie's whispered, "It wasn't your fault."

Meg sighed, "I didn't set the fire, but I am partly to blame. The Claymon wouldn't have come here if it weren't for me."

Sofie shook her head, dismissing the Claymon and the fire. "Not the fire. I am talking about your father."

"What about him?"

Silence grew around the two women and the child. Meg wasn't sure she wanted to hear any more.

"After the fire your father turned silent," Sofie said. "Weeks went by. He didn't do anything to repair the byre roof or to rebuild the house. Your brothers and I did everything. We were living out in the byre then, and every morning, I tried to talk to him. He went to the fields as usual, but Gregory told me he mostly stood at the edge of the farm all day, looking off into the trees. One morning, just before harvest, I reached over to his side of our bed, and it was cold. He had left us in the night."

Meg struggled to understand. "Left? Where did he go?"

Sofie shrugged. "We don't know whether he's alive or dead. If he were somewhere within reach of Springvale, we would have heard."

Meg took her mother's hand and kissed it. She turned it over and stroked its roughness.

"It wasn't your fault," Sophie repeated. "Don't blame yourself. Your father always carried a seed of darkness. After the fire it seemed he could no longer find his way back to the light."

She should have felt grief, but Meg was only angry. She knew very well what this abandonment meant to the family.

"Since the strangers have been here, Lord Stefan has rarely gone beyond the manor walls," Sofie said. "But if he is in control again, things will be different. Gregory has taken your father's place on the farm."

Meg's brother was two years younger than she was.

"He knows what has to be done," Sofie continued. "We have to prove we can make this farm produce as it always has. If we don't, Stefan will give it to someone else. Last autumn we managed to pay what was owed to the manor, but there wasn't much left. Our neighbors helped us through until spring. We expect to do better this year."

The two women fell silent. Betty had fallen asleep.

"That's why you're afraid," Meg said. "You think Gale will tell his father about the trouble here." She looked at the house again, seeing it through his eyes. It was little more than a shack.

Sofie nodded, her fingers busy untangling Betty's hair.

While she waited for Gale's return, Meg drank a cup of milk fresh from the cow and ate two of the small round loaves her mother had baked on the flat stones in the fireplace. Then she worked with Sofie to complete the morning chores. Meg would soon have to make a choice, and the troubles here were going to make her decision more difficult. She chose not to talk about the future, instead telling Sofie about the healer Bethany, and the long winter of lessons.

"I learned to read, Mum."

Meg didn't talk about being able to understand animals, and she didn't say anything more about the dragons either.

As soon as they heard the clatter of the cart in the distance, Sofie sent Betty to fetch her brothers. Gregory, Sam and Jack were at the far end of the field behind the byre, repairing the stone wall around the family's small pasture. They'd come running as soon as Betty told them there were visitors.

After Sofie had wrapped more bread in a cloth for Gale. Meg pushed the farm's wheelbarrow down the dirt track toward the sound of the approaching cart. She planned to wait for Gale on

the other side of a small rise, before he could see the farm. She
was glad he'd arrive before the boys returned from the pasture.
As much as she might resent it, Gale carried authority here as
Lord Stefan's heir, and he knew how to use it. Her brothers
would obey him.

When he spotted Meg waiting by the track, Gale waved. As
the cart continued its slow progress, Meg could barely keep herself from running to meet him, but the spot she had chosen to
wait was closest to where the dragons were hidden.

Before the horse stopped, Meg had pushed the wheelbarrow
behind the cart and was trying to shift one of the two sides of
beef. Gale jumped down to help. The meat was wrapped in
sheets, which made it easier to grip, but it would have been too
heavy to carry far without the wheelbarrow. Even with it, the
rough ground might make taking it to the dragons impossible.

"Will we have to make them come here?" Meg asked. "This
is heavier than I thought it would be."

"We had better take it to them if we can," Gale said. "I want
the people of Springvale to be thinking about the dragons and
talking about the dragons, but I don't want them to see them
again until tonight."

"Did he ask you why you wanted the meat?" Meg asked, remembering the ancient guard sitting on his stool outside the
springhouse.

"He didn't seem to care. The cart and horse were already waiting, ready to carry the meat to the kitchen at the manor. I'm sure
he didn't recognize me, and he is too deaf to hear much. He
seemed to think I was one of the servants from the manor, come
to load the meat into the cart. He was only surprised I was alone.
It was all I could do to drag it out of the springhouse by myself,
and I had to push it up a plank into the back of the cart."

Gale unhitched the horse and led it under the shade of a tree
by the side of the road.

"You take one handle, and I'll take the other," he said, testing
the weight of the meat in the wheelbarrow.

"I need to tell you something."

Despite the urgency of getting food to the dragons, Gale stopped and waited. Keeping her eyes on his face, Meg quickly explained what had happened to her family in the year since they had hidden on the farm – about the fire, her father's disappearance, and the struggle to produce enough crops to satisfy the Manor.

"You're asking me protect them," he said. His face was expressionless.

"That's right."

"Do you trust me so little?" Gale said. "Did you think I would make their suffering worse by punishing them?"

"Your father would," Meg said. "He'd say he's helping them by taking away their responsibility for the farm."

Gale was silent. That meant he was acknowledging the truth of her words.

Meg continued to hold his gaze. Gale might protect her family, but he understood his father's way of thinking. These two men, Lord Stefan and Gale, carried the fate of everyone at Springvale in their hands. If he chose to leave her mother and brothers to try to make a success of the farm, she didn't want it to be only to please her. Meg didn't want to owe him that debt.

The conversation might have become an argument except that, just then, Meg's brothers came running. After a minimum of greetings and promises to answer their questions as soon as possible, Meg and Jack pushed the wheelbarrow with one side of beef towards the fringe of trees while Gale, Gregory and Sam followed behind dragging the other half, still wrapped in its sheet.

Back in the farmyard, Sofie had told her sons only that they had to help Meg and Gale, where they would find them, and nothing else. Now, as they labored toward the trees through the rutted field edge, Meg tried to prepare them for their first encounter with Ruby and Padraik.

When they reached the clearing, the dragons were sitting on their haunches, staring fixedly in the direction from which their meal would arrive. Meg could see from their faces how scared the boys were, but at least she was able to give them more warning than she had when she first encountered Padraik back on Niue.

The boys clustered together at the far edge of the clearing. Meg and Gale pushed the wheelbarrow the last few feet by themselves and dumped the meat out onto the ground. They dragged the second half forward and ripped away the sheets. When the dragons started to tear at the meat, the boys retreated even farther, but they stayed within sight. It was a terrible and mesmerizing sight. Ruby and Padraik snarled as if they were fighting lions instead of eating a meal that had already been killed.

After he had swallowed a few mouthfuls, Padraik raised his head and roared. *"It is good! It is as good as I knew it would be!"*

"You are welcome," Gale said. He went back to gnawing the plain loaf Meg had brought for him.

Seeing that Gale and Meg were on familiar terms with the dragons, Sam and Jack inched closer.

"Wait until they've finished," Gregory ordered.

Meg thought about the moment when she saw her brothers for the first time that day. They were all running, but Jack slowed his pace before he came close to where Meg and Gale were standing beside the wheelbarrow. He had barely learned to talk when she went to the Manor. Next was Sam, who almost knocked her down with his hug. Gregory, the oldest, stayed back with Jack and refused to meet her eyes.

The dragons' scales glowed ever brighter as they continued to attack the beef with talons and fangs, but as their hunger was sated, they became more and more fastidious, offering each other especially desirable bits until nothing was left of their meal except a tangle of bones.

"You can go home now," Gale told the boys, "but don't tell anyone we're here. It must be a secret for now. Come back before it starts to get dark tonight. There's something else I'll need you to do."

Gregory nodded, and the other boys set off ahead of him in the direction of the farm.

Before he followed, Meg said, "Mother told me what happened last spring. I am truly sorry, Greg."

"It's not your fault." His words sounded grudging. It was what their mother had told him to say.

"But it partly is," Meg said. "If we hadn't hidden in the byre, and if the Claymon found no sign of us there, maybe they wouldn't have set the fire. And then maybe our father wouldn't have gone away."

They stood together watching the dragons, who were already growing sleepy again now that they had eaten.

"No," Gregory said. "I saw them that night. The Claymon would have burned the farm whether you hid there or not."

Tears pricked her eyes, and Meg hugged her brother. He stiffened, but he didn't pull away.

42

THE LAST FLIGHT

THE SUN WAS DROPPING below the treetops as Gale and Meg prepared to fly. This might be the last time either of them would ride on a dragon's back, but they didn't talk about how much they were going to miss it.

It was almost time to show the Claymon what a dragon can do. Seeing Padraik and Ruby sitting in the meadow outside the manor gates that morning should have been enough to send the Claymon on their way, but if that didn't convince them, Gale's message should have. It promised the Northerners would be granted safe passage through the Manor's lands if they left at once. If they weren't gone by nightfall, they would receive a demonstration of the dragons' power. And if they didn't heed that warning, Gale promised Springvale Manor and all its inhabitants would burn. The first warning was true. The other might not be, but the Claymon had to believe it.

Even though they wouldn't be flying far, Meg tested the ropes and knots of the harnesses as she always did. Then she dug through her pack and confirmed what she already knew. The jar of soothing ointment was almost empty. Ruby's eye had mostly healed. The skin around the wound looked pink and free of infection. A scab was forming in the empty eye socket.

Ruby no longer was in pain when she flew, but Meg spread a thin layer of the medicine around the dragon's eye socket anyway and tightened the strap holding the patch in place. Then Meg spread the rest of the salve onto other places on the dragons' bellies and sides where the ropes had roughened their skin during the long journey from the northern mountains.

The dragons loved it when Meg doctored them. They rolled onto their backs as soon as she pulled the jar from her bag. This time there was no need to conserve the remaining ointment. After tonight there would be no one to give Padraik and Ruby this attention. When she had finished, Meg carefully stowed the jar and silently vowed to refill it one day.

Through that afternoon, Gale positioned himself high on the hill above the manor. From there, he watched for the Claymon and their horses and longed to see them crossing from the manor to the forest. The day stretched on, but the gate didn't open. He didn't know it, but the vantage point he had chosen was very close to the place where Katherine and Meg first saw the Claymon riding to Springvale. While he kept an eye on the gate and the road, Gale built an enormous pile of brush and collected additional fuel. After that task was finished, the hours until dusk passed slowly. He had spent so many long, cold days and nights travelling from the North that he found it hard to stay awake.

The boys had already returned to the clearing and were waiting with Meg by the time Gale arrived. He explained what would happen once it was fully dark, and then he sent the boys to conceal themselves near the manor walls. He told Gregory to go by way of their neighbors and to ask for help. Springvale Manor had only one gate, and he didn't think the Claymon would leave without their horses, but there was a chance they would sneak out another way. He needed to know as soon as they were gone.

"What should we tell the neighbors?" Gregory asked. "They haven't seen the dragons. Everyone at Springvale probably has heard about them by now, even on the farms, but hearing is not the same as seeing." He glanced at the other side of the clearing, where Meg was retying a knot on one of the harnesses. "How much should we say?"

"Tell them they will tell their grandchildren about the night they saw fire raining from the sky," Gale said.

After a pause, he said, "That isn't exactly comforting, is it? Tell them they will be helping to send the Claymon packing and that, so long as they stay well away from the keep, they will not be in danger. As soon as the Claymon leave, run to the top of the hill as fast as you can and set fire to the brush I've piled there. Keep it burning high, so we'll be able to spot it when we're flying."

After the boys had gone, Meg finished the work of testing the harnesses. She was about to jump up onto Ruby's back when Gale put his hand on her arm.

She stepped back down and waited. It was her turn to listen.

"What is going to happen now?" he asked bluntly. Meg thought he had been rehearsing these words, but they sounded too harsh. He was nervous.

"After the Claymon are gone, you mean?"

"No. Tomorrow. Next season. Next year. I know you've been thinking about it."

"What do you want to happen?" Meg asked. She had been waiting to have this conversation, but his timing couldn't have been worse.

"You know what I want. I want Springvale to be the way it was before. I want everyone to forget the Claymon ever were here."

Meg nodded. She knew Gale wanted to repair all the damage, to return life here to the way it was when he was a boy. Surely, he must realize that would be impossible, especially after what the two of them were about to do. And even when he was a boy, enjoying his freedom, returning to the manor only when he wanted to sleep in a soft bed, life was far from idyllic for most of Springvale manor's inhabitants.

She didn't say any of that. Instead, she said, "Your father is growing old. After a year under the thumb of foreigners, he may be ready to share his authority. Are you ready to accept it?"

Again, Meg pictured Gale as he was before the two of them became friends – rarely at home, always in the fields or wandering inside the edges of the forest.

"I am ready," he said, and quickly added, "And I want you to stay."

Now that the words had been spoken, Meg discovered she had been struck dumb. She couldn't think of any answer that would make them both happy.

When she didn't respond, he chose to think she hadn't heard him. He said, "I want you to stay with me here in Springvale. To marry me and live in the manor."

Meg looked at the ground and shook her head.

"I love you," she finally said. "You know that. You are my closest friend, even closer than Katherine, but you know I can't do that."

"You say you want Springvale to be as it was before," she continued. "I was a kitchen girl then. We never had spoken to each other. A year has passed, and I am not that girl any longer, but Springvale will be the same place, with the same rules. Do you think your father will agree to such a marriage?"

"I can convince him," Gale said.

Meg forced a smile. "I know how persuasive you can be, but getting him to accept this match won't be easy. It will take time." She paused, looking off to the north. "There are places I need to go, and that will also take time, since I will be walking instead of flying. I want to go back to Pallas to see how Katherine is faring, and I want to visit Bethany's farm again. There are books I need."

Meg took Gale's hand. "But I'll return to Springvale by autumn. If you need me, I'll be at the farm then, helping my family with the harvest."

They stood silently for a time. It was almost completely dark when Padraik nudged Gale, almost knocking him off his feet. The dragons had stayed out of the conversation, but it was time to fly.

Gale sighed. That's how Meg knew he had been expecting her answer. "You haven't promised," he said.

"And I won't," Meg said. "You will have a lot to do if the Claymon leave tonight. Having me here would just make it harder. And you might change your mind."

"I won't change my mind." He took her hand and pulled her close. "I'm not like my father, you know. Like you, I've changed in the past year, and I've learned a lot. I'll make sure your family has the time they need to recover from the fire and the loss of your father, and if Gregory needs more help, I'll send it to him."

"Thank you," Meg said, breathing in his scent and already missing him.

There was a half-moon that night. It shed enough light to show the dragons and their riders the shapes of the manor buildings and the surrounding wall. Pinpricks of light pierced the darkness through the slit-like windows of the central keep. Most of the residents would be gathered there by now. Everyone would know about Gale's warning. The message he sent through the wall with the boy had given them a chance. *If the Claymon are not gone before dark, everyone inside the Manor walls will be in peril. You will learn what a dragon can do…*

His warning had not been enough to make the Claymon leave Springvale, but he hoped many of the people would have slipped away to hide on outlying crofts.

The dragons circled the manor twice before heading farther out to begin their first pass over the wall.

"I hope I can do it," Padraik said. *"I've only made fire that one time, and I was angry then."*

"It isn't hard. I've done it lots. Every time the men came up the mountain. Just think about our child. You'd breathe fire if anyone tried to hurt her." Ruby said.

"Him." Padraik said.

"There's no time for that now!" Gale said. *"Go!"*

The dragons swept down, their bellies nearly grazing the wall. There were guards, but they didn't let a single arrow fly before they flattened themselves against the stone, hiding their heads under their arms. The dragons were moving too fast for Gale to see how many of those men were Claymon.

Ruby and Padraik circled the central keep from opposite directions, and as they flew, they screamed. The sound was like the punishing wind that coils around mountain peaks in winter. It was like a hundred birds of prey taking flight at once. The sound alone should have been enough to rid the manor of its contagion, but on their second pass, the dragons added fire. Some of it made its way through the narrow windows as tongues of flame – not enough to kill, but plenty to show what dragons are capable of doing.

Meg and Gale had learned to stuff cloth into their ears to protect themselves from the sound. Even though they were clinging to the ropes, it was all they could do to keep their seats as the dragons spiraled around the tower. They thought they could hear the screams of the people inside the keep. Gale hardened his heart. Getting rid of the Claymon was never going to be done by just telling them to leave.

The dragons slowed and circled farther from the keep, still sending their cries echoing between the manor walls. Small blazes flared wherever their fire touched rooftops below. Tiny figures ran back and forth between the manor's two wells and the flames, braving the dragons to save their homes.

An arrow sliced through the flesh of Meg's upper arm. She screamed and lost her grip on the harness. Archers had climbed to the top of the central tower.

"Steady!" Ruby said. The dragons shot over the keep, sending the archers running for the trap door at its center. They set the roof of the tower on fire. Although the keep itself was built of

stone, the platform was wooden. Built by Gale's great grandfather, his descendants had oiled it well every year to preserve it.

The keep became a torch. This wasn't part of Gale's plan. The platform would soon crumble, and when it did, embers would fall, lighting the next floor and the next until they reached the room where the Claymon and his parents were hiding, along with anyone else who hadn't heeded his warning to leave the Manor.

Up above, the hill was still all darkness. That meant the Claymon had not yet run. The dragons were in a frenzy. Gale feared they had gone too far to stop themselves.

"Padraik! Listen!" No response. Gale tried again. *"Padraik!"*

"Tell me what you want us to do." It was Ruby. *"Padraik can't hear you when he is in battle, but I'll show him what to do. He'll follow me."*

"I don't know how much longer I can hold on," Meg said.

"What do you mean?" Gale said.

"Meg is hurt," Ruby said. *"I can smell her blood. We have to finish this!"*

Gale directed Ruby to fly outside the manor's walls. They made a wide circle, venting their anger upon a hay wain, a broken-down shed, and other targets chosen by Gale until the entire manor was circled by fire. Still there was no signal fire on top of the hill.

The dragons shot back inside the walls and circled the blazing tower once more. Flames already licked from the two rings of windows closest to the top. Gale directed Ruby to fly lower, to the second level from the ground. The dining hall was on that level, the site of every celebration of his lifetime. It was where their treasure was kept, such as it was.

Sensing the dragons were weakening, he told them to target the dining hall windows with the last of their fire.

"Gale! You are destroying your home!" Meg cried.

"I can't stop," he said.

As they dropped, Meg yelled, *"Look, it's the signal!"*

On the hill above the manor, a fire blazed that had not been made by dragons, but she was afraid it was too late. She leaned forward and wrapped her arms around Ruby's neck.

43

EVERLASTING LIFE

THE TIME FOR ARGUING and whining was done. Peter Greystone slashed at the empty air with his sword. His breath came in sobs. The witnesses heard the weapon whistle as Maraba easily leapt away. Greystone froze for an instant, and then he obeyed her command and he ran. He looked clumsy and disoriented as he stumbled through the block below. Soon he was out of sight beyond the burning wagon.

Maraba continued licking her paw for a few more moments before she padded after him. She didn't seem in any hurry to catch Greystone, but Anna had understood the short conversation between Patrick and the animal guide. She knew Greystone wouldn't evade his fate. The big cat just wanted to play with him first.

Patrick was swaying. Anna rushed to give him her arm.

"Help," she called, wrapping her shawl tightly around his wounded leg. Two rebels made a seat of their arms and, against Patrick's protests, they made him sit and carried him down the hill to the improvised hospital.

"Is it really over?" the young woman asked. She had spent the night on the rooftop with the children. A little boy stood with his head against her skirt, half asleep. She held his hand and rested her other hand on her belly.

In summer, this woman would give birth to a child, the first since their return to this ancient city encircled by forest. Pallas would be that babe's home, and the child would know about their exile and return only through stories.

Anna considered the young woman's question. "No, not quite," she said, before heading down the street herself.

By the time Anna reached the woodworker's house and made her way into the makeshift hospital, Patrick was already lying on the sawdust covered floor, and his trouser leg had been cut away. He was awake, and he didn't seem to be in pain. He lay very still with his eyes fixed on Katherine's face. This was the first time Anna had seen Katherine at work as a healer. From now on that is the only way she would picture her. Katherine placed her hands over the deep cut on Patrick's leg, oblivious to Anna's arrival and to her mother working close by.

"There are a few we couldn't save," Ellen said, nodding towards the far wall. She had been tending the other wounded. This pause in her duties wouldn't last long, but she wanted to make sure Katherine could manage one more healing. Closing Patrick's wound should have been easy after everything the two of them had done that night, but now, just before sunrise and after her effort to save Patch, Katherine was emptied. The gift might fail her.

Anna glanced at the figures lying in the shadows and quickly looked away. She didn't have enough courage to lift the coverings to see the faces beneath. She touched Ellen's arm and said, "Thank you."

Anna passed into the yard behind the workroom, where she found Leonides leaning against the wall. He was staring up at the fading stars, smoking a pipe.

"Your plan worked just as you said it would," Anna said. She fell silent as she remembered the scene in the street where embers from the overturned wagon illuminated the bodies of the fallen. Some of the Claymon were dead and would have to be buried outside the city walls. Others were only wounded. What were they to do with wounded soldiers?

Leonides tapped his pipe against a rock jutting from the wall and ground out the sparks with his heel.

"Yes," he said distantly, as if he were thinking about something else. "The Ostarans won't stay long. Now that Greystone is gone, they'll be eager to go home and kick the rest of the Claymon out of their city."

"Devon Elder told me they'll stay two more days to help clear the streets. And they'll have to come back to Pallas. Some of their wounded won't be ready to travel."

Leonides stowed his pipe in his pocket.

Anna continued, hoping he would offer some guidance. "Ellen and Katherine will have to rest. In the meantime, I and others will take over care of the wounded here, and we will try to help the Claymon who are hurt. I had better call a meeting of the council."

She paused to give him time to answer. She desperately needed his advice about how to begin moving forward after so much violence. Even though she was council leader, she and everyone else would be looking to Leonides for direction.

"I have to leave for a time. I'm not certain how long I'll be away," he said abruptly. "And Patrick will have to go with me…" Leonides gazed towards the candle-lit window of his workroom, where Katherine was still trying to mend the damage Greystone's sword had done, "…as soon as he can walk."

"Is it Honorus?" Anna said.

Leonides didn't answer but left her alone in the yard, ducking through the low doorway to the workshop. Anna took a deep breath of cool air. It was scented with the loamy fragrance of the workroom and the forest. She made herself stand up a little straighter, despite her weariness. Besides assigning some townspeople and Ostarans to help the wounded Claymon, who might still be dangerous, she had better organize some breakfast.

When Anna followed Leonides into the house, she found him crouching next to his former apprentice. He rested his hand on Patrick's hair. Katherine must have finished her work. She was sitting nearby with her back against the wall, and Patrick was asleep.

Anna brushed tears away and hurried out of the house and back up the street. It was foolish to be crying over such a small thing, after all they had seen and done.

"When you leave, I'm going with you," Katherine said.

The conversation between Leonides and Anna had carried through the window. She gathered up the bloody rags within her reach and stood up as if the matter was settled.

"You can't," Leonides replied mildly. "You are needed here. But that isn't the reason."

"Then why?" Katherine said. Like everyone else, she respected the old woodworker. If it weren't for him, last night's battle would surely have ended differently. Nevertheless, her tone was defiant. She had decided long ago that no one was going to give her orders again.

Ellen rested her hands on her daughter's shoulders, massaging the tense muscles. "He's right," she said. "Leonides will be taking Patrick to meet his brother. Honorus must not reach Pallas."

Katherine pulled away and turned around to face her mother. "I know that, but I still don't understand why I can't go with them. I have closed Patrick's wound, but what if I didn't do it right? What if it reopens? I have to be there!"

"It won't reopen." Ellen's tired mind searched for a way to explain why Honorus was so dangerous. Finally, she shrugged. "I haven't told you much about Honorus. You have observed him in a dream, but I saw him every day when I was captive in Ostara. I sat near him night after night in the hall. I couldn't claim a headache and stay in my room too often. He would have known if I lied."

"Maybe you can picture it," she continued, "Peter Greystone at the center of the table on the dais, where your father once sat, with me at his right hand, and the magician on his left. It was so hard to make myself think of everyday things – of the design I was embroidering, of what must be eaten from the larder before spoiling, of the beetles on the bean plants, of an ailing towns-woman – of anything except your father. If I allowed Devon and the others to come into my mind for even a moment, the magician would have snatched the thought and handed it to Peter Greystone as if it were another delicacy from a platter."

Katherine still looked unconvinced.

"Patrick has to be there when the Lady and I put this right," Leonides said. "Even I don't know why he must be there, but the Lady says he will have a role to play. Honorus has no power over us or over his brother, but he will use every trick he can to find out if we are trying to deceive him."

"Honorus is far older than he was in your dream, Katherine," Leonides continued, "And since then he has delved deep into sorcery. Because of what he stole from the refugees back in Brethren, he is also physically stronger than when Ellen knew him. He has become a monster. His anger is always simmering, and it will surely flare when we meet him. Are you sure you will be able to do as your mother did? To think of only mundane things when the enemy is standing in front of you, even when you are afraid, and your body is crying for sleep? Because if you can't, all of us will be in danger, and Pallas may be lost."

Katherine turned away to examine the condition of her other patients, including Patch. She crouched and studied his face care-fully. He still showed no sign of waking. It had been risky, enlist-ing Oro to show the old Runner his choice last night. Katherine still couldn't be certain he had decided to return instead of walk-ing toward the heart of the forest.

By the time she had paused by each of the wounded and returned to Leonides and Ellen, her face was set. "You already knew my answer before you asked the question," she said resentfully. "At least take Stormer with you. Honorus can't touch him."

"We thought of that," Leonides said. "But the last time Honorus and Stormer were together, it didn't end well — for Honorus, at least. His mood will be ugly enough without that reminder."

"Go. Sleep." Ellen said. "Find a quiet corner upstairs. Our patients are resting and I will stay here and doze until one of them needs me. By the time you wake up, Patrick may already have returned."

Katherine recognized this soothing tone. It was the one her mother had used through Katherine's life whenever she wanted to ease some hurt or to smooth a childish problem. Now that she was grown, Katherine knew Ellen's words didn't necessarily mean she knew what was going to happen.

The animal guides must have told Leonides that Honorus was drawing near. If Patrick's brother was as powerful as everyone seemed to think, then how did the Lady and Leonides intend to stop him? They must have a plan, but Katherine's tired mind couldn't begin to follow them down that path.

Katherine knelt one more time and smoothed the hair away from Patrick's eyes. Not caring that others were watching, she kissed his forehead. Then she rose, squeezed her mother's hand and climbed the stairs.

"That wasn't easy for her," Ellen said.

Leonides watched Patrick's sleeping face for a few more moments. "No. I have to prepare. Send word when he is awake. If he is still sleeping when I return, I will wake him myself."

By late morning, dappled sunlight illuminated patches of bluebells. Coiled ferns bordered the path, chippies scolded, and a breeze caressed his cheek. Patrick didn't notice any of it. He didn't smell the freshness of the spring morning in the forest or hear the chorus of birdsong.

When he left the workshop, leaning on Leonides, Patrick was certain he wouldn't be able to walk far, but after they met the Lady, just outside the city wall, he followed a little way behind them. Despite the urgency of the errand, the two ancient ones adjusted their pace to match his slow one.

Patrick had always known this day was coming. With battle looming, he had found it easy to put Honorus out of his mind while he focused on the difficult but straightforward task of re-pelling the Northerners. All that time Patrick knew Honorus might have gotten himself lost in the forest on his way to Pallas, but he wouldn't give up until he reached the city and took con-trol.

After Leonides woke him back in the infirmary, the first thing he said was that he and the Lady had a plan to keep that from happening. The second thing was that Patrick had to be a part of it. His old master didn't give him any details. He seemed to ex-pect his former apprentice to trust him as he had when he was a boy. Patrick was in no position to argue.

At first, Patrick's leg felt stiff, but when he put weight on it, the pain was bearable. He was weak, but that wasn't so strange. After all the planning and preparation, fighting in the streets after midnight, and then matching swords with Peter Greystone, why wouldn't he be tired? Based on the condition of the straw around and under him back in the infirmary, he had lost a lot of blood. Still, there was more to his lethargy than battle fatigue and his wound.

The leaden feeling started after Leonides woke him and told him he would have to be present when they met Honorus. That's when Patrick finally named the black, churning mass in his chest. It was dread. It was as if his brother were already casting a spell in his direction, like a fishing net meant to capture and drown anything within its spread.

He could have done without it, but Patrick was grateful for the walking staff Leonides had lent him. It was smoothed and worn by his master's touch. The extra support allowed him to put thoughts of his injury aside so he could consider other things, like Katherine and her serious face as she worked to heal his leg.

Even though the two of them had not seen each other since before the battle started the night before, she didn't say a word when they carried him into the makeshift hospital. She simply ordered his bearers to lay him on the sawdust. It was as if she had been expecting his arrival.

He was still awake when she gently cut his trouser leg away with her knife. It was same knife he had carried so long as a talisman and later returned to her. She only started to talk to him after she had seen the deep cut. Even then, she only said the things she might say to any of her patients – that he would walk again, that he had come in time, and – other things. His memory was fuzzy. He remembered her hands growing warm on his skin, her eyes meeting his own, and then oblivion.

Patrick's thoughts drifted further back, to Maraba's sudden appearance in the street after Greystone wounded him. The Panther wasn't a creature of towns, though Patrick had become used to her appearance in his house at dusk each night. She seemed to come from nowhere, just as she had this morning. She would walk across the top of the wall and leap down to sit next to the deep hearth where he had made his bed.

Patrick had thought he would have to defeat Greystone alone, and he always knew it would be risky. Now he knew he had been stupid to think he could hope to win a sword fight against someone like Peter Greystone. At the exact moment when Patrick realized he was surely going to lose and that all the planning and loss had been useless, the panther stepped between him and his opponent. If she hadn't done that Greystone would have finished him.

As he started to notice sights and sounds around him, Patrick finally understood why Maraba had come night after night to tell him the long story of her kind.

He had been so intent on protecting Pallas and its people that he hadn't thought about the effect Greystone's victory would have on the forest itself, on the panther and all the other denizens of that green ocean. While he spent hours gazing over the trees from the top of his tower, he rarely thought about the creatures living beneath and within the canopy of leaves. The forest was Maraba's home as much as Pallas was his. It belonged to her and to countless others. Humans would miss the forest if Greystone and his like felled it. The animals couldn't survive without it.

That is why Maraba stepped in to deal with Peter Greystone in her own way. By doing so, she secured a future for all of them. By now the Claymon leader must be dead. How did she do it? Did she devour him afterwards? Patrick made himself turn away from thinking about the Claymon's last moments. He had seen enough blood to last the rest of his life. He chose instead to picture the shocked look on Greystone's face when Maraba materialized in front of him.

Leonides and the Lady didn't say anything to each other or to Patrick as they continued walking steadily towards the meeting with Honorus. The magician was as great a threat to the future of the city as the Claymon had been, and the victory against the Northerners would be worthless if this mission failed. As his feet found their rhythm on the faint path, Patrick found himself falling into a forest trance.

Patrick didn't know it yet, but Raven was the guide who set this plan in motion. He was the one who told Leonides the magician was near. Now the bird stayed close as the three drew near to the place where Honorus was camped. The usually talkative raven wasn't in the mood to chat today. He seemed to understand how much rested on the coming encounter. He rested on branches along the way, gliding forward to pace the three humans. Every so often Patrick caught a glimpse of his glossy black feathers through the leaves.

Maybe Honorus didn't know they were coming, but that didn't seem likely. He had his own ways of knowing things. Raven told Leonides they would find Honorus in a clearing to the south, beyond the hills. Whether his brother was expecting visitors or not, he would still be protected by the Claymon soldiers Greystone had sent with him from Ostara.

They were walking south to meet him, but Honorus had come from Ostara, far to the north. His brother must have completely circled Pallas to be approaching it from this direction. Maybe he still didn't know where he was.

According to Katherine's friend and protégé, Stormer, this wasn't the first time Honorus had gotten himself turned around in the forest. He also lost his way when he left Pallas many the first time. This was a long time after the people went to the island of Niue. By then Honorus had lived in solitude so long that he was half mad. By the time the Claymon found him lying in the blistering sun at the edge of the plain and carried him to Greystone, Honorus was barely a dried husk.

The last time Patrick was in this part of the forest, south of the city, he was with Katherine, Meg and Gale. That was after she found him in the cave and broke the Lady's spell. He was nearly sleep walking then. He didn't begin to wake up and start living again until Katherine and Meg found Mabus and placed the sword's hilt in his hand. Before that, his rescuers must have had to travel very slowly. He thought he remembered times when he sat down and refused to budge. That meant the distance between the cave and Pallas probably wasn't as far as he remembered.

Patrick knew he was right when they reached the Celadrian Hills before mid-day. He remembered the slopes as much steeper than this gentle climb. Now the Lady's pace quickened, as if she feared the opportunity to stop Honorus might slip away. Maybe, like him, she was anxious to put the encounter behind her. At first Patrick struggled to keep her and Leonides in sight, but he soon learned to trust his injured leg and adjusted to the faster pace.

The Forest Lady was hardly tall enough to reach his shoulder, and Patrick was not a tall man. As he watched her sturdy figure striding ahead of him, Patrick tried to make sense of her role in all this. If he had to guess her age, he would say she was in the prime of her life, a vigorous fifty-year-old, but this lady in green was an important character in the oldest stories of his people. According to those tales, she had always lived in the forest. Patrick had found reasons to thank, to blame, and even to hate her, but even though she had been walking ahead of him for hours, the Lady was as much a mystery as ever.

She had reshaped his fate after his first battle all those years ago, but the first time Patrick actually met the Lady face-to-face was this morning. When he saw her, she was pacing back and forth as if she couldn't wait to start walking. Patrick's mind was still muddled. He was trying to make sense of the task Leonides had set for him.

She didn't say anything to him when they met, but simply took his hand in welcome. Her hand was warm, and he looked into a face roughened by sun and weather, framed by wild hair streaked with grey. The moment she turned away, Patrick had difficulty picturing her features, and he couldn't have said what color her eyes were, only that they were large and solemn, matching her serious expression.

Patrick had bowed stiffly and said, "Lady."

She did not reply, only offered a slight smile. In the hours since then, she had not broken that silence. Patrick watched her green skirt swish back and forth ahead of him. He had finally woken up enough to notice the fabric shone like silk and was the exact shade of the unfurling ferns. As soon as she saw Patrick could keep up, her pace never varied, and he could sense something of her determination in those footsteps.

Strangely, even though the meeting with Honorus was draw-ing close, the dread that had accompanied him from the infir-mary and into the forest diminished the farther they walked. His head was clearing too. He placed his hand on Mabus's hilt. It was growing warm.

They had reached the other side of the hills when the Lady stopped and held up her hand. "Patrick, come stand by me. We walk together from here."

Patrick heard the low, calm voice for the first time in this world, and he knew he had heard it many times before in his dreams.

Leonides had already taken his place on her other side.

Patrick glanced over his shoulder. The animal guides had as-sembled. He never guessed there were so many of them. How had they come without him noticing? Maraba was there, coat gleaming, showing no sign of her bloody chore. Jasper the bear followed just behind her. Even Lupe the wolf was here, weaving in and out among the trees.

Oro landed on a branch just above and in front of Patrick's shoulder.

"Welcome, friend," Patrick said. The owl's presence reassured him even though he didn't see how the bird could help.

"I was there at the beginning," Oro said. *"I am not going to miss the end. I had a fight with my mate about it. She wanted to be the one to come, but someone has to stay with our owlets. I had to promise I would remember and tell her everything."*

Along with the owl, the trees were alive with every kind of bird, but they were no longer singing. Even the ordinary birds had fallen silent. Patrick held out his arm, and Raven fluttered down and landed on it.

"It is almost time to meet the bad man." Raven said.

Patrick glanced at the Lady, and she nodded.

"Are you the girl's raven, or are you mine?" Patrick asked.

"I have always been my own raven," he said, *"but we are friends."*

The Lady's steps became even and deliberate, as if she were about to take part in a ritual. That's when Patrick realized Woods Runners were there too. They had come as silently as the animal guides. Patrick had thought Patch and Patchson were the last to follow the Lady's ways. He was wrong.

Patrick blinked as they stepped from shade into bright, clear light. They had reached the clearing. They could see that, not long ago, it had been lovely with green grass and flowers, but those had all been trampled by men and horses. Raven flew up to perch on a branch at the edge of the sunny space. The other animals and the Woods Runners stayed out of sight well inside the forest.

A few Claymon soldiers were sitting around a small fire. They jumped to their feet and stared when the Lady and her companions appeared but didn't draw their swords. The visitors didn't seem threatening. The Lady paid no attention to the soldiers but waited silently in front of the single tent at the center of the clearing. It had a chair in front of it. Patrick's brother never went anywhere without such comforts.

The sun beat down. After so much walking in the cool forest, they were beginning to feel too warm by the time Honorus decided he had kept them waiting long enough. He ducked through the canvas and seated himself. He wore his usual cloak with its deep hood hiding his face. He might not understand the animal guides, but Honorus had his own ways of knowing things. It was easy to see he had sensed their approach. Patrick felt a tentacle of the old dread wriggle around his guts and tighten.

"You have come to bring me to Pallas." Honorus made the statement sound like a fact. "It has been a long journey from Ostara. I hope you have repaired and furnished my dwelling."

He paused.

"Why aren't you kneeling?" he demanded.

"The forest is my domain," the Lady said evenly, "yet I do not require my people to abase themselves when we meet."

"I rule Pallas and you and everything else," Honorus sneered. He swept his arm in an arc as if to encompass the vastness of the forest. "It is my birthright. And if that isn't enough, Peter Greystone has granted it to me."

Leonides had warned Patrick to remain quiet until prompted to speak, but he found it impossible to obey as he listened to Honorus' boasting. His brother was the same bully he had always been, and Patrick felt the urge to knock him down. He tightened his hand on his sword's hilt, which was almost too hot to touch.

"Our father was respected in Pallas," Patrick said in a tight voice. "The people chose him. They came to him for advice, but he never claimed to be their lord. You murdered him! That cancels your claim."

The Lady shook her head, signaling Patrick to silence.

"I understand," the Lady told Honorus as if Patrick had not spoken. "Yet I know there is something you want from me before you return to Pallas. I am ready to grant it. I will help you."

Honorus didn't answer her, and the silence stretched so long that Patrick started to think the Lady's plan had already failed. He held his breath as he felt the first icy touch of his brother's intrusion. Darkness filled the clearing, and he fought panic as Honorus entered his mind and began methodically sorting through his memories. His temples throbbed. The pain was worse than the wound from Greystone's sword. This was the test Leonides had warned him about.

As soon as Honorus realized Patrick was useless, that he knew nothing of the Lady's intentions, he abruptly withdrew, leaving his younger brother bent over and gasping. Patrick's skin was pale and clammy despite the sun's warmth.

Leonides moved close to steady him, Patrick felt his master's hand tighten on his arm. Honorus must have moved on to probe the minds of Leonides and the Lady, but they would have ways to protect themselves, wouldn't they?

Whatever Honorus discovered must have reassured him. The animal guides and the Woods Runners remained hidden, so as far as Honorus could tell these three and one raven had come here to meet him by themselves. It probably didn't matter that they couldn't hide their repugnance. In a way, their distaste may have reassured the magician. He was arrogant enough to think they had come to meet him to fulfill a duty. It didn't matter whether they liked him or not so long as they were here to guide him to Pallas. Patrick was right. Honorus still didn't know the way.

Honorus stood and called to the Claymon soldiers. "You have brought me far enough. My people are here, and they will escort me the rest of the way. You may return to your master."

As the Northerners hurried to pack their kit, Patrick wondered what game his brother was playing. Why wouldn't he keep the Claymon with him? He could use them to support his authority in Pallas. Did he really believe he would be welcomed there?

When the Claymon were gone, leaving only one horse, the tent, and the smoking coals of the fire, Honorus finally threw back his hood, revealing his ruined face. Patrick had seen it before, but it still came as a shock to see his brother's skull wobbling on top of shoulders that had been restored to youthful strength. It was as if parts from two bodies had been stitched together.

As a young man, Honorus had been handsome, and he had used that gift to his advantage whenever he could. Now peeling, blotchy skin stretched tight over his skull like pieces of mismatched leather. A few strands of lank, grey hair dangled over ears that were much too large. Honorus straightened to his full height and glared at the Forest Lady.

"I know who you are," Honorus said. "And I know what you did for him." He spat the words as he pointed at Patrick. "My brother. The younger son. He abandoned our parents to work for your servant." He didn't bother looking at Leonides.

"Yes," said the Forest Lady, showing no reaction to Honorus's macabre appearance or to his insult about her companion.

"You are correct. When Patrick was wounded, I gave him time to heal. I placed him in a sacred place, under my protection."

"And because of that he will live forever," Honorus said, bitterly. "That's what I want. Make me immortal, and finish what I started on the beach. I want to be as I once was."

If Patrick had not intervened, if Honorus had been allowed to finish his transformation back in Brethren, the refugees would all have died. As it was, the attack left them weakened, and Meier Steele was killed. Considering what Honorus had done to them, it was a miracle the refugees had been able to follow Patrick across the mountains to return to Pallas. Sensing Patrick was again having trouble controlling his mouth, Leonides caught his eye and shook his head.

Honorus continued. "Restore me. Make me appear as I did when I was young. Make me immortal."

Honorus didn't know that, although time had paused for Patrick while he was in the cave, much as it did for the people of Pallas during their stay on Niue, as soon as Katherine awakened him, he had started to age. The same was true for the refugees. As soon as they left the island, the natural course of their lives resumed. As far as Patrick knew, the only truly old ones were the man and woman standing next to him. Leonides and the Forest Lady might be immortal. Even healers like Gerard and Bethany would eventually grow old and die. Honorus seemed unaware of these realities, and Patrick noticed the Lady didn't explain them to him.

"I cannot do it," she said calmly. "You will have to live as long as you can through your own cunning. There is nothing I can do about your appearance."

"You are lying!" Honorus snarled. It seemed impossible, but the expression on his face became even uglier. "You told me you came here ready to grant my request. You must have known what I would ask. I command it!"

The Lady bowed her head, as if considering his words. When she raised it again, she looked directly into Honorus's eyes and held the gaze. He was the first to turn away.

"What did you see when you looked into my mind?" she asked. In her voice, Patrick thought he could hear something of what he himself felt, that he had been soiled when Honorus rifled through his thoughts.

Honorus didn't answer.

"You saw I do not lie," the Lady said. "You are right. I can restore your face. But it will take time. I do not believe you trust me enough. That is why I cannot do it."

"Explain."

"If I am to give you the things you have demanded, then it must be as it was for Patrick. We must carry you to the cave and lay you there."

The Lady reached into the bag tied at her waist and held up a vial. She removed the stopper and gently swirled the liquid. It was amber, like distilled sunlight, and every living creature within the clearing and the edge of the forest took a deep breath. The potion smelled of warm apricots, strawberries and almonds. Patrick suddenly felt sleepy.

She stoppered the bottle. Honorus looked at it greedily, but he did not reach out to take it.

"It is poison," he said.

"Patrick."

When the Lady said his name, Patrick knew what she was asking him to do. It was obvious. Honorus thought Patrick was the Lady's favorite. He had to drink the potion to prove it was not a deadly poison.

Ever since Katherine broke the spell, and he woke up in the cave, Patrick had felt a deep dread of being unconscious again, of losing control and placing his fate in the hands of others. It is what kept him from sleeping most nights. His heart pounded, but after a moment he held out a shaking hand to take the vial.

"Sit down," the Lady said. "It works quickly."

He sat on the ground. The Lady bent over him and would have tipped a dose of the potion into his mouth, but just as the glass touched Patrick's lips, Honorus snapped, "No. If you give it to him, there might not be enough for me. But before I drink it, you must tell me what you intend to do."

The Forest Lady looked at Honorus with surprise. "I told you. It must be just as it was for your brother. We will lay you in the cave while you are asleep, and you will stay there until you have been restored."

"How long will that take?"

"To restore your youth, perhaps by summer's end. To achieve immortality will take longer."

"That is too long!" Honorus snarled. "Greystone will come. He will take Pallas while I am asleep. When I awaken I will have nothing."

"It is your choice," the Lady said, storing away the vial. "Is it your wish that we lead you to Pallas now? We can be there before dark."

Before she could close the flap on her pouch, Honorus leapt forward and snatched the vial. He held it up to the light, then knelt and drained it. His eyes opened wide, and he fell onto his side.

Patrick, Leonides and the Lady circled around and stared down in shock. Honorus's mouth was hanging open, and he was already snoring. The Lady closed the magician's staring eyes with her fingertips. When they were certain he was asleep, the Lady gestured, and the Woods Runners slipped out from the forest to join them.

"What now?" Patrick said.

"He shouldn't have drunk it all," the Lady said, "At least now there is no danger he will awaken as we carry him to his resting place. It will be just as I said. Honorus did not trust me fully, but he saw enough when he probed my mind to know I told him nothing but truth."

Leonides said, "It would have been to his advantage to ask a few more questions before he drank the potion, though."

"Like how he is to be awakened?" Patrick asked.

"Precisely."

"And the exact terms of his immortality."

Maraba entered the clearing, and Patrick saw a familiar object dangling from her mouth by a chain. It was a small box shaped like a skep, a domed beehive. It was the one Meg once found hanging against the rocks under the waterfall that curtained the cave. That seemed so long ago. It was in another life.

The cat dropped the object at the Lady's feet and backed away.

"Where did that come from?" Patrick asked. He had thought nothing could surprise him anymore.

"Peter Greystone has had it ever since you left it behind in the stable in Ostara," Leonides said. "It became his talisman. It was in his pocket when you fought him this morning."

Patrick didn't bother asking how Leonides knew he left the box behind in Ostara or how Greystone had come to have it.

The Lady lifted the box by its chain, and it opened at her touch. "The charm to wake your brother will be hidden in this case, and the case will be hung inside the waterfall – just as it was for you, Patrick."

Four Woods Runners entered the clearing carrying a litter. One of them was Patchson. They roughly rolled Honorus onto it and lifted the corners.

"Wait," the Lady said, as the other Runners slipped out from among the trees.

"Many years ago, you obeyed me faithfully when I asked you to watch over Patrick. Today you will carry his brother to the cave and lay him on the bier, but after that it will be the task of others to watch over him and to make sure his sleep is undisturbed. It is time for you to return to your lives in the forest."

The Lady continued, "I spoke truth to Honorus. In the cave he will regain his youth, and so long as he stays there, he will never age."

The talking animals entered the clearing and formed a line behind the litter bearers. A cloud of birds swirled around the open space and landed in the trees around its edges.

Last of all, Oro flew in a star shape around the clearing before settling on a branch that stretched out over the trodden grass. *"We will be the watchers, and we will pass the duty to our owlets, our kittens and our cubs forever."*

Maraba spoke up. *"The Woods Runners watched Patrick to keep him from harm. We will watch Honorus for a different reason — to make certain he never threatens the forest again."*

Patrick exclaimed, "Why don't we just kill him?"

He couldn't tear his eyes from his brother's face. Even now that Honorus was unconscious, he saw deep lines of cruelty etched around his eyes and his mouth.

Patrick's words shocked every person and creature in the clearing into stillness. Even he seemed stunned. Was he really prepared to kill his brother in this sunny clearing as he lay helpless?

"While he lives, he will be a danger to all our people and to the forest and the animals," Patrick argued.

The Lady said, "We do not have to kill him, and I will not allow you to slay your brother. You will not return to Pallas bearing that stain. I told Honorus I would lay him in the cave, and that is what I will do."

Patrick still believed it was risky. After all, it was mere chance that Katherine, Meg and Gale found the key, broke the spell, and woke him, wasn't it? What if someone else stumbled into the cave many years from now and found his brother there, his youth restored? They might find a way to awaken him. They wouldn't know how dangerous he was.

"I promise you," the Lady said. It wasn't necessary for her to intrude as Honorus had to read Patrick's thoughts. "I know where the key is. It is safely hidden, and so long as I walk the forest paths, it will remain so."

Patrick turned away from her gaze and nodded. Then he joined the Woods Runners, the animal guides, the Lady and Leonides in the strange procession that would lead them back to the place where the story began.

44

THE END AND THE BEGINNING

IN THE PARK ACROSS the street from the Meier mansion, in the shade of the ancient sycamore tree, a small class of children fidgeted and dozed. During the past two months, a few of the adults had taken it in turns to teach them in the town's traditional classroom under the tree's spreading branches, now open to both boys and girls. The lessons were meant to be another step towards normalcy for the children of Pallas after the years of exile, deprivation, and violence.

Today it was Anna's turn to be the teacher. Her subject was history. What the children enjoyed most was telling and retelling the story of the battle against the Claymon, and especially their own role in defeating the Northerners. The events were fresh in their memories, and even when they weren't in school, they often could be seen running through the streets reenacting the battle. This game always culminated with the fire monster hurtling down the hill. When they got to that part of the story, the children ran from the upper to the lower town, shrieking like demons and toppling over at the very bottom. Their enemies were imaginary. There weren't enough children to form two sides.

Anna had decided it was time to expand the lessons beyond the events the children had experienced themselves. Today she was teaching them about Pallas before the exodus to Niue – about its festivals, its traditions and crafts, and the alliances with the Woods Runners and important trading partners like Ostara.

They would need to know as much as possible about the unique culture of the forest city if they were going to grow up and lead it into the future.

The afternoon had grown warm. Anna sensed she was losing the children's attention, but they didn't know she had a surprise in store. Over the past few weeks, with Patrick's help, she had rebuilt the baker's oven, and she and the other women had rec-reated one of Marios's recipes. They hadn't had a chance to try it yet. It had taken time to find all the ingredients and to capture the yeast needed to make the dough rise.

Maybe it was just as well that they hadn't been able to try the recipe. If they had, the aroma of baking cakes would have given the secret away. The day had finally come to fire the oven for the first time since their return to Pallas. It was already heating, and the dough had been mixed and formed into cakes. If Anna's plan was a success, the children would soon have their first taste of old Pallas.

At the other end of the park, some of the grass had been dug away, and a few small plots were planted to lettuce, sweet peas, beans and squash. The seeds had been sent back to the city by Maron, and even though they were put into the ground later than they should have been, the plants were thriving.

Once Patch decided he was well enough to travel, which was well before Katherine would have released him, he returned to Bethany's farm. She tried to talk him out of going, but since he was her patient, not her prisoner, in the end she had no choice but to wish him well. At least he travelled with Patchson this time. His son would return to Pallas while Patch stayed with Maron in the place that had come to represent perfect peace to him.

Along with the seeds for the garden, Maron sent many other things back to Pallas. Katherine was there when Patchson walked through the water gate, and she was as excited as everyone else to watch him pull bags of nuts and small bricks of butter from his bulging pack. There even were some eggs wrapped in lamb's wool, and not a single one had broken. Maron had sent two more blankets and had tucked a spindle into the bottom of the pack even though there were not yet any sheep grazing on the green. She could not spare enough and Patchson could not carry enough food to feed the people for long, but the gifts lifted their spirits.

The bakers adjusted their recipe to use ground nuts instead of flour. It would change the texture of the cakes, but they might be even better.

While Anna and the other townspeople took inventory of the treasures he had brought, Patchson led Katherine aside and said, "My mother cannot write, so she gave me a message for you."

Patchson paused and took a breath. He frowned as he tried to remember. Katherine knew the next words would be Maron's. "Patch told me everything. You sent him to me, and this farm will be our home until Bethany returns. I know you believe Patch left your care too soon. I promise he will grow strong here. He is asleep under an apple tree. I thank you."

Patchson pulled Katherine into a long hug and said, "That's from Ma too."

Now, as Katherine attacked the weeds that threatened to overwhelm the seedlings, she thought about how close Patch had come to choosing the forest path, about the town's victories over its enemies, and about the losses they seldom talked about. Her serious expression reflected the disquiet she felt whenever she allowed herself to dwell too long on the events of the spring and early summer. Thinking about the past always led to troubling thoughts about the future.

Ellen had returned to Pallas from Ostara a few weeks after the battle to bring home the wounded who had been recovering under Katherine's care. Even though defeating the Claymon in their streets was a triumph for the people of the forest, Peter Greystone actually had brought a very small part of his force to Pallas. Of the wounded Claymon, most left Pallas as soon as they were able to walk, without thanks or a backwards glance, but a few had asked to stay, and they were welcomed to the town.

Most of the Claymon army remained intact, but because of Greystone's overweening pride, he had never appointed a second-in-command, only fawning courtiers. Without a leader, the Claymon who had been occupying Ostara headed for the hills of the north when Devon Elder pounded on the city gates. Not a drop of blood was shed there.

Katherine wondered about the Claymon who had been sent to secure Greystone's claim to far-flung outposts like Springvale. They had been given a taste of power, and they might not relinquish their hold easily. And what was to keep some other leader from coming forward to lead the Claymon?

Her mother assured Kathe that Devon Elder would never allow Ostara to be invaded again, from any direction, but still Katherine worried. And it didn't help that she and Ellen parted after a disagreement. To be honest, they quarreled.

Kathe winced as she tugged on a particularly stubborn weed, imagining her father's reaction when Ellen returned without her again. According to Ellen, Devon still couldn't understand why she couldn't…tug…just return…tug…to that…tug…old life. He wanted his daughter to come home. At last the roots broke free, showering her with dirt. Ellen understood Katherine's reasons for staying here, even sympathized, but she still did her best to convince Katherine to return to Pallas. Ellen admitted she was being selfish. She wanted her daughter close.

When Ellen left Pallas to return to Ostara, Stormer went with her. He had stayed in Pallas after the Claymon were defeated, and during those weeks, when he wasn't helping to clear rocks from the street or take apart the barricades, Katherine noticed him sitting at a distance from the students in the park. When she realized he went there because he longed to know how to read, she returned the book he had stolen from Honorus to him. They spent many afternoons turning the pages together, and she helped him to decipher the letters.

Stormer was a good student, but Katherine found this particular book rather confusing and dull. It was about philosophy, and it was written in a very old-fashioned style, but Stormer couldn't seem to get enough of it. Once he understood the basics, he read during every idle moment, even when Katherine wasn't tutoring him. By the time Ellen returned to guide the recovered wounded home, he had nearly finished it.

Honorus had brought his books with him when he came to Pallas, and they were now stored in two cedar chests in Patrick's house. With his permission, Ellen chose a second volume, one without too much magic in it, for Stormer.

"If you need another, Katherine will send it to you," she told him.

A few days after Ellen left, Abel arrived after having already visited Ostara. He limped so slowly down the path to Pallas there was time for Katherine to receive word of his coming and go out to meet him. Rowen walked sedately at his side, bearing little resemblance to the wolf-dog puppy she had adopted in Pallas the year before. Rowan jumped up and put her huge paws on Kathe's shoulders, but she soon returned to Abel's side. With a pang, Kathe realized Rowan was his dog now.

And then there was the problem of Honorus. She presumed he was asleep in the cave. Everyone else seemed to have put him out of their minds, but Katherine knew the cave was much too close to Pallas. She imagined him lying on the bier, growing stronger every day.

Why had the Lady put him there? Why didn't she kill him when she had the chance? Despite the Lady's assurances, which were supported by Leonides, allowing Honorus to live and heal was a terrible idea. Patrick was uneasy too, at least at first. He had even suggested killing his brother after he drank the potion. Katherine wished he had done it. She had half a mind to go to the cave herself now and plunge a knife into the magician's wicked chest.

She could do it. She had already risked everything for the people of Pallas. She would do even more, but despite her misgivings about Honorus, she knew she would never pass through the waterfall again.

After Leonides and Patrick returned to Pallas – without the Forest Lady – everyone gathered in the street to hear about all that had happened in the clearing and what the Lady had said and done there. Since that day, Patrick had come to accept that the ancient ones had done the right thing, but Katherine still struggled to be as trusting.

She pulled a strand of gossamer silk from inside the neck of her dress and dangled a tiny key in front of her face. Its existence had disturbed her sleep ever since Patrick's return from his encounter with his brother. He didn't know she had it – not yet – but from what he said, the Lady seemed to know it was in Katherine's keeping. Stranger still, she seemed to think it was safe with her.

Katherine had devised a dozen plans to dispose of the key, but in the end all were flawed. She even considered throwing the blasted thing into the coals under the new oven, but what if it didn't melt? It was a pretty, shiny little trifle, cunningly made. One of the children might pick it out of the ashes.

She thought about the day she took it. It was the day she, Meg and Gale woke Patrick from his long sleep. Patrick took the box shaped like a beehive, and Katherine had the key. She was a sentimental fool! She should have thrown it into the pool in front of the cave.

No. That still wouldn't have been safe enough. The current could have carried it into the stream. Someone might have found it. Katherine sighed and turned her attention back to weeding.

45

EVER AFTER

THERE WAS JUST ENOUGH space for Bethany and Gerard to sit side-by-side in the stern of the boat. The sea stretched off in every direction, frothed into small waves by a steady breeze from the west. When two dots appeared above the otherwise featureless horizon, in the middle of their second day at sea, they watched them until they were close enough to make out the shapes of the delicate wings and long tails of dragons.

As soon as she was certain, Bethany laughed and cried, "It's Padraik!" She clung to the side of the boat and grinned at the light sparking from green and red scales. "And it looks like Meg found him a mate!"

Gerard kept one hand on the tiller, keeping the dinghy on an easterly course. Their sail was full of a lively breeze from the west, and that was a good sign. The island of Niue was already out of sight, far behind them.

A few days ago, the book showed them a new picture. In it the two of them were sitting together on the bench in front of Bethany's cottage at twilight. In it they were very old – even older than they were now. Two walking staffs leaned against the wall beside the door, and light poured out through the windows. Somehow, they knew there were visitors inside – all the dear ones they had been missing and had feared they would never see again.

Neither of them had spoken of it, but they had been waiting for and preparing for a sign. The little boat was already as sound as they could make it, and instead of napping in the shade, they had spent their afternoons stitching a small sail from the cloth that once lined the crates left behind by the *Goshawk*.

After the lives they had led before they came to Niue, they were bored, and they were people who needed to be busy. That's what they told themselves as they caught extra fish and dried them in the sun and wove themselves new sunhats, this time with strings to tie under their chins.

They believed their tiny boat had escaped the dragons' notice until the pair swept low and circled, skimming over the surface of the water. The wind from their wings caused sudden turbulence.

"We left just in time," Gerard said, as he and Bethany struggled to keep the boat from capsizing.

"Welcome home!" he called. *"Your hoard is just as you left it, and we have added a few things to it."*

A few weeks ago, he had found a perfect and very rare shell, an Owl's Eye. It had seemed to wink at him when he picked it up. It was just a trick of the light, but he took it to the cave anyway. And just before they left the island, Bethany took off the ring he had given her long ago and placed it on top of the small heap of treasures. "Padraik should have some real gold," she said. "Besides, I don't need a ring to know you and I are bound together."

Gerard was still smiling at that memory when Padraik answered. *"This is my beloved. Her name is Ruby."*

They thought that was the last they would hear from the dragons, but the two circled once more, and this time they flew a little higher and filled the sail so full of the breeze from their wings that Bethany and Gerard weren't sure the stitches would hold.

"When you see the first star appear, while the sunset still lingers to the west, watch for the headland. You don't have far to go," Padraik said.

"You are beautiful," Bethany called with her thoughts, and also with her voice because she couldn't help it.

By the time the boat was under control and on course again, the two dragons had flown on and were almost out of sight.

"Do they mean the first star tonight?" Bethany said. "That doesn't seem possible."

They thought they had been on the island and outside the stream of time, for a little over three years, but that didn't mean the same amount of time had passed back on the mainland. On the island, changing seasons were marked by shifts so subtle they sometimes didn't notice them right away. The wind came from a slightly different direction; a more intense sun baked the beach; the parrots laid more eggs and fledged noisy, greedy chicks. Each night, as the sun sank into the ocean, Gerard made a mark on the cliff face. Strangely, when Gerard went to the cliff face to make his final mark on their last night, before they sailed, the rocks had been wiped clean. The blankness made him feel disoriented, as if no time had passed at all.

"I wouldn't be surprised," he said, but he wasn't sure Bethany had heard him. She was gripping the side of the boat again and pointing at the dolphins that had come to lead them home.

Katherine was still weeding the vegetables when she looked up and saw Meg crossing the park toward her. She jumped up, crushing a bean plant. The children had finished their lessons, and Anna had just led them off to the baker's house, where they would peek into the rebuilt oven and taste cake for the first time since their return to Pallas. Now, hours later, the sun was sinking in the west, but the two young women still sat together in the pool of shade under the sycamore tree. The rest of the citizens of Pallas, even Patrick, had not interrupted the reunion.

After the surprise of Meg's arrival, the hugs, and the chatter of greeting, they both had quieted. Neither of them had dared to hope for a peaceful afternoon like this one. Even though they had so much to say, they chose their words carefully, and they often found themselves sitting silently, listening to the sounds of rustling leaves and distant laughter.

News traveled fast in Pallas. As soon as Anna heard of the dragon rider's arrival, she rescued the last two pieces of the cake before her students could devour them. She put them into a basket and sent them to the girls with the most trustworthy of her students.

The three citizens of Pallas who were killed in the battle for the city had been buried weeks ago in the new graveyard just outside the lower gate. Vines and grasses were already claiming their graves. The rest of Katherine's patients had recovered, or they looked likely to do so.

The remaining citizens of Pallas had agreed without discussion that their ordeal was really over. It might have happened on the day the first child was born since their return from Niue. When they knew the baby girl and her mother were safe, everyone in the city seemed to take a final, collective breath of sorrow and relief and then they continued their new lives. They would never forget the friends and the years they had lost, but they could finally believe in a future out from under the shadow of the Claymon and Honorus.

"How did you know you would find me here?" Katherine asked Meg as they settled themselves for a long visit. "I might have returned to Ostara. That's where my story began, and my parents did everything they could to convince me to return – short of dragging me there."

Without realizing she was doing it, Meg rubbed her arm where the arrow had pierced it. She still couldn't remember how Gale got her to her mother's house, but she remembered his white face when she opened her eyes. He stayed with her while Sofie cut the shaft of the arrow and gently pulled it out of Meg's arm. She wished she could remember some of the things he said during those moments. Maybe they weren't words at all, but only the soothing sounds of a lover.

"I didn't think of that," Meg said honestly. "Isn't Patrick here? Now that the two of you are together, why would you be anywhere else?"

"I'm still living with some of the other women, in the house by the gate," Katherine said. "We see each other every day, but he hasn't talked about the future."

"He will," Meg said. "You know Patrick. He'll be worried that you can do better, that he's too old for you, that life would be easier for you in Ostara. Has he told you to leave?"

"No, but…"

"Then you will have to be the one to speak first," Meg said, practically. "What are you waiting for?"

Changing the subject, Meg said, "I have to go to the farm tomorrow, but I'll stop in Pallas again before I go back to Springvale to help my family with the harvest."

Katherine knew she meant Bethany's farm.

"I want to borrow two of her books. I know she won't mind. I was in the middle of reading them when your mother came. Do you remember? We were skating on the pond. If someone can go with me, we'll bring back supplies, if Maron has anything to spare."

"Patchson can go. I know he has wanted to see his parents, and he can hunt on the way back. We could use some more nuts if she has any to spare. Now that the children have tasted cake, there will be no peace until there is more."

"Help me to find Patchson, then," Meg said. "And I will expect everything to be settled between you and Patrick by the time I return."

Katherine found Patrick standing on top of his tower gazing over the deep green of the summer forest. He had heard her climbing the stairs and turned to greet her. Even though they had seen each other an hour earlier, when everyone met for supper, Patrick still looked at her with the expression he wore whenever they met. It told her she was the person he most wished to see, and he couldn't believe she was really there. No one else looked at her that way.

He had encouraged Katherine to go to Bethany's farm with Meg. If he was concerned about her plan to return to Pallas by herself, he didn't show it, but he was standing at the gate to meet her. The long walk had given Katherine time to realize Meg was right. She didn't want to wait any longer for the rest of her life to begin.

She smiled and took his hand.

"I have come home," she said, gesturing toward the roofless mansion behind her. "It is what I want. You are the one I want."

When Patrick didn't answer right away, she said, "What do you say?"

He pulled her into an embrace and whispered. "You were always the brave one. I haven't dared to ask. I was afraid you would tell me no."

They were still there together when Maraba arrived to recite another chapter from the story of her people.

ACKNOWLEDGEMENTS

I am a slow writer. Thank you to all the people in my life who have waited so patiently for me to finish this book. Emily Cook, Cheryl Bartz, and Linda Enden each read the manuscript and offered corrections and sensible suggestions. I hope when the three of you reread *The Reawakened Forest*, you will see how you helped to improve it. Emily Cook created the cover art for this and the other books in *The Healing Winds Trilogy*. I love all these illustrations, but this one may be my favorite because it stars Oro, the first of the talking animals to appear back in *The Changeful Map*. Most of all, thanks to my coach, editor, publisher, and all-around-everything Doug Cook. This book exists because of you.

ABOUT THE AUTHOR

SALLY STOUT grew up in Michigan exploring the fields and woods of her family's farm and spent a great deal of time in the forests of Middle Earth and Narnia. She has taught English as a Peace Corps Volunteer in the Kingdom of Tonga and in high school and college classrooms. She and her husband weave and bird watch in Frankfort, Michigan.

www.sallystoutbooks.com

Made in the USA
Monee, IL
30 October 2020

45862564R00256